'84

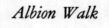

Albion Walk

Novels by Gwendoline Butler

The Red Staircase
Meadowsweet
The Vesey Inheritance
Sarsen Place

ALBION WALK

Gwendoline Butler

Coward, McCann & Geoghegan New York

Library of Congress Cataloging in Publication Data

Butler, Gwendoline.
Albion Walk.

I. Title
PR6052.U813A78   1982   823'.914   82-7447
ISBN 0-698-11172-9   AACR2

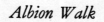

Albion Walk

♪ Prelude

I think that all the great moments of my life have been played out to music in an atmosphere reminiscent of Rosine's, redolent of spices, Bohemian, theatrical. In fact, one or two episodes took place in a theatre, but never upon a stage. I have avoided that fate, thank God, although my mother once confided that I was conceived in a prop bed of gilded wood and plaster used in a scene from *The Balkan Princess,* an operetta in which she had the starring role. But in this, as in much else, her memory may have been at fault. Or she may have lied—she very often had her own reasons for lying. We all do, I suppose.

At the Mansion House dinner I was aware of my Rosine scent. I now have it specially prepared by a parfumeur near Covent Garden; Poiret, its originator, has been dead for decades. I had generously applied Nuits de Chine as I dressed; the scent takes me back to Biarritz and the time of my first successes. My first love, too. Oh God, how long ago it seems, and yet how vivid.

Outside, workmen were building the stands for the crowds who would line the streets for the Coronation of the Queen. They were working all night, so I was told, racing to complete their task. The Mall, Piccadilly, St. James's, Regent Street, all of London was decorated with flags and bunting. In the heart the Old City—here when the Romans came, already ancient when William the Conqueror arrived—the last touches to the display were being added. I remembered the day the new queen was born; they called her mother "The Little Duchess."

The Lord Mayor leaned across to me while lighting my cigarette, and said in a low voice: "In the speech that I'm going to make after this function in your honour and after the presentation to you"—yes, a lovely piece of silver, dating from 1750; I chose it myself from the silver vaults—"I'm going to thank you

7

for your services to the theatre and the arts in London, but I wish I could tell the truth and say it's really for being such a lovely lady."

The Lord Mayor straightened up and turned to his neighbour. I could see the diamonds glittering on his badge of office which nestled in a cravat of fine lace. What a long way he'd come since his barrow in Berwick Market. Then I saw a hint of a wink in his eye. Not so far after all, I thought.

A band was playing in the Egyptian room—offstage, as it were, from where we were dining in state—and I picked up a tune from Noel Coward's *Bitter Sweet*: I was sure it had been chosen for me. I had prayed for a sort of miracle that day as I was dressing, and now it was happening. I looked up and saw Aldwyn smiling at me. How lucky I was to have such a beautiful daughter. She raised her glass slightly towards me in a silent toast. I was becoming light-headed from the champagne, the warm air, and the mingled scents of the roses and my Nuits de Chine; the room began to blur.

I closed my eyes, tempted for a second not to open them. Let them think I was deeply moved, faint, or even worse. I daresay people had been known to die at the Lord Mayor's dinners. For an amused moment I imagined the concerned hum of voices, the discreet bustle about me, the alarm, but I checked myself. There was more of my mother in me than I had suspected. Don't ham it up, Alice, I told myself; if you're going to die, then do it in private.

I opened my eyes decisively. This was far too delicious a moment in my life to lose any of it. An honour from the City of London, a marvellous new show planned for my theatre, and Coronation Year as well. Yes, it was a time for joy, made more precious by the knowledge that I was about to undergo major surgery.

"Ah, Scheherazade is back with us again, then?" It was Louisa, speaking with that faint mixture of Italy and Bow in her voice, which had always attracted me. Her dress was a Hartnell, her jewellery from Kutchinsky.

I opened my eyes wide. "Why do you call me that?"

"Because you are such a divine teller of tales. I have always thought of you as such, didn't you know? Now I say it aloud." She was mocking me a little, but with great sweetness and kindness, just as she always had.

"I was thinking of Vienna and Paris."

8

We were walking through to the Egyptian room. It was crowded with people, most of whom I knew; some I loved, and many I greatly admired. We walked the full length of the room together. The crowds parted before us politely; it was a sort of royal progress.

"What are you going to do for the Coronation?"

"Have a big party," I said. "As big as I can make it. Family and friends. Then the theatre, as usual, and then we're all going to see Noel at the Café de Paris."

"Lovely," said Louisa. "It seems right it should be Noel to entertain you in the evening."

Another step back in time, but how gloriously enjoyable to remember, for a moment, those wild days when I'd first started to manage the Albion, first felt sure that this was really my world. I had known Noel that long.

"What about Matthew?" asked Louisa bluntly. She never flinched from the sort of question angels are supposed to evade.

I thought for a moment. "He'll be there. He is family, after all. Anyway, I've asked him, and I very much hope he comes."

"You do? After everything?"

I smiled at an acquaintance across the room, an old friend from the theatre. I'd put on his first play. Now he had a knighthood and a house on the Riviera.

"Yes, it was my fault too that our marriage broke up. So I've asked him and he's going to fly over from New York. That's where he's been living."

"Oh, we all know that, dear. Hardly a secret."

We'd come to the end of the room, and we both turned round. "I'm off," said Louisa. "After all, I am the hostess, and there's a prince of the blood over there and I ought to be talking to him. No one else is." She leaned forward and kissed my cheek. "A lovely evening—a real triumph for you. And deserved. We all salute you."

"Thank you, Louie."

"I see you too dress at Hartnell now?" She cast a brief glance at the blue and white silk. "But you always have beautiful clothes. It's what I first noticed about you, even when we were all poor."

"It was Poiret; he taught me how to dress and how to wear beautiful clothes."

"You loved that old man."

"Yes. Yes, I did."

"More than anyone else you've ever loved."

"No," I said. "Be moderate, Louie, and don't exaggerate. Not nearly as much as two other people, but not much less than a third."

"Aldwyn? You adore that girl." I didn't respond, and Louie said, "What *did* you quarrel with Matthew about?"

"What do we ever quarrel about in our family?" I said with sudden bitterness. "Property, rights, and style."

"Style?"

"Yes, style. How you live and what you live for. In that area, we parted company, Matthew and I." I gave Louie a little push. "Go and talk to your little prince of the blood. He's looking dreadfully bored."

Louisa walked away. It was, after all, her evening too. I stood there for a moment looking around, enjoying the scene. It was an "orders and decorations" evening, so that the men were as bejewelled as the women.

Then I saw a small, determined figure making its way through the crowd.

"Franny! It's not possible. Is it really you?"

"You think I'm a ghost? You heard I was dead?" He chuckled.

I held him at arms' length and took a good look. Shorter than I by a foot, he had tiny delicate hands, feet that were expensively shod—he'd always had that look of elegance, even when he had opened his first cinema, the Zanadu, at the age of twenty. Now he was totally bald.

"I heard you went nowhere. Never left the Bahamas."

"For *you*. Louie asked me. I came."

"Oh, Franny." I kissed his cheek, which felt like soft, well cared for leather. "You angel." He had been that, literally—my first backer in the theatre.

"For the Coronation, for the Queen herself, I would not have come. For you, yes."

"Thank you, Fran, my dear old friend." All the same, I expected there was some business deal afoot. Franny Hollman had not changed so very much. Though he was approaching seventy, he still kept his finger in all sorts of pies.

"You made me money, Alice. I got my percentage. And I'm interested in what I hear you've got coming up. That new show for next year ..." He lowered his voice. "I have heard rumours."

10

The old devil—he'd heard about Robert Carewe and *The Garden of the Goddesses.*

"I'm not sure if it's really for you, Fran. It's very sharp and angry. Very modern."

"I have an intuition." He tilted his head—it was a familiar gesture. "It may not be such a success, or perhaps events will stop you exploiting it to the full—"

The old fox was up to something. "Not still after the Albion for yourself, Fran? You know I'd never sell."

He threw up his hands in horror. "What a thing to say! You know I am out of the entertainment business altogether."

I had heard so. But with Fran, who could be sure? "We'll talk about it. Will you lunch sometime?"

"The Savoy as always?" We shook hands on it and prepared to part. I was amused at the incident. It is always agreeable when old friends turn up, and even more so when they run true to form. Fran, my loyal old friend, was plotting something. I could read the signs. As well as he had loved me—and I believed he had had genuinely deep feelings for me—I also knew Fran could be unrelenting: friend or foe knew not to stand between Francis Hollman and anything he wanted. He could be devious, too. A gentle alarm stirred inside me.

"Alice." I swung round. I knew those clear, well-bred tones. Flora Charlecote, my sister-in-law and cousin-under-the-blanket. At least that was how she saw herself. There was a fundamental disagreement in the family as to whether my mother and Randolph Charlecote had ever got around to marrying, which not even the lawsuit had succeeded in laying to rest.

"Flora, what are you doing here?"

"Louisa invited me," said Flora composedly. "I don't get invited to the Mansion House so often that I can turn down an invitation. I wanted to come." Flora had made a late but happy marriage to a remote Charlecote kinsman. She was wearing a terrible old white dress that had seen many a hunt ball. She pecked at my cheek and murmured that, after all, we were cousins and she was proud of me. That she was also my sister-in-law she tactfully did not mention.

"I think I'm almost glad you're not selling the Albion," said Flora, suddenly. "We could do with the money. The site would be worth about a million. But it would have been sad—though dramatic—to have to sell just now when you are at a peak of success."

11

"I think you're the one with the taste for drama, not I."

"Oh, we all have that, all the Charlecotes," said Flora. "You'd better go and meet the prince. He looks as though he wants to speak to you."

"I was presented before dinner. Once is enough," I said.

"Guess what?" said Flora. "I was nearly a Coronation casualty. I was walking underneath some scaffolding when a workman dropped a hammer. If it had hit me I would have been dead." Her bright blue eyes gleamed with amusement. "I was nearly off your hands. Make things easier, wouldn't it?"

"No," I said slowly, from the depths of my thirty-odd years' experience of our relationship. "I'd miss you, Flora; I don't see you much. I'm quite sure you don't like me really, in spite of what you say. And I'm not sure if I like you, but I like to know you're there."

Instead of answering, she went off on a tangent. "I hear Aldwyn's got herself engaged to Alexander," she said. "Is he setting himself out to be a judge, or is he grooming himself to go into merchant banking or diamonds?"

How shrewd she was. You must always remember that about the Charlecotes—sharp wits under the country tweeds.

"I don't know if it's come to an engagement, quite," I said cautiously. "Maybe yes, maybe no."

We were interrupted by our hostess. "No more family talk," she said sternly. "Today you are a public figure, and your public wants you."

For the next half hour I gave myself up to the pleasure of being made much of, passing from group to group, in a daze of happiness. Why not enjoy it. This was my moment to savour, a moment I'd worked towards for years.

"A penny for them," spoke a light, pretty voice with darker undertones that would deepen with age. A voice inherited from my mother and from me.

I looked up. "Aldwyn! Bless you, darling. A penny wouldn't buy them. Thousands wouldn't. I was thinking how lucky I was."

She looked excited and a little frightened, as if she were watching for something to happen. I wondered what it was. It never occurred to me that she was frightened for me.

"Can we meet and talk?" she said abruptly. "I've something to tell you."

12

"The flat, dearest? I'm going back there almost at once."

She frowned. "Tonight's difficult."

I supposed she was meeting Alexander. I tried not to wonder too much about their relationship, physical, mental or emotional. "I'll be there all tomorrow. I'm staying up in London for a few days."

Her face cleared. "Yes, tomorrow. Good. I'll come early." She was wearing a pleated white chiffon dress that must certainly have cost her more than she could afford.

"Since when did you dress at Grès?" I asked lightly.

She looked down at her dress with surprise. "Oh, is that where it came from? I didn't know. It was a present."

"Never mind. You look marvellous." She was better looking than I had ever been, and with the Charlecote slender height, a feature I secretly envied. She gave me a kiss and went away.

I started to leave, making for my car.

Louisa came up to me, shrugging her sable wrap around her shoulders. She was older now, but her features were still delicate and fine.

"Darling, what goes with you? You're excited over all this, very dignified and sweet, but not happy." She took another look. "Too thin, my darling, you are too thin."

I gave my head a slight shake, to divert the conversation. I didn't want Louisa to have one of her flashes of intuitive truth. Not yet. Later I might need all the help I could get, but for the moment I would face the imminent operation on my own.

As I waited for my car I thought, with a sense of shock, that nearly all the people who had been important in my life were at that party. Yet there were some notable absentees: my mother, Josie; my former husband, Matthew; my old friend and rival, Maria; and Frederic, whom I had once desperately loved. These people had shaped my past. On the drive home I wondered what would shape my future.

As I opened the door of my flat, memories rushed in. Beneath the darkness lay the Albion Theatre itself. I had a private lift up, these days, but once I had climbed the stairs, past stages, dressing rooms and storerooms to my private apartment. My mind went back to the beginning, to the first time I had seen the Albion, just as the Great War ended. I thought about my early struggles, my successes and my despairs. I recalled tragedies—the death of my first great star and the murder of my cousin—and triumphs, like the night I saw Noel Coward applauding and cheering me on.

I loved my flat, but it had black memories too. I had sat out the Blitz there, waiting every night to be burned or blown to pieces. The Albion *had* been hit—at night, thank God, when the auditorium was empty—but high above Albion Walk I had been safe. I remembered those noisy, bloody scenes now with a sort of retrospective pleasure. I had come through.

I also remembered the night I had run through the flat, banging on the furniture and shouting against Matthew. Did nights like that imprint themselves on the walls and the furniture?

I had lived through dark days. I had gone through black doors bravely and had come out the other side. I was about to face another very dark day, and walk through a door, perhaps never to return. I had to face that thought.

The flat had seemed empty when Aldwyn had first moved away, but I had adapted well, and now I liked being on my own. I had decorated the place myself, the labour taking me back to the days when I had worked as a Martine for Paul Poiret. I suppose his ideas of the way things should be done still influenced me. I used mirrors on walls and doors, and I remained very fond of stained wood.

My sitting room had cherry-red and grey stained wood furniture, and I had painted a mural of a landscape in sunlight on one wall. I loved it, though Aldwyn raised her eyebrows when she first saw it. Her own flat was furnished with expensive, pale Swedish furniture that to her generation represented the ultimate refinement of living. She did not understand my Ruhlmann sofa, nor its significance in my life. Nor my Queen Anne mirror, whose walnut I had touched up with gilt. Horace Walpole would have approved, but my Aldwyn did not. She was her father's daughter in so many ways. They kept in touch, I knew. Well, why not? Matthew kept in touch with Maria, too, so I heard.

I wondered what they said. Did they talk of the past? I found myself dwelling more on the past because my own future seemed so doubtful. I knew that I had ahead of me an operation that was certainly dangerous and potentially fatal. So I looked back instead, back to my youth.

14

Someone, it may have been my own daughter, once asked me how a little cockney like me fetched up at an art school in Vienna.

"I was dumped," I remember answering briskly. "By my own mother. I was dumped in Vienna."

Part One

♪ Chapter One

Vienna in 1913. "A magic city" was the phrase I heard used of it later. But magic is a cold, misty word, and prewar Vienna was full of vigorous, decided life, with nothing misty or mysterious about it. The Viennese were a healthy, hearty people who enjoyed life.

In 1913 Josie was in Vienna, singing in an operetta; her prospects had looked promising, but had proved illusory. She had accepted the soubrette role in *The Bohemian Girl,* lured by the amount of money and the luxury of the apartment she was offered. Or she said she was so enticed, but I think now a lover was involved. I seem to remember laughter behind closed doors, and blushes over unexplained gifts of jewels and flowers.

Not that Josie didn't blush easily. It is, after all, not clear if even my father was her first lover. I rather think he wasn't. But she had certainly adored Randolph Charlecote, and when he left her—and me—she minded very much. I was young then, but I remember the tears, floods of them, and every drop was genuine. I did not know then what parted them, but Josie's extravagance might have been a factor. Or perhaps my father just got bored with her. I think she always hoped he would come back to her. Perhaps he would have, if he had not been killed. The Charlecotes, on the whole, are faithful to their loves.

The May family, in their way, had their own brand of fidelity. I loved Josie. Whatever she did to me as a child, whatever were to be our quarrels when I was an adult, I loved her. I think she loved me too, even when she left me in Vienna.

Josie had groaned again.

"What is it, Mum?" I remember clutching her arm.

She was breathing gustily. "Keep your voice down, kid. I don't want the landlady to hear."

19

Privately, I thought Madame Augustin *must* be hearing.

Josie rolled over on the sofa. "Oh, the pain in my guts—sorry, love, shouldn't use that word. Ladies don't say guts. Not that I'm a lady. You are though, being a Charlecote. They don't use words like that. Don't know what they say. Entrails, p'rhaps," she gasped.

I could tell she was only talking to stop from groaning.

"Still, there's lots of things women have to do that ain't strictly ladylike. As you'll find out. The way we're supposed to behave and the way we do behave—two different things," she finished breathlessly. Then she gave a scream and drew her legs up, convulsively.

She reached a hand blindly and I took it and held it. "Are you all right, Josie?" I asked.

A spot of blood appeared on the sofa and increased until a trickle was spilling to the floor.

"Get Madame Augustin," whispered Josie.

I rushed out to where Madame was standing in the hall outside, listening, as I had known she would be. I gasped out my message, but she already seemed to know it all.

I was pushed aside to sit on the stairs, desolate and scared, while she went in to see Josie. Presently she reappeared and hurried off down the stairs, coming back with a woman who was clearly a nurse.

No one took any notice of me. I sat there too wretched and miserable to cry. I was convinced that Josie was going to die. "Oh Josie, Josie," I said to myself. "I love you. Don't leave me." I had had one or two frightening glimpses of what it was to be alone and penniless. I felt helpless in this alien world where I knew hardly anyone.

The landlady came out of the room carrying a bucket. I stood up.

"Don't get in my way, child."

"What's the matter with Josie?" I demanded urgently. "Is it something she's eaten? Is she going to be all right?"

"Eaten! That's good. Eaten!" And rocking with laughter, the woman passed down the stairs.

That casual joke from that silly, thoughtless woman made me feel like a stray cat that has been kicked into the gutter. But I was a stout-hearted child, not easily cowed; I didn't cry. I gritted my teeth and resolved to take this rotten battle on and win. I didn't know it was going to take my life to do it.

Then the nurse appeared at the door, and was kinder. She told me she was sure my mother would get well, and to be a good girl. Josie was carried down the stairs and taken off in a strange little covered pushcart like a baker's van. No one told me anything, but I discovered by running behind the van that we were going to the hospital.

The hospital was horrible, with grey walls and the smell of carbolic. Forgotten, I crouched outside the ward where they had taken Josie and heard the word "abortion." When a nurse pushing a stretcher went in, I followed unnoticed. The ward was a high, narrow room, and at first I could not make out where Josie was. Then I saw she was in a corner bed opposite the door with a screen around her. I tiptoed across and crouched in the shadow of the screen.

I could see her face, white and still. Her eyes were closed. "Josie," I whispered. She didn't seem to hear. I reached out and touched her hand, which was deadly cold, except for the palm, where it burned red hot.

I was sure she was going to die. I was only surprised she was not dead already. I still saw the blood spilling on the floor. For me the nightmare had begun that morning when she had surprised me by saying she wouldn't be going into the theatre, didn't feel up to it. She had never missed a performance; she crawled onto the stage whatever the state of her health. The Mays always did. We went on.

"Mum," I said, touching her hand again. "Josie. Alice is here."

She opened her eyes. I felt she didn't know me. "It's Alice," I said urgently.

The woman in the bed next to Josie started to moan. No one took any notice. It was a terrible noise; I could sense death in the air. I started to cry.

Josie said in a weak voice, "Sorry, kid." She stretched out a hand. I linked my fingers with hers and hung on. If Josie died, somehow I would go with her.

How did I get away from the hospital in the end? I think a doctor noticed me and Madame Augustin turned up, cuffed my ear for being a nuisance, and took me away. Josie got better, came back and was soon as bouncy as ever. Then she left me.

She told me herself, with a bold front, behind which I am now able to see a sharp misery. At the time it seemed to me the

21

final betrayal: I'd been abandoned by both my parents. She was going to New York, and I was not.

"I can't stay without you, on my own," I cried.

"Oh, don't look at me with those big eyes. Honestly, I hate big eyes, they can look so bloody accusing," and she turned away to study her own face in the mirror, touching her hair and patting colour on her cheeks. "You're old enough to understand about money."

"Yes, I know, but, Mother—"

"Call me Josie," she said inexorably. "I don't want a big girl like you calling me Mother. The show's closed and I'm pretty broke. You know how things have been since I was ill. You can read the writing on the walls with the best, I'm sure. Nothing wrong with your wits, I will say that. You're a clever kid. Good with your hands, too." She glanced down at the painting I was doing as I sat on the floor. Her shoulders sagged, as if she was suddenly weary. "I've got you into the Werkstaette. That's because you've got artistic talent."

"And what's the Werkstaette? An orphanage? A place for left children?"

She ignored me. "It's because you've got talent. You're lucky. It's a school to train girls with artistic gifts—you know, bring them on. Make them artists." She looked at me hopefully.

"What do we do?" I asked bleakly. "It sounds like a sweat shop."

"I don't know where you get that language," she said, in outrage.

"Or my knowledge of the world? From you, of course. From your lousy, rotten knowledge of it."

For a moment I thought she would slap my face, her hand jerked angrily towards me and I got ready to feel the pain and not show it, but instead her hand dropped, and she turned her head away. "This is bad for me too, Alice," she murmured. She dabbed at her eye with a tiny lace handkerchief. "Show some mercy, kid."

"Tell me about the Werkstaette," I said.

"It's a good place," she said eagerly. "Only started about four years ago by a friend of Count Henri's."

"Oh, him." I blamed that handsome Viennese aristocrat for what had happened to Josie.

The Werkstaette was the result of a noble idea, that of training young girls of the poorer classes, who were possessed of artistic talent, to develop that talent and earn their living from it. They were to be craft workers rather than artists.

I remember how I inspected my new home cautiously, like a little cat. First impressions were favourable enough. I liked the look of the plain well-lit building with its no-nonsense air. I felt I could tolerate the head of the school, the Director, Josef Hoffmann, although he had a strict face. But I was wary about the matron, Frau Paul, who looked after the girls. As for Annette Lucifer, who taught drawing, I knew an enemy when I saw one.

Josie said good-bye in the rooms allotted to me.

"Good-bye, kid." She kissed my cheek. "Look after yourself. I'll write to you. You've got my address in New York?"

I nodded. "In my diary." I kept my diary in a locked book. Josie regularly picked the lock and read the diary. Thus we knew each other's thoughts. It was a way of communicating.

"Well, don't lose it."

I shook my head. "I won't." Nor did I, but it was of no use, because Josie never got to New York. She travelled via Paris, and somehow she got stuck there, and I heard no more of the show in New York. Nor did she ever send me an address. I was more aware than ever of being abandoned.

When Josie had left me, I deposited the bag with my clothes on the bed, sat down on my bedside chair and surveyed my new kingdom. I thought of it as that, although the room had another occupant, at the moment absent.

I studied her bed and possessions. On her chest of drawers was a drawing of a beautiful young woman, bejewelled and wearing something resembling a crown; beside it stood a candle and a little pot of flowers.

Like an altar, I thought. I believe I knew even then, in my cynical and worldly young heart, that there was something unreal about the lady in the picture. I had lived long enough in the theatre world to recognise a touch of it when I saw it. I wondered if she said her prayers to it.

My gaze shifted to the bed, on which rested an embroidered nightdress case of pale pink satin that I instantly coveted. "Maria," it said in pale blue satin stitch. I went over and picked it up. It told me something about Maria: she was a neat sewer, and she liked her possessions, of which she did not appear to have many. Not nearly as many as I, who had in my luggage as many as three stuffed Pierrot dolls, two silver-topped scent bottles, and a genuine tortoiseshell comb, studded with brilliants. All were once the property of Josie and had been acquired by me when she tired of them. Maria's brush and comb were of simple wood with her initials burned into them. Presumably, since Maria shared a room with me, she too was "different."

I stroked the satin case and put it back. I wouldn't have my own in pale pink and blue; mine would be scarlet and black.

"What were you doing with my nightdress case?" said a cold voice from the door.

I turned. So this was Maria! a short, dark-haired young girl with a riot of shiny, black curls of which I was at once bitterly envious, since my own hair was straight and ordinary. I tried to do things with it, like curling it on my cheeks in what Josie called "kiss" curls, or cutting it into a fringe across my fore-head, but I was never satisfied with it.

"What were you doing?" repeated Maria.

"Admiring it," I said honestly. Maria had an interesting face. I thought we might become friends. But not if she thought I was pinching her things. Though I had lived in a world in which people did steal, I had always remained fairly honest. But I didn't blame her for being suspicious.

Maria went over, adjusted the position of the satin envelope on the bed, and gave it a pat. I saw then that she had not suspected me of theft, she was just a girl who loved her possessions and did not like them interfered with.

"Like to look at my stuff?" I spread my belongings out on the bed and started to dispose of them in my chest of drawers. "Help yourself," I said. "Choose what you want from this lot." And I indicated dolls, lace handkerchiefs, scent bottles and silk stockings.

Her eyes went round with surprise. "Can I?"

"Of course. Go on. I mean it."

Her hand hovered over the stockings. "Not those, they have runs," I said.

"But silk—to wear silk against the skin, how soft."

"Well, go on, have a pair. I've got more than one. But have something else as well."

"Really? Truly?"

"Yes, honestly. I'd like you to. Here, have this scent bottle. It held attar of roses."

24

"Oh!" She took it up, unscrewed the top. "Oh, yes, you can smell it, the whole bottle smells of roses. Oh, it's so sweet and clean, it goes right through my head."

"It's yours, then," I said.

She took the bottle, polished the top gently with her hand and went over to her bureau top and placed it reverently by the picture of the woman, talking softly to herself while she did so.

Frau Paul called us to supper then, and it was when she saw the display on my bed that she scolded me. Luggage was not to be placed on the bed. In fact, no objects were to be placed upon the clean bedspread (she turned a blind eye to Maria's embroidered nightdress case). It was a firm rule of the school and by rights I should earn a "black" mark. As it was, it would be saved up and only be inflicted on me if I earned another one.

The child of the free and easy life, I was a little daunted to be tied up in a mass of rules and restrictions. I think Maria saw my apprehension.

"They are strict here, but fair, and the food is good," she said. "Only keep out of the rat house," she went on with a sinister giggle.

"What's that?"

"Where we go for punishment."

Thus encouraged, I went with her to supper: a good, thick soup with crusty bread, meat in a savoury stew with beans, and fruit for dessert. She was right about the food, it was tasty. Maria was always correct on such matters, I later discovered.

We ate at one long table, and for a few minutes I found the crescendo of girlish voices hard to bear. I was a naturally ebullient child, however, and soon I would have been glad to join in. But no one spoke to me.

Exhaustion overtook me as we prepared for bed. I undressed quickly, noticing with surprise that Maria undressed completely beneath her petticoat and then manoeuvred her nightdress of heavy cotton over her head so that I didn't even see a bare leg. I slid into a cast-off of Josie's, made of pale blue ninon. A lump suddenly arose in my throat and I knew I was going to cry.

"Yes, you cry now," said Maria. "Tomorrow you will be better." Her voice was consoling, she had been through it all herself.

The truth was Maria had invented her own support in this

difficult world, evolved her own fantasy. That night she let me into it.

"Alice," whispered Maria. "Can I ask you something?"

I came awake again. "Yes, go on."

I had to wait a long while before she said: "You speak English."

"Well, go on."

"Will you teach me to speak English?" I was stunned into silence, and the silence worried Maria. "It is very important to me," she said.

"All right. I'll teach you. Of course."

"Oh, thank you."

Then I had an idea. "But if I teach you English, will you teach me better German in return?"

"Gladly." In the darkness Maria reached out a hand and took mine in a firm grasp. "That is a bargain, then."

"Right." I closed my eyes, ready to sleep. I wasn't planning any teaching at the moment. But Maria hadn't finished.

"You see," she went on, in a quiet but confident voice. "It is very necessary for me to learn English."

"Oh? Why?"

"Because of my birth, my descent," she said.

"Oh, but I thought—" I began, and then stopped short.

"What is it you thought?"

"Well, from the way you go on—about what you own, and the way you talk—I thought you'd been born in an orphanage."

"One is not born in an orphanage," said Maria. "One is placed in an orphanage. Still, it is clever of you. Yes, I was brought up as a foundling."

"Oh, I am sorry, Maria. Mothers are awful, or they can be. Josie is a real tartar when she's in the mood, I can tell you, but I wouldn't be without her." It seemed easier for Josie to be without me, but I decided not to dwell upon that side of it.

"But I have a mother, too," said Maria in a whisper.

"Well, of course you *must* have, but not to know who she is . . ."

"Oh, I know," said Maria, with utter certainty. "They tried to keep it secret from me, for reasons of state, but I know. I guessed." She added reverently: "I think I always knew in my heart. I knew I was not the child of ordinary parents."

"Who is your mother then?"

26

"A princess."

"Oh." I considered this statement. "How do you know?"

"My body told me early on," said Maria, with confidence. "Maria, it said, you are not the same as these other children around you. My hands, to begin with. I have very delicate long fingers, not a peasant's or a working person's hands at all. Anyway, I *felt* different."

"You have a lovely voice," I said. I appreciated voices, and Maria's was deep and sweet.

"And then one day," went on Maria, "the Mother Superior of the home where I was being looked after told me that my baby clothes, those that I had worn when I was found on their doorstep, were of the finest possible quality. 'Fit for a princess,' she said."

I suppose it was possible for even a Mother Superior in charge of an orphanage to be a silly woman, although you'd think she'd have had silliness knocked out of her by the job. She must have known the sort of girl she was talking to.

"Did she show you the clothes?" I demanded.

"No. They'd been destroyed. Or so she *said*. But perhaps they'd just been taken away."

"Why would anyone do that?"

"Evidence of my existence, you see. I suppose my mother wasn't married to my father. Either he wasn't well-born enough or else there were reasons of state why they could not marry." She gave a deep, romantic sigh: she had it all worked out.

As I tried to sleep I heard her voice going on: how she had drawn a picture of her mother, from imagination, but she thought it would be a likeness. How one day her mother would claim her, and she must be ready.

I pretended to be asleep. I was embarrassed by the insight I felt I had into Maria's heart. Poor Maria, or maybe lucky Maria; it was a good dream while it lasted. As I drifted off I heard Maria saying confidently:

"After English, French. God will surely send me a French speaker next."

I didn't settle down easily at the Werkstaette. Life with Josie had not made discipline easy to me. And I was full of resentment—angry with Josie, angry with myself. I felt lost and deserted.

I reacted by breaking every rule, and by being as rude to the

Director as I could be. But I was more interested in the teaching we received, more absorbed in the work we were expected to produce, than I wanted to admit. I was even glad for a moment when my efforts received praise. Afterwards, however, I was angrier than ever. So I started spoiling my work deliberately. One day I tore up the drawing I was making and threw the pieces away. Annette Lucifer hit me on the knuckles with a ruler.

Suddenly I hated these women who ruled my life with their whims. I rubbed my knuckles. No one had ever hit me. Josie never. Before I knew what I was doing, my anger boiled over and I hit Fraulein Lucifer on the face. There was a moment of horrified silence, and then I was hurled off to Frau Paul, who shut me in the punishment cupboard.

It was dark in there with only a narrow crack of light coming through the bottom of the door. I found nothing to sit on so I crouched on the floor near to that crack. Something touched my leg. "Keep out of the rat house," Maria had said. I screamed. Now I was in the rat house.

I shouted and banged on the door with my fists. "Let me out! Let me out!"

No one came. I continued banging and shouting till my knuckles were bleeding and my voice was hoarse. "I hate you all," I sobbed. "I hate you."

I kept my eyes to the crack of light because I had a deeper fear even than the fear of rats. An irrational, terrible fear. This place was coffin-shaped and had the odor of dirt. The darkness seemed to press on my eyelids with physical strength. I couldn't face inwards because the walls and ceiling of the cupboard were pressing on me too. I began to feel I would choke; I could hear my heart banging in my ears. It was like being buried alive.

I started to cry, tears squeezing themselves under my lids. Desperately I pressed nose and mouth against the bottom of the door, trying to suck in the air.

I don't know how long I lay there, but I began to be aware of a gentle tapping and a voice calling my name softly.

"Alice? Alice? Can you hear? Answer me. It's Maria." Another little tap on the door, and the whisper again.

"Can you hear me? Yes?"

I sat up. "Yes."

Quickly she told me that she had stolen the key to the door, and was about to push it through to me. I was to wait a few minutes so that she could get away, then let myself out.

"Yes," I breathed. It was all I could do to speak, but she heard, gave a last rap at the door as if to encourage me, and went away. I could hear her feet on the floor. Blessed, blessed Maria.

I had the key in the door and turned before her voice had died away in my ears. The corridor outside was empty; I ran to the lobby. A thick alpaca cloak hung on a hook near a side door. I recognised it as Frau Paul's. I grabbed it, threw it on and ran out of the door into the street. At first I just ran, not caring where I was, just breathing in the free air. But after a while I stopped, and threw the key to the cupboard into the gutter. Let them find it if they could.

All the time I had been running something had been banging hard against my side. I put my hand down to discover what it was. A purse, a hard, round leather purse—Frau Paul's. There were bank notes inside. I knew now I had money for a real escape.

Without realising it, I had made my way to a broad main road along which carriages and trams were travelling. Dimly I recognised where I was from my days in Vienna with Josie. I knew I could walk from here to the main railway station, from which ran the great continental express linking Vienna with Paris and London.

A soft rain was falling. A lamp-lighter was going from lamp to lamp pulling the chain that made the gas flame within the mantle. I stood in the cobbled forecourt of the station wondering which way to go. Cabs bearing travellers were rattling past me on either side. A crowded omnibus drew up at the kerb, and the passengers hurried off towards the trains. I thought I saw a face I recognised. It wasn't anyone from the Werkstaette, but I couldn't place who it was. I sank back into the shadows by a wall.

But I soon realised that in this whole concourse no one was interested in me, for all of them were intent on getting their luggage and themselves to the train on time. I could see the label "Hotel de Louvre, Paris" on the trunks of one group. Josie was in Paris. Paris it would be.

I was not so stupid as to think that there was enough money in Frau Paul's purse to get me to Paris, but it would buy me a ticket to somewhere. Life with a theatrical troupe had taught me there were ways of travelling on the cheap. You could always hide in the lavatory as the guard went by.

I made my way towards the Paris train. Passengers were already arriving for it, and, when a couple started to argue with the man inspecting tickets, I managed to slip behind their luggage and get on the platform. Then I stood behind a pillar waiting for the right chance to board the express. I mustn't be on too early, or I might get turned off before it drew out of the station. I wondered what was happening back at the Werkstaette. They probably hadn't noticed I had gone yet.

A pile of trunks and a small tower of baskets were being handled by sweating porters near where I stood. They were theatrical baskets, full of costumes and props. THE HIGH JINKS COMPANY, I read, THEATRE RIVOLI, PARIS. And there was that trunk for the Hotel de Louvre again. Half a dozen pretty and fashionably dressed young women, as well as several men, were preparing to board the train. They were all giggling and joking, obviously delighted to be off, and talking among themselves in a mixture of French, German and English. Obviously a cosmopolitan lot, and equally obviously, to my knowledgeable eye, the "High Jinks" company on the move. I thought I could join the crowd already assembling and slip aboard unnoticed. I came out from behind my pillar. I had recognised one of the girls; she was called Fraulein Lotti Menken, and was a soubrette-style actress, perenially youthful unless you saw her close, when she was suddenly older. It had been her face I had recognised earlier that evening; she had visited Josie once.

She was standing with a young man who had the most beautiful face I had ever seen. He turned and saw me, and our eyes met. For a moment he seemed to study my face, then he turned gravely away. He was dark haired, with regular features and a sensitive, perceptive look in his eyes, which were deep set under level brows and with lashes exceptionally long for a man. There were lines of humour about his mouth. He looked both youthful and gentle.

Cries of welcome from the actresses drew my attention to a figure hurrying down the platform, hat pushed rakishly to the side of his head, arms full of flowers for the girls, and a great smile on his face. It was Count Henri.

He saw me, and instantly, startled recognition came into his eyes, he said, "Alice!" His hand came down heavily on my shoulders, and I gave a cry.

30

The young man turned round and lifted the hand away. "Steady on," he said gently. "Don't hurt her." He smiled at me.

Well, Count Henri was no fool. He soon had the truth out of me. I was hustled back to the Werkstaette in disgrace. I knew I wouldn't escape the minute he saw me; no one escaped from Count Henri. I had heard Josie say so.

I was not re-imprisoned in the punishment cupboard. I'm not sure why. But at night I had terrible nightmares. Once I woke up screaming.

"Maria," I sobbed, holding on to her. "The dark comes down, and then there is earth on my mouth, on my eyes, forcing itself up my nose."

Maria put her arms round me and stroked my hair in the dark. "Just a nightmare. It is over now."

"I'm buried alive. That is how it is to be buried alive."

Maria hung on to me, trying to quieten me, but to no avail. "Maria, I saw the baby, and it was alive. Do you think they buried it?"

Maria asked no questions, nor answered any, but continued to hold me tight, as if she had her own nightmares and did not wish to add mine to hers.

Silently she comforted me. Night after night she saw me through. A bond was forged between us by those nights, that I could not break and which, I think, was equally strong for Maria. Two little lost girls together.

One day the Director came into our studio with another man. I was too young to guess his age, but I know now that he was thirty-three years old. He had a stocky, muscular figure and a natural elegance. But what I marvelled at chiefly was the perfection of his clothes. My mother's men friends had been what she called good dressers, and, indeed, had been clothed by the best London tailors, but this man was something else again. He wore a tightly fitted overcoat that reached to just below his knees; it was double-breasted with a large and beautifully tailored collar. Collar and cuffs were bound in what looked like satin and there was broad satin frogging across his chest. The material was so soft and thick it looked like velvet, but I think it was really cashmere. He carried a gleaming silk hat in white-gloved hands. On his feet were the best polished boots I had ever seen. He was not handsome, with slightly protuberant

31

black eyes and a big moustache, yet good humour made his face pleasant to look at. I had seen many attractive men in Josie's company, and many who wore beautiful clothes, but I had never seen a man like this before.

He and the Director advanced down the room between the aisles of desks, stopping here and there for a look. Judging by the bored, sceptical look on our visitor's face, I had the distinct feeling that he found the paintings of most of the Werkstaette pupils to be too formal and conservative, as indeed I did myself. The Director's face took on a puzzled frown when he saw my board, but his companion woke up.

"And who is this?" He spoke in a heavily accented German.

"This is our English pupil," said Herr Hoffmann. "This is Alice May."

"English? Ah, the marvellous English. I have some English customers, a duchess or two, a countess. No royal princesses, alas. They are not allowed; they must dress from Bond Street, but it matters not. They have no style." He twinkled at me, pouring out a stream of English, just as heavily accented as his German.

"You're French," I said.

"This is Monsieur Paul Poiret," said the Director reprovingly. "From Paris."

"And what is this I see?" said Paul Poiret, picking up my abstract.

"Oranges," I said, hanging my head.

"But what colour, what freedom of movement, what rhythm. And so natural."

I raised my eyes and looked at him: he meant it. "They don't look like ordinary oranges," I said.

"They look like *your* oranges." He held my drawing at an arm's length, screwed up his eyes in a look with which I was to become familiar. "And they would look splendid on a wall. I see them as wallpapers and curtains. Delicious. So suitable for a room in which to breakfast." He turned to me and said: "My dear, will you become a Martine?"

I stared in uncomprehending silence.

"I can promise you exciting work, real artistic freedom, and as you become more and more useful to me, a good wage."

Nervously I croaked out: "What are the Martines?"

He threw open his arms wide: "They are everything: they design all that houses need—furniture, wallpapers, curtains, china, whole rooms. The Martines design houses, the Rosines make scent, and I create beautiful ladies."

This miraculous man, like a visitor from another planet, a god, seemed to take everything for granted. He had come to Vienna to visit the Werkstaette. He had started a similar school of his own in Paris named after his daughter Martine.

"Poiret—the Martines," I heard Maria breathe. The names obviously meant something to her. "Can I come too?"

"If I go, you come," I said firmly, and I meant it.

We went to Paris as 1913 became 1914. I suppose there was a Christmas that year, but I remember nothing of it, so overwhelmed was I by the totality of Paris. The street smells, the traffic noises, the clothes (the expensive ones, at least) completely disarmed me. I adored it. Life suddenly seemed larger and brighter than I had ever known it.

With Paul Poiret we were, of course, at the heart of an exclusive world. Poiret was almost master of Parisian society then; his word as to what smart women wore, or used for scent, or how they decorated their houses, had the force of law. If a woman did not choose to wear his clothes exactly as he had designed, he dismissed her from his atelier, no matter what her rank. He used beautiful girls as models for his clothes, but his best advertisement was his elegant wife, who might almost have been created to wear his clothes. In a way she *had* been so created, and by Poiret himself, for he had fallen in love with her when she was only sixteen.

When I saw her that first time she was wearing a grey duvetyn suit (skirt and jacket, we called it) with a turban of the same material and a long muffler of dusty pink, the same shade as her knee boots which showed through a slit in the skirt. Denise Poiret was the embodiment of Poiret's "look."

The Martines, as Paul Poiret conceived them, were craftswomen who could turn their hand to anything—designing curtains, wallpapers, and bathroom tiles, painting furniture, creating frescos, and working for the theatre as well. He had created an energetic, talented centre for the decorative arts, and Maria and I were proud to be so important a part of it. Paul Poiret's fertile mind also invented the Rosines, who made and sold the most delightful perfumes. A chemist had devised the scents, but Poiret's nose had selected those which would appeal to his discriminating customers, and it was he who had chosen their names: Le Coupe d'Or, Nuits de Chine, Le Balcon, among others. I remember, the first time I went into the Rosine shop on an errand for Poiret, standing there and sniffing in great breaths of ambergris, musk, and geranium. These subtle and sensuous scents settled my sense of smell for the rest of my life.

At Martines, our talent was thought sufficient for itself. We had little supervision; we were given our tasks and left free to design as we wanted. Maria and I ate breakfast and lunch at the Martines' headquarters in the Faubourg St. Honoré and we were placed in lodgings around the corner, lodgings that were simple and small but mercifully free of any authority, except perhaps for that of the concierge, an elderly and very deaf lady who maintained a total and complete reserve towards us.

My first project as a Martine was to design a backdrop for a play Poiret was working on. I remember the thrill of seeing it grow before me, and the excitement when I was told it would be used.

Josie got in touch with me as soon as I arrived in Paris. The Werkstaette and M. Poiret had both told her of my move to Paris. She telephoned me at the Martine workroom, telling me that she was going on tour.

She sounded low key. "It's been downward time, kid," she said. "Still, I'm working, and we'll be back in Paris soon."

"Which theatre, Josie?"

"I'm not sure yet," she said, evasively. "And who knows, your old Josie may hit the high spots yet. I never stay down for long, do I?"

"No. Don't you want to see me, Josie?"

"I do ... and I will soon. I bet you've grown into a beauty! Tootle-pip, darling. I'll send a card."

"And an address," I shouted, but it was too late.

Paul Poiret found out that Josie's next show in Paris would be opening at the Théâtre Monique on the Rue 'Rose. Two weeks later Maria and I made our way there.

The Rue 'Rose was sleazy and the Théâtre Monique was sleazier still, and I quite feared for my poor Josie when I saw her name in small letters underneath the title: *Les Périls de Pauline.*

Maria and I paid for tickets and took our seats. The auditorium was full enough, although the audience was hardly the sort to bring out the best in an actress. They were making a fair racket with laughter, jokes, and fidgeting around, and I couldn't say they hushed expectantly when the curtain went up. In fact, a low whistle came from one or two points in the house. Josie did not play the part of Pauline, for which she ought to have been grateful, since most of the whistles, catcalls, shouts and fruit were directed at the buxom girl who had that role. The girl was a rotten actress, no doubt about it, but neither producer nor management had given her much support. The costumes and sets (twelve slow changes) looked as though they had been picked up at the Flea Market.

Josie appeared towards the end of the first act. Her part was negligible, a lick and a spit. She gave it what she could, but it was apparent that she wasn't pleasing the audience. She wasn't helped by her costume of a tight-fitting lamé, bronzing with age. My spirits sank at the sight of her.

I made no comment to Maria, who was sitting quietly by my side. She knew very little about the theatre, but she had taste and she knew quality—or the lack of it—when she saw it. At the end of the show, no one got much of a hand from the audience. There was not even the spirit in the house for the odd hiss. We all rose sadly and departed. I took Maria round to the back of the house to see Josie.

I knocked and went straight in without waiting for an answer. Josie was sitting at her make-up table, cleaning her face. Her eyes caught mine in the mirror.

"Hello, kid," she said, tonelessly. "So you got here."

"No thanks to you."

Josie turned round to face me. "I was ashamed." She spread out her hands. "Well—look at me." She had put on weight and there was grey in her hair. "When I think of some of the parts I had in London. I was a star. . . . It's a wicked world, the theatre. One day you're the top, then the next no one wants you. You remember that, Alice."

"Even a lie would have been better than silence," I said.

"Do you think so? Funny, your father said that once. Sorry, kid."

I introduced Maria. "Hello, dear," said Josie. "Sorry to plunge you into our family affairs, but that's how we are."

"It's interesting," said Maria, and she meant it. I could see

35

her studying this specimen of the, to her, unknown genus, "mother." I hoped she would not accept Josie as average for the type.

"Thanks," said Josie, swinging back to finish cleaning her face. "You and I ought to get on then."

Maria smiled. "I'd like to."

"Don't adopt her as your mother," I advised. "Because she won't do."

Josie turned again, this time to look at Maria. "Haven't you got a mother of your own?"

Maria thought about it, evidently considering what to say. "No," she said at last. "I'm a foundling."

Josie opened her arms wide, as if to adopt us both, although she had really not done all that well with me.

"Come and have supper with me, girls," said Josie briskly. "I'm ready now and could do with a snack."

We went round the corner to a little café where Maria and I drank coffee and Josie had coffee and brandy. She poured the cognac into her coffee and drank it down in great gulps. "I needed that. You may not think much of that show at the Monique, but it feeds me, and it has come to that."

"What about New York?"

"An illusion, the fairy vanishing act, like so much in my life. And me without a penny."

"Oh, all right," I said grudgingly. "Apologies accepted. At least *I* was eating."

When we parted we were a harmonious family group, into which Maria had miraculously merged, and I had Josie's address firmly written down. I wondered if she was living there alone. From her demeanour, somehow I thought she was.

Within the week Josie had burst in on me at the Martines. "My luck's changed: I've got a new show with a good part. You brought me luck, kid. I'm on the up and up." I could tell she was excited. As always with Josie, she looked young and beautiful when she was happy. Even her clothes were new and very becoming. Soon she had left the cast at the Théâtre Monique and was rehearsing for *Tic-Tac,* while I was busily engaged in creating my set for the third act of *Plus ça Change.*

From the start of the new show, Josie was particularly happy. It took me a bit of time to associate this with a young man called Frederic Lothar. Then Josie came to "my" first night and I went to hers, and there was Frederic on the stage, singing, always beautifully, to Josie's soubrette role. As far as I remember, she was maid to a duchess, and Frederic was valet to a prince. Frederic was the young man I had seen on the station in Vienna. He was older, as was I, but as beautiful as I remembered him.

"I've seen him before Paris," I murmured to Maria, who was sitting by my side. She was silent, unable to speak, following Frederic with her eyes, nor did she utter a word until the curtain went down.

Then she said, "Can we go backstage?"

I was determined to go, in case there was a chance of meeting the beautiful young man. Josie hadn't asked us, but that wouldn't stop me.

"Come on," I said to Maria.

There was not such a crush backstage as might have been expected, and the stage-door man let us in without a murmur. Still, no doubt, *Tic-Tac* would see Josie through to midsummer as she anticipated. She was usually right about that sort of thing. I could see the routine bottles of champagne and the baskets of flowers going to the dressing-rooms of the principals as we went along to Josie.

There was even a bottle in her room too, but not yet opened. I suppose she was keeping it for someone special.

"Hello, Alice. Good of you to come."

"As if I wouldn't."

"What did you think of the show?"

"Tip-top. And you were brilliant. Sparkling."

"Catchy tunes, aren't they?" She was powdering her face with a big swansdown powder puff on a long ivory wand with an African's head as a handle. Pure Josie, that. "We might be going on to London and then New York."

There was a knock on the door and Frederic walked in. He was wearing a silk dressing-gown and carrying a tray on which was a sandwich, a cup of coffee and a glass of brandy. "Here you are, Josie, food and drink. Hello, you two girls." He smiled at us both, but he smiled particularly at me. "Haven't I seen you before?"

"Yes, once. On a railway station in Vienna," I added. "Count Henri—you remember?"

"Good lord, was that you? How you've changed. Grown up."

From that moment I was in love with him.

He asked me to go with him to the English Thé Salon in the

Rue de Rivoli, where we could dance. That was the beginning.

We danced beautifully together. But perhaps it would have gone no further if Paul Poiret had not asked me to design the costumes for the ballet called *Semele and Jupiter*. I asked Frederic if he would act as a model for me, and to my surprise he consented. I was the innocent tempter.

I had a tiny studio with the usual platform for the model under a north light. I wore a trim, blue smock, and worked away with crayon, the complete professional. He was a good model, but a little shy, to my surprise. I felt him flinch as I adjusted the purple velvet mantle over one bare shoulder.

Tentatively, shyly, I stroked the skin. I was naive and heedless, a young Pagan in my awakening to life. Later on a man who knew me well said, "Alice, you always were a sucker for anything beautiful . . . And if it moved and talked, well, you wanted it more."

I couldn't resist kissing Frederic. Of course, we'd kissed and cuddled at the tea room, but this was different. As I kissed him, I giggled. Frederic said that giggle was like a bubble on a glass of champagne. It spoke of gaiety and freedom and lack of restraint. My giggle released us, and my laughter carried us forward, so that I was soon happily conducting my own undressing, and vigorously cooperating in that moment of union, arching my back, and laughing.

I'm glad I laughed then. I thought that was how love should always and forever be. The loss of virginity seemed a small price to pay for such great happiness.

I didn't realise then that the loss of virginity is emotional more than physical: it had opened my mind to love. I had lost a little of that invulnerability against the world I was struggling to achieve.

There was never much conversation between me and Frederic. If we talked it was of theatre gossip, or about our dreams for the future. What we had in common was a strong physical love to which speech was not essential. And we kept our affair a secret. Love affairs often were then; people were more private, and we were at the age to find secrecy romantic. Moreover, I did not want Josie to know; I feared her influence.

What drew Frederic to me? Easy enough to see what attracted me to him: he was beautiful to look at, with a deep, soft speaking voice, which I adored. But why did he love me? Being in love is a more complex business than I thought it was in those days. I believe now what drew Frederic to me was my anxiousness to love. I had offered my love to Josie, but she hadn't really wanted it. Or not on the terms I was offering. Josie wanted her freedom and took it, whereas I wanted desperately to be settled.

As that year turned towards summer and the days grew longer and warmer, Frederic and I made little expeditions outside Paris. One Saturday afternoon we took a cab to where you could hire a boat, and then made a river trip down the Seine, and had lunch together at a riverside café. I wore a white cotton organdie dress sprinkled with hundreds and thousands of multicoloured dots which I had painted on myself. It was a dress never to be forgotten. To paint it at all had taken me over a week. I was glowing in my first heedless, happy, physical relationship. The touch of Frederic's hand on my bare shoulder, the weight of his mouth on mine, these obliterated all else, and transfigured my whole life. There was a trembling, tentative innocence about it all. I see that now. I also see that not only was I the initiator, but mine was the energy and desire that carried us along.

Maria knew. I had said nothing, confided nothing, but nevertheless she knew. Once I saw her nostrils quiver like an excited animal. It was almost as if she could smell love's odour. I think it made her physically angry, and her anger only made me colder to her.

"I hope you fall in the river," she said, as I put on my hat, a large white straw.

"Oh, Maria." I wasn't really taking much notice of her. This naturally annoyed her even more. "I can swim, you know."

In a sudden aggressive voice, she said, "There's a girl in the chorus of Josie's show that absolutely hates your guts. She'd do anything to get level with you."

"Why should she?" I asked, bewildered. "I don't believe it."

"Don't you? Well, we shall see." Her eyes shone with dark fury. "We shall see," and she pushed me through the door of our room and banged it behind me so hard that Madame la Concierge came out of her little parlour at the bottom of the stairs and looked at me.

Maria got her way. I did fall in the river.

Frederic was rowing and we were drawing in to our landing-stage. I was standing up to climb ashore when the wash from a big motor launch, full of laughing soldiers with their girls, hit our little craft and tumbled me into the water. "Bother, Maria," I remember thinking as I fell. "This wouldn't have happened if she hadn't wished for it." Frederic had to hurry me off in a cab.

I was sitting in Frederic's dressing-room, wrapped in a great towel and sipping hot brandy and water, when Josie sailed in.

"Freddo," she began, and then she saw me and stopped. Her face became terrible, like an angry mask. "So," she said. It was like a scene from some dated melodrama at the Lyceum that Josie would never have played in. I wanted to laugh and cry at the same time. "*You!* What that bitch from the chorus said was true. Well, I've closed my eyes to a lot of things that I must now speak about. You are a lying little slut—cold-hearted, like your father."

"I've never lied!"

But she swept on! "As for you, Frederic, taking advantage of a girl—"

Frederic became very angry. "You don't know what you are saying," he said in a cold voice.

Josie gave a hoot of disbelief. "And as for you, Alice," she proclaimed. "You can go away and start packing your things. I shall be sending you home, to England, tomorrow!"

"Josie!"

But the door had slammed behind her.

Next day Paul Poiret came into the Martines with a grave face. He stood behind me for a moment, studying what I had done. I was working on a new theatre decor for him, this time a revue. "Very nice," he said. "Good. You have talent. So," he went on, "your mother wishes to send you home. A pity."

The relationship between us had grown steadily over the last few months; I was no longer just one among his pupils. He was a man who liked and understood women. It was no accident that he designed clothes, scent, and furniture for women, and no accident that the schools of workers he had recruited, the Martines and the Rosines, were young females. But he was an autocrat. I had found him tyrannical and high-handed on occasion. However, if one refused to surrender to him, he was perversely charmed. I argued with him, contrary to all the rules, and prospered. Looking back, I see that he slipped neatly into the hole left by the father I had hardly known. In the all-femi-

40

nine world in which I lived, he was the male dominator. Then it seemed natural; later our relationship changed.

I swung round. "She can't do it."

He raised his eyebrows slightly. "Probably not, no. But there are other considerations." He drew up a chair and sat down looking at me. "It might be sensible for you to go."

"Why?"

He didn't answer at once but hummed a little tune, picked up my sketch and studied it. "You live in a little world of your own. A theatre world. I do the same myself, so I understand. But reality intrudes. It may be about to do so."

"You mean Frederic?" I faltered. "But we love each other."

He stood up. "There are more important things in the world than love, alas. Like war. You had better go back home to England." He sounded kindly. "We will make arrangements for you."

There it was again, that moment when life picked you up like a parcel and posted you on. But I was older now, and this was not Vienna, nor was I penniless. I was a young woman who earned her own money and who had a lover. Not London—what would I do there? My place was with Frederic.

I didn't show any of this. I kept a controlled face to the world, but I made up my mind.

When my work ended that day I went round to where Frederic lived in a single room over a grocer's shop, around the corner from the theatre. Not a smart place, but good, plain, simple lodgings. Frederic was sitting in an armchair by the window, reading a newspaper and studying a score. He never smoked because of his voice. I lost no time in telling him. "They *are* going to send me back to London, and I won't go, not without you. We must run away together."

Frederic got up. "Yes," he said, in a serious voice. "I have been thinking it may be the only way and all things considered, I believe we should go together to Vienna and get married there quickly in case France and Germany go to war."

I had packed my small valise. "I am ready." A war couldn't change me. What was a war compared to love? If we parted now we would be separated forever. I knew I must cling to the deepest relationship I then had.

"We will go after the performance tonight. I cannot let them down for that, you understand." I nodded. "Dearest darling, I wonder if I'm right to let you do this?"

41

"We must, we must," I said urgently.

I waited for Frederic in his rooms until he came back from the theatre. We hurried to the station together. For the sake of economy we were taking a fast train to Belfort, which was a major fortress town where we could get a bus to the Swiss frontier. Our carriage was almost empty and Frederic held me in his arms as we bumped through the night.

But events moved too fast for us.

I fell asleep, to be awakened by the train grinding to a stop. The train stayed in the station for a long time. Outside we could hear shouts and the sound of other trains, but ours stayed where it was.

Presently Frederic got up and looked out of the window. Then he turned back to me. "Will you look out and tell me what you see?"

I poked my head out of the window. "I see trains on either side of the platform. Trains and trains. And soldiers, everywhere there are soldiers." I was scared.

Frederic got out of the carriage, and walked down the platform, heedless of my frightened beseeching of him not to leave. Very soon he was back.

"General mobilisation of the French army," he said. "It has come more quickly than I expected. By the morning France and Austria and Germany will be at war. England will soon follow."

"What shall we do?"

Sadly he said, "Get your bag and get out of the train. The guard says that this one will never move tonight. Across the platform is one that will return to Paris."

"Back to Paris?" I was bewildered.

I let him lead me across the platform to where another train stood. Something about his expression aroused a terrible fear in me. "Frederic—you are coming back with me?"

"No." He took my hand and pressed it between his two. "No, dearest love, I cannot come. I must go back to Austria. You must see that; your country and mine will soon be at war. They tell me there is an omnibus which goes to the frontier. I shall take it."

"Then I'm coming with you." I was trembling.

"Alice, no. It is too late. If we could have been married before the war started, all would have been well. But now it is too late. We could never be married in time. I don't know what may happen to me, and how could I risk leaving you alone in a country at war?"

"But I'm English. England won't fight." Tears were streaming down my face. Once again I was being abandoned.

"I think she will. No, Alice. You must go back." He pushed a piece of paper in my hand. "That is my address in Vienna. Try to write." For a first time I saw him as a German. "I will join the army, of course. I shall fight for the Emperor. I must."

He jumped out of the carriage and walked rapidly away. I tried to follow but a soldier standing by the door pushed me back with a laugh. "Let's keep the German whore from her lover," he said.

"I'm English, I'm English," I cried, vainly trying to get past his burly figure. He only laughed in my face; he didn't care, he didn't like the English any better than the Germans. There was nothing personal in his interference in my life. It was just a display of blind, peasant maliciousness. He gave me another push so that I fell backward into the train. The door slammed.

The train was moving; I scrambled to my feet and hung out of the window. Across the crowded platform I just made out the figure of Frederic.

"Frederic!" I shrieked.

He heard me and turned. I stared at him, tears pouring down my face, till the train rounded a bend and sped forward into the darkness.

I shall never forget that moment. I staggered to the side of the train and was violently sick. I sat huddled against a door, cold and desperate. No one took any notice of me. "He's gone. Frederic's gone," I kept saying to myself, muttering it like an incantation to exorcise my pain. But the pain grew worse as the reality had time to sink in. I had lost my lover.

When I got back to Paris the city was strangely unchanged. But there was no denying the sight of soldiers in buses and lorries being driven past. Some people cheered at the sight; others stood in sullen silence. It was very early morning, but I was able to buy a newspaper. There had been a terrorist killing in Bosnia, Austria had declared war on Serbia, Russia had mobilised and Germany had declared war on France and Russia. Soon England would be dragged in. The world was standing on its head.

I tried to hide in my room, seeing no one, but Maria wouldn't let me.

"Your mother is looking for you," she said.

"She knows where to find me." I didn't look at her.

"She does *now*. You weren't here last night." She gave me an accusing stare.

"Not what you think," I muttered. "We were running away to get married, but the train was stopped—" I didn't go on; I could not talk about it yet. "Anyway, Frederic's gone," I said, the pain was such that I could hardly talk.

"I am going too," said Maria. "You can tell Monsieur Poiret for me. We are enemies now." Her hard face frightened me.

I sat down on my bed and watched her. She finished packing, locked her bag, tested the weight to see if she could carry it, and then put on her hat and coat. Then she announced bleakly, "I'm going to the Gâre de Lyon to see if I can get a train to Italy, and so on to Austria that way. Italy is neutral."

"I'm coming."

She gave me a long look but did not refuse my offer. Silently we set off together. We were almost halfway there on the Metro when I said, "It's bad there at the station. I don't know what trains are running."

"There'll be something. I'll manage."

Again we relapsed into silence, a silence not broken until we were in the station itself. Maria left her bag with me and went to investigate. Then she came back and picked it up. "Good-bye, Alice. There's a train to Turin in half an hour. No seats but I can stand."

"Maria—" I pulled the piece of paper with Frederic's address on it. "I want you to have this. I might not be able to get in touch with him, but you can. Write to him, or go and see him for me."

Suddenly we were hugging each other and crying.

"Good-bye, Alice. God keep you."

"And you too, Maria." The tears were flooding out of my eyes. "My best, my only friend."

I could see Maria was struggling to say something that was important to her. At last she came out with it. "Thank you for everything, Alice. You have made me a person. Before . . . I was just nothing." She kissed me, then she held out her hand. "An English handshake."

We shook hands. I wondered if I would ever see her again.

I stayed in Paris, enduring a stormy scene with Josie.

"You deserve whatever you get, Alice. You've asked for it. I've brought you up badly, that's what it is."

"You didn't bring me up at all, Josie, but I've learned a lot from you."

I thought she was going to slap my face. Then suddenly her anger collapsed and she kissed me. "Sorry, Alice. I love you, kid."

"I know Josie. I love you, too."

For a moment I longed to lean on her shoulder and tell her how miserable I was. But she drew away and powdered her nose. Emotion was over for the day.

"I'm leaving. The show is closing. It was mainly for English and American visitors anyway, and now they are rushing home. I'm going to London. Want to come?"

I shook my head.

In a low voice she said, "I want to say I'm sorry for what I said—about your father. He wasn't what I said. Nor are you."

"That's all right," I said, awkwardly.

"As a matter of fact, I loved him."

"I've always known that."

"And we were married whatever they say."

I was surprised. "Is there any doubt?" We used Josie's maiden name of May, but that was a professional matter.

"We were married according to Scots law," said Josie briefly. "His regiment was in Edinburgh. You just say you are married in front of at least two witnesses, and that does it. A handfast marriage, it is called."

"So why did he go, Josie?" I had always wanted to know her version of it, and I had never dared to ask before.

"I suppose I played him up just once too often," she said, evasively.

In Josie's parlance that meant only one thing. "You mean you had a lover?"

"Yes." She shifted her gaze and fiddled with a cigarette.

"Lovers," I corrected grimly, reading her profile accurately.

She turned her face in full protest. "Oh kid, don't sound so condemning. Men *like* me. They like you. You'll find out . . ." She gave me a searching look. "I reckon you have already."

I turned away. I could not bear to mention Frederic's name.

We parted without much more said on either side. She kissed

my cheek and I could smell her scent. No one could ever wear scent like Josie. I realise I have spent a lot of my life trying to reproduce that quality of Josie's and never succeeding.

After Josie had gone, and one week after that day in August when England declared war on Germany and Austria-Hungary, I realised that I was pregnant.

I was entirely on my own. I longed for Frederic, for Josie even. But strangely, it was Maria I missed most. I needed strength and she would have been strong for me.

I remember looking at the old doctor's face as he told me and seeing the hair growing out of a mole in his nose, thinking simultaneously that he looked like an old woman and that I was as good as dead.

I packed my bags and told my landlady I was leaving for London. She thought this wise. In time of war one was better with one's own people. She nodded sagely.

It was a lie, of courses. I was not going to London. But I dared not let her guess my real intention. She got me a cab to take my bags to the railway station. I left them there "to be collected." It was an anonymous place and I sought anonymity.

I went for a walk along the banks of the Seine. The evening was fine with a dark, blue sky full of stars. Paris in August was deserted by "le beau monde," but there were plenty of people like me around. Shopgirls walking with their lovers—many already in uniform—housewives hurrying home with a bottle of wine and a fresh baton of bread for the evening meal, lone men and women walking as idly as I was.

I was saying good-bye to Paris. Good-bye to the world.

I bought myself some violets from a woman selling flowers at the kerbside, and I walked along smelling them occasionally. No one would miss me, no one would notice I was gone. Darling Frederic, I thought, our dear young love, too dear for my possessing. Even what I have left of you inside me, I cannot sustain. I stood looking down at the Seine for a long time. It was tempting to imagine myself sinking beneath the quiet waters. But I knew that way was not for me.

Carrying my violets, I walked to the Martine workrooms. On the way I stopped at a bar and bought a measure of cognac in a bottle. It was a long trudge, so I was tired when I got there. I had a key, since all the Martines were trusted with keys if the

46

comings and goings of their work seemed to warrant it. I often worked late.

I let myself in, turned on a light and walked to the cupboard where were stored all the materials we used: oils, paints, acids and spirits. I took down a bottle of spirits of lemon which we used for removing paint stains. The crystals, easily dissolved in alcohol, stripped the die from leather and wood and textiles with ease. I remembered what the last Martine to use it had said as she put the bottle back on the shelf. "Take half an ounce of that stuff and you won't live ten minutes. The fastest and surest of poisons."

"Have you ever known anyone to take it?" I had asked.

She gave me a look. "Have I just? Didn't my own aunt down a dose with me watching? Took it in a glass of absinthe. I didn't know what it was. Out like a light she went. Gone."

"Why did she do it?" I had asked.

My informant had just shrugged. Now I thought I knew the answer to my own question.

I measured out half an ounce of the crystals and dissolved them in the glass of brandy. Ten minutes, I thought, just ten minutes. That's nothing. I picked up the glass and drank about half. Immediately I had a burning sensation in my mouth, and I vomited. The room around me began to darken.

Suddenly a voice sounded in my ears, and an arm came round my shoulders to steady me.

"My child, what have you been up to?" It was Poiret. In the gathering darkness around me I saw him pick up the bottle of salts. "Oxalic Acid." He pushed the bottle aside angrily. "Why did you take it?"

"It seemed the right thing to do," I muttered, already aware that it was not.

"How much did you take?"

I knew that I would have lapsed into unconsciousness if he had not forced me to concentrate. "Half an ounce," I managed to say, but he was answering his own questions.

"Of which, merciful heavens, you have drunk less than a half." I heard the glass fall, as if he had knocked it over.

The next passage of events is confused in my memory. I remember being forced to drink a chalky liquid, and then the arrival of a doctor, and my removal to a hospital bed.

I was treated with great gentleness, possibly because Paul

47

Poiret had placed me in a private clinic. Nothing could have been less like the hospital in which Josie had bled and bled, yet our predicament was the same. When I cried, I cried for both of us.

Poiret asked me later why I had not sought advice and help from him, hinting that he could have solved my problem for me. I didn't tell him the truth. I didn't say that because of what I had seen in the hospital in Vienna I feared abortion. I knew that I couldn't, as things were in society, bear the child, so my own death seemed preferable. I'd been wrong. I knew now that I wanted to live. I was going to take life with both hands and make what I wanted from it.

9 Chapter Two

The war was a hard time for Paul Poiret, but our "Monsieur" bore it gallantly. No Don Quixote ever went off to war more inappropriately attired—wearing a self-tailored uniform and riding in an immaculate limousine. The car had to return, but he kept the uniform, though the great couturier became, simply, a tailor working for the army of the Third Republic.

"One must do one's duty, Alice," he said. He looked at his elegant, manicured hands with much sadness. "Nature did not intend me to be a soldier, but I will fight on all fronts, public and personal. Paul Poiret is still the master."

Nevertheless, I believe he half realised that his domination of the Parisian world of high fashion was over, and it brought about a dangerous point in our relationship. Men uncertain of their professional future sometimes seek confirmation of their strength in other fields.

He took me to dinner at Maxim's, and told me how much he

admired me. Taking my hand in his, he said, "You have become what I admire most; a woman with a style of her own. It is not my style. I do not say so. It is your *own* style." He looked at my hair. "The short hair, the 'bob,' it suits you. You have become a beautiful and desirable woman."

I took a deep breath. "I too admire you, cher maître. You have done so much for me. Everything that my own father never did."

With a gentle, self-mocking arch of his eyebrows and a sad smile, he withdrew his hand. "Thank you, my dear child. And I congratulate you; you belong to the postwar world already. You have found your place."

We finished our dinner, and discussed work plans. I was thoroughly absorbed in Poiret's work, designing for theatrical productions, straight plays, comic operas, and, as people became more desperate for amusement, revues. If there was no other work for me, I sold perfume in the Rosine shop.

During this period I wrote regularly to my grandmother, whom I remembered as a short, plump, pretty woman with big blue eyes and white hair. Josie sent me an occasional post card.

Although the guns could be heard in Paris when a big push was on, and although the city itself was shelled by Big Bertha, the great gun, there was a frantic gaiety in the air, alien to the elegant world of Paul Poiret. The dances, the clothes, the hair styles, all were different. Poiret detested it, but I joined in. I was very young, after all, and could not be unhappy all the time. I went to parties where *la jeunesse folle* of society and artists danced to the rag and the shimmy. Skirts were going up, heels were higher, hair shorter, and make-up more obvious. The Rosines sold powder, rouge, lipstick, and eye-shadow. Actresses had always "made up," and now ordinary women did so; I did it myself. I was joining my own generation and moving farther away from Poiret's world. Daughters always leave their fathers behind.

Slowly, as the war continued, it could be seen that the whole world was abandoning the style of Paul Poiret. Flamboyant, exotic clothes were gone like the Russian princesses who had worn them. Sporty, simple, easy clothes were the fashion now. I think I knew intuitively that it was my new world that was being created, and this enabled me to bear the terrible tensions of the war years. I had no news, not even through the Red Cross, of Maria or Frederic.

One day I was working in the Rosine shop when a remarkably beautiful woman came in, escorted by a British officer. He was on leave from the trenches, I supposed. I knew the woman, Elise de Court, a popular actress who had begun making films. She was lovely to look at, with doll-like features and a froth of yellow hair and big blue eyes. She had the reputation of taking her men for what she could get. I presumed that this expedition to Rosine's was part of this process. I felt sorry for the officer, but no doubt he felt it was worth it.

I was packing essences in an alcove at the back, so that I could observe without being noticed. The British officer was a handsome man with long, elegant features. He looked too good for her.

I could hear Elise de Court. "Oh, come on, Charles," she was saying in that high, fluting voice of hers. "Tell me which scent you prefer," and she sprayed herself liberally with "Nuits de Chine." "Or this one?" She applied another.

"What's that one called?" he drawled.

"Connaise-tu le pays?" Elise had a name for playing with fire.

"Yes, I connais very well, and so do you, Elise," he said, with a slow smile. "Let's have that one, then."

He's on to her, I thought, and somehow I was glad of it.

Elise took the biggest bottle of Connais-tu le pays she could get.

When they'd gone I asked, "Who was that with Elise? Charles something. She called him Charles." I mimicked Elise.

Fanny Levin, who was serving, laughed. "Oh, isn't Elise awful? You can't blame her, though. She'll only be at the top for such a little while, looks like that don't last, although she makes up superbly. No, he's not called Charles. That's Colonel Charlecote. Gorgeous too, isn't he? Very brave, they say. He has the Victoria Cross. No real money, though, but I suppose Elise feels she's doing her bit."

"I don't think Elise is doing too badly," I said, going back to packing a red velvet box for the Duchess de Calenta. I was so absorbed that I packed the wrong colours of lotion, powder and eye make-up giving her make-up for a blonde instead of for the strong-nosed brunette she was.

So that was my father; I had seen him in the flesh at last. He was very like the photograph Josie still kept. It was a shock, and yet exciting also. He was very attractive.

I had a good look in the mirror when I got back to my room that night, but I didn't feel that I resembled him at all.

The next day Paul Poiret came into Rosine; I thought he had some new theatrical project to talk over. When he found me, he drew me over into the alcove, and sat me down on the padded velvet seat. I could see my own face reflected in the mirror on which the Rosines had painted sprays of lilac and mimosa. It was spring, 1917, a bad year.

"How's your mother?" he said. "Heard from her lately?"

"She's touring, first company, with *The Bing Boys.*"

"I thought you might wish to see her again. There is a chance that I might design for a London show, sometime next year, the war permitting. A man called Cochran has asked me. I am thinking about it. Who knows, perhaps we shall have victory by then? *Afgar,* he says it is to be called, and the oriental background demands my presence. If I go, I shall ask for you: we work together well."

"That's marvellous." I was very pleased.

Poiret started humming a tune. "You have been a good little soldier, eh? Like me."

I knew him well by now. "What is it? What are you about to tell me?"

"I have had news of Frederic through my client in Sweden. Not good news, I am afraid, child. The report was: 'Missing, believed killed.' " He fell silent.

Missing, believed killed. We all knew what that meant in those days, and what the chances were.

"Poor child," murmured Poiret. "Poor, poor child."

Did he mean me or Frederic?

That night I did something I had never done before. I stopped for coffee and brandy at a café near the Rue de Rivoli. I usually took breakfast there, the proprietor had become a friend, but even to him I did not explain what had happened. I was holding my grief tightly to me along with the guilt I felt about the baby, a guilt I could never now purge by telling Frederic.

I had one more coffee with brandy, and then another. It

51

didn't exactly dull the pain, but it stopped the feeling that I was shaking all over. I had my shopping bag with my supper in it at my feet, and my picture portfolio on the table. In spite of my chic clothes and bobbed hair, I daresay I looked exactly what I was: a working girl and an artist.

I was still sipping my coffee when a bunch of English officers came into the café and seated themselves about a round table. One of them was Colonel Charlecote. I looked at him and smiled. I wonder what was in that smile and what chords it struck in him? He got up, came across to me, and stood there for a moment looking at me with a serious face, so that I saw he could be formidable when he chose. Then he said, in French: "Why is a nice little girl like you sitting in a café getting drunk and smiling at strange soldiers?"

In English, I said clearly: "I'm not drunk, or not very. And you're not a strange man; you're my father."

He stared, then drew a chair up and sat down at the table. "My God, you're Alice."

"Yes. Josie's daughter—and yours."

"How did you know who I am?"

"You were pointed out to me in a shop. I work in Rosine."

"Ah," he said briefly, remembering the occasion. He seemed a bit embarrassed.

"Yes, *ah*. You want to watch Elise. But I expect you know that."

"I can see you're a woman of the world." His face was still serious, but amusement was lined up behind it, waiting to break through. "Now I understand the smile. But why the brandy, and why the tears? You're really too young for the brandy." All the same, he waved to the waiter and ordered some for himself.

"But not for the tears. I've just heard that someone I was fond of has been killed."

"Casualties have been heavy lately." He drank his brandy; his hand shook a little. "It could be any of us. We have our life till the next bullet or the next shell. That's all we can count on." He patted my hand. "Poor child. French, was he?"

"It's not quite what you think," I said, in a stony voice. "He was one of the enemy. An Austrian. I heard through Sweden. Missing, believed killed. But that's really dead, isn't it? I don't suppose you're so sympathetic now."

He still held my hand. "Doesn't make any difference to me.

I've got past that easy knowing whose side I am on. Patriotism, and all that. I'm not on any side now, except the side of surviving. I want to come through. He didn't survive; he was a man. I can be sad with you."

"Is that how you all feel?" I said.

"Yes, underneath. We don't talk much, but we're just hanging on, trying to survive. There'll be some new American armies coming in soon. They won't understand what we've learned, they'll still be trying to win battles. So they may win the war for us. I expect they will. But we will have died for it. No, I'm sorry for the poor chap, whether he was German or Austrian. I might have killed him, and if I hadn't killed him yesterday I might have to go out and kill him tomorrow. He'd do the same to me. That's how it is. But it doesn't mean I'm not sorry, Alice."

He drank some more brandy, which did not make him drunk but loosened the tautness of his nerves.

He stayed with me and forced me to eat a large dinner with him. He himself ate little, but continued to drink brandy. I did most of the talking. I told him about Paul Poiret and the Martines; I told him of my ambitions in the theatre. Finally I told him about the baby and my attempt at suicide. I felt surprisingly lightened by my confessions to him. Though he didn't say much, I felt his sympathy and was warmed by it.

"Don't take it too much to heart," he advised. "Put it behind you now with the memory of the poor fellow who's dead. I've learned to bury my memories. You do the same."

With the brandy, and the food, and the generally high emotional temperature, I was brave enough to ask him a question about Josie.

"What's the state of the game? Are you married to Josie? Did you ever get married to her?" He hesitated. "She says you did. I want to know."

He was still hesitating. "We played a game of marriage. I don't think I ever went out of my way to disabuse any of the stuffy Edinburgh matrons of their idea that we were married."

"Josie says that's enough in Scotland: she called it a handfast marriage."

"I suppose I thought of her as my wife then," he said, looking down at the table. "Things went wrong after that, but we were very much in love. Not very dependable, I'm afraid, me and Josie," he said apologetically.

"I think I'm glad to be a Charlecote," I said.

"I shouldn't be all that eager to join the Charlecotes. Heaven knows, we've got our quota of lunatics among us. I've got one cousin who is near enough to a criminal, and a violent one too. Mad, bad and dangerous to know. And I have a nephew who is probably my son since I had an affair with my sister-in-law." He was much drunker than I'd thought. "I ought to have stayed closer to Josie," he went on, unsteadily. "My fault. I very much regret that I did not. I am proud of you, now that I've seen you, Alice. Damn it, I'm determined you shall inherit something from me other than my damned temperament. Nothing much to leave—my eldest brother has everything while he lives. I don't expect to survive him, *he* has a Staff job, but I have something, and you shall have it." His voice was ragged; he said: "I'd like to write a letter to my solicitor." He looked about him. "Waiter, bring me a pen and paper."

"He won't have a pen or paper," I said. "It isn't an English club. This place will be closing soon."

"What do you know about English clubs?"

"Enough to know they are not like a bar in the Rue Castiglione." I stood up, catching the waiter's eye. "Come on."

I walked him to my apartment on the Rue Caumartim. He sat down heavily on a chair and lit a cigarette. "Have a gasper?"

"No, thank you."

"You've got this place nice. Reminds me of my mother's sitting room at Charlecote, somehow."

I produced writing paper, pen and ink, but he sat there without moving. When I looked I saw his hands were trembling violently.

"I get these fits," he muttered. "Some brandy, for God's sake."

I kept none, but I knew my neighbour below, a young medical student, always had a bottle, and I ran downstairs to borrow it. When I got back, Randolph had the pen in his hand, making a fist of it. But he had knocked over the ink and was looking at it helplessly.

"Sorry," he said, his voice jerky. "Not usually as bad as this." Then panic broke. "Oh my God, Allie, I can't go on."

"Don't call me Allie." Suddenly I was furious.

"I did when you were little."

54

"Take the brandy. I was never little. I grew up too soon, thanks to you and Josie."

I held the brandy to his lips, his own hand being too unsteady.

"It's not fear," he muttered. "Don't think that. Not fear in my mind. But the body's had enough. It's developing a mind of its own. I'm so terribly afraid, Alice, that this body of mine will run away." He covered his face with his hands. "I know I'm going to die, but I want to do it decently, not with a bullet in my back." I saw his shoulders heave.

I stroked his head, trying to comfort him. All my own anger had evaporated.

"This is just between you and me, Allie?"

"I'll never mention it."

"That letter." Blindly he stretched out a hand.

"Here, let me help," I said. I moved to sit beside him.

An hour later he left, more or less in his right mind. "I'll send you a card when I can," he said. He took the letter I had written to post himself.

No card came.

Some months later, in the early autumn, I had a letter from his solicitors telling me that Colonel Randolph Charlecote had been killed in action, not long after our meeting. He and his elder brother had died within a few weeks of each other. His youngest brother had been killed in 1915. There were now no male senior Charlecotes left, only the younger generation. Randolph had left me as a legacy the lease of an old London theatre, The Albion in Albion Walk, off the Strand, the freehold ground of which belonged to the Charlecote family trust. The lease had something under twenty years to run, expiring in 1933.

In September 1917, the doughboys duly arrived on the battlefronts and, as Randolph Charlecote had predicted, the tide of war began to change.

Early in 1918, Poiret took me with him to London to help him costume *Afgar*. I also had a theatre to claim. My London life had begun.

Part Two

ℐ Chapter Three

When Aldwyn asked me questions about my early life in London, I used to pretend I had forgotten, but really I only had to close my eyes and the whole scene sprang to life in my memory. Some details were sharper and more painful than I was ever going to let Aldwyn know. She felt she had a right to my past, but some of it was my secret.

It was strange returning to my native country. I had been a child when Josie first bore me away, and now I sometimes looked older than I was and sometimes younger. For business purposes I was evasive about my age; I was carrying a lot of responsibility for *Afgar,* and I needed to seem old enough for it. But I soon discovered that almost everyone in my circle was young, not perhaps as young as I was myself, but still incredibly young for the work we were doing. We almost created the bright new image of the decade that followed just by *being* young and brilliant. Society picked it up after us, when they saw the image had chic, but we made it.

As soon as we arrived I left Poiret at the Ritz ("So convenient for the theatre"), and took a taxi to Albion Walk. I got out at the end of the short street, a cul-de-sac at the back of the Stand, and went on foot.

Whatever Albion Walk had been like in its heyday twenty years earlier when my father had purchased the lease for his beloved Josie, that heyday had decisively ended with the war. Bombs had fallen in the middle of the street, destroying two small shops which had once faced the theatre. The other shops were empty and sad. The theatre itself was now used as a club for soldiers from the Dominions and Colonies and was called The Empire Club. I knew at a glance that the Club was for the lowest ranks and not for officers; nor did it appear to me that even the "other ranks" had a good time there or chose to come

59

in great numbers, so woebegone and run-down was the Albion. And yet when it was built it had been a pretty theatre, designed on classical lines with a graceful pillared portico, stucco front and well placed windows.

I approached to study the melancholy sight. Splinters from a bomb had scarred the pillars, and the explosion had broken several windows, which were boarded up. No one had thought it worthwhile to do much in the way of repairs. As I went closer I could see that playbills going back before the war still clung to the walls. *A Stranger from the Sea* had been the last play performed there. Lifting up layers of tattered paper I saw that some years earlier *The Merry Miller* had preceded *A Stranger*. Josie had appeared in *The Merry Miller*. I liked that thought. It made me feel at home.

I walked back down Albion Walk, and at the end of the road I turned and surveyed the little perspective. Then, quite calmly, but with tremendous inner force, I made up my mind what I was going to do: I was going to take up my lease of the Albion and restore it to its former glory. It was London itself that gave me confidence. I seemed to breathe in vitality and energy with its air. Paris, by comparison, was a sad city, drained by the war. My ambition did not stop there. While I was about it, I would do something about the terrace of shops opposite. I had learned my lessons from the Martines and the Rosines well. I could just see those small early nineteenth-century shop-fronts housing elegant boutiques for the sale of scents and furniture and curtains and carpets in the style of the Martines. I was sufficiently sensitive to the way the world was changing to realise that such shops in such an area would prosper. It would need money, though, that elusive stuff called capital, of which neither Josie nor I ever seemed to have much. We had capital inside us, however, in the form of inexhaustible energy and creativity.

There was someone else looking at the Old Alby. As I stood looking at my theatre I saw a man come out of the building, through the stage door, and then lock it behind him. He had a large bunch of keys in his hand. The sight annoyed me. They were my keys. What was he doing with them?

I walked over. "Were you looking at the theatre?"

He gave me a surprised stare from steady blue eyes, but he answered "yes" politely enough. A tall young man, his face had the tense, lean look that all young men's faces had then who had so far survived the war. He wasn't handsome in the way Frederic had been, but he had a pleasing face. An arch to his eyebrows and a firm set to his mouth suggested he liked his own way. He didn't look old enough to have been through the lot, but I guessed he had seen enough to mark him. He had a limp, so perhaps he had "stopped a blighty one" and had been sent home. The one word was, apparently, all I was going to get because he started to walk off to a car parked at the kerb.

"Wait, please," I said. "Can I have a look round?"

He turned back briefly. "I don't think so," he said, still politely. "I'm sorry." Perhaps something in my expression got across to him, because he added, "It's not open to the public. The roof's dangerous. Anyway, it's going to be pulled down. A hotel is going here."

"What?" I was astounded. "It can't be. It must be stopped."

"That's for the landlord to say. The theatre belongs to the Charlecote family." He was wearing shabby, casual clothes and I assumed he was a clerk employed either by the family or their solicitors.

"They may own the land, but I have a lease of the theatre, and you can go back to your employers and tell them I don't intend to relinquish that lease."

There was a short pause while he studied my face. "I think you'd better consult your solicitors," he said. "I can't say anything. Sorry," and he got into his car and drove away.

"I shall," I shouted after him, angrily aware that already I had a fight on my hands. Then I took my cab on to the last address given to me by Josie.

We crossed the Waterloo Bridge. There were the Houses of Parliament, and Big Ben in the distance. We ran down into Lambeth. Here was the good old Elephant and Castle.

"A right turn soon," I said alertly to the driver, just in case he thought I was not a Londoner. Suddenly Vienna and Paris had fallen away and I knew what I was. I belonged here.

"Here we are. Ladybrook Grove. Not much grove about it, eh?" The taxi driver gave an asthmatic laugh. "Can't see a tree." We stopped, he unloaded my bags, and I paid him.

I looked around me with interest. A faint memory stirred. I could just remember this terrace of simple houses, stucco-faced, three windows to a floor, with a basement to each house. Some were a bit shabby, but as a group they had a solid friendly air. I was glad to see that Gran's was newly painted.

There was an open motor-car drawn up outside number 32 and as I looked, there were peals of laughter and Josie ran out of the house adjusting a scarf round her neck. She got into the car with a young man.

I stepped forward, "Hi!"

Josie turned round. "Oh, my God," she said.

When I think of how Josie had treated me, her offhand ways as a mother, her neglect of me when I was with her and her downright rejection when she abandoned me, I ought to have hated her. I never could, though, because I could always see her point of view. I *was* a drag on her life and career.

"Thanks," I said, but I could see how she felt: her escort, although older than I, was noticeably younger than Josie. How tiresome for her to have a daughter turning up and claiming her as mother just when she was off on a spree.

He was a tall young man wearing a British officer's uniform with a red armband, signifying that he was on leave because of wounds. There was something familiar about his face, but I could not place it.

Josie leaned forward and spoke to him. I think she must have said something about seeing him later because he gave me a curious look, shouted "See you then" to Josie, and drove off.

"I was having lunch with him at the Savoy," said Josie plaintively to me. "You don't know how hard it is to get a good meal these days, with rationing. I was looking forward to it."

"What did you tell him?" I asked.

"Nothing much. Depends how long you're staying," said Josie, meaning that she would only acknowledge me as her daughter if obliged to.

"I'm going to be working here with Poiret on a show of C.B. Cochran's at the London Pavilion," I said.

"Cocky?" and Josie opened her eyes wide.

"And planning to stay. Can't you see my bags? Haven't you heard about my theatre, the Albion?"

"Yes, and it's a dump." Tears sprang in her eyes. "Oh, and when I think of the lovely place it was. A tragedy."

"I know. I've seen it. I'm going to alter all that." I heaved my bags up the steps to the house. "Grandma in? Not dead, is she?"

"That'll be the day," said Josie. "Take more than the Kaiser to kill your Gran."

She came into the house with me. As soon as the smell hit

62

me, memories came flooding back. Grandma's house smelled of furniture polish and brass cleaner and good food. She was a splendid cook and a ferocious housecleaner. As a child I had been in awe of her and I wondered how I would feel now in my new sophistication; I had an uneasy feeling that Grandma May would break through it. The house was tall and narrow, part of an early nineteenth-century terrace. Grandma, early widowed from an actor, let rooms, but there always seemed to be space for some of our numerous relatives who came and went, like Josie, and for the same reason: most of them were connected in one way or another with the theatre.

There were three groups. First the Mays. Far and away the most numerous, they were the descendants of my grandfather's brothers, so they were Josie's cousins. She herself had been Grandma May's only child. Then came the Davenports, who were Grandma's kin; she had been a Miss Davenport. Their aristocratic name belied their needy status: there never was a well-off Davenport that I knew of. Finally, there were the Cooks, who were related to us through Grandma May's mother, Vicky Cook, of music hall fame. The Cooks had a finger in many pies, from antiques shops to scent stalls in Berwick Street Market. I rather liked the Cooks, but Josie always said they ought to have had an R in their name after the C. There was something about a fur coat one of the Cooks had swindled her out of years ago.

I wondered if there were any Davenports or Cooks resident in the house at this moment. "I suppose there's room for me, is there?" I turned to Josie.

Josie totted up on her fingers. "There are three permanent gentlemen guests. Dickie Davenport is in the top attic, and Ellen May is in the basement. Maida Cook seems to be perching here at the moment, too, more's the pity," she added viciously. "You can come in with me. I'll probably be going off on tour soon, anyway."

"Oh?" I was getting my bags into the hall.

"Number One Tour: *Going Up*. It's coming on at the Gaiety in a week. I'll be taking it out in Evelyn Laye's part." She sounded pleased.

Grandma May came surging up from the basement, and surging was the word. Always plump, she had become definitely fat, seeming to make nonsense of the stories of semi-starvation Josie had hinted at.

63

"Thought I heard voices. Why, it's little Alice."

"Not so little now, Gran. I've grown."

"You could say the same of me," and she gave her deep bass laugh. "Come and give your old Gran a kiss. Glad to see you back. I always told that wicked Josie she should never have left you behind."

"It was for her own good, Mum, and see how well she's done. Working for Cochran, no less. Well, I'm off. See you after lunch. Bobby's waiting round the corner for me," and with a wave she disappeared to her lunch at the Savoy.

"Can I stay, Gran?"

" 'Course you can, love. Always room for one more." That was her philosophy, and not a bad one. Certainly, it had seen her through a lot.

"Who's Bobby?" I asked, because there had been a look on her face I wanted identified.

"Bobby Charlecote," she said, pressing her lips together. "One of *that* lot. She can't keep away from them, Josie can't, and he's years younger than she is. He's a cousin of the other one."

"My father," I said soberly.

"Yes, sorry, love, your father. God rest his soul, since he's dead. A brave man, dear, but not lucky for us. 'What have these Charlecotes got, Josie,' I said, 'that attracts you so much?' But she doesn't seem to know. Here's your room."

When I had unpacked my bags, I took out the solicitor's letter that had told me of my father's bequest and made a note of the address.

Next day I went round to do battle at the firm of Griggs and Griggs. Since my letter had been signed William J. Griggs, I asked to see him. I suppose I had expected a grey-haired Dickensian figure, but instead he turned out to be a jolly, red-faced little man with a tiny hump on his back.

He greeted me cheerfully and said he knew exactly who I was and that he was surprised to see me, since he had believed I lived in France. He answered my questions in a businesslike way. In a few crisp sentences he told me of the terms of my lease. I had another fifteen years to run, which seemed forever to me, but which he hinted might one day come to seem less than infinite. The lease had the usual "dilapidation" clause, by which I must hand back the theatre in good order to the free-

64

holder at the end of my lease. There was also a clause forbidding me to leave the theatre "dark" for more than six months without forfeiting my lease. The latter was in abeyance at the moment because of the war, but could eventually be invoked.

The situation was complicated by the fact that the freehold of the theatre was owned by the Charlecote family: they owned the whole block of land. What my father had done, in fact, was to buy the end of the lease of the theatre his family owned. William Griggs conveyed to me that the Charlecote family had planned to buy me out, not expecting me to want the Albion.

Plainly no one had thought about me seriously. Now they would have to. I kept silent. Instinct told me to leave the ball at his feet. He kicked it.

"I shall have to talk to the Charlecotes, Miss May. You see that, I'm sure. We must have a little conference. As it happens, I am seeing Mr. Matthew Charlecote later today. As the eldest surviving male cousin to the young heir he is in charge of the estate." And he gave me a little outline of the Charlecote family. There had been four brothers, all killed in the war. The eldest son dead, my father dead, and Matthew's father, who had been the youngest son, dead. Only the son of the third brother survived. There were lots of cousins, it seemed—including Bobby Charlecote from a collateral branch—but the main family had been wiped out by the war.

"I'd like to see Matthew Charlecote too," I said firmly.

He huffed and puffed a little, but I got my way. I was sitting there when Matthew Charlecote walked in to keep his appointment.

I got to my feet in surprise.

"So it's you. You are Matthew Charlecote." It was the young man I had seen leaving the Albion Theatre. I had been deceived about his clothes by living so long in France and so close to Poiret; I saw now that he wore his clothes in the English style, as if they were already old. They looked casual, but the jacket was beautifully cut and of excellent material.

"I plead guilty," he answered with a note of amusement. Suddenly I remembered Randolph Charlecote's remark that one of his nephews might also be his son. From what William Griggs had said only Matthew was the right age. I looked at him, assessing all this: I still thought him attractive, but certainly no wave of fraternal feeling swept over me.

65

"Nice day, isn't it?" he continued calmly. "I'm glad you came to see Griggs. And if you remember, I advised you to see him. I think you need advice."

"I can look after myself. And I don't like being condescended to."

"Nothing like that was intended. I just want you to understand the situation as it is. Morning, Griggs."

It didn't take them long to let me know that the Charlecotes wanted to sell the land on which the theatre stood and would be glad to see my lease fall in. They were not therefore disposed to be generous over the clauses relating to the state of the theatre and the use of it. William Griggs wrapped it up a bit, but I understood. I had about six months to put the theatre to rights and make it live again.

"Now you see the position," said Matthew Charlecote. "Impossible. You can't do it." Something about his manner maddened me.

"Nothing's impossible," I said. "I'll do it." And I was running down the stairs and out of the building before they could say another word. I felt as if the farther I got away from them the better chance I had.

I went back home and told Josie, whose only response was to say, "I told you so. You're shaking all over."

"I hate that Matthew Charlecote," I said. "Just hate him."

So there I was installed in London, back with my own family, my eye set on restoring my own theatre, and six months in which to do it.

I did what was required of me in *Afgar*. My job was to help with the designs for the costumes and set. Through colour and line, textures and patterns, I had to bring to life the ideas of my mentor, at a time when London was short of almost every material. But I managed, and *Afgar* was a huge success for everyone concerned. The leading lady, Alice Delysia, became a great star through it. It did me a lot of good too, but it parted me from Paul Poiret. I knew, and he knew also, that I would never return to work in Paris—at least not on our old terms.

"I have launched you in London, Alice," he said. "Shall we meet again? Who knows?"

"I'll never forget what I owe you."

"We can't part like this."

It was evening and we were both free. "Come and have supper with my grandmother. I'd like you to meet her, and she wants to meet you. She's heard so much."

We took a taxi to Ladybrook Grove, where we were welcomed by Grandma May and given a tripe and onion supper at the long table in the kitchen, together with Dickie Davenport and two of the lodgers, both actors "resting" temporarily. It was the first time I had admitted anyone into the most private part of my life, and we both knew it would not have happened if I had not felt utterly confident of my status. I had outgrown my life with Paul Poiret.

"And you've put all the past behind you?" he asked, just as he left.

I knew he meant Frederic. "There are some things that one never gets over. But there are remissions. When the pain comes back it's as bad as it ever was. But in between, one forgets."

I kissed him good-bye. He had no money to lend me—cash was tight with him too—but he spoke to Mr. Cochran, and Cocky came up with a loan of two hundred pounds. This enabled me to get an architect into the Albion Theatre and have an assessment made of the damage. A builder fixed up a tarpaulin on the roof so that at least the rain was kept out. I reported progress to Mr. Griggs. Each time I did so, he shook his head.

I began to feel like a character out of Dickens, living just one step ahead of the bailiffs. I had a little calendar by my bed on which I marked off the days and weeks of the few months of my Albion deadline.

Because I was working for Cochran, I was moving steadily forward into the society where I wanted to be. I began to acquire friends of my own age who belonged in the theatre—adventurous, ambitious souls like myself, who meant, by their talents, to conquer this world. If it seems heartless of us to have been so full of ourselves at this terrible time in Europe's history, I can only say we were young. It was not our world that was being destroyed but our world we were making.

Three of my allotted six months passed. I was saving hard, but it wasn't enough. The roof was not leaking, but the inside of the theatre looked as if an army had camped there. Indeed, it had been used as a recruiting centre for six months in 1915.

It was Bobby Charlecote, oddly enough, who gave me an interesting bit of information. We met one morning at The Double Domino, which was a sort of club, quite casual, that some of us formed so we could meet without outsiders gaping at stage folk. Josie had been a founding member. Bobby *was* an outsider, to my mind, but he came there anyway. He was stage-struck, I guessed, as well as Josie-struck. I was working on a production of Mr. Cochran's called *Cherry*. Melville Gideon was doing the music.

"I hear you're trying to put the old Albion to rights? Seeing that it was damaged in a Zeppelin raid, why don't you ask for a government grant to repair it? You'd get one."

"Would I? I didn't know." Mentally, I chalked one up against Mr. Griggs, who should certainly have told me.

"Comes of being out of the country. Don't suppose the Frenchies do that sort of thing. Self-help there, I daresay."

"It's clever of you to know."

"Considering that my family owns the land the theatre stands on, it's the sort of thing I ought to know. Not that it's my property, you understand. Belongs to a young cousin who is bossed by my wicked cousin, Matthew. Well, second cousin. I spring from a junior branch, which is why I'm not as well heeled as dear Matthew."

"I've met him. Is he wicked?"

"He's confoundedly boring and tiresome, at all events. I wouldn't mind sticking a spoke in his wheels."

"You're not much like your mother, I must say," observed Grandma May, at supper that night.

"Am I not? This soup is lovely, Gran."

"Just potato, dear. No, now Josie at your age, surrounded by all those lovely young men you work with, would have been in love by this time. Had an affair, too, I expect. Proper little beggar, she was. You don't seem to notice men."

I could have told her that I was still protected from love by the memory of Frederic, but I couldn't talk about it even to her. So I kept quiet and ate my soup.

"You look tired," she said.

"I've been trying to find a builder who will do the repairs on the Albion for me for next to nothing, and *that's* tiring," I said. "I think of learning bricklaying and plastering." I was only half joking. Any Martine worth her salt would take on such a job.

After a moment's thought, she said: "Why don't you ask Benny Cook to do it for you?" And to my raised eyebrows, she said slowly, "Keep an eye on him and he'll do you all right. You *do* look exhausted."

But it wasn't just fatigue. I had the Spanish flu, the first victim in that household, and not the last. People were going down with it on every side, and many of them died. I was nearly one of them—I was more ill than I had ever been before. My temperature shot up, I ached all over, and my head was full of terrible pictures of the war, in which men rotted in trenches or hung screaming on barbed wire, and all of them had Frederic's face.

While I was lying in bed, convalescing, the war ended. I heard a wailing of sirens, and the noise of car hooters.

"What's that?" I asked Josie, who was the only one in the house on her feet, and complaining all the while.

She handed me a cup of tea. "The war's over, and they're happy. They're all happy, poor fools." There were tears in her eyes. For the first time I asked myself what the war had meant to my mother, and whom she had lost in it. Was it my father she mourned?

"Mr. Phillips is very ill," she went on. Mr. Phillips was one of the lodgers, a gentle old man. "I think he's going to die."

"Not Gran?" I said, with sudden anxiety.

"No, not Gran," said Josie, wearily. "Although she's bad, too."

Grandma remained wheezily alive but Mr. Phillips did die and surprisingly, bequeathed all he had to my grandmother. She in turn handed the money over to me to help with the Albion. I think she was just glad that the war was over and she was alive, but it did pose an interesting question about her relationship with Mr. Phillips. I began to realise what it was to be a woman in the May family.

I was just on my feet, but still feeling weak, when the builder sent a young workman to the Domino, where I was drinking coffee, with an urgent message.

"We're into trouble," he announced.

"What is it?"

He was the sort of young Londoner who hated talking, except out of the corner of his mouth. "We dunno—water," he said, reluctantly. "Better come, miss."

We went down the staircase into the basement where the

69

floor was covered in a thick skin of foul-smelling water. I had nightmare visions of health regulations and sanitary inspectors.

A huge flagstone had been raised in the floor to reveal a lower flight of stairs cut out of large masonry blocks. I went down the stairs, picking my way with caution. In the dim light I could see that I was in a narrow tunnel. Even in my distracted state I took in that that stone work looked massive and immensely old. I thought it might have been a water conduit from Roman London that had been taken over by some medieval builder as a drain, and been in use ever since. The tunnel sloped gently down in one direction. Just within my vision was a long roll of something covered with fungus and embedded in the pale growth was what looked like a face, a dark blue face with pouting distorted lips and swollen eyelids.

"It's a body," said Bill.

I just stared. Nothing in my life before then had prepared me for what I saw, and I felt sick. Also, I knew the theatre world, and I knew that from henceforth the Albion would be a theatre with a "name."

Over the next few days little bits of information trickled out from the police. The body was that of a man in army uniform. At first it was concluded that he was a deserter who had hidden away and somehow become imprisoned. Then it was discovered that he had died from a blow on the head: he had been murdered.

"The police'll soon find out who he is," said Benny. "He'll have his army papers on him. They'll track him down."

But we learned there were no papers on him and his identity remained a mystery.

"He was a countryman, though, I reckon," said Benny, who seemed to have access to what the police knew. "He had a hare's foot in his pocket. That'd be for luck. Didn't bring him much luck, poor fellow."

"Oh, it's bad luck finding a body in the theatre like that," mourned Josie, when we talked it over. "Poor old Alby."

"One success and everyone will forget the jinx. You watch."

Josie was incredulous. "You haven't got a show."

"I'll get one, of course. Do you think I'll let this stop me? It's all publicity."

Josie was shocked at my hardness. "You'll go bankrupt."

I shrugged. "You can't lose what you haven't got. I'll find a backer." Life with Poiret had taught me techniques, and work with Cochran had introduced me to plenty of angels. There was a good deal of money floating around London at that moment.

Josie tried a different tack. "Who'll trust a good show to a girl?"

"My friends," I said. I was gathering about me a lively group at the Double Domino. Ben, Johnny, Tess, Meggie and Peter. No one was working regularly, but each was full of ambition. They were the nucleus of a group that was to grow with my life. Others floated in and out—Rex, Noel, Edith, Helen—lucky names, lovely names. I had a special place in that crowd because I was known to be neither an actress nor a writer. Thus no one was jealous of me. And I was the possessor of a theatre, even if it was "dark."

Josie said, "Well, until you make your fortune, I've got a job for you. Viola Tree wants some help in her revival of *Pygmalion*. She's got Stella Campbell in it, so she's got her hands full." Josie laughed. "Viola's always been a good friend to me. I knew her when she was a kid. I worked for her old man." Viola was the daughter of Sir Herbert Beesbohn Tree, a famous actor-manager of the days before the war. I knew Viola had gone into management. "It'll be good training for you working for Viola. I just hope Stella doesn't eat you up for breakfast, that's all. She's capable of it."

Stella Campbell was a beautiful and luminous actress; she had been the first English Eliza Doolittle; Bernard Shaw had fallen in love with her, and all her subsequent affairs had been legendary. So too, alas, were her temperament and her temper. She was generally thought to love her Pekingese dog more than any man. I wanted to meet Stella Campbell, but I wasn't sure if I wanted the job with Viola Tree.

"Oh, by the way," continued Josie. "A packet came for you. I left it in the hall."

It was a small square packet, and when I opened it I saw it contained a short note, and an object wrapped in tissue paper. The letter was from Matthew.

"Dear Alice," he wrote. "I came across this in the course of my work at the Red Cross. We sort out a whole heap of personal possessions, German as well as Allied, because it sometimes helps establish identities. In this case, all I can tell you is that the watch

71

and photograph were brought back from a dugout, overrun in the advance of the Summer of 1918. Of course, I recognised you at once. Probably I should not do this, but I send you the watch because I thought it might mean something to you."

My hands were trembling as I opened up the tissue paper. Inside was a soldier's pocket watch, made of base metal, and with a portrait of the old Emperor Franz-Joseph hammered out in profile on the lid. It opened up in my hand, and in the lid was pasted a photograph: a girl standing in the sunlight. I was that girl. Standing behind me, clearly visible, was Maria.

Oh, it was strange and painful to see her face again, and to recall so vividly the day the photograph had been taken by Frederic. I covered my face with my hands, the past rushing back at me. At that moment I loved Frederic, and missed Maria, as if the years in between had never been.

From Matthew it was a kind act that misfired. With this letter he entered into my very private world. Every time we met he seemed to rip off a layer of my skin and touch a nerve; I hated him then.

I controlled myself, and went back to Josie. "Just a note from Matthew Charlecote with something that was lost," I said. "Of course, I'll write a polite thank you. And I'll take that job with Miss Tree," I went on. No doubt I should have accepted anyway, but the photograph pushed me into it. I wanted to be busy, to have people about me, people with no pasts connected to mine.

"No one can give a brush-off better than you, Alice," observed Josie.

I went to work for Viola Tree, hoping for, but not getting, a sight of Mrs. Patrick Campbell.

Later, there was an inquest on the dead man, but no further facts emerged, and I put the matter to the back of my mind. But it brought me publicity and I was interviewed by the London *Evening Herald.* I was a name.

"Body in theatre unidentified," said the headline. "Young owner-manager says work will go ahead."

I put the newspaper aside. We were all sitting around a table at the Domino, drinking coffee and eating toasted buns. It was midmorning. For some there it was breakfast; for others, the particularly hard-up, it was breakfast and luncheon combined.

A tall woman appeared at the door of the Domino. She had greying black hair showing beneath a black satin cloche and wore a satin and fur coat with the air of a goddess going to seed. She was rather out of breath from descending the stairs to our basement club.

"My dears, I imagined myself descending into hell," she announced in resonant tones, "and now I am here it is a very heaven." She was not shouting, but her diction was such that her words reached every corner of the room.

"It's Mrs. Pat Campbell," whispered Peter.

"So it is, my dear, so it is," said Mrs. Pat, who obviously had excellent hearing. The fur on her cloak moved and revealed itself to be a dog, not a pair of cuffs and a muff as I had thought. "And I am looking for Alice May."

I held my hand up as if I was at school, and she came over.

"My dear, I knew your mother. And your grandmother, for that matter. If you should see her, just mention that Stella Campbell sent her regards and she will understand."

"Oh, I will," I said. "I shall see her this evening."

"So soon?" she cooed. "Don't people live a long time, these days?" The little dog barked assent from her bosom. "I thought she would have been gone long since. My dear, I have a lien on your services. Your employer is allowing me to borrow you."

"Miss Tree?"

"Dear Viola," said the honeyed voice. "Yes. We have struck a bargain: she will do this for me, and I will do *that* for her." In a stage aside, she went on, "She wishes me to perform in a play by my old lover, Mr. Shaw. And when I say lover," she said, reducing her voice even lower, "I do not mean there was much active participation in that sport, for he is all of the intellect and I prefer a lover younger than myself. For so wears a woman to a man." Her voice became brisk. "In which I disagree with Shakespeare who, as ever, underestimated the *tenacity* of women. Cordelia should have hung on, not up. I would have done. And Desdemona should have bitten back." She repeated the last two words which evidently gave her pleasure. Then she stopped playing and concentrated her formidable fire power on me. "You know Vienna, I understand?"

I was startled. "Only very little."

She bowed her head, like a queen receiving the crown. "It will suffice for my humble purpose, I am sure. In Vienna I have a dear friend who is in dreadful circumstances. We must succour even our late enemies. I want you to go bearing a hamper from Fortnum and Masons and a small sum of money. You will travel first class. I insist upon it. I would go myself but for dear Moonbeam here." The little dog, hearing its name, barked. "I cannot leave her behind, and if once we go abroad together we can never come back. I could not risk quarantine for her, my dear." The huge eyes expressed unspeakable emotion. "Those horrid dogs in there—she might be raped."

I travelled first class all the way to Vienna, with a sleeping-berth in addition. "That's Stella Campbell all over," said my grandmother when I told her. "Not a penny to bless herself with, but does she spend!" When sending her regards she refused to explain why Mrs. Patrick Campbell should be especially memorable to her except to say that the lady could be "shocking" and that "a gentleman's legs were involved." Certainly Mrs. Campbell could be shrewd.

Later on I discovered that she had a more than charitable motive in approaching her old friend. Ferdinand Pascal had written a play, the fame of which had reached her. She wished to appear in it, and plays suitable for Stella Campbell were no longer easy to come by. Certainly, when I arrived with my luxuries from Fortnums and Treasury notes in an envelope, he looked more surprised than pleased at first. Living in Vienna then was hard, but he seemed to think that as the down payment on an option for his beautiful play it was not enough.

There was a sadness resting on Vienna those days which even I, young and heedless, could see. I had an address for Maria that I had got through the Red Cross. After I had done my business for Stella Campbell, I went there. A cabbie with a worn, old horse took me to the street in a working-class suburb. Maria had moved, her address unknown. But I was told she worked in a hospital.

I took the cab on, hoping neither horse nor driver would collapse and die on the way. I found Maria on her hands and knees scrubbing the floor of a corridor. I knew her at once, although she was very thin and looked undernourished. I also thought that I had never realised what a beautiful woman she was. Perhaps girls do not perceive that sort of thing about each other, or perhaps we had been too close. Anyway, I now stood outside us both and saw what she was. Just for a second the thought came into my mind that maybe her mother *was* a prin-

74

cess after all. The notion did not last long, because Maria raised her head and saw me.

She recognised me as quickly as I had recognised her. Carefully she took the soap out of the water, dried her hands on her apron, and sat back on her heels, looking at me. There was not much welcome on her face, but I was not surprised. I knew that look. Austria had been beaten in the war, and Maria's expression was the expression of defeat, wary and cautious.

But there was another thing. I had been incredibly tactless: Maria was wearing a sacking apron over a blue uniform; I had on a new jersey two-piece with a low belt that hung on my hips. The outfit was very pretty, even though it had been very cheap, purchased from a stall in Berwick Street. Josie said that the garments were manufacturers' samples, or else had tiny flaws which the big shops would not accept, and that this was why one got such excellent prices. Now I saw that Maria hated me for my elegance.

"So you've turned up," she said, and she got to her feet. She had grown an inch or two since I last saw her, and was now a tall, fine-boned young woman.

"You've kept your English up, then," I heard myself say.

"We had English prisoners of war in this hospital. I helped nurse them. I myself saved the lives of two."

"Thank you," I said, humbly.

"No thanks are needed. I did my job." She wasn't going to relent. She gave a fierce look at my clothes. "Nor need you suppose that because you see me scrubbing floors this is the only job I could get. I do this work out of the love of my country. In war it is one's duty to serve. It still is." Which is more than you seem to have done, she was saying with her eyes. "And now you have come here to patronise me in our defeat." But I saw she was trembling. She didn't hate me really, not Maria. It was her pride, and hurt pride always made Maria cross.

"*No*, Maria." I faced her out. "It's true the war has not been as bad for me as for you, but I have had my troubles, too. No one is untouched. Have you any news of Frederic?"

"So that's why you came," she said slowly. "He was reported missing, believed dead."

"I heard that, too. But he must be dead, or he would have come back by now."

"I don't think he's dead," said Maria suddenly. "I would know. In my heart I would know." As I stared at her in sur-

75

prise, she said, "I loved Frederic also. You weren't the only one. I would know if he were dead."

"He must be," I repeated. "The war's been over some time now, Maria, time enough for things to get sorted out."

"Every day one hears of cases of people turning up," she said. "You don't understand how it is, being on the beaten side." I could see she was crying. I was crying myself. We had drawn together, and I had my arms round her. He's dead, I thought.

"Is the Werkstaette still there, Maria?" I asked.

"Gone. All gone."

"What about the Aristokraten Theatre?" This was where Josie had played.

"Oh, that's still there." She was smiling through her tears now. "They've got a revue there now. All American jokes. For the Occupying Powers. But quite funny."

I could feel how thin Maria was, the bones sticking through the skin. I couldn't leave her here, almost starving. I had seen what conditions were like in Vienna.

Suddenly I heard myself say what I had come there to say, my deep unconscious purpose bursting through into speech. "I've got a theatre now, Maria. One of my own. Come to England with me and we'll work there together. Do come, Maria. There's nothing for you here."

I was a sort of magpie in those days, plucking up bits and pieces from this person, this place, and building them into my life, my theatre. Maria could be part of it.

ℐ Chapter Four

London in 1920 was the gayest city in the world—determined to forget the war. But there was much unemployment, in the theatre as well as elsewhere. It was not an auspicious moment to reopen the Albion. Yet at the Double Domino the mood was hopeful: new plays were about to be written, new songs were composed on the piano, and the new style of acting ("Natural, dear, and not too refined," as Noel said) was greeted with enthusiasm. I was happy. I had not forgotten Frederic, nor my own private tragedy of the child, but I was young and that hopefulness would triumph.

Every day Maria and I were at the Double Domino, where I now had a table of my own. Josie joined us occasionally. She was "resting," but doing so in her usual restless way. I was using her energies by making her take part in the redecoration of the foyer and cloakrooms of the Albion. The designs, a London street scene with lots of fashionable men and women, some of them with easily recognisable faces—the Prince of Wales, Gerald du Maurier and Lady Ottoline Morrell—had been traced out by Maria and me, using techniques learned at the Martines. Floating above the street scene on a white cloud was a bevy of theatre ladies, such as Evelyn Laye, Josine Collins, Gertie Lawrence, and Delysia. For luck we had a small figure of Paul Poiret in every scene. The murals were in black and white with Poiret in *grisaille,* so that he looked like a ghost. I thought he'd appreciate that. The only touch of colour was on Gertie's lips, which were bright red, and I thought *she'd* appreciate that. I mean, it gave her star billing, didn't it? There was a *trompe l'oeil* door in one wall and through this door was the clearly recognisable back of Noel Coward, just departing.

It was a sight to see Josie wearing overalls and brandishing a paint brush. "I don't have the figure for trousers, dear," she protested. But she wore them and smiled happily when she heard one of the workmen pretend to whistle for the "lad."

In the evenings, Maria and I joined her. I was back working free-lance for Cochran, Viola Tree, Charlot—anything to turn a penny—and Maria was selling perfume. We often went to the Domino for a drink and a sandwich late at night. The place was at its brightest and best then—and one night I thought I found there the perfect show with which to launch the new Albion.

The room that night was particularly crowded and, looking through the smoky atmosphere, I thought I saw almost everyone who was struggling upwards in the London theatre as well as a few established stars. A good many of them had come from the first night of the new Charlot revue, *Wild Geese*. Judging by their faces, the show had not been a scintillating success.

Then three people filed silently into the room, heads down: Noel, Bobby and Harry. Only when they had sat down at their table nearby and started to laugh did we realise that, in fact, their gloomy entrance had been an act. Or had it? With Noel, one never knew. I had heard they were in trouble with the new play. I went over to him.

"I hear you've had a great success in Manchester with *I'll Leave It to You*," I said cautiously.

He replied that it wasn't a success with the management, who were not going to bring them to London.

Josie came over to talk.

Noel dragged forward a chair and ordered champagne. For her, he said, raising his glass. Josie looked pleased. He told her she represented "old" theatre. "You are our past and our traditions." Perhaps Josie was less pleased at this, and her face, beneath her shining shingle and arched eyebrows, grew long. He told her she had been a show in herself.

"You had to be. Some of the management I was with, I can tell you. Talk about stingy."

"Managements—" and they were off, swapping the usual horror stories, most of which we all had heard before. There is an obsessive quality to theatre talk. I caught snatches. ". . . skedaddled, twenty of us stranded in Morecombe with a shilling between us," and, "like a goldfish bowl, Josie, no privacy at all. Now I'm not *shy*, but . . ."

I broke in. "I'll bring you into London, Noel. I'll open the Albion with *I'll Leave It to You.*"

Noel's bright, narrow eyes looked thoughtful. He didn't accept, didn't refuse, but was suddenly very businesslike. We agreed to meet in Ebury Street the next day.

"I wouldn't do it," said Josie, as we went home. "Don't let him have the Albion."

"Why not?"

"He'll walk all over you," she declared. "A real little Mr. Know-all. Touch of genius, I grant you that, but he'll be too much for you." And she shook her head.

"We'll see about that," I said.

The next day I was as early at Ebury Street as was consistent with good manners. Noel was breakfasting, leaning up against a red satin headboard and smoking an Abdulla in long, careful breaths. The air was heavy with the scent of Floris's Roman Hyacinths.

I dropped a box of Charbonnel and Walker's chocolates on the satin bedspread.

He relaxed against the quilted satin, his eyes gleaming with life and mirth, twice as alert as almost anyone else and as clever as a waggonload of monkeys.

He rummaged for the "right" chocolate cream.

"Well, you asked me about what I was thinking, and I told you." I ate a cream myself. "Josie thinks I shouldn't take you on. Says you'll be too much for me. Of course, you arranged for me to find you *en scène* this morning. In bed. Breakfasting, red satin and all." I looked round the room and at Noel sitting in state. "I know a stage setting when I see one. Therefore, if I am worth impressing, I think you are quite keen for me to have the play. So let's do business, shall we? And no bandying words."

Our hands went together into the chocolate box, and met over a violet cream.

He got to the violet creams first, and took two, which he somehow managed to eat while still smoking.

Before I left we'd decided that the Albion was to open with *I'll Leave It to You,* starring Noel, to be cast and directed by him, and under my management. Only the money remained to be settled, and somehow I knew he would not be difficult about that. Nor was he.

But I was living in another world as well as the theatre world. One war had ended, but another war was just beginning, an economic war. By the 1920s a depression was starting. Not the Big Brother that was to come at the end of the decade, but a little sister that gave us a taste of what would be. Men who had returned from the war to enjoy the treasures of peace—a land fit for heroes, Lloyd George had promised them—found they couldn't get a job. Officers sold motor-cars, or used their war gratuities to buy chicken farms in Sussex or fruit farms in Kent, which promptly failed. Other ranks took the dole and waited for jobs, which were at a premium. My friends and I had no jobs and no money to speak of, so we noticed the pinch less than most; we were accustomed to it.

But for me and the Albion the consequences were serious; all the sources I had meant to tap for money to put on a show seemed to have gone dry.

"It looks as though 'angels' are dead," I said dismally to Josie, who was out of work herself, and therefore helping Gran with the cooking.

"Oh, they die regularly, dear. But there's always a fresh crop of hopefuls. Or else the old lot are born again. It gets into the blood, I think, gambling on the theatre. Better than cards or roulette. So you hang on."

"I don't know if I can. Not in this instance. I had Noel on the phone saying he wants to get things tied up. Lady Wyndham says she will let him have the New Theatre."

Lady Wyndham, who had been Mary Moore, the actress, was what I hoped and aspired to be. She managed three theatres, Wyndhams, the Criterion and the New.

"Oh, so *Carnival's* coming off, is it?" asked Josie acutely.

"Going on tour."

"With Matheson Lang?" When I nodded, Josie looked pleased. "I know him; I'll try for a part in the touring company. I don't suppose Isobel will want to tour. She hates touring, and she doesn't need the money since she married. I might get her part. Well, it's an ill wind, dear. You go down and I go up." Josie went off humming. Dinner that night was cooked by Grandma, who was a better cook than Josie, but meaner with her materials. Perhaps she had to be. I sometimes forgot that she ran Ladybrook Grove as a boardinghouse and that it had to make a profit. A family boardinghouse was something Noel and I had in common. I paid my way, of course, as did Maria, and Josie too when she could, though money had been in short supply with her lately.

80

One thing all of us suffered from in that house was how to look well dressed on no money at all. But we all had our tricks for solving the problem. Josie, for instance, had a shop in Soho she patronised where used models from Lucille's and Madame Ironmongers were sold at dirt cheap prices, so that if you did not mind being one season behind with the fashion—Josie did not—then you could buy couture clothes for very little. What you also had to do was to keep thin since the models were of elegant proportions; so poor Josie was caught in a constant struggle against her weight. Her bosom, in particular, gave her a lot of trouble, and she had taken to flattening it down with bandages. Grandma May was horrified and proclaimed that her bosom was a woman's greatest glory, but Josie felt she had all too much of her glory for the present mode. Maria and I, being younger, had less trouble here. My great resource was the stall in Berwick Market owned by Eugene Milling and managed by his wife, the beautiful, dark-eyed Louisa.

I admired Louisa, and over the silk stockings and underwear she sold so cheaply we became friends. I took Maria to Berwick Market and went there often alone after working in the Albion. I could walk across in a few minutes, have some coffee at a small Italian restaurant on the corner, and then talk to Louisa, whom I found shrewd and sensible as well as a beauty.

"If you're hard up, then you ought to try our stall in Petticoat Lane next Sunday," she advised me one evening after I had become a regular customer. "Prices are lower there. Different sort of people shop there, you see. Up here you get girls from all the offices and smart shops. They like to look smart and have the money to pay for what they want. Everything we sell here is the newest thing. Now in Petticoat Lane it's housewives shopping for the lowest prices. But the stuff there is good," she assured me. "You can trust us."

"I do."

She leaned forward confidingly. "If the two stalls do well, then we mean to open a shop. Nowhere too smart; I've got my eye on a shop the other end of Oxford Street. The lease falls free in eighteen months and I don't think the present renters will renew, if you understand."

"Yes," I said briefly. I knew all about leases.

"But, of course, trade's pretty slack at the moment, so we shall have to go steady. Still, we aren't doing too badly compared with some," she said modestly.

I knew that Louisa and Eugene were ambitious, and I could see them achieving their ambitions. What they sold had good quality and style as well as being low-priced. I gave Louisa credit for the style, and Eugene for maintaining the quality and price.

"If we do set up shop, what about you doing it up for us?" Louisa knew all about my life in Paris with Paul Poiret and my training at the Martines, just as she knew I had the present lease of the Albion. We were both entrepreneurs in this part of London; it gave us something in common. "It would be good publicity for us, you see, your having worked for Paul Poiret. We'd use that in advertising. So we'd pay well." She had it all worked out.

"Just let me know," I said.

Maria, who had been picking over the stockings at the other end of the stall, came wandering back. "Pretty clocks on your new stockings," she observed. "I like the little arrow head. I will take this pair."

"Oh, don't take the pale grey, take the pinkish ones," pleaded Louisa. "So much newer."

"But they will make my legs look fat," said Maria.

"Ah, but that's what the clock prevents." Louisa put a hand in a pink stocking and drew the silk down over her arm. "You see? It slims the ankle."

While she was wrapping up the stockings which she had successfully sold to Maria, she said, "You know Mr. Cochran, don't you? I've got a cousin who works in his office. She says he was asking for you last week."

"Oh." I thought about it. He hadn't offered me any work for some time—possibly he had some now.

"I haven't seen him lately."

"You ought to get in touch," she advised.

"I will."

Maria and I took a bus to the Elephant and Castle and walked from there to Ladybrook Grove. It was a warm spring day and the buses and trams rattled past us. I bought a bunch of daffodils and a cauliflower from a street trader and carried them in my arms.

"Now why did you buy those?" asked Maria, tripping beside me in her high heels and short skirts, "when we are walking home to save the fare?"

"One to look at and one to eat. Both to enjoy." But I was

low-spirited in spite of my bright words. "What does money matter?" What did it matter, indeed. It was everything.

Josie was back when we got home. She called up from the kitchen: "Cup of tea's on the table." She was already drinking hers. "You look down in the mouth. Take two lumps of sugar. Gives you a lift. Thanks for the cauli." She lit a cigarette. Over her chair was slung a chunky brown fur coat, somewhat the worse for wear. She called it mink. "I'm a bit down in the dumps myself."

"You didn't get the part?"

"You're a mind reader." Then she started to giggle. "See my coat? There were three of us in there, all wearing the same coats. We were all in the cast of the old *Flora Dora* company in Manchester when a bag man there had a sale of bargain mink coats. All the principals and chorus bought one each, men as well as women. You can't mistake us. Whenever you see one of us in one of those coats you know we were in *Flora Dora*. But three of us in one room . . . !" She stood up. "I'm going to bed early—I *did* get an audition, and not a bad part, either. In fact, the best I've had for a long time. So your old Josie's got to look her best tomorrow. See you. Chin up."

"Why?" I asked. "Why do I need a chin up?"

She shrugged. "Because rumour has it that Noel has other plans for his play than the Albion. No hard feelings I'm sure. Business is business."

The next day Noel signed (or his father did, Noel still being underage) a contract with Lady Wyndham. I was bitterly disappointed, but as a consequence of that loss important things happened to me.

On the same day I went to Mr. Cochran's office at 49 Bond Street to see what, if anything, there was in Louisa's story that he wanted to see me. I had to wait in his outer office together with the usual huddle of actors, actresses, showgirls and authors hoping to catch his eye. Among them I saw Dickie Davenport looking well groomed but miserable. He had been out of work for some time, and that went for most of the other people there. There was a sound of music and laughter from the inner room. I thought I recognised Jack Buchanan's voice. He had recently appeared in C.B.'s *Her Dancing Man* at the Garrick, not a particular success, but it looked as though they were now considering another show together. If so, Charlot, Jack's old

83

backer, was out in the cold. Rumour had it that when things were going badly for Charlot, he took to his bed, and rumour also had it that he was spending a good deal of time in bed lately. But he had a new show opening that night that might change his luck. I was going to see it. At the Strand there was a new revue with a Russian troupe—*La Chauve-Souris*—which the critics called "pure theatre."

Louisa's cousin identified me at this point in my thoughts and took me in to see Mr. Cochran. He was leaning back in a chair looking jocund, rosy and well groomed. He greeted me cheerfully with a double "Hallo." He had a funny way of saying things twice. I often thought he used it to give himself time to think. In this instance, I believe he was trying to remember who I was. Then the association came to him and he knew what he wanted to say: He had seen his old friend Paul Poiret in Vienna. They had been looking over a show he was bringing to London, and Poiret had particularly asked that my attention should be drawn to it because he thought I would be interested.

"If he says so, then I am sure I will be. He always knows." I was pleased to be remembered by my old friend. "I'm afraid he has been having a bad time." Word had filtered through to me from Paris of the decided manner in which fashion had shifted away from Poiret's style. Women had bobbed hair, flat bosoms and short skirts, and were no longer interested in the exotic flamboyant style of his that they had once loved. The rising star in this new world was Chanel, and the world which admired her mode could not nourish Poiret. Cochran arrived in time to hear.

Cochran responded that *everyone* was having a bad time; *he* certainly was. His eyes glittered and went cold. He informed me that the show he was bringing in from Vienna had more acts and artistes than he could use, but in order to get the stars he had had to accept the lot. Then he offered me, for the Albion, at a discount, the acts he did not want. Not at *too* much of a discount, of course. Business was business.

I knew he was making me a good offer, albeit a thoroughly commercial one. I could take his material and build a show.

"Give me time to think," I said.

He said I could have a day. I should contact Frank Collins, his stage director.

When I got back into his outer office one of the girls waiting there, a tall, fair-haired girl with huge blue eyes, long legs and tiny white teeth stopped me. "You're from the Albion, aren't you? Didn't they find a body there?" She looked at me curiously.

"Yes." I was prepared to be short.

"Murder, wasn't it?"

This time I didn't answer.

"I seem to remember something about that theatre—you know, during the war. I *heard* something." She tried to concentrate; it seemed difficult. "Only I can't remember what. Was it something to do with drugs?"

"If you think of what it is, tell the police," I said.

"The Old Alby's no joy-house backstage, as I remember. Needs rebuilding. That's what I think."

I was silent. That kind of talk I did not wish to hear. "Tell the police if you remember anything," I said again.

I returned to Albion Walk deep in thought. Someone had let Mr. Cochran down, no doubt, but he had made me a good offer; I'd be a fool not to take it and work in association with him.

"*If* I can find a backer," I said to Josie the next day. She had come to my office to tell me she'd been offered a new role and was triumphantly happy; but she was holding out for more money.

My temporary stage manager, a thin lad called Alec Fiesta, who wasn't going to stay if he could better himself, pushed through the door and shouted, "There's a man outside says he adores you."

"Do I know him?"

"Don't think so. It's Fran Hollman. Owns the Xanadu picture-house round the corner. I don't think you've met him."

"How can he adore me then?"

"From afar, I suppose. Shall I let him in?"

"What's he like?" I was trying to think if I *had* ever seen Francis Hollman; I certainly knew his name. You couldn't live in this bit of London and not know it. As the owner of the Xanadu he was a power in the land.

My stage manager shrugged. "Thin and small. Nothing much to look at. Snappy dresser, though."

"Oh, well, let him in."

A voice said: "I'm already in, darling."

No one had told me how young Fran Hollman was. A skinny young Londoner in tight-fitting clothes worn with a dash, he looked about twenty, although he was older than he looked.

I got off the desk rapidly and straightened my skirt.

"Saw you at the show last night. At the Prince of Wales."

"The revue? *A–Z?* Marvellous, wasn't it?" I was enthusiastic. So was Francis.

"Charlot's best to date. I've always thought he would touch Cochran, but I think he's beaten him now."

"Oh, Cocky goes for bigger things—covers a wider range," I said loyally. "Still, it was lovely."

Together we broke into "Limehouse Blues":

> "Poor broken blossom
> And nobody's child
> Haunted and taunted
> You're just kind of wild."

"That Gertie," said Fran. "Isn't she something special."

Josie pursed her lips. "Personally I think she overdoes it a touch. A little holding back is needed. Restraint is the mark of the true 'artiste.'"

Franny gave her a sharp look and started to hum another tune from the revue: "And her mother came, too."

I giggled, but Josie had been at the Prince of Wales as well, and saw the point.

"I knew *your* mother before you were born, Francis," she said.

"I won't hold that against you," said Fran amiably. "Nor will she."

"She's dead. Poor Ada's been gone a couple of years."

"And who should know better than me? But the guv'nor's still alive and well."

"Your language. Well, I'll leave, Alice. I have an appointment with my agent at twelve." She walked towards the door, a little cloche hat with a pink feather snuggled on her cheek, a gay and insouciant figure.

"Oh, I hope you're in luck, Mum," I said.

"The luck will be his, if I accept the part," said Josie grandly. "Good-bye, Mr. Hollman. Remember me to your father."

Fran watched her go. "Good old Josie," he said. "She never lets go, does she?"

I was brisk. "Now, what is it you want, Mr. Hollman? Apart from adoring me."

"Call me Fran. Worship from a distance, it is, Miss Alice. Entirely respectful. Platonic, even. I want to put money in your theatre. Back a show. Or a bit of one. I know you need the money."

"Ned Latham's offered," I said thoughtfully. Lord Latham was famous for his support of theatrical ventures.

"Oh, go *on.*"

"It's true. But not enough. He's heavily engaged with another outfit."

"And we all know who that is."

I didn't answer, not wanting, at that point, to exchange backstage gossip with Fran.

"My money's as good as anyone else's," said Fran.

"Better, maybe," I said. I knew his reputation about money. It was impeccable.

"And to tell you the truth, I've always fancied the old Alby. Been a lucky place for me. I had my first good idea on business walking past. I remember that sort of thing."

"So it's not me you admire, but my theatre," I murmured.

Fran smiled. "Both. I admire style and beauty when I see it. You and the Albion both have style and beauty." But I instinctively knew he loved objects more than people. It was his strength and his weakness. "So I adore both of you. Does it matter?"

"No. I accept your offer. Your money is *growing* money, Fran. Some money is dead money and will never produce growth. Yours will be fruitful to me and the Albion."

"Good."

"What a pity you didn't come forward earlier before I spent all my own money on the building."

"I am interested in plays and people, not bricks and mortar."

"And?" I sensed with Francis there would be more.

"And what?"

"Well, what else do you want out of it?"

"To you, four and a half percent," he said calmly.

I looked at him quizzically.

"And your company. Let me take you around. Restaurants. Shows. I have never had the company of a truly elegant woman." He held out his hand. "Agreed?"

87

After a moment's hesitation, I took his hand. "Agreed."

That day, I called Frank Collins and accepted Cochran's offer.

9 Chapter Five

I was completely part of the theatre scene of London. And oddly enough it was with Fran that I enjoyed it most. Together we saw most of the plays and revues then running. As well as being my theatre and Noel's, this was the theatre of Jack Buchanan in *Battling Butler,* the theatre of Ivor Novello and of Gerald du Maurier. It was the theatre of such bright revues as *London Calling* and *The Co-Optimists,* and such imported musical comedies as *Oh, Kay, Sitting Pretty* and *Show Boat.* It was the theatre of P. G. Wodehouse and Jerome Kern, and Sigmund Romberg and Oscar Hammerstein. Though times were hard and managements were pushed for cash, there was glitter. The two Astaires danced, Cole Porter wrote hits, and the Prince of Wales sat in the stalls. I discounted all that Josie had said about the theatre dying; it was obviously very much alive.

Later, theatre historians tried to divide it into the theatre of the "chic," peopled by Noel and Co.; the serious theatre, where Mr. Shaw was God; and the theatre of the matinée idol and the afternoon tea tray, which was neither chic nor serious, but was immensely profitable. I suppose I aspired to all three. It was a big world, and yet a small one: you might not know everyone, but there was always someone who did, ready to pass on the latest tale. And there was always some talent we were all secretly watching, a talent that would stretch the limits of our world whether it was Meggie Albanesi or John Gielgud, or, later on, Peggy Ashcroft or Laurence Olivier, or, even later, the lad Richard Burton. Among ourselves we always knew whom to watch. We didn't have to wait for James Agate to tell us.

"Get your coat," Fran said one evening. "I'm taking you out. A little voyage of discovery. Somewhere different."

I grumbled that I was busy, but I obliged. Somehow one did with Fran. "Where are we going?"

"I'm going to show you a little vulgar life. You're getting too classy mewed up in this place."

I looked at him, surprised and a little hurt, but Fran took no notice. I already knew that Fran never acknowledged what he didn't want to see.

"Don't you want to do anything more with your life than this place?" he asked as he bundled me along. "There's a lot of things you could do. Or ought to want to do. See the world. Get educated. Learn about people. You don't know too much. Well, now you're going to learn about me."

"You must have other girls in your life, Fran," I complained as I got into his car, a square Morris. "Why educate me?"

"You're the most malleable."

"That's what you think. And I ought to warn you," I said seriously "that there's no hope for you. I'm in love with someone else. Still in love."

"Of course you are," he said comfortably. "A girl your age is bound to be hopelessly in love. Someone you know, is it? Or some star you've never met?"

"You don't take me seriously."

"I take you very seriously, baby girl." Francis was not tall, and I liked tall men, but he had such immense bounce and élan that size did not seem to matter. And he was very attractive. Mildly sinister, I always thought, but perhaps that added to his attractiveness. "I hope you're hungry," he said. "Because you're going to eat good working-class food. I want you to know where I came from, and where a place like the Albion draws its strength."

He drove south of the river, down a busy main road full of buses and trams, then round a corner to a stall sheltered under a railway arch. The stall was brightly lit with flaming, fishtail gas jets, and a savoury smell floated towards us.

"The best jellied-eel stall south of the river," he announced. "But you can have your eels hot in parsley sauce with vinegar. Meet Sam, who owns it." Sam extended a large hand.

Everything about the stall, including Sam, was immaculate. Sam wore a stiff blue and white apron and a broad smile as he ladled out the eel stew.

I tasted mine cautiously: the eel came in large round chunks of white flesh with a core of jagged backbone inside, and was mild and pleasant in flavour.

"By rights you ought to follow up with a glass of stout, but I'll let you off that."

He didn't allow me long to eat, which we did leaning against the stall while lorry drivers, dock workers and peddlers came up for a quick meal. They all seemed to know Fran. They didn't look at me particularly. Perhaps Fran brought girls here often.

Then we were on the move.

"Now where are we going?"

"Underneath the Arches." He gave me a sideways look. "Know what that means? No? Call yourself a Londoner?"

We drove down a short road lined with market stalls, the end of which was blocked by a line of railway arches. Underneath the arches a whole world of entertainment was spread out: a small boxing ring, a fortune-teller's booth, a shooting-range, and a merry-go-round. One arch was entirely given over to small, rubber-fendered cars tearing round and round to the accompaniment of screams from the occupants. Other arches were filled with more noisy, flamboyant amusements. Across the span of arches ran a streamer of red and yellow announcing CHARLIE'S CHINESE FAIRGROUND. There wasn't a Chinese man in sight—not even a Chinese lantern.

"Take a good look round," said Fran. "This is where I came from. That's where I started. See that stall over there—the one selling peppermint rock and ice cream? That's where I made my first fiver. I was ten. It was illegal. I ought to have been at school."

"When did you give it up?"

"I didn't." He moved me in that direction. "I still own it." Of course, Fran never gave anything up. I ought to have known. "That was me, fifteen years back. Barely tall enough to see over the top of the counter, but I knew how to take the money in. Come on. Let's have a ride." Fran urged me towards the merry-go-round, pulled me onto a dappled mare and climbed up behind me, gripping me tightly round the waist. "Ride a cock-horse. I own this too," he shouted. "That's how the money spins."

Spin was the word—a kaleidoscope of colour and noise started to whirl beneath me. The fairground was just waking for the evening, with more stalls opening their shutters and young couples wandering around. Music and lights surged on, pouring out life against the gathering dark. I could smell hot dogs cooking, and detect the sweet, caramel scent of cotton candy.

"Do you own the whole place?" I shouted back.

"Not quite all. But I could if I wanted. This is where show business starts, and me with it."

He helped me off, as the music and movement slowed to a stop, then he put an arm round me to steady me. By this time he'd been recognised, and friends were coming over, shouting a welcome and shaking hands with him; everyone shouted in Charlie's Chinese Fairground. It was the year the Prince of Wales started to wear trousers with wide legs, "Oxford bags," they were called. The smart dressers of the fairground all sported Oxford bags in vivid checks. I could see that Fran was liked and admired here. "Good old Fran," and "What's the latest, Fran?" came from all sides. He was their big success story, what they all wanted to be, and what some might be.

He led me through the crowd. "Can't stop. Come on, Alice. We're off to the Deptford Hippodrome: George Robey is topping the bill."

George Robey was a magic name in English music hall. Frock-coated but collarless, wearing a round, archaic bowler hat, and carrying an odd little case, he had ridden to the theatre that night on an elephant, and the animal was squatting on the kerb, looking wise and alert, as we arrived.

Fran parked his car beside it. "Watch over it for me, Jumbo. We're not going into the stalls or a box, we're going to sit well back in the pit and eat oranges and peanuts. That's how to enjoy life."

He sat there himself, holding my hand, eyes concentrated on the stage. He was fascinated, completely under its spell. It told me something about Fran and his dreams. Occasionally he looked at me triumphantly. "Enjoying yourself? I knew you would: this is where the theatre gets its energy, and don't you forget it. It's not a holy ritual, but a bawdy living."

Performing that night were Fred Emney ("gin is common stuff, but we keep it in the house in case of measles,") the Brothers Griffith, and Nora Bayes, who sang "Tears in My Eyes." They loved Nora, but she was no Gracie Fields.

Billy Bennet came on before George Robey. With his black, shining quiff of hair, bristly moustache, and seedy black jacket, he clumped onstage in his hobnailed boots. Straightforwardly bawdy, he knew what his audience wanted and he gave it to them.

Robey hardly needed patter, playing with his audience as he pretended to detect a misplaced laugh, offering them a tantrum of anger, before embarking on a rumble of philosophical digression. He had them in stitches with the raising of one sad eyebrow. And somehow, one never forgot that elephant.

Fran and I were laughing helplessly together. "Good girl," he said. "Now you see what it's all about. And you know where I stand."

He put me in his car and drove me home. Before he let me go he put his arm round me. I let it rest for a minute then I gently removed it. He was muscular under the gaberdine. I liked the feel of muscle under fine cloth.

"There are some girls who are afraid of sex, and some who aren't. Your cousin Maida is one of the former, and that's why she gets into trouble, she invites it. You're not afraid."

"No," I said. "I'm not."

"So why do you tie yourself up so tight?"

I could have told him about Frederic, even about the abortion. He would probably have understood. He had let me walk inside his life that night, but I still kept my frontiers manned. My experiences with Frederic and his baby remained private territory.

He didn't wait for me to answer. "Lovely old place, the Deptford Hippo."

"Could do with some fresh paint."

"Not worth it." I looked at him. Now it's coming, I thought. "I own it, I'm going to pull it down. Put up a cinema." He grinned. "This is its last week." He opened the car door. "Good night, baby girl."

92

He kissed me, a gentle kiss, but that last remark had given me a taste of how ruthless he could be.

As I put myself to bed I remembered his words about my cousin Maida. Could I read a warning into them? I knew that my grandmother was worried about the way she lived. She was seen everywhere with Bobby Charlecote, but he was certainly not her only protector.

Even Dickie Davenport had whispered to me hoarsely that he hoped she knew how to look after herself. "A greedy girl," he had grumbled. "And not above biting the hand that feeds her. And I don't mean your grandmother." He winked.

The feet of workmen sounded up and down Albion Walk. The stage lighting was fixed thanks to the work of Steele MacKay, the great innovator. The mechanics of the stage remained too expensive to finance with Fran's money: I was determined not to get too deeply into debt to him. There was a look in his eyes, sometimes, that reminded me he could always hold me in his debt. I didn't want to become like Maida and bite the hand that fed me—and I was not going to be Fran's mistress. I had had a windfall from an unexpected source; Paul Poiret had sent me a letter and a handsome cheque—only a loan, but no interest was required, merely a promise to repay if he ever asked. But I still had to watch the money.

I did not have a sliding or an elevating stage, although in planning the new theatre I had hoped for both. Such equipment would come, but in the meantime, to satisfy Josie, who was still rooted in the "old" theatre, I had the trap door repaired. I stood on it afterwards and that day it seemed to me haunted ground.

To make a profit I had to sell something besides entertainment. The Albion had a bar on which Maria and I performed miracles with the paintbrush. We painted a mural of Queen Victoria's Diamond Jubilee when, by going to the top of the building, it had been possible to get a good view of the procession passing down the Strand. When I was rich I was going to have my offices up there.

Next door to the Albion were the two empty shops that I now opened, keeping one for myself and renting the other to a florist. In my shop, Menus Plaisirs, I arranged luxurious items from France, such as petit-point handbags and lace handkerchiefs, and satin and lace underthings. I also sold French perfumes, including, of course, those from Rosines. We kept Menus Plaisirs open till the curtain went up on the evening performance. I also retained a small stake in the flower shop. Together the two enterprises brought in a modest profit, which I turned over to running the Alby.

Everyone said I was a good businesswoman. I had one firm rule about both the Albion and Menus Plaisirs: we all shared the work. I sold tickets in the box office, if necessary, and even served teas in the intervals. The tea trays were a great thing at the Albion: we prided ourselves on the neatly arranged tray passed along the rows between the acts at matinées. Because I would turn my hand to anything, so would the others, and even stage-door Stan was pressed into service to sell perfume at Menus Plaisirs with a Shakespearean flourish.

My office was in a tiny slip of a room backstage. I was my own business manager; Alec Fiesta was stage manager, since he now thought I was going to be a success, and Maria was, albeit reluctantly, going to do front of house. All decisions were mine, and that was how I wanted it. I tapped the fund of theatrical knowledge in my family. The Mays had lived and died in the theatre for generations. They knew all there was to know. I talked to my grandmother, and I asked Dickie Davenport for advice, and they both said that, in the end, it all depended on flair. If I had that, I would be a success. And they thought I had it.

Apart from the May family, Francis Hollman was my chief confidant. He obviously thought I had something too, but whether it was flair or just my ownership of the Albion that drew him, I could never decide. Needless to say, Maria's arrival in London had made Francis ask questions, and he knew where to go to get answers. We were sitting in my office when he let me know how far his investigations had gone.

"Still dreaming about your dead lover?" asked Francis, striking a match for his cigarette.

"What do you mean by that? And I wish you wouldn't smoke those terrible gaspers."

"I know everything about you, girl. Make it my business to know. Frederic, he was called, wasn't he? And my cigarettes are the best Abdulla Virginians. No common smokes for yours truly."

It was Josie who had told him, I suppose. "I'm thinking about my profits, not dead lovers," I said sharply.

"Good girl," he approved.

"If I can't make the profit I need out of chocolates and whisky, then I shall sell something else. I've learned my lessons from Poiret. I'll sell scents and make-up for women. Not the ones I sell in the shop, but a special scent, packaged for the Albion. I'll make a selling point of that to attract the wealthy girls."

"They're all rich now," said Francis. "Not a poor girl around. You look at 'em in Bond Street and Regent Street. Beautiful girls like you," he said, trying to get a kiss, but I easily evaded him. "Give him up, this Frederic of yours. He's dead and gone. And you never had him anyway."

"You do keep trying, don't you?"

"Forever. Never give up." I didn't realise then that he really meant it.

The Cochran show went into production and my share was handed over to me, bringing with it its own producer, a temperamental man named Bill Ackroyd. The theatre then was like a feudal monarchy with Cochran as the king. A number of lesser magnates, such as Charlot, ranked just beneath him with a pyramid of lesser fiefs below. In this instance, Cochran had come back from a triumphant European tour bringing his spoils with him and presenting me with the highly strung Bill and some half dozen singers and dancers of questionable talent.

I had gathered together a writer and composer, a handful of performers who would turn their hands to anything, and an idea: the Albion should bring in a revue about itself, a survey of its history.

Josie had introduced me to Meggie Repton, with her two friends, Peter Duvier and Ben Street. Meggie was one of the best young actresses of her generation. Peter and Ben both acted then, but later were to turn to directing, and in Ben's case to writing as well. They were a highly talented trio. And Meggie was beautiful.

At the Domino I sat at my table with Peter, and Meggie and Ben and mapped it all out. Peter had a half dozen sketches planned before we'd finished our drinks, and Meggie and Ben were already improvising a song and dance.

"I want it to be quick, lively and spontaneous," I said.

"The great trouble is going to be your Austrians," said Peter, with a frown. "Some dichotomy there."

"No, not at all." I was decided. "The dancing pair can sing the Napoleonic Polka, and the singing act can join in the Viennese Waltz scene for Queen Victoria's birthday and lead the big patriotic finale to the first part with the Crimean War. And all their dances can come in there." I was making notes fast on a page. "We do several of the little play scenes—both serious and funny. Then some vignette street scenes—street sellers with London cries, comic and sad, that sort of thing."

"I like that," said Peter. "I can do something with that." He waved his hands. "We can bring the second interval curtain down with a street scene."

"And then the third act is straight contemporary: what we're doing *now* in the theatre. Then we project the Albion's future."

"I like that even better," said Peter, starting to tap his feet. "No trouble there. Why are you frowning?"

"My real trouble is Bill Ackroyd."

Meggie frowned. "I haven't seen him around. None of us know him. He can't be one of *us.*"

"Oh, don't be so parochial," said Peter.

"No one's ever called me that." Meggie was hurt.

"Oh, sexually no, dear, I grant you, the world's wide open to you, but intellectually—."

"He's from Australia," I put in hastily. "Drifted in with the tide. Cocky found him in America, I believe. But I've got him and I've got to use him."

"Bring him to the Domino and let's meet him," said Ben.

I brought him. He and Peter took an immediate fancy to each other, which made my life a lot easier. I didn't know then I was starting off one of the great love affairs of the twentieth century theatre.

Thus from widely different elements was *Parade* produced, and yet I knew I had stamped it with my own mark.

I issued an announcement:

Alice May
proudly announces the triumphant revival of the Albion Theatre under her management, with new lighting and new decorations by Alice May and Maria Beck, late of the Martines, Paris. The Albion was built in 1782 by Robert Armistead, burned down in 1840 and rebuilt by William Mann. Rebuilt again in 1896, the theatre was closed in 1915 and

used as a recruiting centre until it was hit by an enemy bomb.

Miss Alice May submits a new production to her friends. It is a revue called

Parade: The Passing-Years
Being pictures picked from the past
of the Albion Theatre, alternated
with music, dancing and laughter
From the Prince Regent and the great
Napoleon
through
Victoria, the Empress, and Kaiser Bill
to
the Jazz Age

Maria and I had an argument over the wording of this announcement; she wanted a separate sentence all to herself. There was no doubt that she felt herself in competition with me. I wondered why, but I couldn't come up with an easy answer. In a way, we always had been competitors, but I thought the war had wiped that out. I wanted to help her; I *had* helped her. Perhaps she resented my assistance. Anyway, she was pushing me, and when pushed, I tended to push back. So the announcement of our opening appeared as I had written it.

I felt I needed something more than the usual press announcements. I was an early exponent of the publicity device, a quick learner—I remembered George Robey's elephant. Here again, Maria and I clashed. She thought the idea vulgar.

"Why does Pola Negri have a leopard for a pet? Not because she likes its teeth. Display, Maria, display. That little touch of fantasy that opens up a world."

But she couldn't see it. "I still say vulgar."

"Since it's the Albion, I ought to get a British lion, but it would bite James Agate. I know, I'll get a bulldog."

So I hired an out-of-work actor, dressed him as John Bull and got him to walk up and down outside the Albion with a bulldog. I didn't know then that the man drank.

I started to get plenty of publicity in the newspapers. "Girl Manager reopens the Albion" and "Alice May lights up the Alby" and, in *The Times,* "Miss May's production plans: an interview with London's newest theatre manager." Photographs

97

and interviews of me, Bill, Ben, Meggie and Peter appeared in *Theatre World* and *Stage,* as did the news of John Bull and Dog.

I was conscious all this time of eyes upon me. Fran Hollman's eyes, for one. Maida Cook's, for another. Yes, Maida was watching me, broodingly, even angrily. I saw her often at the Domino with Bobby Charlecote. Thank goodness she wasn't living at Ladybrook Grove. And yet I didn't get the impression that Maida disliked me; she was watching me more as if she had something on her mind. In the world she moved in there was no doubt much to worry her.

"She is a bad girl," Maria said solemnly. Bad to Maria meant sexually active.

At about this time, I discovered Maria had been making the rounds of the theatrical agents looking for another job. That hurt.

"I want to be your equal," she said when questioned.

"You are, Maria."

"You think so? Very well, then, I want to be your better."

"You'll never be that," I said quickly. I could be as prickly as she was. "And lay off me and my family." Maida was *my* cousin, after all.

Ellen May, who worked at Lucille's as a fitter, told me that Maida had been in there ordering many dresses and several pairs of evening lounging pajamas, then newly in fashion; Ellie had no idea who was paying for them, unless it was Maida's protector, but one thing was sure, Maida was spending freely.

"I nearly died when Maida walked in, bold as brass," Ellen said. "She pretended not to know me. Bobby Charlecote was with her. I don't think he was paying, though, only helping her to choose. He's not got that sort of brass. Good taste, though, better than Maida's, *he* knew what to go for."

The Cochran revue opened to a chorus of false praise the day before *Parade* opened at the Albion. After their first night I went round the back to offer felicitations and congratulations. Plenty of people were there already: Jack, Bea, and Gertie and Noel; Ivor on his own, and Elsie, Gladys and Allie—a roll call of the rising theatre, friends and rivals all. Fran Hollman escorted me; Josie came with us, excited and exuberant, and Maria accompanied her.

"It won't run, you know," Josie whispered. "I could see James Agate frown. He didn't like it."

Across the room I saw my cousin Maida with Bobby Charlecote. Maida had a small part in the show. Josie waved to her.

I suppose the cast knew the show was a flop; there was such a sense of forced gaiety, and everyone was drinking too much. The party overflowed from the star's dressing-room out into the corridors, still littered with props of the last scene. I wandered towards the stage, holding my glass of champagne. It was an anxious and tense moment in my own life. Tomorrow the lights would go up at the Albion. I *had* to succeed, and all around me I could see what it was like to fail.

A tall, thin man was dismantling part of the machinery that had brought in the finale. He seemed to be moving mechanically, as if only his body operated while his mind was far away. The show had arrived complete with its own mechanics, I recalled, and now that I had seen the extreme complexity of the last scene I could understand why.

Maria came up behind me. "I have left the party. So dull. Shall we go home?"

"What about Josie?" I said, not taking my eyes off the man.

"Still drinking champagne."

"And Fran?"

"I can't see him."

The man turned his face towards me so that I could see his features. Older than I had thought, older than he should have been, old past my imagining. A thin white silk scarf was wound round and round his throat.

I heard Maria catch her breath. Slowly I went forward and held out my hands. "Frederic," I said. "Poiret must have sent me here to find you."

It had been Poiret who had suggested my name to Mr. Cochran for the Austrian act. I guessed he had known about Frederic and had devised this way of bringing us together, without the responsibility of interference.

Although much thinner and older, Frederic's features were essentially the same. But his expression had changed. All the life and affection that had animated him had gone. I spoke calmly, but I could feel my heart racing, and I had to control my breathing. My mouth was dry; I thought I might faint. Shock, joy and alarm succeeded each other in my mind. In one moment, my whole world had changed. But why didn't Frederic speak?

"Frederic," I said. "It's Alice. I know I've changed. Grown up, cut my hair, put on make-up. But I'm still Alice."

Behind me Maria muttered something I could not hear. She caught at my arm, dragging me back so that we stood side by side. Dimly I resented her action.

He didn't answer, hardly even looked at us.

"Frederic, mein Liebchen," said Maria.

He smiled at us. It was a polite smile, and not unkind, then he walked away.

This time I held Maria back. "Don't follow him. He doesn't know us. He's forgotten us both." She tried to pull away. "No, leave it, Maria. We know where he is, and how to find him. Leave him for now."

We left the party, Maria and I, and went home together, leaving Josie and Fran behind us. Not much was said between us on the way.

"It isn't a natural forgetting," said Maria suddenly.

"No. It would be the war. I expect he was wounded . . . And even without that, he might have lost his memory. There's what they call shell shock. It happens, Maria."

Maria went to her bedroom in the basement and I crept upstairs to my room; I think Grandma May was awake because I heard the springs in her bed twang as I went past, but she didn't call out to me.

I lay unsleeping in my bed. I felt physically sick. Josie and Fran came back in the small hours. I listened to her affectionate farewells to Franny and I heard her singing as she came up the stairs. She crashed into her bedroom, stumbled out again, flushed the lavatory, had another little sing, and hiccuped herself gently to sleep.

I didn't let myself think about Fran; I had enough to deal with in Frederic. Darling Frederic. I realised that terrible experiences lay behind him, inevitably making a barrier between us. Perhaps he hated me now for being English, as I thought Maria hated me sometimes for this reason. But I thanked God for the affection for Frederic that awoke again. It was what I wanted.

When the noise of Josie's going to bed had passed, I got up and went downstairs to Maria's room. Whether we liked it or not a bond had been forged between us that was stronger than our individual wills. I knew she was crying; she knew I would come to her.

But there was something puzzling about her reaction to Frederic, something I could not quite put my finger on.

100

I went up and put my arms round her and hugged her protectively.

"Don't cry." I gave her a comforting squeeze. "After all, he's alive. Back in our lives again. And we owe that to Poiret. I think he sent him to us."

"Yes, but he didn't speak to us."

Maria, who had slumped against my breast, sat up. "I shouldn't have let you tell me what to do. Why should you give orders?"

"He loved me," I said. "And I loved him." Again I had that strange feeling she was keeping something back.

"That was in the past; you know what it was. We don't know what he feels now."

"I must still show love," I said slowly.

"Go back to bed, Alice," said Maria. "You look worn out, and you have the Albion to think of."

"Don't say it like that."

"Well, I am jealous of you, Alice. You have so much and I have so little."

"We can share."

Maria smiled. "Some times you are so naive, Alice. Share, indeed. Go on, go to bed. You look after your theatre and leave Frederic to me."

"I needn't choose between Frederic and the Albion," I said, getting up from the bed.

I thought she was laughing at me. I could sense that Frederic and I, and Maria too, were caught in a tragic joke, one perpetrated by what Thomas Hardy called the "great comedian in the sky," but I also sensed that Maria saw more of the joke than I did.

We kissed and went to bed. I didn't sleep. I was out of the house and on my way to the Winter Garden Theatre before Maria was up. I knew I had to act.

A few solitary figures were moving around backstage. I went from one to the other, staring silently in each face, trying to identify Frederic. I found him in one dark corner of the stage, preoccupied with another piece of machinery. Slowly I approached. I understand that the trauma of war might have taken away Frederic's memory. Now that I was closer I could see a scar running from temple to jaw. A blow like that, I thought, might knock out almost anything. But the human mind is tough; something of himself had remained, because he

101

had come back to the theatre. Part of him knew he belonged in that world. He had forgotten me, but I thought that I could break through that tiny aperture he had left in his memory, and bring him back to life.

"Frederic?" I said.

He turned and looked at me. So he knew his name, but that could have been relearned. Soldiers carry identification papers. He knew he was Frederic Lothar because someone would have told him.

"Frederic," I went on gently, "it surprises me to see you doing this work, instead of singing." I had to remind him of myself gently; I must not alarm him. I had slipped naturally into German, surprised to find how easily it came back to me. "We did know each other well once, Frederic. We were in Paris together. Say you recall it. Do you remember *Tic-Tac* and the Rivoli Theatre? And Josie? And Alice?" He was looking at me with a pathetic, puzzled stare. "But then you were a singer, Frederic. What has become of your voice?"

He picked up the great hammer that lay at his feet and swung it at the machinery. A fury seemed released inside him, the blows came cracking out. An old workman came running across; he took the hammer from Frederic and put an arm around his shoulders, making soothing noises as he did so, and turning Frederic's face away from me. "Whatever did you say to him, miss?"

But he didn't wait for me to answer. Over his shoulder, as he helped Frederic away, he said, "Can't you see the poor fellow can't answer you back? He's got no voice. He's dumb."

So it was with this burden on my shoulders as well as my own desperate need for success that I went to my own first night in the Albion.

Tension is infectious. Maria decided she had to leave Ladybrook Grove: she would be gone by the next day. I had told her about Frederic, and this was how she reacted. It would be better for us to be more independent of each other, she told me.

Josie, scenting drama, chose to put her penny's worth in. "You two," she said. "The way you kick it around. This is a man you are talking about. Not a football."

Maida's addition to it all was probably accidental, since she was not sensitive to anyone's emotions except her own. On the way to the Albion I saw her coming out of the stage door of a neighbouring theatre. I knew she had a small part in the play currently running there. She was carrying a case.

"What's up?" I said. It was Maida's habit to spend the day sleeping.

"Collecting my things. I'm chucking it in," she said briefly. "I had a few lines to say in my show and they're being cut. Well, I couldn't stand that. Get someone else, I said, but yours truly is out. A girl has to think of her status." She had diamonds in her ears and a fur stole slung over her shoulders, but there were dark shadows under her eyes and a bruise on one cheek. Life wasn't all honey and roses for Maida. For a moment, as she raised her eyes to look at me, I saw fear at the back of them, fear about something direct, physical and violent. Then the shutter came down and she was all smiles.

"Give my love to Gran. I've got a good billet. Tell her I'm in the money. Ta-ta, love." Then, unexpectedly, she offered sympathy. "Chin up, Alice. So what if your man's lost his voice and his memory? Josie told me. Alice is lucky, I said, a man you can really love is a luxury a woman can't often afford, never mind what he hasn't got."

Backstage there was the usual tension and excitement that made the atmosphere electric. From this mixture of pain and hope came the nervous energy to fuel a success. Without it the opening would be like bread without yeast. We all knew that, yet it was still a time to be endured.

The smell of greasepaint is compounded of so many different elements: the scent of make-up, of talcum powder and eau de cologne, the sweat of anxious human bodies, together with the tang of the fixative used by the makers of wigs and false hair, which can penetrate even to the auditorium. I used to say I could smell a production of King Lear a street away.

The doorman, whisky on his breath but stone-cold sober with the terror that consumed us all, alerted me to the expected just-before-curtain-rise quarrel. There is always one, and this time it was between Bill and Peter.

"It's nerves, we all know it's nerves, but there'll be blood flowing if you don't step between them," Sam said.

"I'm not stepping between them in this dress," I said, crisply. I was wearing the prettiest dress I had ever owned, beaded chiffon, pleated from my hips, and I had no intention of getting blood on it. "Where are they quarrelling?"

Sam nodded towards a door. "In the Gents."

I walked over and banged on it. "Darlings," I called in a loud voice. No answer, but a listening silence. "Darlings, stop that quarrel and get out of there. I need all the help I can get tonight. Kill yourselves tomorrow on your own time."

Then I stalked off, not waiting to see if they came out. I knew they would. We had to have one emotional explosion backstage on opening night. Now that it had taken place all would be well.

Out front all was movement and gaiety. I stood watching the crowds arrive. The press was there and even a man with a movie camera making a film of us for a newsreel. Many worlds were represented. Josie was well known and liked in the theatre, as was Gran, so the theatre had turned out in force to support us. Besides, one more theatre meant one more chance of work. From the Cooks and the Davenports had come rows of friendly faces. I could see Francis, his face all grin. And there were Eugene and Louisa, wearing their best clothes and their usual sparkle. For the occasion Louisa had sold me my straight, beaded dress, which had once belonged to Dorothy Dickson, so that this wasn't its first appearance in a theatre. Noel was there, looking serious. And so were Peter and Ben. All my particular friends from the Domino, together with the proprietor, Hannah Less, who rarely went anywhere farther than her own bar. The sight of a tall woman, aflutter with bright, strange clothes, whom I knew to be Lady Ottoline Morrell, alerted me to the fact that the Albion might become intellectually fashionable. Of the social world I could see Lady Louis Mountbatten, Lady Diana Cooper and Lady Londonderry, as well as several Guinesses and a clutch of Tennents. We didn't have a royal prince, however, and that was a loss. From the theatrical world I saw as many as could take the time from their own productions. Noel was there, but not Gertie; Maria Tempest came (she'd played in the Albion years ago), and someone said they saw Somerset Maugham laughing. Doris Zinkeisen came to see my sets. Michael Arlen had a stall. Sitting next to him was Basil Dean. Once again I saw James Agate in the audience, but this time he was looking optimistic. Oh, how much I hoped we got a good notice in the Sunday *Times*.

I suppose I had expected almost all these faces, but what I had not expected was a solid line of Charlecotes in the front row. I knew who they were: they looked like my father and they looked like each other. Bobby was sitting awkwardly in the middle of the family. Assembled together, they looked handsome and forceful; a set of tall, heavily-built men and Junoesque women. There were more women than men; the war had been hard on families like the Charlecotes. But the women had had their fatalities too. One of Lady Charlecote's daughters-in-law, the mother of the heir Edward, had married very soon, but Matthew's mother had been killed in a Zeppelin raid. I was never to see them all again as a group. Perhaps it was the last time they met like this themselves. Matthew Charlecote was placed at the end of the row, with a pretty young girl sitting next to him. When he saw me across the aisle he gave me a friendly bow.

Josie, standing beside me, drew in a little hissing breath. "That lot here," she said. "Who'd have thought it? Come to check on their own property, that's what this parade means."

"Do you think so?"

"Sure of it. Ever see a more property-conscious lot than them?"

"Oh, I don't know. They look very handsome." And prosperous too, I thought, although the women's clothes, while solidly and beautifully made, were not smart. Smartness, that mixture of moment and mood, was the quality everyone sought just then.

"They hate me," said Josie, with some satisfaction. "And it's mutual. I married their precious son, and they hate to admit it." *Won't* admit it would be more accurate, I thought. *"You've got a friend there, at any rate,"* she continued.

"Who? Bobby?"

"Bobby!" Josie brushed away the suggestion. "No, Matthew."

"Never." It was more than likely he was my brother, but I could hardly believe it. Surely I would have a sense of it?

"Oh, I know that look; I ought to. Don't you have anything to do with him. I'm warning you, now."

I didn't know what Josie was playing at, but I couldn't stand it now. I walked away from her. I had to be on my own. I was fighting to control my feelings. The crisis time was almost upon me.

For a little while my whole world was contained in this theatre. All my dreams, all my hopes for the future, all my ambitions depended on what happened in the next few hours. Everything, all at once, was being put to the test. I felt that either I succeeded now, or failed forever.

On every side I felt the tension. It was enjoyable as well as terrifying. That's how the theatre is. We were all infected. Backstage, in the dressing-room, that was to be expected. But the girls serving in the bars, and handing out the programmes were just as jittery. They were all on my side, because it was their job and their future too. Muttered comments of support and slaps on the shoulder came at me as I walked about nervously.

I had faith in the show, of course, but in those last few minutes before we got under way I felt all sensation ebb away, until it was as though I had nothing left inside. I kept reminding myself that it was a good show, with a witty, concise book, joined to delightfully tuneful music that people would go away humming. It combined old tunes and new brilliantly. I knew it did, but I was still miserable. I thought of the truly dreadful dress rehearsal that had gone on all night and only pulled itself together at the last minute. That was said to be a good omen. I hoped so, but I still felt sick.

On impulse, I went round to the chorus's dressing-room, where the girls were powdering their backs for each other in the usual good humoured fashion, to wish them good luck. They gave me a cheer. I marvelled at them when I thought of how tired they must be, their feet aching and bleeding from the solid, pounding hours of rehearsal not so far behind them. And yet they glittered with confidence and happiness.

One of the girls ran after me and flung her arms round me in a hug. "Honey, honey, honey." Chorus girls can be like that. She was a little cockney hybrid, half English, half Russian, a beautiful dancer.

"Honey, yourself," I said.

Reassured, I returned to the front. The moment had come. The house lights went down, the curtains went up, and by halfway through the first act the occasional ripples of laughter, together with the sense of tension created and held, gave me my first hint that things were going well. I stood at the back watching. By the end of the first act I knew for sure that my unpretentious but first important production was a success.

I went out to the cloak room, vomited into a basin, cleaned my face, and put fresh make-up on. Then I went back to my position to clench my hands and watch. Triumph gradually mounted within me. When the final curtain came down to a thunder of applause I could enjoy it. Later, there was a party for us all. I stood a little apart, watching.

I felt as though a little bubble of good fortune, with me inside it, was floating right up and over the Albion. Beneath the bubble and enjoying the most tremendous party onstage were all my friends and most of my relatives. The first person out to me was Noel, a smile spreading from ear to ear and a cry of triumph on his lips. I did enjoy that moment of my success.

I did not need the champagne to feel intoxicated; I held a glass in my hand to sip occasionally, but the traditional cold tea would have done me as well. Presently someone put a record on a gramophone and we all began to dance. I did a good foxtrot, so I was usually in demand as a dancer. Tonight everyone wanted to dance with me, and I was passed on from partner to partner, laughing and happy. In that intensely superstitious theatrical crowd it was as if I was the symbol of luck and to touch me would bring good fortune. I kept an eye out for Matthew Charlecote to see if he would join the dance, but he remained on the edge of the group, watching us.

Eventually I gasped that I was exhausted, extricated myself from my latest partner who was getting amorous, and wandered towards the rest of the party. All around me were groups of happy people, chattering and laughing. Supper was just about to be served and I made up my mind that I would eat it in Matthew's company. I walked towards him.

Out of the corner of my eye I saw Josie approaching. Not entirely steadily, I thought. Gin and success always did go to Josie's head. Or perhaps she really was determined to wreck my life. I accused her of both things. She was wearing a dress with a little silver train, and Bobby Charlecote managed to tread on it: Josie slapped his face, accusing him of doing it deliberately.

Matthew greeted me warmly and introduced me to the tall, pretty, gawky girl he said was his sister Flora. Apart from a desire to tell her that she should not wear green, I had no interest in her—only in Matthew.

He gave me a smile that I realised had great charm. "At heart all of us Charlecotes are in love with the theatre. There's enough of it in me to make me glad the Albion's alive."

"Thank you," I said, surprised and touched.

Josie broke into the moment, clutching her train and out for blood. "I want you, Alice. Come and pin me up." She glared at me and Matthew. "What are you doing, anyway?"

A middle-aged female Charlecote forced her way through the crowd and confronted my mother. "You've just broken my son Bobby's nose."

"Oh, rubbish. And what if I have? He can have it reset. Or lopped off. All you Charlecotes have long noses. Down which to look. You've always looked down on me and I've had enough. I was lawfully married to your bloody Randolph. All this, all of everything—" her arm swept out in a wide arc, knocking over a tray of drinks which spilled themselves over the Honourable Mrs. Charlecote's white brocade. Josie gave an evil laugh.

Matthew interrupted her, his face serious. "Everything what?" he asked.

"It all ought to belong to Alice. It *does* belong to Alice. By rights. If she had her rights."

Matthew and I stared at each other.

"And, by God, I'm going to law to prove it. I'll prove my marriage at the Old Bailey."

"Oh, *Josie,*" I said. Even I knew the Old Bailey was for criminal cases.

But for Josie the hunt was up. "You're all swindling Alice out of her rights. It should all go to Alice as Randolph's heir. Down the family, that's the way it is—Randolph's elder brother didn't have a child so that makes it Randolph's and then Alice's."

Matthew was white. "If you go on like that, we shall *have* to take you to court," he said.

"You will?" said Josie, drawing herself up. "You will? It'll be me that starts it. You can leave it to me. And as for you, Madam,"—this to Mrs. Charlecote—"you can cease your weeping and mewing, because I am about to leave," and picking up the remains of her train she swept out, saying to me as she did: "Those last lines were from *The Daisy of Pimlico*. Splendid exit, what?"

"Damn it, Josie. Don't dig up the foundations all round me. Let me get on with things in my own way. I can build a bridge with the Charlecotes. I think I like them now I've seen them." I was as angry as she was, glad to see her leave the theatre.

I was going back to my party, to salvage what I could, when Dickie came rushing in.

108

"Alice—the bulldog's got away and it's chasing Basil Dean down the street."

"Oh God, what an enemy to make," and I hurried off to see what I could do.

I found John Bull slumped against the main entrance, eyes closed. "Where's the dog?" I demanded.

"Gawd knows, dear," and his eyes closed again. "I saw him haring off down the road after a bitch."

Noel emerged, looking helpful. "I should get back to your party, Alice. That tall cousin of yours, who, I might say, obviously has an eye for you, has just told the one with the bloody nose exactly just what he can do with it." His gaze studied the road. "I believe I see the other two protagonists coming round again, critic first. Leave this to mother."

Eventually the party came to an end, and I got home. I felt exhausted, but I knew I wouldn't sleep. I had a triumph. But I also had Frederic. What was I going to do about him? Was it love I still felt? How could it be? We didn't seem to know each other. Then there was Josie. What was about to happen there?

Gran had got Josie to bed when I arrived. She was crying by that time, jolliness having given way to self-pity. But she was still muttering about revenge.

"Keep her away from Walter Cook while she's in this mood or he'll have her in the courts before you can stop her, that's all," said Gran. "What happened about the dog?"

"Oh, you know?" I said wearily. "Dickie told you, I suppose?" She nodded. "Oh, it was all right in the end. Sybil Thorndyke caught him and she was able to calm him down."

"Who? The dog?"

"No, Basil Dean. It was Stella Campbell's fault, really, her Peke's in heat. She should never have had it with her. It upset the bulldog."

Gran gave a hoot of laughter and stumped up to bed.

But Noel was right on one thing: the helter-skelter down Albion Walk of impresario, dog, and distinguished actress, with the rising young juvenile actor grinning broadly in the background, was splashed all over the newspapers. I discharged the man, but I was obliged to keep the dog; Alby was to be with me for the rest of his life.

The day had not quite ended for me. Maria was sitting on

my bed, waiting. "I didn't come to the theatre. How did it go?"

"I noticed," I said briefly. "A triumph. But my mother got into a fight. And the bulldog bit a critic. Why didn't you come?"

"I went to see Frederic. You'd been. It was my turn."

"Go on," I said. I knew what was coming.

Maria smiled. It struck me at once that she did not seem dissatisfied. "I found him. You were quite right; he cannot speak. I also saw the old workman who befriends him. He says he thinks the condition is an hysterical one. He seems to understand—he served in the trenches, too."

"And Frederic himself?"

Again that quick smile. "He did not know me, of course, but I was able to speak to him in Austrian—proper Austrian which he recognised—not the way you talk, which is the way a foreigner talks." Then she produced her little victory. "And I showed him that photograph of the two of us." I nodded. "The photograph was proof I had been his friend, and for a moment, just for a flash, the curtain lifted and he knew me. I saw it, Alice. Then all was blank again, but it will come back. He knew me."

She could not hide the triumph in her eyes, nor did I blame her. Compared with me, Maria's case was easy. She loved Frederic and would fight for him. I envied her for her simplicity. I had been like that once. But she had gone, that girl who had loved Frederic so simply and whole-heartedly. She was lost inside a complicated stranger with new ambitions and drives, who admitted the existence of other men, like Francis and Matthew, and who carried a cold burden of guilt. No, there was nothing simple about my reaction to Frederic now.

"I owe Frederic a life," I said aloud.

The next day the papers were full of praise. The Albion was news, and *Parade* a success. The box office reported a deluge of bookings. I went round and stared for myself at the queue already forming.

It ought to have been one of the happiest days of my life.

I dropped in at Gene's stall in Berwick Market to buy myself some new silk stockings.

"I laddered my best pair chasing a dog."

"So I heard." Louisa gave her delicious giggle.

"You don't look like the girl of the moment, though," she said as she wrapped the stockings. "See our new wrapping

110

paper? Got our name on it. A big step forward. Like you and the Albion. Remember to keep those seams dead straight. And wear them inside out; they look finer. Go and get yourself a drink, for heaven's sake. Wish I could join you."

Slumped silently over a drink at the Domino, I was joined by Noel. No one ever had a more sympathetic sense of silence than he. I started to talk. I told him of my worries. I told him about Frederic, not going into detail. But then I didn't have to: without doubt the story had gone the rounds by now, and with embellishments. The drama of Josie's quarrel and her attack on the Charlecotes he knew already. But I had my own details to pour out over the martinis. "There's Walter Cook, he's a cousin, and a solicitor. On the shady side of the street, in my opinion, too. My family history is complicated. You know that. But it's even more complicated now."

Walter Cook had discovered new information emerging from the war records that made it clear my father had survived his brother by several days, and had therefore, at his death, been the owner of the family estate, Causley, and all that went with it. From the day of his death Josie now asserted, I ought to have had *everything*, and she meant to see I got it, if she had to go to law to prove it. Moreover, said Wally Cook, even if the marriage could not be proved, then I probably had a good case on account of the letter my father had written expressing a wish I should have all he could leave. A lot could be built from that, Wally thought. I hoped we could keep the letter out of it.

"Gran calls Wally Cook our evil genius. But I don't think we need one."

"Few families do."

"Family relationships ought to be kept out of law-courts." I had my own reasons for not wanting any digging around in my family roots. There might be too much, including some behaviour of my own, to uncover. It might be a good idea to look at a law book and find out what the law on forgery was. I knew you didn't get your hand cut off any longer, but socially they probably had your head. "Family relationships—well, they're so entwined; aren't they?" There were in the Charlecote family, anyway, if what Randolph Charlecote had confided drunkenly was true.

"Oh yes, dear," said Noel cheerfully. "Like convolvulus. Or bindweed."

It was at this point he formulated the great truth that came

111

to be known as Noel's Law: the period of one's great professional success is not always, perhaps never, the time of one's greatest personal happiness. He had one other piece of advice: that I should go to see Causley for myself.

Because of this, or perhaps because of the martinis, I took a railway ticket to Newcastle, and from there hired a car to drive me to Causley House where the Charlecotes lived. I walked up the drive and stood looking at the big house that might be mine. It had a dramatic position on rising ground, framed in trees, with a strongly modelled façade, bay windows, turrets, gables and chimney stacks. The front entrance was splendidly symmetrical and flanked by a pillared portico. I thought it both beautiful and impressive.

Now that I'd seen Causley, I found I wanted it. But I wanted the Albion and my way of life in the theatre, too. I wanted to share in the male-dominated world of property and career. I tried to look into a future in which I had these things and Frederic also. I couldn't seem to get a clear picture of his part in it. Property and success bring their own rights and obligations, but so also does love. Could I pay the price demanded for both? Did I even want to? And yet Frederic was so very, very vulnerable, and my heart was tender towards him.

𝒢 Chapter Six

I came back to London at once. My short absence had been noticed, of course, but it established the idea that I did disappear occasionally for brief spells, and no questions were asked.

Noel's advice had been right in one respect: now that I'd seen Causley I certainly knew how I felt about it. But I still had to make up my mind what to do about Frederic. I wanted to do what was best for him. Or so I told myself.

I let the problem simmer while I got on with the Albion and its problems. One of our sketches had drawn the belated disapproval of the Lord Chamberlain, who was demanding we alter some lines. I could foresee more trouble with him. Everyone said he was attempting to impose prewar conventions on the postwar world and it wouldn't do.

It was not until the second evening after my return that I saw Frederic. He was waiting at the stage door with a small bunch of white lilac. It was so much what the smart young Viennese man-about-town would have done, so decided a throwback to what Frederic had been, that I wanted to cry. He had dressed for the evening in what was obviously his best outfit of neat trousers, a crisp white shirt and a dark jacket. The contrast with the expensive, smart clothes he had once worn so beautifully gave me a lump in my throat.

I put my hand out for the flowers and then bent to sniff the sweet smell of lilac. Had he ever given me lilac before? I couldn't remember. "How did you know how to find me?"

He looked amused, and produced a newspaper with the photograph in it.

"I am so glad that you have come." I looked around me. We were not alone. There were stagehands moving the sets and members of the cast slowly filtering through to the dressing rooms and hence home. There are lots of dark corners in theatres, but few for quiet conversation. "Let's go into my office." I wondered where Maria was; she had been in the theatre earlier that evening. For all I knew, she could be working away at the accounts in my office now; she turned her hand to anything that needed doing. But the room was empty although the lamp on my desk was burning and there were signs that someone had been working there recently. "I was writing letters," I said nervously. "I'm trying to set up a new show. One must have one in hand." Frederic nodded as if he fully understood.

"Let's have some coffee." Maria and I had a gas burner on a table, with a kettle and a jug, so that we could have the frequent cups of tea and coffee that had become so essential to us. "I think there might be some brandy in the cupboard." I began to rummage along the shelf where we kept our cups and saucers. "I have some on hand for emergencies."

Frederic shook his head. I remembered that he had never

liked brandy. He was not so much changed, then. I began to prepare the coffee, and while it was brewing I put the lilac in a jug. Frederic sat down easily in a chair to wait. I saw that he had learned to manage without speech, and that while things were running easily he did not fret. He would have to fight against that, I thought; we would have to make him fight. It would not do to become passive. Now I saw the fury I had called up the other night as a good sign rather than a bad one: he hadn't given up feeling yet.

As I talked, I was deciding what to do. Frederic had come to me, I could not let him go again. Fran had been right: Frederic needed medical advice. Presumably he had had help when he was first wounded, but in the rout of defeat I doubted if it had been much. Anyway, it had not been enough. The loss of his voice and the loss of his memory must be related. If one came back, perhaps the other would too. I didn't know which I wanted back first.

I handed Frederic a cup of coffee. I pushed over the sugar, but no milk; I remembered that he drank black coffee. He smiled at me.

He picked up the cup and raised it to his lips. Frederic had a sensuous mouth, the upper lip long and clearly outlined, the lower curving beneath it like a bow. And yet, it wasn't a womanish mouth; it looked hard and firm. I wondered what it was like to be kissed by that mouth. How strange that I could not remember.

Frederic drew a piece of paper towards him and with a pencil he wrote: "I apologise because I made a noise. I was angry."

I shook my head. "But I understand. I was tactless." And I thought, I shall be tactless again if necessary. "Is that why you brought me the flowers?"

On the paper he wrote: "No. The flowers are because you said you were my friend."

"Yes. I knew you in Vienna first, and then in Paris." I did not go beyond this simple statement.

This time he wrote: "You are very young."

I laughed, and drank some of my coffee. Go easy, I told myself. It would be so easy to frighten him; I knew he was easily frightened. But I put my hand up and held it to his lips, my forefinger gently tracing the outline of his mouth. I felt his lips move beneath my touch.

114

The lights flickered and went out. I knew it was Stan, the doorman, turning off the main fuses before he left. The Alby was so old and the wiring so rotten, that I had decided all fire risks must be eliminated, and so the last person to leave the theatre threw the fuses.

I went to the door and called: "I'm still here, Stan. I'll do the lights."

There was no answer, but the lights surged on. "Thanks," I called down the empty corridor. Then I heard the distant closing of a door. In the recess of the backstage I could see the shape of Mrs. Siddons's four-poster bed, curtains and all.

I went back to my desk. The palms of my hands were damp. Even Meggie, who had so many lovers, waited, more or less, to be asked. I knew from the way she talked there were certain conventions one observed.

I took Frederic's hand and put it against my own lips, brushed it gently with a kiss and said, "I called us friends. We were more than that. We were lovers." I fluttered my fingers across his cheek.

Frederic looked at me in surprise as I led him towards Mrs. Siddons's bed. It was a strange time and a strange place in which to reunite, but then I remembered what Josie had said about my own begetting. Perhaps there was something in heredity, after all.

I drew him down and kissed his lips. "We must go back, Frederic," I whispered, "and heal the past."

Did he understand me? I had a moment of incredulity at my own wildness and Frederic's too, before past and present came together and overwhelmed us both.

The bed smelled of new paint, and the mattress had hard lumps. Afterwards, I looked at Frederic for an explosion of memory, of speech returned, but there was none. So much for romance, I thought; it's not going to work. Part of me will always belong to Frederic, but there is so much more of me now that does not. All my theatre life, which I value and can't give up, separates me from that girl I was.

I turned to Frederic. There were tears in his eyes. He was looking at me intently, weeping for what he could not remember, or utter if he did.

"Oh my dear love," I said. "I'm trying to bring you back. I'm trying."

* * *

115

Frederic believed me when I told him that he had once been in love with me. The alchemy between us still existed, he felt it, but he was shy and cautious. Since his injury many people had tried to unwrap his past for him, but he had never been able to accept the reality they offered. His past and his future had been severed. Apart from his singing, he had no trade. Yet he had turned naturally to the theatre because it had seemed home. I thought there was hope in this, a sign that memory was only dormant, not dead.

Underneath, the old Frederic was there intact. I *had* to believe so. I was less sure that the old Alice lived inside me. I think she had died in Paris, and this immensely complicated newcomer lived in her place. I had not told him about the child and I guessed I never would now.

I forgot to put water in the jug of white lilac, so that the blossoms soon died. You could take it as a symbol, I thought, that I too remembered some things and forgot others. That was our tragedy.

But all the same, the excitement of romance flickered like a candle that had been relit. I had the same quick feeling of happiness when I was going to see him, the same longing to mention his name, to talk about him to those who would listen. For a little while there was a sparkle in our life. I didn't realise that I would have to work to keep our happiness.

I kept up my own life: I had to. One success was not enough. I had to be working towards the next one, and already in my office at the Alby I was doing business. Authors, actors, agents, and producers streamed through my small room offering plays and projects.

Money was always a problem, but I had ideas, and at my table at the Domino I discussed them with my friends. People were in and out of work—some in shows, some not, some hopeful, some in the depths of despair, while others like me were moving energetically towards what they wanted. I had part of what I wanted, but I had to work to keep it.

Maria thought I was being too tough. But I explained, "I am a woman on my own."

"And Frederic?"

"For the moment, he does not count. When he gets his voice back, finds his memory, then it will be different."

Maria's expression did not change. "If he ever does."

On Francis's advice I had taken Frederic to a famous throat

specialist in Wigmore Street, and he had referred us to a psychologist. This man, trained under Dr. Freud in Vienna, advised me to go on with my relationship with Frederic as I had begun. It felt strange to have one's love life arranged by doctor's orders. Even Meggie had not achieved such sophistication. "Accept what he can give," the psychologist said.

Maria and I met daily by arrangement either at the Domino or at the Alby. That day we were at the Domino.

"You don't know what he will remember," she said ominously.

"What does it matter? I shall have given him back his life." And then—because she was very jealous of me, the relationship between us stretched to the very limit—I said, *"We* will have given it to him."

"Thank you." She bowed her head over her coffee.

"The coffee's rotten at the Domino these days," I said, uneasily.

"The coffee's the same. It's you. You're not happy, are you?"

"Not exactly. How can I be, with Frederic the way he is? I have a sense of achievement in my own life—that counts. But love, human relationships count too. I'm beginning to learn one can't have everything at the same time. Or not for long."

"But one can have nothing for a very long time," said Maria with a wry smile. "That, *I* am learning." She picked up the newspaper that I had spread on the table between us. "How famous you are getting."

"Oh, that." I had been interviewed by *The Daily Mail,* and the reward for being a docile and accessible subject had been a large spread of photographs and comments, together with the headline: "A new eagle in the theatre: Alice May in her eyrie." "It's all good publicity for the Alby." We were bringing in a second edition of *Parade,* taking some sketches out and adding some new ones, while freshening up others. The new revised *Parade* would last us another few months, I thought, especially with such publicity, but then I must put on a new show. Noel had one in hand, but I wasn't sure if it was a winner, and there were certain scenes in it that went too close to my relationship with Josie for comfort.

We left the Domino together, since none of our own special crowd were there. We said good-bye in the street, I turned towards the Albion and Maria made her way to Fran's head office, two rooms in Madeleine Street, where she was assisting in plans for the decoration of his fourth cinema. I had my head in a nest of spring flowers, calling itself a hat, and my shoulders wrapped in a seal collar, since the day was cold. Louisa had introduced me to a tall and handsome young man who had already designed a few stage dresses for Alice Delysia and was ambitious to do more. She thought we might do business. He was also setting up a small couture house and that had brought him to talk to me about Paul Poiret, whom he regarded as a sort of god. From his collection I had ordered the dress and coat of mulberry panne velvet which I was now wearing. He had made me a special price, since I was a good advertisement for him and would presently be ordering clothes for the new play—God, Francis Hollman and the producer being willing. He was installed in two rooms in a house in Mayfair, up and down the stairs of which ran Gladys Cooper. But she had not so far allowed him to dress her, remaining loyal to Molyneux.

I remember that day so well because so many strands in my life came together in it. I remember my hat, and the fact that I had an exciting evening engagement, and that I was both happy and unhappy.

I had a surprise meeting in my office with Wally Cook, evil genius to our clan. It was our first meeting face to face. He looked what he was, smart and oversharp. He was older than me by ten years, immeasurably older in wiliness. His ostensible reason for coming was to tell me that Josie was determined to go ahead with the lawsuit against the Charlecotes. Since I knew this by now, I waited to see what would follow. To my surprise, he wanted to warn me against Maida. "Cousinly interest," he called it.

I knew all about his cousinly interest: it had introduced Maida Cook to the man, Frank Drews, reputed to control the importation of Black and White "coco"—cocaine—into London. I didn't use dope myself, having seen some of its worst consequences in Paris, but there was usually some cocaine floating around Mayfair if you wanted it. People said it was harmless, that it just gave you a kick, but I knew better. I don't know if Maida herself took the stuff—I thought not—but I had wondered about Bobby Charlecote. He was very jumpy sometimes.

It seemed Maida was quarrelling with Frank, and over Bobby at that. Wally thought this dangerous.

"For what it's worth, I think Maida's really in love with Bobby Charlecote," I said.

"And that's the danger. She'll lose her head. Not see what's good for her. Let that girl kick her heels about and she'll create havoc. You don't want the Albion to get a bad name."

For the first time it struck me that he did genuinely fear for Maida and dread violence.

I wonder if Wally winced as he left, seeing that he passed a policeman. The policeman was Inspector Doggett and he came to tell us that they had discovered the identity of the man murdered in the Albion. He was called Thomas Wooler and he had come from Causley. I absorbed this fact silently. It made a definite link between the dead man and the Charlecotes, who were the ground landlords of the Albion.

"And, of course, you've been to Causley lately?"

"Are you watching me?" I asked sharply.

He shook his head. "We just happened to have a man there that day who recognised you."

He went on to tell me that local feeling was that joining-up was the best thing Thomas Wooler had done.

"He may have been glad to escape," I said.

"Very likely." His pale, opaque gaze gave nothing away. "It remains a mystery why he was in the Albion. He had no connection with the unit that used it as a recruiting centre."

"Was he killed in the Albion?"

"Yes, he was. Not killed elsewhere and brought here dead. He was killed where he was found. He may have come here because of the Charlecote connection. Although, by all accounts, he was not a man for sentiment."

"Perhaps he met someone he knew," I said.

Inspector Doggett nodded. "This is his photograph, as he was when he was alive," he added. On the table he placed a photograph of the head and shoulders of a young man in soldier's uniform. A bold, bright face stared out at me. It was the sort of photograph many soldiers had had taken on leave. "I wondered if you ever saw him?"

"But I couldn't have done. I wasn't in London when the Albion was used as a recruiting centre; I didn't come here until 1918. The Albion was hit by a bomb and closed in 1917."

"Ah, but he was not killed as early as 1917. The doctors think he wasn't killed until some time in 1918. So he didn't die as early as you think. You *might* have seen him about the place."

"No." I shook my head. "No, I've never seen him. Nor did I have anything to do with the Alby till I started renovating."

"Not at all?"

"Well, I came here once." I remembered my visit the day I had arrived in London, when I had seen Matthew Charlecote. "But I didn't go inside."

"Thank you, Miss May." He pocketed the photograph. "Oh, come, I didn't think you would have seen him, but I had to ask. Now, may I have your permission to question one or two of the staff? I gather some of them go back to the days before the war?"

"Yes. The doorman does, I believe, and one or two of the stagehands. Yes, of course you may speak to them. But they were all questioned by one of your colleagues when the body was first found." My voice died away. Silly of me, I thought— different man, different questions.

Suddenly, I said: "He didn't do drugs, did he? Take cocaine?"

"No, Miss May," said the inspector, his face calm. "No, Miss May, he didn't that we know of. Why do you ask?"

"I don't know. Just thought of it." But at the back of my mind a faint connection traced itself between Maida's protector and the Albion. The notion was so tenuous that I shook my head to get rid of it.

I was thinking so deeply about this, that his next words came as an unexpected shock.

"I believe you have a Mr. Frederic Lothar here?"

"Yes," I said, not pleased to be asked. "I suppose you still keep a check on all aliens, especially former enemy aliens, and pass the word around among you. But he reports to the local police station every month, doesn't he?"

"As far as I know," said Inspector Doggett. "No trouble there at all. An interesting and tragic case, poor fellow. Is his wife to join him?"

"He's not married," I said.

"Isn't he? I understood he was a married man."

"No."

"Ah, my error." He held out his hand. "Good-bye, Miss May."

I think I knew even then that there was a link between

120

Maida Cook and her two lovers, Frank Drews and Bobby Charlecote, that would somehow reach out and touch this dead man at the Albion. The nature of that link was as yet a mystery to me, but that money and violence came into it I was sure. Walter Cook's money, and Frank Drews's money, and Bobby Charlecote's lack of money, together with Maida's love for Bobby were all pieces in this incomplete mosaic.

I had a gramophone in my office on which I played music to help me through the bad patches. I wound up the handle, adjusted the horn and put on a record of "Sitting Pretty" with Queenie May singing the Jerome Kern song. It was an American record brought back by a friend of Josie's.

Just then Maria came in, to bring me a message from Francis. She stayed for a moment, listening to the tune.

"It's a wheeze, isn't it?" I said absently. We listened to the record through again, then I turned it off.

"About Frederic," I said. "Do you think it's possible he was married during his time in the army?"

Maria's expression did not change one iota. "Well ... one day he'll tell us."

"How hard you have become," I said.

"No, not hard at all." She went towards the door.

"I wonder if he wants to remember, wants to speak again," I said sadly. "After all, who knows what he may have to tell us?"

"Ah," said Maria.

"But he *must* remember, we must get his voice and his memory back."

"So it is *you* that is hard," she said, shutting the door with a little snap, leaving me sitting with a surprised look on my face.

Then I got up and put on another record: Jack Buchanan singing a number from *Toni*. All the time I was on the look-out for new ideas, new artists, and new writers that I might use in the Albion. Because I was so young and poor I had to try and catch the new performers on their way up. I could not afford the established stars; I had to make my own. To a certain extent I had already done this. Meggie Repton had appeared in *Parade* and had made an immediate impact. As a result, I had had her agent on the telephone telling me that Meggie would not be available for the new edition of *Parade*. She had received an offer to play with Tallulah Bankhead in New York. Meggie hadn't had the courage to tell me herself, but I couldn't blame her. It was a great chance and she was right to take it.

121

For that night, since I was a success and a woman of some interest, I had received an unexpected invitation. It was almost a royal command. Semi-imperial, anyway, and from a lady who ruled a small world. The huge white card bidding me to an evening party in Bloomsbury, in Gower Street, was sent by Lady Ottoline Morrell.

The large nineteenth century house, in a district that was intellectual but not "smart," had been rented for the season only, but it already bore the mark of Lady Ottoline's vibrant personality. She was a handsome, big-boned woman, dressed in peacock colours and wearing a sort of turban of purple silk, caught up with a yellow opal set in diamonds.

The house was crowded with guests; all the reception rooms were jammed with chattering people, and some even stood on the stairs. Slowly, speculatively, I picked my way through, knowing no one, but amused to be present. It was an accolade, of sorts, to be invited.

Then I saw Matthew leaning against a wall, a glass in his hand, making conversation with a slender bespectacled woman, but watching me.

Lady Ottoline had seen I was observing Matthew; she screeched across the room in that piercing tone of hers, "Not so handsome as your father," thus announcing my paternity. Josie's claims about her marriage and my Charlecote inheritance were being repeated everywhere at that time: it was the gossip of the day. Perhaps that was why I was invited.

Then Lady Ottoline made an observation that was of great importance. "They're violent men, those Charlecotes," she said. "Like all that generation. The Grenfell boys were the same, and others as well, then. It's gone now. That dreadful war—and how easily they stepped into it, saw the natural venting of it." With those words, Lady Ottoline added her farthing of influence to what I made of my life.

Shortly after this Matthew detached himself from his wall and came over to talk to me. I found him amusing and entertaining. All the while I was wondering if he was as violent as our hostess claimed. I thought I was aware of an uneasy energy crackling through him. There was no denying that I found him attractive, but I held back, full of profound reservation. Honour, and a kind of duty, bound me to Frederic. I had picked up a masculine set of ambitions and had to observe a male sense of responsibility. In my case I had a conflict of emotions about

Matthew, the sharp side of which, when it showed itself, had a cutting edge almost akin to hate. He attracted and alarmed me all at once.

As I stood there waiting outside the house for a taxi, with the noise of laughter and music streaming through the opened windows, I became aware of a figure standing in a dark corner watching me. I recognised Frederic. He must have followed me. Perhaps he had often done so. I realised then that he had very strong feelings for me, and that I had handled him badly and hurt him.

I had a very strong temptation then to break off our relationship. His intensity frightened me. How the pendulum had swung. Looking back I could see that in our early days in Paris it had been I who had been the most engrossed. Now it was Frederic. And with a flash of intuition I realised that all he had left now was his pride and his relationship with me. A relationship that must have seemed, in many respects, almost unreal to him. He had only my word for it that we had met and loved before. Sometimes I thought that his memories of Paris would surface, but they never did. I had never told him of the child; it would have been wanton cruelty. Suddenly I felt tender and protective to him, just as I might have felt towards that child. I knew I could not leave him in the cold.

Within the next few days I had moved Frederic into my apartment at the top of the Albion. I had assumed my responsibilities as a woman of property.

𝓰 Chapter Seven

In the climate of the time, taking Frederic in was a brave thing to do, since there was no question of marriage. Fran Hollman said there was a time to call in debts and a time to extend them, and invited me to dinner at the Savoy. Louisa looked troubled, and said she would come and see us, but she couldn't bring Gene as he was "very strict about that sort of thing." In my world it was all right to have love affairs, but better to be circumspect. You could be the object of gossip, but you should not openly flout the laws. Josie and I were both bad about keeping to this set of rules. I was particularly to be remarked upon because not only did I keep Frederic in my apartment, but I also went out to dinner with Fran.

My dinners with Fran were part of my theatre world. For Frederic I deliberately tried to create another world, a romantic one. I meant to make up to him for all he had lost in the war; I had to compensate for my clumsiness with extra love. Except when business demanded, I was always home to have dinner with him, and I cooked it myself. With candlelit dinners and good wine, with love and passion, I tended the love between us.

Frederic did his part. I never made a gesture to him but it met with a loving response. I grew to feel a lifting of the heart at his shy smile that was echoed in his eyes. Lacking speech, Frederic had learned to communicate with his eyes. But sometimes I caught a lost look there, and I guessed memories, hidden deep inside of him, were trying to come through. I always tried to be specially tender to him at these times.

I took him to Brighton once for what was meant to be a sort of honeymoon. We walked by the sea and visited the Prince Regent's Chinese fantasy building. Then we went back to a room I had had filled with flowers. I had ordered champagne and caviar. They seemed to bring on one of his bad moods. As I watched him struggle with it, I realised sadly that if we married I would have to be both husband and wife. No, Brighton was not a success. We were better locked in our own private world. But it is hard for worlds to stay private. Reality will break in.

Josie and I quarrelled, naturally. She was back at Ladybrook Grove since her show was about to come into London after its provincial tryout. "You're like a babe in arms about human nature, and especially men's," she said.

"Do you understand Frederic better than I do?"

"I understand about human dignity and having your nose rubbed in it," said Josie, with feeling. "Because it's happened to me. Yours truly knows all about that. You're lucky he hasn't just walked out on you. Or killed himself."

"I've thought about that," I said.

"Or you."

I looked at her in surprise. "Frederic's very gentle."

"Oh, you and Maria," she said irritably. "Babes in arms, like I said. You don't know about love. You just don't understand." She got off the bed where she had been sitting and brushed the bits of lint from her skirt, which was fashionably knee-high. "But you'll learn. I'm off. I'm going to see my lawyer."

"Walter Cook, I suppose?"

"Yes, and you'll thank me one day."

I wondered what effect Frederic's move would have on Maria. She soon let me know. She was busy working for Francis Hollman. I saw sketches of the interiors she was designing for his new cinemas and they were a world away from the Moorish fantasies he had started with. Stark, angular, clean, Maria's decor caught the eye. I was busy too, preoccupied with plans for a play to be brought into the Albion when the revue went out on the road.

One day, about a week after my quarrel with Josie, I came into my office to see Maria neatly piling all the presents I had ever given her on my desk. It was ridiculously like a wife leaving home, and I wanted to laugh, except I felt more like crying.

"I didn't do this before," said Maria calmly, "because it might have seemed like anger, and I want you to know this is a considered opinion."

London had changed her as it had changed me. She was outrageously smart these days, tall and slim, with her hair cropped even shorter than mine into the back of her neck. That, with her Austrian accent and the monocle she had taken to using, made her an absolute knockout. God, how we had both transformed ourselves into "twenties girls." Even Maria's fantasy about her royal mother had been converted into the contemporary idiom: people whispered that her mother was a Russian princess, married to an Austrian who had gone back to Russia in time to be killed by the Bolsheviks.

I pushed my discarded offerings into a drawer. "I'll keep them till you want them again."

"I'm not leaving the country," said Maria. "You're not getting rid of me that way. Don't think it. I'm a success, just as much as you are, perhaps more."

"I know it."

"So I shall stay. Besides, it is necessary I should. I will be here to pick up the pieces when you have broken Frederic into bits."

All this time I was looking for my new play. Scripts were constantly sent to me; aspiring authors even came to read their work aloud. One young man camped on my doorstep for a whole night, ready to get at me first thing in the morning. Naturally he hadn't written a very good play. I knew what I wanted: it had to be contemporary, it had to be fast-moving, and it had to have a small cast with not more than two sets— one, if possible, since money was tight. And since I was losing Meggie to a successful New York production, it had to have two leading roles, male and female, of more or less equal weight. Casting would be easier that way.

By arrangement I met Noel at the Domino. We talked about my need for a good play. Noel said he thought he could put one my way.

It was a late spring and the intimations of economic trouble that had already shown themselves throughout the country began to grow stronger. Money was tight; there was a good deal of unemployment, especially on the stage. The theatre was moving, but no one seemed to know where.

All the time I had the threat of Josie's lawsuit with the Charlecotes looming over me. If it could have been over and done with quickly, I would have been glad, but such things take time. Slowly, slowly, the sword of Damocles was being hoist above my head by my own mother, but I did not try to

126

stop her: this confrontation between the Mays and the Charle-cotes had to come about.

Noel sent a new play round by special messenger, one of those sturdy little uniformed lads who used to cycle around the town whistling the latest hits. The play was *Maid in Chancery;* the author, Giles Oliver, himself an actor and the son of an actor.

When I'd read it, I telephoned my thanks to Noel. My only reservation was that Giles wanted right of choice over casting. But as it happened, he gave no trouble at all.

Giles and I sat companionably side by side in the stalls watching the chosen audition. Over the years these sessions took on a certain monotony, though I always sat in on them if I possibly could. But so early in my career, the occasion still held great excitement for me. We were watching a curly-haired, twenty-year-old girl who had already been singled out for criti-cal praise, and who probably would have achieved everything we all thought she would but for an early and disastrous mar-riage. Still, she was doing beautifully that day.

"She read the first scene for me last night in my office," con-fided Giles. "But this is even better. Lovely, Adela," he called out. "That'll do for now."

"Toodle-pip, darling," and with a wave, she floated off.

We ticked Adela off our list and went on through the small number of players that remained. The male juvenile lead was hard to cast. Size was the difficulty. Giles was not tall and, since he was the leading man, was determined not to be towered over. So we auditioned all the shortest young actors in London. They were prettier than some of the girls, I thought. Juveniles really had to be good looking in those days if they were to have much chance. But the lad that Giles's eyes rested on with most approval was untidy with badly cut hair. Tim Braby. He had a wild, fierce look in his eyes. I knew him by reputation as one of the few actors with political convictions that showed; he was a member of the Labour party. A troublemaker, I thought, but he was what Giles wanted. He had already read through for us privately and had more or less been given the role. Now he had arrived to run through a scene with Sophia Blake, who was to play the part of the Dowager.

Sophia, an elegant, white-haired grande dame, arrived at that moment. "Darlings, not late, am I?"

127

"Lovely, Sophia, bless you. Lovely to see you. Shall we start?" said Giles obligingly.

She read badly, hardly bothering to raise her voice, and certainly making no effort to project herself.

I raised an eyebrow.

"She hates to audition." Giles breathed at me hastily. "In fact, we don't dare use the word."

Now Tim Braby stood there watching while Sophia finished her speech. I could see that he found Sophia's performance distasteful. But he waited patiently, though he did give her a baleful look.

To Giles, Miss Blake said: "You know I like to have my wig from Perroquet? And my shoes from Bianchi's?"

"Of course, Sophia," soothed Giles.

"As for my dresses, I won't worry you, provided you use either Molyneux or Worth for the third-act dress. I'm not fussy. You won't find me difficult."

Giles gave me a broad wink.

When I talked it over with Josie next day, she commented, "You want to watch Sophia. A holy terror she is."

We were shopping at Leichner's for stage make-up for Josie. She was sitting in front of a large mirror trying out sticks of various shades.

"I'd have thought young Tim Braby was the trouble-maker there," I said.

"Oh no, you won't have any bother with him. He's too hard-working and ambitious to cause trouble."

I tried to question her then about Walter Cook and the lawsuit, tried to laugh her out of it. But Josie knew how to be evasive when it suited her, and she was so then, turning away with a joke about the Leichner mascara not running however much you cried. "So suitable for the witness-box!"

However, she proved right about Sophia Blake. I attended rehearsals for *Maid in Chancery* as often as I could, partly out of curiosity and partly to keep an eye on my property. Rehearsals took place in a disused chapel in Farthing Street, not far from the Albion. The odour of dead sanctity and dust were heavy in the air, but the acoustics were excellent and the rent virtually nil. A marvellous freehold to own, I thought, and wondered if I could buy it. But that was being like Fran.

A scene between Tim and Sophy was coming to an end. As far as I could see Sophy was still walking through her part, although everyone assured me that she would "give" when the time came. I could see that Tim Braby was getting more and more upset by her deadness, but he was controlling himself. Then he fumbled his words, lost his timing and the cue.

"Again please, Tim," murmured Giles.

This time Tim, although getting his cue right, was quite wrong on movement, leaving Sophy floating around in mid-stage on her own.

Without looking at Tim, Sophy addressed Giles in louder and more potent tones than any of her part in the play had so far evoked. "You really can't expect me to give a good perform-ance with such painfully amateur support. I'm afraid I can't continue." And she laid her script down on the floor, and walked away.

Tactfully, I left Giles to deal with her, and I went to a win-dow to look out. There was a builder's yard beyond and I in-terested myself in a pile of bricks. Behind me I could hear Giles being sweetly reasonable, and Sophia being bloody unreason-able. Giles got her back into the rehearsal eventually, but within minutes she had Adela in tears.

"It's all right," Giles whispered to me. "We're doing fine, really." I wondered, especially when I knew I was going to re-fuse Sophy her last-act dress from Molyneux.

That night he telephoned to say that Sophia had withdrawn from the play. He was evasive about the reason, but finally, in an embarrassed voice, admitted that Miss Blake took exception to the "moral tone" of the management: she meant me and Frederic, of course.

"Well, damn her, then," I exploded. "How many husbands has she had? Three?"

"But I think what's really behind it is that wretched dress . . . Couldn't it be Molyneux? Couldn't you manage it?"

I let him persuade me and for a day or two I believe things went smoothly. Then Sophia gave her part up again, claiming once more that she could not be happy with the management. She went around saying that she had never liked the play, any-way. There were rumours of a better offer elsewhere. Even of a fourth husband.

"We're up a gum tree," Giles said.

He despaired, and I had to prop him up, while busily run-ning over in my mind a list of all available and unavailable ac-tresses: Gladys Cooper, Violet Vanbrugh, Irene Vanbrugh,

Cathleen Nesbitt. What about Marie Tempest? Was she really tied up?

Josie said, "I told you so. You won't get much support from Giles, either. You'll have to be the man there. I knew his father. Such a beautiful man, lovely actor. No strength, but lovely projection. Dead now, poor chap. Would join up. No call to, because he was lame in one leg. Killed within a week. Oh, I did cry. We all did. He was much loved." Josie was a great source of information about the theatre, although I was never sure how far to rely on what she said.

Three days after Sophia bowed out, Giles flew into my office. Marie Tempest's husband had telephoned him to say his wife was interested, since her other play had died. Within the hour he had called on Miss Tempest, with flowers, and he could now announce with triumph that Miss Tempest was definitely engaged.

"She says she's read the play already and is longing to do Helen Cathcart." Giles was triumphant. He put his hands on my waist and whirled me round the room, stamping and shouting. "Lucky us. Lucky us." Then he stopped dead. "Oh, I'm afraid there's one thing, love. *All* her dresses will have to come from Molyneux."

For a few days all went well. Then Adela announced she was marrying a duke and would be leaving the cast.

"A real duke?" demanded Giles. "Anything less and I'll hold you to your contract."

But yes, he was a real duke, and really in love with Adela, who had an enormous diamond ring to show for it. Of course she said she'd go on acting, but not in *this* play.

"So I suppose we're up your gum-tree again?" I said to Giles.

But the gods were on our side. In New York, Meggie's play was postponed and finally put off altogether. "If you can fix a part for me in the play, I can appear," she cabled.

"I'll fix *her,*" he said. But really he was jubilant. "We're all together again," he said. "The three musketeers."

Meggie's cable demanded all *her* dresses to be by Molyneux too. I groaned, but accepted.

We met her off the boat-train, and she smiled and waved at us and at the press photographers. She was extremely excited.

"Guess what? On my last night in New York I saw a ghost," she announced dramatically.

130

"Whose ghost? Did it walk on Friday?" asked Giles flippantly. "Are *all* these your bags?"

"It was my own ghost. It passed at the end of the corridor. I recognised me at once."

"What did you do?"

"I bowed and said good evening. One should always be polite, even to one's self."

The press loved the ghost story and wrote it all down. We got some marvellous publicity out of it, and Giles, Meggie, Miss Tempest and I appeared in the *Daily Sketch*—all of us smiling idiotically, with the exception of Miss Tempest, who looked serene.

Everyone thought I must be very happy. They were wrong.

If outsiders had seen more of the picture they would have known that Frederic and I were living in a state of neutrality, with little evidence of the consuming passion that they may have imagined. On the day I brought him there, Frederic had walked all through my apartment, looking at everything from the large sitting room, which had a view of the Thames, to the small kitchen and the bedroom. He surveyed everything, and then came back. He wrote a question on a piece of paper and pushed it towards me: "Do we marry?"

I shook my head. "No. Not yet."

He didn't ask for an explanation. He simply went into the spare room I had allotted him, closed the door, and did not come out until the evening meal was ready. Even then he did not come until I went to the door of the room and opened it. He was sitting on the bed, playing a game of patience. For a moment the picture of quiet resignation stopped me speaking, then I said: "Dinner is ready."

On his pad of paper he wrote: "I am sorry. I did not hear you knock on the door."

"I didn't knock; I just came in."

Very carefully he wrote on the pad "Please to knock."

Thus was the stage set for our life together in the Albion apartment during this period. It was an uncomfortable time for all. I would like to have consulted Maria, but pride forbade. However, I suspected she saw Frederic on her own, and thus had a shrewd notion of the state of affairs. Fran knew too, I think.

131

I was wretchedly unhappy, though to the world outside I was a successful, sophisticated young star.

I had the uneasy sense of violence building up around me. Unemployment was high and rising and there was discontent with the way the government was handling things. The miners were on strike; the trade unions were making threatening noises. But other events were about to engulf the Albion and me.

One day, when we were well into rehearsals for *Maid in Chancery,* Josie walked into my office to let me know that Walter Cook had engaged a detective to search for witnesses to the fact that Josie and Randolph had lived as man and wife. She hoped there were some still around. "Still, knowing Wally, I expect he'll dig them up from the graveyard if he has to."

"How much is it going to cost?"

"Nothing."

"Oh, Josie, come on!"

"Well, Wally gets a cut when we win."

"And if we lose?"

She was silent. "Oh well, your Dad gave me a set of black pearls, about the only thing of his I've got left, he used to wear them as studs, and he had them made up as earrings for me. I'll hock them. I was saving them up for my old age, but why worry? I don't suppose I'll have one." With her blond Eton crop, short pleated skirt and blue and white sailor jacket, she didn't look old enough to be my mother. No one had made the transition from youth to triumphant middle age better than Josie. "Wally says he means to get it into court in the next few weeks. Oh, I hope there won't be a general strike that will hold things up."

"I hope not," I said soberly. "Josie . . . I won't join you in the lawsuit. You're on your own."

She pretended not to hear me. She got up from my desk where she had perched herself. Josie always perched lately, it was part of her youthfulness. "Look after yourself. If there's a strike, will you be able to keep the Albion open? I should try— it'll be like the war, and the troops will need amusement." I could see that Josie had every intention of enjoying the national strike, if she possibly could.

She wasn't the only one. Millions of her fellow countrymen turned out in crowds to man the buses and trains and open food canteens, and seemed to regard it as a cross between a small war and a Bank Holiday on Hampstead Heath. Some of the strikers appeared to take the same attitude, although I suppose for some, especially the miners, who had already been out for months, it was in bitter earnest. I didn't feel as bold and unafraid as Josie.

The first I knew of the strike was the silence. My apartment on the top of the Albion caught all the noise of traffic in the Strand, as well as the distant rattle of the trams along the embankment and the rumble of the trains over the bridge to Charing Cross. I was so used to it that I hardly noticed it; I loved the incessant vitality of the great city. I had gone to bed planning a special window display in my luxuries shop in Albion Walk to celebrate the birth of the little York Princess; I woke to silence. It was a fine, sunny May morning. I could hear the birds, but no trams rattled, no trains swung across the bridge, no boats hooted on the Thames. A great stillness had come with the dawn.

I raised the window and listened. Far below I could see a uniformed policeman walking down the road. The sound of his boots on the pavement floated up to me. I drew on a dressing gown and ran down the narrow stone staircase and out through a narrow door beside the stage door. The policeman had just reached the Albion.

"Is it the strike?" I asked. "Is that why it's so still?"

"Yes, miss. General strike, started at midnight, on orders of the general council of the trade unions." He spoke with sombre relish.

"I suppose policemen can't?"

"Oh no, miss, that would be mutiny." He sounded shocked.

"It's terribly quiet." I shivered in the cool morning air. "I never thought a revolution could be so quiet."

"Lor' bless you, miss, there won't be a revolution. We shall keep control. The government's got everything in hand. You can trust Mr. Baldwin. And our Army lads'll hold steady. You go upstairs, miss, make a cup of tea and go to work as usual. Listen to the wireless—you'll hear everything there."

After I'd had my cup of tea, I went back into the street to see what was going on. Perhaps childhood memories of Parisian talk of communes and revolutions had made me expect troops and armed policemen and barricades. But Albion Walk and the Strand was much as usual, except quieter. As I walked I

133

could see that the traffic was building up, with every car filled to bursting point. One or two buses sailed by, manned by obvious volunteers and crowded with passengers all in high spirits. One bus had a large Union Jack on the front and a notice saying: WE GO ANYWHERE, FARES BY ARRANGEMENT.

I walked along, marvelling. So far I had not seen a striker, but then I saw a group of three in front of the National Gallery, which was open but not attracting any great press of customers. I wasn't sure why it merited a picket of three strikers, although the broad pavement was a good place to parade and the flight of steps gave a position of command. An elderly special constable in an armband was trying to move them on, but in the friendliest possible way they were not going.

"What were you in the Great War, guv?" asked one of the strikers.

"A general, my man."

"Haven't you come down in the world then, constable?"

There was loud laughter, and when I looked back, cigarettes were being exchanged as though the men were fraternising in the trenches.

Their experiences in the war had made both parties better able to play their part in the strike with order and dignity.

I turned back along the Strand towards Albion Walk. Most of the shops were opening although later than usual. I wondered what would happen about the theatres and about the Albion in particular. One of Fran's glittering cinema palaces was around the corner from Wellington Street in Wellington Row, so I went along to see what was afoot there, and to take advice from Fran if he was there.

The great man, all five foot five of him, was standing outside wearing a pale grey trilby and a Charvet tie. "Business as usual, eh, Fran?" I said.

"Sure, darling," he said, in the pretend American accent he had been trying out lately and through which his basic Cockney shone like steel beneath the brass. But his American went with his tan and white shoes and the thick horn-rimmed spectacles he kept in the top pocket of his suit. Gene's brother made his suits and put in a special pocket for him.

"I shall open the Albion then," I said decisively. "Curtain up on time."

"Of course, love. And dinner afterwards, eh?"

134

"I'll see." Strengthened as usual by contact with Francis, I hurried back to Albion Walk.

The telephone was working again when I returned and an air of normality prevailed. As the day wore on, people began to arrive full of stories of how they had managed to get lifts into town. There was a general air of excitement and congratulation.

"I waited for a Rolls-Royce to pass the corner and then I got a lift in *that,*" I heard a dancer saying with satisfaction. "And I'm going to supper with him after the show, then a lift home. There's always a silver lining, isn't there?"

I telephoned Ladybrook Grove. Gran answered at once. She sounded as sturdily confident as ever, for she let me know, without hesitation, that she was not a strike-breaker and would not be out "doing her bit." On the contrary, she would have a cup of tea ready for any striker who knocked on her door. Anyway, she already had her hands full with Maida, whose illness seemed to anger her.

"Good-bye, Gran, look after yourself. I'll get across and see you as soon as I can."

Gran's words about not being a strike-breaker had made me think. Whose side was I on?

That afternoon I attended a meeting of the Society of West End Managers to decide whether we should keep our theatres open or not. In fact, there were several meetings, but the one I attended was the largest and was held in the cocktail bar at the Savoy Hotel. One by one we drifted in: Lady Wyndham, Charles Taylor and Arthur Collins from Drury Lane, George Grossmith and Teddy Laurillard, and others whose faces were less well known to me. I saw Clive McKee putting in a watching brief for C. B. Cochran. I had Frederic with me because he had insisted on coming. Whether he came to protect me or to see what was going on, I was not sure. I felt in him an attraction towards violence that was disturbing. But I thought he was better with me than away from me.

Noel and I vied with each other in the interviews we gave— "Young Lions of the Theatre"—but since I was one of the youngest managers, I took an unobtrusive seat at the back and listened. Inwardly I debated the big question: would I keep the Albion open at all costs, or support the strike and let it go dark?

It speedily became apparent to me that there was no support

135

at all for the strike among the managers (not unnaturally, I suppose, when the economic position of the West End theatres was considered). Those who were in favour of closing their theatres had only the hazards of keeping open in mind. Would their property be damaged? Was there a chance of arson? How violent were the pickets? Would there be any audience to play to? William Gaunt, who did not belong to the Managers' Society, was the prime exponent of the latter belief and all his theatres—His Majesty's, The Winter Garden, The Adelphi and the Apollo—were closed.

My own decision came quickly and spontaneously. When the managers of the Garrick, the Prince of Wales and the Palladium announced that it would be business as usual, I added that the Albion would open and play to the matinée audiences as well. They gave me a muted cheer for that declaration. And it was I, from my seat at the back, who suggested that we make an announcement to the press.

"There *are* no newspapers," said someone.

"But there is going to be a government paper," I called out. "Let's get our news in it."

So the next day *The British Gazette* carried an announcement about which theatres would be opened and which closed. It was also I who thought of approaching the British Broadcasting Company with our news and a request to let our audiences know. I made some enemies over that, I think; we are a noticeably touchy bunch in our profession.

The Albion opened and the evening performances went on as usual. We had a good house, one determined to enjoy itself. The feeling that things must be kept going was working to my advantage. All the same, I wanted to get ahead with *Maid in Chancery*, which had a marvellous court scene, always a winner, and I knew that if the strike went on for too long this could be difficult. Time was not on my side. I remembered Gran's words about not breaking the strike, but I knew that the Albion and its future mattered most to me.

Next day I came down to my office and at once caught the tension in the air. The girl who helped me with the letters and the books was standing by my desk with her coat and hat still on, and Stan the doorman was talking to her. They both swung round when they saw me.

"Good morning, April, you got here all right?"

"Oh yes, Miss May. I walked most of the way and then got a

lift in the most beautiful open tourer: two young undergrads from Cambridge giving lifts all round. No, it was all easy—till I got here." Her eyes were bright with excitement and her voice was portentous.

"What do you mean?"

Stan answered for her: "There's a picket line formed outside."

"What? Outside the Albion?" It seemed incredible: theatres weren't being picketed. We were making do with emergency lighting, but supplies for the bars were getting through. And actors weren't on strike. It might come to that one day, but it hadn't yet. "Are you sure?"

"Take a look, Miss May. See for yourself."

"Stage door or front?" I queried.

"Both," said April eagerly. She was enjoying it. "I saw the crowd outside the front as I came down Albion Walk."

"Crowd? Is it a crowd?"

Once again Stan interrupted. "No, not a crowd. Only about half a dozen, all told." He started as if to say something else, then stopped short. "Come and have a look, miss."

I followed him out to the stage door. Three young men in working clothes stood there looking pale and tired. I closed the door and went back into the heart of the theatre. "They don't seem much of a threat," I said.

"Not that lot, no," agreed Stan.

I walked through the auditorium and out into the foyer. A light, decorative iron grille was drawn down across the face of the theatre when it was closed. Later in the day it would be folded back and the box office would be open. The metalwork was in an art nouveau pattern of roses and lilies. Through the heart of a lily I could see a man's face staring at me. He was cloth-capped, with a muffler around his neck, but by no means undernourished; and he looked determined. He moved away, and behind him I saw half a dozen more men. They seemed to have brought with them all the apparatus of those intending to stay: a brazier, stools, and a big notice which read: SUPPORT THE STRIKE. THIS THEATRE STAYS CLOSED. There was a kettle boiling on the brazier and mugs of tea were being handed round.

"Here to stay, I reckon," said Stan.

"I agree."

"There's a young woman among 'em, too," said Stan.

137

"Is there?" He meant me to see something, as I knew by the tone of his voice.

The young woman moved away from the brazier to hand a mug of tea to one of the strikers, and I saw it was Maria. Our eyes met; she held my gaze for a minute, then deliberately turned her back on me. I stood there, swallowing; I felt quite sick. I was frightened of Maria at that moment. I knew I could not face her, and I stumbled back into the theatre.

I didn't ask myself why Maria hated me; I knew why: it was Frederic. On cue, he appeared in my office. Somehow he had learned what was happening outside. I supposed April had told him. She was fascinated by Frederic and hung about him as much as she could. Frederic had on a top coat and carried a thick stick. He managed to make it clear that he meant it for my protection; I shook my head. "I don't need that sort of protection. There won't be any violence." But I had the uneasy feeling that both Maria and Frederic wanted violence.

I consulted with Stan; we decided to let the police know, if they did not know already, that we had a picket at the Albion. Stan put on his coat and said he would pop round to the station, where he had a friend or two. "Better than telephoning," he said.

"Will they let you through?"

"Sure. And back again. I can jolly my way through."

He was soon gone and not long in coming back, when he gave me a quick nod. "They're sending a couple of men round now, and more this afternoon in time for the matinée."

April gave a little squeal of excitement and I glared at her. I noticed that Frederic was sitting in a corner, reading the paper and drinking a cup of coffee. April again, I thought with irritation. She had put a cup of coffee in front of me, and I drank it mechanically.

I knew I had to go out there and face Maria, but I couldn't bring myself to do it yet. It was rotten of her, I thought, when I'd done so much for her.

At lunch time I went up to the roof of the Albion and craned my neck to get a look at the Strand. I could see a convoy of food lorries from the docks passing along with the army in support. Butter was going to be short, we were told, but there would be plenty of milk. Everyone knew that a cup of milky tea with two lumps of sugar was the best thing for shock. Hyde Park was the milk centre for London at the moment.

I tidied my hair, put on some lipstick, and straightened the seams of my stockings, then I ran down the stairs to confront Maria. Appearances did give strength.

Stan gave me a wary look as I stalked past and I heard Frederic's feet behind me. Out of the corner of my eye I saw that he had the stick with him. I turned round and shook my head, giving his shoulder a gentle push backwards. He shook my hand off angrily; I shrugged and let him follow.

The girl who sat in the box office was crouched miserably in her seat, staring at the scene before her. The protective grille had been drawn back from the front of the theatre but no member of the matinée audience had yet set foot beyond it. Outside, on the pavement, the first arrivals were being held in check by the strikers' cordon. Two middle-aged women and a girl were standing in the road, not even being allowed to set foot on the pavement. A police constable listened to the argument that was going on. One of the women was putting their case for being allowed through, and the strikers were solidly ignoring her. The woman who was doing the talking motioned to her companions that she was going ahead, and she started to move towards the theatre. The strikers linked hands and formed a barrier in front of her. She stopped. The girl called her back, and after an angry word with the strikers that I could not hear, she went back to where she had been. Maria moved a pace forward from her group and stood staring at me; in her face was challenge. I knew I must act.

I realised then, with a shock of shame, that I was a coward: I did not want to get hurt. Something of this must have communicated itself to Frederic; he came to stand by my side. By this time more members of our would-be matinée audience were turning the corner into Albion Walk. By ones and twos a small crowd was assembling. Unobtrusively some more policemen had arrived as well.

I had the sense that I'd already let the scene get out of hand, that I should have spoken to the strikers before this, made a speech, a demonstration of some sort, to persuade them to go away. Trying to leave Frederic behind, but aware that he was behind me like a shadow, I walked out of the theatre.

As if she had been waiting for my move, Maria came up to me. The big man who seemed to be the leader took a step to join her. As he did so he poured the remains of his cup of tea on the ground in front of me. It spilled on my pale stockings; I gave a scream. Frederic jumped from behind and his stick cracked down on the big man's arm. I was aware then of shouts, of bodies pressing forward and of Maria's angry, distorted face. I heard a policeman shout.

All my protective feelings for Frederic surged up. I tried to turn towards him, but someone, a policeman, I think, held me back. I was forced to watch as the big man swung round and punched Frederic on the jaw. Frederic's head jerked back, but he stayed on his feet. The big man looked angry, but there was a white, furious expression on Frederic's face that was even more formidable. He charged forward again, his stick cracking down on the man again. Another man interfered, striking a sideways blow at Frederic to try and deflect him. I heard Maria call Frederic's name. He didn't seem to notice. She saw me and shouted across.

"Stop him, Alice. He's doing this for you. Stop him. Or they'll kill him."

Desperately I called out. "Frederic, Frederic, I'm coming." I wrenched myself away from the policeman, but a striker dragged at me, twisting my arm. Then I heard Maria screaming.

A brick seemed to come out of nowhere and Frederic fell to the ground, blood on his face and around his mouth. His eyes were closed. Maria dropped to her knees by his side and started to wipe the blood from his face. He did not move. There was despair in my heart. Once more I had somehow failed him. At that moment love for him was strong within me, mixed with a kind of passionate regret.

Dimly, I was aware of the police getting the strikers away down the street, and of Stan talking to the theatre crowd. I heard someone call for an ambulance.

"Oh Maria, is he dead?" All anger and rivalry between us had melted away, on my part at least, and I think on hers also because she said: "No, no, of course not. But he had a blow on his head. That is bad. I think he cannot take any more damage on his head."

He may die then, I thought. My mouth was dry and hard inside. Behind me I heard the ambulance arrive. Albion Walk had gone quiet. There were people in it still, but they seemed infinitely far away. A policeman helped the ambulance men lift Frederic onto a stretcher.

As they moved him, his eyes opened, and, incredibly, he spoke. "Maria," he said. "Maria."

140

Frederic slipped back into an unconscious state after that one repeated word. Maria and I followed the ambulance on foot to the Charing Cross Hospital—the old actors' hospital—where we waited until news was brought to us. "A strike casualty," I heard a nurse call him.

The injury was not a serious one, but the blow had fallen on the old wound and seemed to have reactivated old pressures. Frederic did not come round. Day after day he lay in deep unconsciousness. Maria and I visited him, sometimes together, sometimes alone, but he neither stirred nor spoke again. Once or twice he opened his eyes, but they seemed to say nothing.

The strike dragged on. Every day the Albion opened as usual, but after the first day audiences were sparse. My apartment above seemed empty without Frederic. I did not ask Maria to move in with me; we were friends again, but our lives were now totally apart.

One day Sir John Simon rose in the House of Commons and declared the strike illegal. That later turned out not to be true, but at the time he was believed. The trade union leaders drew back. Early one morning I woke, disturbed by a noise. I lay in bed for a moment, wondering what the noise was, then I ran to the window and poked my head out. I could hear the rumble of a train along the embankment. The strike was over. The next day, while Frederic was still unconscious, everyone, except the miners over whose bodies the strike had been fought anyway, went back to work.

9 Chapter Eight

I announced the final performance of *Parade* and set a date at the beginning of June for the opening of *Maid in Chancery*.

I loved working with Giles Oliver. He seemed to bridge both my worlds, for his father had been a close friend of Randolph

Charlecote and had loved Josie too. Giles was full of plans for the future and even had a property in mind, a comedy set in a girls' school. I felt that my professional future was full of hope. But show business is a merry-go-round. There was the cinema's threat to think of, as Fran reminded me.

I settled to the final preparations for *Maid in Chancery*. All the business side was my share, while Giles performed the creative miracles required to make pages of script come to life.

No one from the police spoke to me further about Thomas Wooler, since it was so patently obvious I had told all I knew. But older members of the theatre staff, those few who had worked at the theatre during the war, were interviewed more than once and were asked to look at various photographs of Thomas Wooler to see if any memories could be aroused. The manner of the two policemen who hung around the theatre was puzzling. The police had not joined the strike, of course, but I thought that as private people these two might have sympathised with it because there was sometimes a kind of radical aggression apparent in their stance. I felt that they regarded the theatre as part of that glittering and indulged world of rich people one saw reflected in *The Tatler*. I wondered what questions they asked the Charlecotes. But the Charlecotes were so grand, and so much a part of the ruling class, that I expect they were handled with deference. In any case, they were protected by their lawyers as well as their status: they had William Griggs and I had only Walter Cook.

I kept away from Walter as much as I could, but by degrees I was being dragged into his net. I was working on publicity for the opening of *Maid in Chancery* when Josie arrived in my office, planted herself on the edge of my desk, and swung her slender, elegant leg under my nose. It was a Wednesday, as I remember.

April stopped typing and looked up in admiration. "Oh, what *lovely* stockings, Miss May." She greatly admired Josie and had her autograph in the programme of Josie's last show. "What colour would you call it?"

"American tan," said Josie, surveying a ginger leg. "Bemberg's best." Over her shoulder to me she threw, "See if Gene can get you some: one and nine a pair, fully-fashioned, mind."

"You didn't come to see me to talk about stockings, Josie. What is it you want? Is it money?" My hand went out to the cashbox. I was Josie's banker and held what savings she could make. It was the only way to keep her solvent. Otherwise, everything went on clothes, furs, and jewellery, before she had paid any essential bills, not to mention income tax. Josie never believed in the reality of income tax till it hit her in the face.

"No." She stroked her ankle. "I'm quite flush at the moment. Long live films, I say; I've had three weeks in *Lavender's Blue* at Kew. Lovely. The director says I'm photogenic. That's what they call it when you photograph well. As if I didn't know— only Gladys Cooper sold more postcards than I did in the old days." And it was true that Josie's neat, lively features did photograph beautifully. She had been one of the picture postcard beauties of the days before the war, with her face shining out from every newspaper shop. Or so Gran had told me.

"You should have handed the film money over to me to bank, then," I said. "Come on, what is it?"

Josie took out her powder compact and touched up her face, licking her lips before she put on lipstick, and tugging at a kiss curl on her cheek. "Do you like this hat?" It was a black satin cloche with a silver buckle. "You're such a giver, Alice. You ought to be more of a *taker.*"

"Josie!" I said, warningly.

She put her lipstick away in her vanity case, gave a quick look at April, decided she was a safe audience (which she was not), and said, "Wally says you've *got* to come in with me on this case. Join in the plea, be a plaintiff."

"Oh *no,*" I said. "No, no, and no!"

Josie went on, undeterred. "He says it won't look so convincing if you don't join me. People will wonder why not and raise their eyebrows. You wouldn't like that, would you, Alice?"

"I wouldn't mind. I'm used to it."

"Frederic, you mean?" said Josie shrewdly. "I've always been against that, as well you know. How is he?"

"The same," I said. "I go to see him every day. But he's not come round. Perhaps he never will."

"You poor kid." Josie squeezed my hand. "I remember how it was when your father went." She put her hands to her face. "Oh, it seemed such a waste, all the men that were killed in that war. That's why you must stand by my side."

"Your logic defeats me."

"Oh, I hate you when you're sarcastic, Alice. You never got that from me. Nor your father."

"It must be natural wickedness. I won't do it, Josie."

143

April had gone back to her typing, but was listening to every word. No doubt every word she heard would be faithfully transmitted to her family in Deptford. Next to my cousin Ellen May, she was the biggest gossip I knew.

"Alice, you must." A hint of desperation was creeping into my mother's voice. Still, I ignored it: Josie could be a fine, natural actress.

"I'm busy, Josie—you know, letters, designers to see, costumes to check over—I'm doing the clothes and set for *Maid,* did you know?"

"Look, Alice, it's true about money: I've been earning, and although I haven't handed the money over to you to hold like I promised, I haven't spent it either, or not so much." A new black hat, a silver buckle, a bottle of perfume—I calculated quickly—yes, only a moderate expenditure for Josie. "But I've collected a few bills. From Wally Cook for legal services. He'll let them ride. After all, he's my cousin. But he says I've got a *moral* obligation to him to go ahead with my case."

I was remembering my interview with Randolph. Had he called Josie his wife? No. He'd said he thought of her as his wife. But had there been a reservation in his voice? I recalled the half smile on his lips, the thoughtful way he had spoken. There *had* been a question in his voice.

It made me distrust Josie; I felt she too wasn't being totally unreserved. She was keeping something back. She had that look about her. But then, I was keeping something back too.

"I don't believe we'll win," I said.

"We will. Of course we will if we stand together. You're Randolph's daughter, damn it."

I wondered what Josie would say if she knew of Randolph's allegation about his nephew-son.

"Are you telling me everything?" I asked Josie.

"Are you?" She countered. "Do you ever?"

"All right, Josie," I said, removing my arm. "You've got what you want: I'll stand with you."

When I saw the relief in her face then, I knew how much she had depended on me, and how anxious she felt. "How much money will this run us into?" I asked.

Josie hesitated. "Thousands," she said.

"Oh, my God."

"You've got the lease of the theatre. You're making a profit there," she said swiftly. "You can raise money on it."

"I already *have,* to get the Alby going."

"From Fran Hollman." How well briefed she was. "He'll let it run."

"At a price." I wouldn't have put it past Fran to have an arrangement to their mutual benefit with Walter Cook, whereby my debt to him would be increased. I trusted Francis, but he liked to pull strings and he wanted me at the end of one.

"We're going to win," said Josie. "And then we'll have no money problems."

"Have your way, Josie."

All the same, I might not have gone ahead with it if Matthew had not turned up in my office the next day. He walked in as if he owned it, as he probably felt he did. He had brought with him a small pot of flowers, which he planted on my desk more like someone delivering a declaration of war than trying to placate a kinswoman. "From my sister Flora," he said. "She grows them." He looked at the bright leaves. "Dracaena: dragon plant. No one else has this sort."

"Kind of her." I pushed the plant to one side. It looked capable of eating me. "You came to bring me a dragon?"

He smiled, and his face looked younger and nicer. "No, that was just an excuse . . . I wanted to ask you something." He took in a deep breath. "Will you give up this case, Alice? Couldn't we come to a compromise . . . a settlement . . ."

"Money?" I asked.

"Yes." He nodded.

Fury rose inside me and prevented me from speaking. A mixture of emotions created the anger. He attracted me. Surely I couldn't feel like this about a brother? And then there was Frederic. What about loving *him?* It all boiled over into resentment that Matthew could think I would take money.

"Clear out," I said. "Clear bloody out. And take your bribe with you." I saw his face change, the smile disappear. "God knows I've done things I'm ashamed of. But I've done what seemed right to me, never mind anyone else." I was on the verge of a confession to him, only he didn't know it. I waited to see if he picked anything up. If he had questioned me then, I might have told him everything. But he didn't. I went on, "And I've never done anything for a bribe."

145

"It's not a bribe. Please, Alice, please." He was pleading with me, desperately in earnest. "Do be reasonable. We are simply recognising you have some rights. We could settle out of court. Litigation is always a mistake."

The fact that I thought so too did not make me less angry.

Matthew came up close to me and put his hand on my chin and tilted my face towards him. "Look at me, Alice. I've noticed you never do unless you have to. Why not? I swear I'm not a monster."

I kept very still, like an animal that fears to be captured. "You've not been happy with that man you've lived with; I know you haven't. You were born to be happy, Alice. It's in your face, in your eyes . . ."

I thought he was going to kiss me; I dared not let it happen. I jerked my head away. "Leave me alone."

He winced. Not at my words, but at my face.

"That's it, then?" His hands dropped to his side, and he stepped back. His face had gone white.

"Yes." There was no going back. "See you in court."

He didn't answer, but simply turned away and went out. Not angrily, but sadly.

I sat there after he left, till April came up to me and took the potted plant away from me reproachfully. "You're tearing it to bits, poor thing," she said.

Every day I went to see Frederic and told him all my news, just in case he could understand. I did so on the evening of Matthew's visit. He never stirred.

"Oh, Miss May," said the Sister, as I said good-bye. "You have a terrible rash on your wrists and hands. Whatever have you been doing?"

Great red weals had appeared on the back of my hands and on my forearms. I think it was a reaction to some juice exuded by Flora Charlecote's plant.

"I've been fighting with dragons," I said.

The court was crowded. The well where we sat was full of lawyers and clerks and officials, and the public benches were crammed to bursting point. The judge, as he faced us, looked like a small, alert bird of prey with hooded eyes.

What I had not been prepared for was the publicity attendant upon the lawsuit. I had not realised that society would

146

take so passionate an interest in all of us, and that seats in the court would be fought for by the rich and the well-born and the famous. As I looked around I could see faces I recognised— many of them well known. In each was the same expectant look I had seen in first-night audiences. Josie and I were part of the Season. It was socially "done" to see us in court. Even the judge's wife was there, and our own counsel's wife and mistress.

The press appeared in force. There had been a lot of startled comment in the newspaper about the baronetcy going one way and the estates another—not usual in British society, I gathered, where a kind of noblesse oblige still ruled. One newspaper went so far as to attribute the split to the Causley estate being in Northumberland, an ancient kingdom, where the old English inheritance rule of "gavel kind" had applied.

Several weeks had passed since my encounter with Matthew and my pledge of allegiance to Josie. The period had been filled by the slow cranking up of the legal machine. On Walter's advice Josie had employed a private detective to track down possible witnesses to her married state. She had searched her memory and produced the names of half a dozen men and women who had known her and Randolph in Scotland two decades ago. They had all trouped together in the company of *The Belle of Bath.* She and Randolph had entertained them all frequently, but their ways had parted, and she had never seen them again. "Except perhaps Elsie Ellis," she said when pressed. "I did afterwards see Elsie Ellis."

The detective must have been efficient at his job, because before the case came into court, he had produced three old friends of Josie's, complete with their memories of the Scottish tour of *The Belle of Bath,* and had hopes of tracking down a fourth, Elsie Ellis herself.

My grandmother did not approve of anything that was happening. "You'll have to watch Elsie," she said. "She liked her drink, as I remember."

Thus, trailing family quarrels and private suspicions, the case of May and May versus the Attorney General came into the Court of Probate, Divorce and Admiralty for judgement. Josie and I as plaintiffs, called Charlecote May Josephine and Charlecote May Alice Laura, "prayed the Court to decree and declare that Josephine May and Randolph Charlecote were legally married by the mutual exchange of matrimonial consent,

147

in Scotland on a date unknown, and that therefore Alice Laura May Charlecote was from the moment of her birth their legal child and heiress."

We got no further than this before the attorney-general rose to say that he did not admit the claims of the petitioners, and prayed the court to protect the rights and interests of the Crown. Sophia Charlecote, widow of Henry Charlecote, then intervened and put the plaintiffs to the proof that the marriage was valid and the birth of Alice Laura was that of a lawful child. Matthew Charlecote also intervened, acting on behalf of his nephew Eric Edward Charlecote, to protect the said Eric Edward Charlecote's interests and dignities as heir to Henry Charlecote. They had their own counsel present also.

"One step forward and two back," I murmured to my counsel.

"This part is purely formal," he whispered. "I told you how it would go."

Nevertheless, I felt that from the beginning the whole balance of the case was tilted against us because the strength of the English legal system was directed towards supporting those in possession.

There ensued a long discussion between the counsel and the judge about what was called "Lord Brougham's Act," a piece of work that seemed at first hearing to bring Josie's Scottish marriage into grave jeopardy. I stopped listening after a while.

Josie sat next to me, trying to look interested in what was going on, but only succeeding in looking bemused. She was dressed for the occasion in a plain navy blue coat and skirt, with a little blue hat; she looked young and pretty. I recognised the costume as one which had been worn by Gladys Cooper in *Randell versus Rex,* and which Josie must have borrowed from the wardrobe mistress for the occasion. After all, Gladys Cooper had the judge and jury in tears in that one, didn't she?

When I started listening again, I found that witnesses were about to be called. Josie had to prove by witnesses that she and Randolph had lived in Scotland for three weeks before declaring that they were married. If she couldn't prove those three weeks of residence then we might as well pack up and go home. But I knew from Josie's satisfied smile that there was going to be no trouble with this one.

And indeed, the first witness to this fact was soon produced: a well-groomed elderly man, with a green carnation in his but-

148

tonhole and carrying a grey topper and a silver-topped stick, stepped blithely into the witness box. He bowed to the judge and blew a kiss to Josie. She looked pleased but was sensible enough not to respond. "Good old Clive," she whispered. "Haven't seen him for years. Clive Jerome: principal in *Belle,* danced like a dream."

The judge turned an expressionless stare to Mr. Jerome, and the abashed actor became a quiet, old man, waiting rather nervously to be questioned. But he was a pro and his evidence, which bore out Josie's story, came across clearly after a few preliminary questions.

"Did they live together as man and wife?"

"Oh, yes. Everyone knew they lived together."

"And did you believe them in fact to *be* married?"

"I remember hearing them say, laughing, that they had come to Scotland to *be* married."

I suppose I thought there might be some savage cross-examination, but perhaps I'd seen Gerald du Maurier in too many court scenes, because after a few polite questions about his memory from the attorney-general, Mr. Clive was allowed to go.

The judge whispered something to one of his acolytes and rose. The morning's session was over; it was time for lunch.

It was at lunch that I first took in how avidly people were watching me and Josie. Walter Cook, showing some taste for once, had taken us to a quiet restaurant nearby in Chancery Lane, where they specialised in sea food. But even there we caused a stir. We were the notorious mother and daughter whose private lives were scandalous. Of course, they had all heard of my relationship with Frederic by now. The day before, when I had gone for my daily visit to the hospital, there had been a press photographer, and that morning in *The Daily Mail* there was a picture of me entering the hospital under the headline "Singer's fortieth day of unconsciousness."

Frederic had not been unconscious for forty days and he was no longer a singer. Still, it was evidence that I was being observed. Oh, well, it was also publicity for *Maid in Chancery,* which was about to open. I had deliberately, flagrantly allowed that it should play during the period of the lawsuit. Some people said that I deserved what I got.

I kept my head high, ate my *sole Meunière,* and allowed Wally to refill my glass with wine. Not to my surprise, Fran had slid into the seat opposite mine.

"Mustn't be selfish and keep all the pretty ladies to myself," said Walter, genially.

"Hello, Fran." I spoke without enthusiasm. "How do you think it's going?"

"I'm enjoying every minute of it," said Josie; she looked round the crowded restaurant like a queen greeting her public. "I'm going to show those Charlecotes."

Fran and I looked at each other and a silent shrug passed between us. "Oh, come on, Alice," he murmured. "Don't pretend you aren't longing to wipe the smile off Matthew Charlecote's face."

"Oh, you're so sharp you'll cut yourself," I said, all my sophistication draining away and a phrase out of little Alice May's varied past popping right out. I hated Fran for knowing so much about me.

In the afternoon things heated up a bit. Mr. Clive Jerome appeared in the witness box again, minus his green carnation, and my lunch sat heavily on my stomach. This time, the attorney-general was noticeably less polite and managed to extract the information that Clive Jerome had had a stroke and that his memory might be suspect.

The next witness, brought by Josie's side, was a tall, slender man, wearing a black coat with a velvet collar and carrying a wide-brimmed hat. He was called Felix Sinwood. A strange name for a strange person, I thought. Josie looked surprised, and murmured that she did not trust him and never had. All the same, under Sir Roland's gentle guidance, he testified that in his memoirs he had described a dinner party in Edinburgh at which he had been a guest of Josie and Randolph and where Josie had acted as hostess; she had been treated by all the guests as the wife of Randolph.

"I suppose that's something," conceded Josie.

However, under cross-examination from the opposing counsel, Mr. Sinwood gave it as his opinion, as a critic and man of the theatre, that so far from three weeks have been spent in Scotland rehearsing *The Belle of Bath,* not more than three days had been put in. Three weeks' residence was what was necessary to make the marriage stick, and he knew it, the old devil. Josie's case began to look a little dented; her smile dimmed.

Sir Roland must have been expecting the attack of Felix Sinwood, or of someone very like him, because no sooner had Felix stepped from the witness box than his place was taken by

150

a very well known face indeed: Charles Madison was called by the defence. His family's roots in the theatre went back to Garrick and probably even to Burbage. His grandfather had acted for the young Queen Victoria at Windsor, his father had built a theatre, and his daughter had just left for Hollywood. It told me something about Josie and her standing in the theatre that he was willing to come.

With a few crisp sentences, delivered with his usual style, Charlie Madison gave his opinion that a show like *The Belle of Bath* might well have needed several weeks' rehearsal in Scotland and that if it had needed it, then it would have got it, since it had been produced by the very careful management of his old friend Albert Duckett. Madison gave a convincing performance. He didn't even look at Josie as he left the witness box. I felt like clapping. Indeed, a murmur of applause started up in the body of the court, most of whose members had been part of an admiring audience of his many times before, but a swift stare from the judge hushed it.

Josie cheered up. I knew by now what Sir Roland was trying to do. It appeared that there were three ways of creating an irregular yet binding marriage bond in Scotland, which the incursions of Lord Brougham and his Act had not materially changed. There was a marriage "de praesenti cohabitis," in other words, by living together as man and wife. Then there was "marriage by declaration," which meant that Josie and Randolph had to have called each other man and wife in front of witnesses. So far, they didn't appear to have done this. The third route, which seemed to have been invented by Sir Roland, was what he called "tacit" consent, and it looked the most likely winner for us.

Sir Roland was trying for evidence on any of these three ways of proving Josie's marriage, but in order to make any start at all, he had to prove that she and Randolph had stayed together in Scotland for three weeks or more. Thanks to Charles Madison, I thought he had. The matter rested after Charles's evidence.

The Charlecote family had appeared en masse in the afternoon. In the morning only Matthew had been present and I had managed to avoid looking at him. I had heard him, though, because he had a note in his voice to which I felt peculiarly sensitive. Now they were all there—Sophia Charlecote, and Flora, and Matthew, together with a lad whom I took to be

151

the boy, Edward, all seated next to each other. Edward was talking to William Griggs. The boy had a sensitive and intelligent face but was physically fragile. Whatever happened to the disposition of the estates, the baronetcy would remain with him.

Thus ended the first day of the trial. I thought the case could go either way.

On the second day I could not bear to stay in court; I took Josie there, wished her luck with her evidence, and fled. I went to the theatre, where everyone was lolling around in the exhausted state of those who have rehearsed, quarrelled, made up and rehearsed again. I didn't escape from the case even there. They all wanted to know how things were going and seemed surprised I could not say.

"Not well, I think," I said. "Josie seems to treat it as a stage show in which a good performance will bring in the right verdict, but I've looked at the lawyers' faces and I'm sure that's not how it is." I turned to their worries. "How's the play going?"

Giles frowned. "It's good. I hope it's sharp enough, that's all. Everything has to have a razor's edge on it since *Hay Fever.*"

We were the postwar theatre where sophistication was all. *Hay Fever* had closed and so had *No, No, Nanette,* but other productions were looming over us.

"We've got stiff competition coming up," said Giles. "There's G. in *Oh Kay,* and they're spending forty-five thousand for Jack and Binnie in *Sunny.* We shall get the critics and the reviews, but what will the gallery girls think of us?"

"You'll drag them in, Giles," I smiled affectionately. "They love you. It's your profile, darling. And Meggie." I turned to where our star was polishing her nails with a buffer and a block of pink chalk. "They love every bawdy moment of Meggie."

"I'm not bawdy, dear. You've never heard me swear. I never swear."

"No, Meg, but behind you is the story of your life." I smiled. *"That's* what they like."

"I suppose if we are going to have a hit with *Maid,* then something else is going to go terribly wrong."

"Yes. You never win all round, do you?" agreed Giles.

"I expect you'll lose the case," suggested Meggie cheerfully.

"Yes, I expect that will be it," I said, but I didn't accept it as the answer.

Giles left us and Meggie said, "Giles is so beautiful. But I couldn't love him."

That might be his luck, I thought, since Meggie destroyed the people she loved.

"Anyway, I don't think he likes girls, do you? His father didn't, *really.*" She looked at me speculatively.

"Shut up, Meggie," I said. "Sometimes you are foolish."

"It's the disease of the times, love. We're all rotten now."

I looked at her. With her elegant bones and great chic, she was one of the most positive people I knew. But sometimes she frightened me.

"Oh yes," she said, lighting a cigarette in its long holder. "According to all the old rules, I am rotten to the core. But I don't lie and I'm dead loyal to my friends."

"Is that enough?" I asked.

"It's all you can expect. You're the same. We can't help ourselves, you and I; we are children of our time."

That day Josie gave her evidence; she was in the witness box for nearly the whole session. I was told she behaved beautifully, and she seemed optimistic. "But it's hard to tell," she said that night.

On the day following other witnesses were taken. One, William Dagtown, once groom to Randolph, was hostile to Josie, but she was recalled to the witness box to attest that she had reproved him for ill-treating a dog. To the animal lovers in court, which included most of the audience, this disposed of William Dagtown.

I appeared briefly to say that I had been born and believed my parents to be married. Calling myself May was a professional matter only, I said crisply. My hands were sweating when I left the witness box, happy to have got away lightly. Or so I thought.

I went back to the Albion after giving my evidence. In the *Evening News* was a photograph of me hurrying from the court to the theatre. It was the night on which *Maid in Chancery* was opening. I was at once plunged into the tension and muddle of the behind-stage drama. On the one hand was a white-faced Meggie saying that she had "dried" completely at her run-through and was never going to remember a word, and on the other there was Giles, calm but dead quiet, stalking through the corridors. As actor and producer and writer, he bore a heavy burden. My burden was the Albion itself. Over and above everything else, I knew that I needed a big financial success to carry on.

From the minute the curtain went up and Meggie revealed that she had not forgotten her lines, *Maid in Chancery* was clearly a hit. On every side I heard the murmur of praise rising up. You can always tell when an audience is getting what it wants; satisfaction shows in every tiny movement, every nuance of every passing comment. In the bar at the interval people drank quickly, eager to get back. We sold fewer chocolates than usual. This play was too important for chocolates.

At the end the audience stood up and clapped and cheered, and the gallery girls shouted. We had to wait for the critics in the morning, of course, and Giles said that he, for one, was taking nothing for granted. I slipped away from the celebratory drinks in Meggie's dressing room and went up to bed.

I was drinking coffee in the morning when the telephone rang; I thought it must be Meggie ringing to ask if I had read the reviews, which were spendid. But it was Gran.

"I thought you'd like to know that Maida was confined last night," she announced.

"Confined?" I said stupidly. "Confined where?"

"Not where—with, you silly girl. She's had a baby. A boy."

"Good heavens," was all I could say.

"Oh, yes," said Gran, triumphantly. "You never think of anything like that, do you? Nor did Maida till it happened. Well, good-bye then. I suppose I stopped you reading all your notices?"

I was thoroughly awake now. "Wait a minute, Gran. I want to ask you something. Do you know of any reason why Elsie Ellis's evidence could be a danger to Mother?" Gran had not been in court at all, and, knowing how she felt about Walter Cook, I had not expected her to be.

"Elsie? No, she's a good old thing. She drinks a bit. When's she giving evidence? In the morning? You ought to be all right, but you want to watch her after lunch."

It was afternoon before Elsie Ellis was called. She had got herself up for her appearance in court, with a red fox fur collar to her coat-dress of white serge. She held a matching muff, although the day was warm, and wore a little hat, decorated with Parma violets. A bunch of violets was pinned to her ample breast. Her face was pale, and as far as I could tell, she was dead sober.

154

She made a cheerful and obliging witness, readily admitting to having known both Josie and Randolph. Yes, she had been a member of the *The Belle of Bath* troupe, and certainly it was her memory they had stayed at least three weeks in Scotland. "It might have been four," she said generously. But Sir Roland did not take her up on this. I suspect, like me, he was beginning to worry about the flush rising in her neck and cheeks. Elsie's pallor now looked more like a liberal sprinkling of lavender face powder than a natural colouring.

Yes, she agreed, Josie and Randolph had lived together as married people in Scotland, and she had quite thought of Josie as Mrs. Charlecote, although she could not recall if she had actually used that name. Probably she had. Then she dropped her bombshell. "I was ever so glad about the second wedding. I went along and sat at the back, quiet as a mouse . . ."

"The *second* wedding?" asked Sir Roland, in a careful, emotionless voice. "What wedding was that?"

There was a moment of dead silence and then a subdued hum of comment arose. The judge glared around him and the court went quiet again.

"The one in St. Martin's in 1905," faltered Elsie. "The secret one. Have I said something I shouldn't?"

Minutes later in Sir Roland's chambers, the court being adjourned at Sir Roland's request, Josie was in tears.

"I didn't invite her; I didn't know she was there. It was supposed to be a secret. We had a road sweeper and a window cleaner as witnesses. She must have crept in and sat at the back. I didn't see her." She dabbed at her eyes. "It was just to be a romantic church blessing on our match. What difference does it make?"

"It makes this difference," said Sir Roland, putting his hands together. "If it was necessary, then the Scottish marriage was not legal; and if it was secret, then it goes against your plea that a manifest marriage, which is above all open, was declared in Scotland."

Succinct, I thought. Even I could see that Josie had cut her own throat.

"So we've lost?" I asked.

There was a long pause before Sir Roland answered. "Perhaps not," he said. "Perhaps not. You saw your father in Paris, Miss May?"

I nodded.

"I think I will be calling you again, Miss May," he said thoughtfully. "Be a brave girl. Rally your forces." He didn't say any more, but he didn't need to. I knew what he meant.

After a consultation with the judge and the counsel for the other side, my recall was permitted.

Slowly the court filled again, the judge reappeared, and I took my place in the witness box. Unlike Josie, I had not dressed specially for the occasion, but Louisa, who had perhaps foreseen what might be required of me, had chosen my clothes. I wore a neat, grey suit with a little matching cloche of soft velour. A touch of pink showed at the neck from a pleated blouse. At the last minute Louisa took away my black gloves and made me carry white ones. The clothes invested me with a school-girlish, ingénue air. I think Louisa felt instinctively that such a look would stand me in great stead.

I did feel the protection of my appearance—as women do—but not, perhaps, in the way Louisa had expected. It gave me the courage to be myself—not entirely admirable, not one to emulate, but able to do what had to be done.

Sir Roland started very quietly; he had changed his shirt since we last met, I noticed, and now wore one with a pale grey stripe. Changed his shirt and changed his cuff-links to heavy silver ones instead of gold. What a dandy he was. Somehow this thought gave me courage, and I lifted my chin and smiled at him. Sometime later Matthew told me that gesture had touched him deeply.

Sir Roland took me back over my meeting with my father and how it happened, discreetly engaging the sympathy of the court.

"And you never saw Colonel Charlecote again?" My father had been promoted Colonel just before his death.

"No. He was killed shortly afterwards."

There was a hush in court.

"Colonel Charlecote was talking to you quite freely?"

"Yes. Oh yes."

Everyone was listening. It was a hungry silence; they knew something good was coming.

"No holding back—quite frankly?"

"Yes." I just breathed the word.

"He acknowledged you as his daughter?"

Had he? Hadn't he just called me "Josie's girl?" "Yes," I said clearly.

156

We had talked it all over in Sir Roland's office before; he knew I had thought Randolph a bit drunk—wild with wine and his return to the trenches.

To my relief the letter written at this time was not mentioned.

There was a pause. Then Sir Roland asked, "He thought he was going to be killed? He sensed it?" He let his voice drop in sympathy. His voice was one of his tools, and he knew how to use it.

"Yes, I did think so. Not at the time. But afterwards I was sure that was what he had felt."

I tried to keep my voice steady, but in spite of myself it trembled slightly. I felt a movement of sympathy in the court.

"And you had already lost someone very dear to you. Or thought you had. And it drew the two of you closer together?"

"Yes, that is true," I said in a low voice. "Or so I thought."

"So what we have is the testimony of a man believing himself about to die, a man who was, indeed, about to die. A loving, true-hearted man." Sir Roland cast a wary eye at the judge to see how he was getting away with this statement, the foundation of his new examination of me. I couldn't read the judge's impassive face, but apparently Sir Roland was satisfied, because he paused for dramatic effect.

We were coming to it; I braced myself and got ready. Sir Roland looked at me with sympathy. "You must be absolutely sincere," he had said in chambers. "Speak only from the heart."

Then in a quiet voice, but so beautifully modulated that every syllable could be heard throughout the court, he asked me what, in the last conversation, had been said about my mother. Had he spoken of her?

I was conscious of drawing all my forces together to speak. "Yes," I said loudly, clearly. "He did. He called her wife."

There was a satisfied rustle throughout the court. I continued: "They were married in Scotland. He implied they were married there."

"And the second marriage? Was that mentioned?"

"No. Never. I never heard it mentioned. For him, the Scottish marriage was what counted. I'm sure of that."

"Did he say anything else?" questioned Sir Roland.

"He said that he regretted moving apart from my mother

157

and me, and that he wanted me to inherit everything that was his."

"And after your conversation," said Sir Roland, apparently speaking to me, but really addressing the court, "this gallant gentleman went away and scribbled a few words to his lawyer acknowledging his responsibilities before going away to die."

It was all over then, and I knew it. I heard Josie crying softly behind me. Across the room my eyes met Matthew's.

Had I lied or had I told the truth? For a moment I couldn't be sure, and then I felt a great, blessed, inner conviction that, although I had done the best I could for myself, I had expressed the real truth of what Randolph Charlecote had been saying. I knew now what he had meant: he had thought of Josie as his wife, and me as his heiress. In his heart he acknowledged us.

I have only the most confused impressions of the short cross-examination that followed, of the judge's withdrawal to consider his verdict, and then, when it was given and we had won, of Matthew coming across to me to say, "We won't dispute it. There will be no appeal. I expect there will be a lot of legal delays even so. But you must come to Causley. Only give my grandmother a bit of time." He was speaking, in spite of the awkwardness of his words, with a desperate honesty. What is truth, I wondered—your truth or my truth? Can we bind the two together and somehow make a go of the whole business. I wanted to do so very much. And at that moment the way ahead seemed clear.

It wasn't to be clear at all, however.

I went into the Albion the next morning thinking that they would all be happy for me there. So they were, I suppose, but Meggie said, "You're the little Cinderella girl now, aren't you? *After* the ball, when she's won the golden crown." Then she sighed, and said she supposed I'd lose interest in the Alby now. That hurt.

I wondered what reaction I'd get from Maria when we met, as we probably would, by Frederic's bed. While I had been in court, she had taken on the major part of visiting him.

I had something to offer Frederic now. Life had taken so much from him, perhaps I could now repay him. My terrible, barely repressed guilt for the loss of his child welled up all over again. I never seemed to be able to put it behind me. I hurried on to the hospital.

158

Frederic's hospital was crowded, there had been a bad accident on the railway, and they were still bringing in the casualties. It looked like a battle station, with the corridors lined with the wounded lying on stretchers. There was a terrible smell of smoke and blood in the air.

"It was in the tunnel near the station," I heard someone say. "They're still bringing them out."

I hurried past the stretchers, trying not to look. I'd never make a nurse, that was certain.

They had moved Frederic from his room and for a moment I stood there with my heart thudding in the belief that he must be dead. But the Sister caught my eye from behind her desk and waved me into her ward.

"He's in that bed by the window," she said, giving me a huge, bright smile. "Sure, and he's better." She had an Irish accent that was most pronounced when she was happy.

I hurried down the ward. Frederic, propped up on pillows, was in a bed by a window. Maria was in a chair by his side, her face turned towards Frederic so that I could not see her expression. But I could see Frederic's, and I stopped. I felt as if I had had a blow, just below the heart.

Slowly I went towards them and stood at the end of the bed looking at Frederic.

"Welcome back, Frederic," I said, and I smiled. I am proud of that smile. If a record book is kept anywhere, I hope that smile will stand to my credit, to be set against all my bad behaviour.

Maria sat firmly in her chair without speaking, but she raised her hand in a sort of salute. Her expression was expectant and alert. I had never seen her look more totally in control. She didn't mention the court case. She had just come through to her own particular victory. I read that much in her eyes, even before she spoke.

"The noise of the victims being brought from the railway accident roused him," she said. "The sights and sounds were like the war. He thought it was the war still and he was a casualty."

"I can understand that," I said. My throat and mouth were dry.

I had had so many signals about what was coming. The whole of Maria's behaviour since our very first reunion in Vienna had been telling me the truth if I could read it. Now she stretched out a hand to Frederic possessively. "We were married in Vienna before he went off to fight. He thought he'd never see you again, and I loved him very much. He grew to love me too. Frederic's my husband, Alice."

Briefly she explained that she had kept quiet about their relationship because I had the money and the resources to help Frederic, whereas she had none. After all, she had no idea if he would ever regain either memory or voice.

Frederic said only one word, "Alice?" It was a plea for understanding.

I stared back. For a moment I couldn't respond, I couldn't speak, couldn't even move. I put my hand to my eyes; I discovered I was crying.

"It's a shock, I know," said Maria. "Say something."

"I don't know what to say." I was struggling to keep my self-control. I knew I must not scream or shout. "Sorry, I can't make sense."

Why was I apologising? Suddenly I felt hot anger. "You bitch, Maria."

She didn't answer, just hung on to Frederic's hand.

"I've just walked over a land-mine. One you planted and left waiting for me, Maria. Yes, I am angry. Yes, I am hurt." I looked directly at Frederic; I could hardly work out what I felt about him. "I'm not sure what I'm going to do, Maria, but don't count on me giving up."

"There's nothing you can do."

"Frederic?" I said. "Say something. What am I to you? What will you do? Tell me."

I knew I had lost when he turned to look at Maria without answering.

I left them then without another word. Outside the hospital I damned them both. The tears were rolling down my face. What was I going to do? What was there left for me? Those two had made a fool of me.

No, said a small, inner voice. You made a fool of yourself. Pick up the pieces and get on with your life.

I think I walked along the embankment. I hardly know where I went, only that I walked till I was exhausted, deep in self-examination.

Later that day I made my way to Ladybrook Grove. I pushed open the front door and let myself in. The house was quiet; it had about it that warm, waiting feeling of a house empty of the people who normally live in it. I knew Gran had every room occupied, but at this time of the day they would all be out working or looking for work.

The friendly listening silence comforted me a little, and I stood there for a moment absorbing it. Then I went into Gran's own sitting room, into which the lodgers only went by invitation, and sat down to wait for her.

Presently she came, bearing a tray loaded with teapot and cups. "Saw you go past." So she had been there all the time. The kitchen was in the basement. "I could tell you were miserable. Yesterday, I suppose?"

"Not entirely." I took the tea and sipped it. "Where's Maida? And how is she?"

"Maida's in a nice, little nursing home run by an order of Anglican nuns," said Gran. "I hope they're both learning something from each other."

I sipped the tea which was radiantly hot and full of transferred vitality from Gran. "Poor baby. I suppose it will look like that dreadful gangster."

"No, he certainly will not look like him," said Gran, in a strange voice. "He will look like Bobby Charlecote."

I put my cup down on its saucer with a little bang. "How nasty. How very nasty." I took a dislike to the boy at that moment. "Are we never to get out of that particular cycle?" I could hear my voice rising. "Is it going to go on and on?"

"Looks like it, doesn't it?" Gran sounded cheerful enough about it.

"Well, keep him out of my way."

"That's not a pretty thing to say."

"No." I looked at her. "Gran, I'm so unhappy. I've been stupid. Worse than that, I've been made to feel a fool. And I don't like that, either."

"Oh, it's pride then, is it? So tell me."

"No, not just pride—pain, sharp pain." I would like to have had the relief of tears, but I felt dry inside, cold and parched at the same time.

"You ought to be on top of the world with all you've got," she said.

I looked at her, so wise and competent, everything that Josie and I didn't seem to be, and the hurt poured out of me. I told her everything. Beginning with the baby and ending with what I had just heard. "Frederic—last night he became conscious again. And with the return to consciousness his voice came

161

back and with it his memory. The doctors always said it might be like that—they called the amnesia and loss of voice hysterical symptoms. And when he came to himself, he thought he was still in Germany."

"Well, of course."

"But he remembered all about himself. Remembered . . ." I swallowed, the words clogging my throat. "He remembered that he had been married to Maria before he went back to the front that last time." Now I was crying: angry, hot tears were pouring down my face. "He's been married to her all this time. Maria *knew,* and she never told me."

"She has her feelings too," said Gran gravely.

"She knew," I repeated. "And never said." Maria and Frederic, which of them did I feel had betrayed me more? "Oh, Gran, yesterday I had a theatre, someone I loved, friends, we'd won the court case, and now it's all gone sour."

I could feel anger building up inside me, and I knew that somehow it would have to come out.

9 Chapter Nine

Maid in Chancery got great publicity. It was the show everyone wanted to see: there were queues down Albion Walk and around the corner. I had an enormous success on my hands.

I suppose the plot accounted for that great popularity. The author had hit on a story that seemed to echo contemporary worries about the way society was going and the place of women in it. I don't know if it accurately represented reality, but many people saw it as the twenties in a nutshell. It was about a poor little rich girl torn between a promiscuous, selfish but beautiful mother and an alcoholic father, and her struggle to free herself from the Lord Chancellor's wardship in order to salvage one parent and to create a happy romance for herself. The author had provided her with a suitable young man. But the young man had an incipient drinking problem, and the girl discovered in herself the seeds of her mother's weakness. Well, I won't tell you the conclusion except to say, as one critic did, "It tore at the heartstrings." I read it again recently and it seemed contrived but powerful. Of course it had gorgeous parts, so the actors loved it. Everyone had at least one good scene, and the leads had several.

But again and again I caught that note of scepticism in the voices of my theatre friends. Now I was the Charlecote heiress I was not one of "them." So once again I was in that curious position of having gained a professional peak, while my own personal life seemed to crumble around me. Part of me was happy, another part desperately sad. There was a raw patch inside me that would not heal.

Francis Hollman was prompt with consolation for one loss. He appeared the morning after I had learned about Frederic and Maria.

"Don't you go marrying Francis," my grandmother had warned. "You can't marry Fran." I had replied that no one could, that he wasn't real.

"Sorry," he said, sitting himself down by my desk and offering me a cigarette from a silver case with his initials on it. "For you, I mean. But water under the bridge now."

Of course Francis knew all about Maria and Frederic, as did everyone in the Albion, although they had the tact not to mention it to me. Francis had no tact, and frankly I found that easier to deal with. Tact can be very damaging to self-esteem.

"Yes, they've been married all this time, and Maria never mentioned it." I couldn't help letting that rankle, though she had told me her reasons. She had no idea when or even if Frederic would ever regain his voice or his memory and claim her as his wife. Meanwhile, I had the resources to help him, and she had nothing. It was simply good sense to keep quiet.

"You want to face up to the whole business," advised Fran. "And you're not doing it. I can tell you're not. Get it out of your system. Then put it aside."

He took me out to dinner. He was learning his way around the world and we went to the Savoy. After all, as he said, from

163

where his head office was, the Savoy was his local. His chain of cinemas was expanding rapidly, and the style of building was changing as well. "The suburbs—the better-off, middle-class suburbs—that's where I'm going," he told me over cocktails. "Lewisham, Eltham, Croydon, Orpington, Stanmore, Harrow, Wimbledon," he ticked them off on his fingers. "I've got the finances behind me; I'm not managing on a shoestring. Eugene's got a friend, a cousin; we've kept it in the family." They were not really related; he meant that the complicated network of social relationships starting from neighbourhood and school worked as well lower down the social scale as for people like the Charlecotes. "I see the buildings differently, too: they're going to be functional in style. Nice sharp angles and clean lines. Maria helped me there. She made me see the old fuss was out of date, we've got to be modern now. Up to date. She says I'm a bit late already to be contemporary, but she's introduced me to an architect from Paris."

"You're talking too much, Fran," I said, coldly. I almost hated him for trading with Maria—it seemed disloyal.

"I'm trying to impress you, Alice," he said, leaning across and putting his hand firmly on mine. "And you take some impressing. You are now a rich girl."

Then he told me he was copying me and having an apartment for himself constructed on the top of his rebuilt cinema off the Strand. "They call it a penthouse," he said solemnly. "That's what Lady Louis Mountbatten calls hers in Park Lane. To you and me, love, it's the top floor flat." And then he told me there would be an empty suite with my name on the door.

I thought about it. "I don't see what that would get me, Fran," I said eventually. "Except a change of address."

"I'll make the offer again," said Francis. "And then we'll see."

It sounded more like a threat than a promise.

"It's the Albion you really want, not me."

"Well, I'm trying the best way I can to get it," he said, with touching honesty.

"Who's your architect?"

"A man called Ruhlmann," said Fran. "No, he's not Viennese, although he may sound like it. He's from Paris. A friend of Poiret's. That's how Maria got his name." So Maria was in touch with Poiret? That interested me. Secretive Maria.

"He did the Paramount cinema in Paris, and the Yardley

showrooms in Bond Street. Lovely stuff. I popped across to Paris for a look-see. He's expensive. Real class. But for me, nothing but the best." This was true. Francis had genuine feeling for excellence, which he desired, above all, for himself. But he also knew how to get his money's worth. "Then we will do copies for the suburban chain of houses," he went on. In retrospect, Francis, although he always emerged with a profit, was one of the chief creators of public taste in the decade which followed.

His final words that evening were again about Frederic and Maria. "There's a lot of anger ticking away inside you, and that's not good. See Maria. Talk things over. That's my advice."

As soon as Frederic was well enough to leave the hospital, they had moved into some furnished rooms that Maria had found in Soho. We would be neighbours.

Josie, with her usual skill at clearing out from a difficult situation, had landed herself a part in a tour leaving for Australia. She came in to see me before she left.

"Sorry, kid. I'm glad to be going, but I feel bad about leaving you holding the baby."

"Not literally," I said grimly.

"No, Maida's doing that. She's had a bad time, poor girl—a haemorrhage and an abscess. Aren't women unlucky? Do me a favour; go and see her."

As I looked at my mother's face, fine-boned and pretty, brows drawn in a look of concentration, I felt anger at my dead father who had not valued her at her true worth.

"All right. For you, I will."

"I want to earn what I can in Australia," went on Josie. "Because I'm deep in debt to Wally Cook, and he'd like his money back." She gave me a shamefaced look. "Not entirely the law costs ... I had a couple of little flutters that went wrong." She knew I hated her gambling.

"Wally hasn't said anything to me, but I'll help you. I have money now—or I will have." It would take time before I could handle any of my Charlecote inheritance.

"It's me he wants it from, I think." Josie checked her face in the mirror of her compact. "He's always wanted his claws in me, but I can fight him off, never fear. No, I'll get the money, some way. He may be a bit pushed himself," she said thoughtfully. She licked her finger and smoothed her eyebrows, plucked to a narrow, arching line, and said, "Yes, I reckon he's got his money troubles, too." Her face was thoughtful. "By the way, I had Matthew Charlecote in to see me. He was trying to be friendly. But it was you he really had in mind. He likes you, Alice."

"Did you tell him about Maida's baby?"

"Good heavens, no," said Josie. "I left that to you. Or Maida." Josie kissed me good-bye.

"Take your world, Alice. We won that lawsuit. That mattered to me. It's all yours now. Make what you like of it."

And she was gone. I wondered when she'd come back, and what sort of a world I'd have created when she did.

To keep my promise to Josie I went to see Maida in her nursing home the next morning. She was hardly an ideal patient, dropping cigarette ash over the bed and on the baby, whom she refused to breast-feed because she thought it would ruin her figure. "I made them give him a bottle; I can't look after him, anyway. It's back to work for me." Her voice was indifferent.

She confided that Frank Dawes, angry over the baby, was demanding back all the jewellery, furs and cash he had given her. Maida was evasive about how it was to be managed. She seemed half scared, half sympathetic, wholly comprehending of his dilemma, as only a woman of her type could be. "But I think he's short of the ready himself. He's had the police breathing down his neck, which is bad for business. Also, I reckon he has gambling debts to Alfie Romeo, and owing that one is trouble."

I looked at the baby in the crib beside her bed. He looked a real Charlecote to me.

"What would you say if I told you he was Matthew's kid, really?" asked Maida maliciously.

"I wouldn't believe you," I said at once.

"Well, he isn't. And you can believe that. I just thought I'd try it to see what you said."

"You'll get yourself killed one day."

Maida giggled. "You fancy Matthew yourself, although you won't admit it. And why not? At least he's a proper man."

I shook my head.

"What's the baby's name?" Years later there was a psychological technique known as aversion therapy, designed to make you dislike something you were naturally drawn to. Maida was an early and spontaneous exponent of the art, turning it against herself and her child. If she wanted me to dislike them both heartily, then she was going about it the right way.

"Alexander. Pick him up. Why don't you? He won't bite."

"No."

From the depths of me there came an uncontrollable reluctance to touch the child. Maida had kept her child; I had aborted mine. Guilt is a very unreasonable business, and mine now made me terrified of and repelled by the baby. From the very beginning, I had a deep and difficult relationship with Alexander. And from the cradle I think he knew it; he looked at me almost accusingly.

Maida saw my reaction and must have been angered by it because a spirit of idle wickedness prompted her to suggest that I report Maria to the police on account of the lies she must have told them when applying for a passport. "She had a husband all the time and she knew it," said Maida. "I'd get her sent out of the country if it was me."

I went back to my apartment over the Albion, and poured myself a glass of brandy. I asked myself why I didn't do just what Maida suggested to get even with Maria. I went as far as dialling the police station, but I put the receiver down. I was angry, but I wanted a more personal revenge.

Then I telephoned Maria and asked her to come round at once, if she could. My tone implied she had better. "You know the way. Just straight up the stairs."

I left my sitting-room door open and sat there waiting for her, sipping my brandy. I rarely drank, but it seemed a night for it. I filled the glass again.

Presently I head Maria running up the stairs. She strode straight in, and then stood staring at me. I must have looked wild. I got up and gave her a drink. "Sit down. I'm going to tell you something: I'm going to get you sent back to Vienna."

"How?" She gripped the glass so her knuckles showed white.

"Through the police. I'll say you told lies. You did."

"I don't believe you."

"Wait and find out," I said defiantly.

In measured tones Maria said: "I don't believe you because it would be contemptible. And you are not contemptible."

I shrugged. "You cheated; I'll cheat."

Maria sat down on a chair opposite me, and studied my face. She seemed to be thinking things out.

167

I could feel the brandy mounting to my brain. "We've got to have this out. About Frederic. He was mine. Now he's yours."

"Put like that, it is offensive," observed Maria coolly. "You are drunk."

"Join me," I said, and poured some more brandy in her glass.

"I am not going to apologise for what I did," she said, her voice cold and steady. "I did what had to be done. What seemed good to me."

"You should have told me. I thought I was your friend." That was part of the hurt.

"I used to get very angry at the way you treated Frederic," Maria said. "Sometimes angry at the way you treated me. You were so bloody generous."

"Have some more brandy." I stood over her with the bottle. "If I'm so generous, drink some more."

"Thank you." She inclined her head. Her monacle fell into the glass. She picked it up and wiped it.

I laughed. "You look a fool in that."

"I can understand your jealousy."

"I'm not jealous. I just want to hit you."

Maria laughed. "You would find I can hit back."

I slapped Maria's face. Without hesitation, she struck me back. The blow stung, and I reacted by giving her a hard push.

She fell back, stumbling against a chair, which crashed to the ground. She grabbed my skirt and dragged me down with her. For a moment, I was winded.

Maria wrapped her arms tightly round me, rolled me over, and began to bang my head on the floor. There must have been some dirty fighting in that convent-orphanage where she had got her early education.

I think I may have been shouting; Maria was deadly quiet. But we were both concentrating on giving as good as we got. I dragged myself away, scrambled up, and emptied a vase of roses over Maria. The water was stale and stinking. She gasped and looked around for something to throw at me; she found a chair and dragged it towards her. I grabbed her hair.

Suddenly Giles and April were in the room. "Stop it, stop it, you two." He was separating us. "You're mad. Or drunk. Or both."

I had never seen Giles so furious.

"Drunk," said April, picking up the brandy bottle.

I looked from Giles to Maria. Suddenly sobered, I didn't

know whether to laugh or cry. It seemed better to laugh. I guessed Maria felt the same. "Sorry, Maria," I said. "Scene over."

I thought our friendship was over now. Certainly it had taken a blow. But as I sat alone that night, I realised there was a solid link between me and Maria of the kind that siblings know.

Next day the story went the rounds; both Giles and April were gossips, if friendly ones. It was just one more tale in the saga building up about me.

I learned something about myself through that episode, but, unfortunately, not enough. I seemed constantly to be educating myself about myself and I still had a lot to find out. But, at least, having behaved badly to Maria, I felt I had somehow squared our account, and I could settle down to put myself back together and get on with my life. Formal, if watchful, relations were resumed between me, Maria and Frederic.

My fight with Maria helped to clarify my feelings for Frederic. He was kind, gentle, and he had his pride, but to me he had become a "cardboard lover," as the song said.

With her impeccable timing, Josie had left the scene at the right moment. I plunged into work to deaden my feelings, discussing a new play and tidying plans for two touring companies. These would feed from our London productions once they were past their peak of attraction, and so extract every ounce of profit from them while leaving the Albion as a show case for new productions. For the first time I had a feeling of financial ease: money was coming into the box office fast, and although I shared it with Giles as author and producer, mine was the larger part. In addition, I had the Charlecote inheritance to look forward to, although I was finding that money from an estate, especially such a tangled inheritance as mine, is slow to turn into money in the bank.

I received a formal request from the lawyers to visit Causley, followed by a polite, if chilly, letter from Lady Charlecote. I had to go. I shopped for suitable clothes. Tweeds, little wool dresses for day, evening clothes. I wanted to look right. I was still very thrifty in personal matters, and still searched for my dresses from Louisa's racks. They had two shops now, and, like Francis, were thinking of moving into the suburbs with a circuit of small shops. In professional matters I was more willing to spend, using the services of a new young designer to provide some of the dresses for Meggie. Louisa was late to hire a designer herself. The one I used was marvellously skilled with the draping of a bodice and the pleat of a skirt. Fashion was tilting towards the romantic again, and this was the style he excelled in. So I had one dress from him for the Charlecote visit, a dress of pale aquamarine silk, embroidered with seed pearls across the bodice. Someone whom I later loved said the decorations reminded him of the artificial flower memorials to be seen in French cemeteries.

If ever a dress could be called unlucky, this one could. It witnessed violent quarrels and got an introduction to murder, but it was marvellously becoming and survived the war and "bundles for bombed-outs" (who wanted to face the Blitz in green silk and pearls?). It still hangs in my cupboard.

The first time I wore the dress I saw Maida and Bobby Charlecote sitting together at a table at the Embassy Club. I was surprised to see them in such a place, surprised to see them together, surprised—really—to see them at all. I could tell by Maida's expression that they were quarrelling. Suddenly she got up and rushed from the table. There were tears in her eyes. Bobby Charlecote looked my way but pretended not to see me. His face was white and angry. In a little while he left too, white gloves in his hand, black ebony stick under his arm. He always carried that stick. I shall never forget seeing them there that evening. That next day I went to Causley. A difficult visit in itself.

I was not yet the owner—many legal formalities had yet to be gone through—but the Charlecotes behaved as if I was, throwing open all doors to me with a sort of proud politeness that was like a blow in the face. It isn't true that onlookers see most of the game. They only see the ball moving; they don't feel the impact, the bruise, the blood under the skin. Outsiders might have said how well we were all behaving, but we were actually wounding each other all the time.

I took a taxi to King's Cross and then caught the midday train to Newcastle-upon-Tyne. From Newcastle I took the local train to Causley Halt, where the Charlecotes' car was to meet me. It was a bright, cold afternoon, full of a golden light that made the countryside luminous. An aged chauffeur came forward, touching his cap as I stepped from the train. He had no trouble identifying me, since I was the only passenger for

Causley. "I'm Badstock, Miss," he said. "Mr. Matthew told me what you looked like. A very pretty young lady, he said." He put me in the car, tucked a fur rug around my legs, and we set off. Conversation between us was impossible since we were separated by a glass barrier, but he turned around at intervals to give me a friendly smile. There was absolutely no danger in this, except perhaps of driving into the ditch, since no other vehicle passed us on the narrow road.

I leaned back on the pale fawn cushions and wriggled into a position where I could see my face in the mirror. Hair shingled, a marcelled wave folded softly on one side, a fur collar drawn up about my face, I thought I looked both chic and sophisticated. Francis had given me a boutonnière of violets to bring me luck. I bent my head to the scent of violets, then looked in the mirror to apply a touch more lipstick. I felt I needed all my worldly wisdom in this encounter with my aristocratic relations. Matthew told me later, with amusement, that the Charlecotes were not at all aristocratic, simply "a good gentry family." But when the car ran up the drive and stopped before the great grey portico of the house, and Sophia Charlecote came out on the steps to greet me, she seemed almost regal to me.

I drew back for a moment to look up at the house. It was even more impressive than I had remembered. I felt awed that it was mine. Then I went forward to Sophia and shook her hand. The chauffeur disappeared round the side of the house with the car and my luggage, and I followed Sophia's tweeded figure into the hall, where tea was laid out beside a blazing fire. Officially it was spring, but the air was cold.

"Had a good journey? That's not a bad train." She sat herself down before a tea tray, heavy with Victorian silver, and picked up the teapot. "Cream? Sugar? Flora will be in soon, she's out with the dogs. And Matthew will be driving up from London. Poor boy, how he hates living a London life, but his work demands living there."

"Cream, please," I said nervously. "But no sugar." I tried to edge away from the heat of the fire, which was burning my face while leaving the rest of me distinctly chilled. My hostess was warmly wrapped in thick green tweeds and ribbed woollen stockings, while I was wearing a little cream wool stockinette jersey suit with silk stockings and was thus unprotected against the really wicked draught that blew about the hall. Our little encampment of sofas, tea table and screens was like an island of

171

feminine civilisation in the great male starkness of that hall. I got my first real taste of what Causley Hall was like that tea-time, and nothing I saw later really contradicted what I sensed then, although later friendships and associations softened the picture.

Causley was built for men: in the great hall they could meet the tenants and neighbours, in the library they could entertain their friends, in the dining-room they could overeat, looked down upon by generations of male ancestors. Women had the drawing room for their tea tray, or the boudoir, or a corner of the hall. Causley even had a bachelors' corridor and a men's entrance to be used after a day out with the hands or the gun.

It must have been impossible for a young woman to grow up in such an atmosphere without feeling oppressed, and I think Flora did suffer in this way. But she accepted it as part of the natural order of things: women were a lesser species. Not physically, however, for Flora was well-built, with a handsome face, and was as tall as I was, though my bones were narrower. We ought to have looked alike, being blood relations, but I was never sure that we did. While I was at Causley I studied all the photographs of my father as a baby and a lad, seeking a resemblance of my own face. I started that day at tea. While I sipped the strong Indian brew handed across to me by Sophia Charlecote I studied some miniatures of boys, obviously brothers, arranged in a circle around a portrait of a young woman.

"My sons. And me as a young woman. I was no beauty, but a good breeder." Without self-pity she took me through the sad litany; the war had decimated the males of the Charlecote family. "My youngest son, Matthew's father, went first, before Christmas 1914. One of the earliest casualties. He married young. A lovely girl," she pointed to a picture on the wall, "but flighty. Killed in a Zeppelin raid in London." I looked at the picture of a beautiful woman with a mass of fair hair. She would have been younger than Josie, I guessed. Had she been the sister-in-law of whom Randolph had spoken? It seemed likely. Lady Charlecote was going on: "One son was in the navy: that was Edward's father. He married a banker's daughter. She's remarried and lives in New Zealand. We never see her. My eldest boy never married, alas, and he and Randolph were killed in France, as you know." To the boy Edward, child of the third son, had descended the baronetcy. I had almost everything else.

"Where does Bobby fit in?"

"Bobby is the son of my husband's younger brother; he married a cousin." Bobby was clearly an unhappy subject. "You've met his mother." Indeed, I had: she was the lady who had nearly come to blows with Josie at the Albion. "Of course, there are Charlecote cousins and kin all over the country. But they are collaterals only. The Charlecotes of Causley are the direct line since the thirteenth century. The baronetcy is early, one of the first James I created."

And Edward looked so delicate, I thought, as I finished my tea.

After tea I was taken to my room.

"We don't dress," she said, leading me up the great oaken staircase, polished to a high degree of danger. "Just a little tea gown."

I had a lovely tea gown to wear, and the green silk dress for the big dinner tomorrow.

Act two began with the arrival of Matthew. He drove up in an open sports car. I was wearing my little tea dress, which bore no resemblance to the fluttering laces and ninon adorning Sophia Charlecote and which, to my tutored eyes, had come from Paris, well before the war. Flora had not yet appeared, and I was wondering if the Charlecotes went to cocktails before dinner.

I had already formed some impression of the house. At the heart of it was the great hall which was an Edwardian creation, built and thoroughly furnished about twenty years ago. My Martine-trained hands longed to brighten it up, for the heavy carved furniture and green velvet hangings were oppressive. A seventeenth-century tapestry hung on one wall, depicting the martyrdom of St. Sebastian, and on another wall was a huge Delacroix-type picture of a bloody battle. An elaborately carved gallery, under which climbed the staircase, stretched across one end of the hall. Upstairs was a long corridor from which opened the doors to the bedrooms and which ended in yet another staircase of meaner proportions than the first. Sophia told me it led to the "bachelors" wing, which was hardly ever used now but had been a vital necessity in the days when they had entertained on a big scale. I knew about Edwardian house-parties and nodded wisely. Bachelors on one side of the house, young unmarried women on the other, and the married

173

couples disposed of in the middle of the house, with arrangements made for lovers visiting at night.

The center of the house was much older than the Victorian additions and my bedroom had beautiful panelling. It was furnished comfortably, if unexcitingly, with wicker furniture, painted white, and a good deal of pleated pink silk. I found it very cold, however, and hurried over my dressing.

But the house was already exercising a charm over me; I found myself luxuriating in its sense of identity and purpose. It was a house built with great love for a family to live in.

From a window in the hall I saw Matthew drive up and hoped he had not seen me staring, but he had, and waved. Then he came leaping up the steps and under the portico in the hall.

"Hello, sorry to be late. Did Grandmother give you a drink? No, she wouldn't. I say, what a whizz of a dress."

He shook me a cocktail—a "sidecar" he called it, rather nasty and strong—and I sipped it. Girls like me who managed a theatre and had had lovers *ought* to enjoy cocktails.

He sat down with his drink. "You've changed since I first saw you. That day at the Albion, you remember?"

"What was I like then?"

"Bold. Nervous. Young."

"And what do I look like now?"

"Successful. Young. Still nervous."

"I am."

The next day Matthew took me for a drive in the neighbourhood. I thought him a little more wary of me than before. I wondered what he knew of me and Frederic. Moving in the circles he did, he would have heard the gossip, but all he said to me that came out of that world was "I saw your cousin Maida Cook with Bobby: she looks ill."

"Yes—I saw them too, at Quags. Quarrelling, I thought."

It was a clear, but blustery day. Matthew drove an open Humber tourer, but he wrapped me up well in rugs and furs so that I did not mind the sharp wind. He drove me down a steep hill that curved towards the village, a long winding street of grey houses. An immense quiet hung over it all.

"Causley," he said. "Don't suppose you saw it in the dark."

"No. Did you know," I said, "that the man whose dead body was found in the Albion was Thomas Wooler from Causley?"

174

"Yes, I knew. I had the police round to see me, asking questions."

"Did you know him?"

He paused before answering, to check the road was clear. "I'd heard of him, I think. When he first disappeared he was talked about."

"I wonder what he was like?"

"A bad lot, so I believe."

"I wonder who killed him. And why in the Albion?" I mused. "Did the police say much to you?"

"Very little, indeed. I expect they know more than they are telling, though. They usually do. Look, we're out of Causley now and into proper country. Do you notice the walls? Dry flintstone walls are special to Northumberland."

At the top of the hill he stopped the car and let me examine the neat precision of the walls. Below stretched a tidy patchwork of fields and woods. A flock of thick-fleeced Northumberland sheep grazed on a hillside, across which one sole figure of a man was walking, attended by his dog.

"Are they lambing?"

"No, that's over now for the year."

"How peaceful it looks."

"Yes, so it is. I used to long for here when I was in France." He turned to look at the noble sweep of the countryside.

"You didn't like the violence?"

"No." He sounded surprised. "How could anyone?"

"You must have been very young then."

"Not so old," he admitted. "It wasn't a time to grow old in. Come, let's get on. I want to show you a mining village. I wish farming was more prosperous. I'm afraid the hill farmers are having a bad time."

I looked at the countryside with more understanding after that and could see the signs of poverty, gates and farm buildings in need of paint, a rusting, broken-down piece of machinery in one corner of a field, arable land left without a crop.

Suddenly we were going through another sort of village where the houses clung together on a hill looking down on an industrial landscape in miniature with pit-head buildings, and cranes and slag-heaps of coal. A line of railway waggons lay in a siding. Nothing looked in use, though. In the streets of the village groups of men stood at street corners.

"Why aren't they working?" I asked.

175

"Don't you read any of the newspaper except the theatre page? Depression. The strike didn't help, either. The miners stayed on strike weeks after the others, but it didn't do any good. They're going back for less money. And for others there's no work at all."

"Oh." I was beginning to see the background to the economic pressures the theatre was feeling. "Do you Charlecotes own a mine?"

"Yes." He pointed to a distant village. "Over there is Varleyhead Colliery, nicknamed Lionheart. At present as idle as the rest."

"You must have been very rich once," I said. "Perhaps you still are."

"No. Not rich. Just comfortable. And now we are rather less rich and less comfortable." He looked at his watch. "Better get back for lunch." He turned the car round and started to drive in the direction of Causley. His face was thoughtful, and I got the impression he was getting ready to say something. "My grandmother is very fond of young Edward. She doesn't want anything to come in his way." He did not look at me, but his profile was severe. "She wants him to have everything, or almost everything he would have had if . . . well . . . if."

"I'll do what I can. Can't promise anything, though. I expect he's a nice kid. But I've got to find my feet." I shrugged. "And I've got responsibilities like the Albion. I don't know what fat there is to spare on the estate. Not much, I suspect. It looks pretty run down to me."

Matthew said quickly, "We've had a bad time up here. Agriculture's not booming, and taxation's heavy on estates like this. We had tremendous death duties. There's a lot to be still sorted out," he ended gloomily.

"I know. The lawyers told me. You're in debt."

He laughed. "We've nothing left to mortgage . . . except the Albion." He looked at me in question. "Would you?"

"No," I said fiercely. "I'll never touch the Alby."

"You can't sacrifice all this—" he indicated with his hand— "for the sake of a theatre."

"The theatre's the only thing earning efficiently at the moment as far as I can see." I turned on him. "Look, I'd ask you to recall that before the lawsuit, which I won, the only thing I had of my own was the Albion. And now it looks as though the cost

176

of winning is I have to share it. Well, no. The Albion is out of it." I'd really hoped to tap the Charlecote money for the Albion. In fact, I'd already borrowed from Fran on the strength of it. Fear sharpened my anger.

"You can't ditch your responsibilities to Causley. You'll find out." He added: "I hoped you'd see that after a visit here. I told Gran you would. You have double responsibilities now. I wanted to show them to you."

I swallowed hard, tears were not far away. "Thanks," I said bitterly. "Thanks for telling me. I came here partly because I thought your grandmother wanted to meet me as my father's daughter. I was quite wrong. She just wanted to look me over. I daresay some of you don't even believe I *am* his daughter, and it may interest you to know that looking at all the family portraits I wonder myself. I don't see any resemblance and I am glad of it. That would be a twist to the plot wouldn't it? If it turned out that I wasn't Randolph's child at all? I'm sure you think Josie capable of it. I'll do my best for this place, don't think I won't, but for the Albion I will *fight.*"

If we hadn't been in the middle of nowhere with nothing but rolling green hills and narrow fields all around us, I think I might have tried to get out of the car.

Matthew drove the remaining miles to Causley Hall in silence, but as we drew up outside the house and prepared to get out, he said: "If it's any comfort to you, I have never seen the Charlecote likeness in you so strong as now, when you are angry." And there was a strange note of something like respect in his voice.

That evening there was a dinner-party for me to meet the neighbours and local bigwigs. Behind good manners and polite masks, they were consumed with curiosity about me. Even while they were talking to each other they were studying me. I didn't mind too much. Their attention wasn't unfriendly, merely watchful. No judgements had been passed upon me yet—they were waiting to see how I behaved.

The party was Lady Charlecote's last great flourish. After this, she and Flora moved out to a small house on the estate, and the big house was closed up and deserted. The estate office near the stable-block remained in use, and Matthew arranged for me to have a cottage in the woods to stay in as I wanted. He fitted up a room in it with maps of the estate, so that here I could study the accounts and records of Causley and learn my way about.

I went up to Causley on my own in the next few weeks, trying on my new role as Chatelaine to see how it would fit. It felt strange. Once I went into the big house and wandered through the shuttered rooms, trying to imagine what life in it had been like and to relate it to the Alice who had grown up in Vienna and Paris, been befriended by Paul Poiret, and who now sought her career in the theatre. Nothing seemed to match. I couldn't see myself living there. Too many ghosts, too many mice.

There was dust on the chandeliers, the gold on the great wall mirrors was worn, showing the red enamel underneath, the damask curtains were faded. They hadn't spent a penny on decoration for years.

I thought everything could do with a good infusion of working-class May blood. I was a success at the Albion; I had lifted the theatre up out of the mud. I'd do the same here. They *needed* me. The farm workers and the miners would know I was the same class as they were and pull with me. I think I saw myself as Alice May, heir to all the Charlecotes and their saviour, bringing down the third-act curtain to a thunder of applause.

The news of my ambition was received coldly at the Albion. If I had expected support, I didn't get it. Shrugs and blank faces greeted me.

Meggie Repton said, "You know what we feel? We feel you're no longer one of us."

No longer one of that wandering tribe, those itinerant dwellers on the theatre street, the descendants of Burbage, Garrick and the Crummles, the acting profession.

"Damn you," I said. "It's not true: I'm exactly the same."

But no one who has gone through the sudden change of status that I had experienced could emerge exactly the same. I had an estate, I was owner of Causley, so how could I line myself up with the troupes of players? There was a barrier between us now.

The weeks passed, and became months. I went to Causley as often as I could. The house appropriated by me at Causley had originally been a gamekeeper's cottage and was then lived in by a retired housekeeper from Causley, whose possessions still furnished it. She seemed to have been a friendly soul with a

178

taste for Victorian oil paintings of animals. I didn't know it, but my living there constituted in itself a breach of what the country thought good manners and was a lively source of gossip. I ought to have been under the same roof as Lady Charlecote, or not there at all. Some said I had my lover living with me. No one minded that he was invisible, that just added spice to the mystery.

In fact, I was very lonely, since the only people I ever saw were the estate bailiff, a tall thin Scotsman, and Flora, who called several times to stare at me—half admiringly, half nervously—as if I was some strange wild animal. And Matthew, of course.

I reserved the midweek for the Albion. *Maid in Chancery* looked settled for a good run; it was playing to full houses, and I thought we would be safe for months. But I was already looking ahead to the next production of a play called *Rendezvous* that Giles had brought to my attention.

During this period I avoided Maria and Frederic. She was still working for Francis. Josie sent letters and postcards; they were cheerful, but told me little of herself. I didn't know what had become of Maida's baby, but Maida herself was seen racketing around the town. I was living an energetic social life myself at the time, so I knew. No one could say Maida looked happy, however, which made me rush to *my* mirror to see what my face said. I was thinner, the bones in my face sharper, but I could see that, at last, I had developed into my own particular style: modern, chic, and casual. Paul Poiret, my old friend, would have been proud of me.

That year a wave of expectation swept through stage circles, and the cause was *Show Boat*. Even before the musical crossed the Atlantic we knew all about it. The word had run ahead that it was stupendous. *Show Boat* had been drawn from the novel by Edna Ferber; the book and lyrics were written by Oscar Hammerstein II and set to music by Jerome Kern. I went to the first night at Drury Lane as Francis's guest with Louisa and Gene.

That day I had had a telephone call from Matthew asking if I would meet him at Causley to talk estate business. For the first time I had refused. He too travelled regularly back from London to Causley.

He was working in the City himself. From things said, I knew that he was with a firm of jobbers in the Stock Exchange, traders in shares. "Only a sort of apprentice," he had said once. "And rather old for it, too. But the war put me behind in all that." Ever since we had come near to quarrelling on the tour of the Causley estate, he had not been speaking freely to me about himself. He was keeping his distance. And I, for several reasons, was keeping mine.

On this occasion, Matthew had urged me to come up, and seemed disappointed and a little anxious when I refused. Perhaps he sensed a thought that was forming at the back of my mind: how in the end I should have to cut the ties that bound me to Causley, sell it and concentrate on the theatre, the only life I really knew.

At dinner before *Show Boat* Louisa was particularly lively; Eugene never said much, but he took everything in and was really the source of many of the stories Louisa recounted so amusingly. I knew so much more about Louisa now than I had done when I shopped for silk stockings from her stall. I knew that she was the eldest of three sisters left motherless early and had had to keep a sharp eye on the two younger girls, one a dancer and the other a salesgirl. "Both *good* girls," she assured me. Her parents, and Eugene's, had come from the same small village in Southern Italy, a village the family still visited every summer. But Louisa and Gene were thorough Cockneys and felt entirely English.

She had dressed us both for the evening, herself in silver and me in black. Skirts were very short that season, the shortest ever, although there was already a hint that the hemline would drop and, in anticipation, my dress had a sharp dip to one side that was called a handkerchief point. I was in a mood in which every sensation seemed heightened. And *Show Boat,* with its nostalgic scenes of show folk on the Mississippi in the 1880s only intensified that mood. Paul Robeson sang "Old Man River" in his deep, tender voice. Marie Burke and Edith Day, who played Magnolia, both acted with plaintive beauty.

When we got to the scene in which the husband, married to a woman in whose veins ran negro blood, stabs his wife's hand and drinks from her wrist so that he too may have mixed blood in him, I had tears running down my cheeks.

Francis gave me a quick look. Then he put his arms round my shoulders. "Alice, love, do you want me to cut your hand and drink your blood? Glad to oblige."

180

"No," I was dabbing. "Fran, you are a fool."

He still had his arm round my shoulders. "You're burning hot. Louisa, I think this girl's got a fever."

"It's hot in the theatre," said Louisa soothingly. "Alice, are you all right?"

"Perfectly. I'm fine."

But that night, after *Show Boat* had come to its triumphant last curtain, I excused myself from the others, brushing aside their protests and Fran's disappointment, to hurry home. There I changed my clothes, packed a bag, and got into my little car to drive through the night to Causley. Just before I left, I telephoned the Dower House to leave Matthew a message that I had changed my mind and would be coming.

All through the night, as I drove, my mind kept returning to the image of blood drawn, falling, mingling. My pulse raced.

When I got to my cottage, I built a fire in the grate and made some coffee. Matthew soon came striding through the door, with a couple of his mother's little dogs at his heels. "I came straight over. Can I have a cup of that coffee? Thanks. Nice fire." He was warming his hands at the blaze. "Glad you changed your mind. Why did you?"

I didn't answer directly. "I went to see *Show Boat* last night. Have you seen it?"

"No. Read the book, though. What did you make of it?"

"Oh—nostalgic, romantic, more than a touch melodramatic, but full of catchy tunes. Oh, it'll do well. Probably run for years."

Matthew was staring down in the fire. "Good coal. Coal from the Lionheart Colliery, isn't it? You can always tell the way it burns."

"I don't know. I expect so. There's always a bucket left for me to burn."

"I want to talk to you about Lionheart." He sighed. "As well as about the farms. Trouble never comes singularly."

Agriculture was in a bad way in that decade and was to stay that way till the next war. I had misjudged the farm-baillif—he was doing the best he could. Looking at the accounts I could see how prices for corn, barley and milk were dropping all the time. Money from Charlecote investments was being used to prop up the farms. I was sharp enough to have caught on to what the country had decided would be a solution to the Charlecotes' problems: I should marry Matthew. In romantic love

181

stories it is the poor, dispossessed heroine who marries the rich intruder. We would be able to put a nice twist in it.

"Go on," I said. "What is it about Lionheart?"

Matthew picked up the poker and stabbed at a lump of coal; it fell apart in a splutter of sparks.

"Bloody silly name. My grandfather had a taste for the dramatic effect. He had the money for it. I'm so sorry for those poor devils there."

The miners of the Lionheart Colliery had come through the long strike, which was the cause of the general strike and which outlasted it, with less in their pay packets after the layoff than before it. They were angry. "Damn Bolshy," was how Mr. Binyon, the mine-manager, put it. Still looking at the fire, Matthew told me he was afraid there was going to be violence at the Lionheart Mine. He wanted me to go with him tomorrow to a meeting of the men and talk to them. "Will you do it? It's why I asked you to come here."

I agreed readily. I had so many plans for improvements at the mines: I wanted to better working conditions and get the miners out of their terraced cottages into decent houses. I had similar plans for the whole estate. But I knew Matthew thought I was spending too much money; he had already pointed out that double death duties (Randolph having survived long enough to inherit Causley nominally) were now payable. The estate was tight pressed for cash.

"So far, all you've been to them has been someone with London clothes and a pretty face," he said, turning from the fire to look at me. "I think if they meet you then they will know you are genuine."

"I *am* genuine," I said. "I'd be willing to put more money in the mine. I think we should—"

He interrupted me: "Money. Yes, that's something we certainly ought to talk about." He pulled a paper out of his pocket. "Let me run through the expenditure you have committed yourself to in the next year." He started to read out. "You have promised repairs to six cottages on the North Lane Farm, repairs to three cottages on Barlon Farm, complete rebuilding of two—"

I broke in, "These are all things that needed to be done. People can't work efficiently from slums."

He read on: "You are putting in electricity, and water mains all over the place—"

"If the farms earn more, we can afford more," I started to say.

"And I suppose you'd like to make similar improvements with the Lionheart? Of course. So would I. But where's the money going to come from? Don't you think Binyon and I haven't been struggling for months, years even, to keep the mine alive? You thought you could sweep in here like a fresh wind and set us all to rights. God forgive me, I even hoped you could. I was willing to help. But I can't stand by and let you make a fool of yourself."

Matthew had stopped walking round the room, and we were confronting each other.

"That's what you really wanted me here for," I said slowly. "Not to escort me to the mine. You wouldn't care if they spat in my face. It was to say all this."

"I didn't know you'd act so quickly with all these schemes," he said.

"Behind your back, you mean? Go on, say it. It's what you think."

"I'll tell you what I think: I think that in running the Albion you have shown great flair and efficiency. You know the theatre, but you don't know a single, bloody thing about running an estate." He got a grip on himself, and said more coolly, "I'm going to show you the estate records for the last hundred years."

There are moments that are turning points in one's life, whether recognised or not at the time. From that hour I realised that property imposed its own limitations, and that you could be pinched for money while possessing much. I understood the Charlecotes, and Matthew in particular, from then on. More, I no longer felt so detached from them. Necessity bound us together. Over the generations the estates at Causley had been put together, piece by careful piece—by inheritance, by marriages, and by purchase. It was a family holding and not to be exploited by one person in one generation. I began to see also how frail were the financial props on which Causley rested.

Working together relaxed some of the pressure between us so that it was easy to sit afterwards by the fire and drink sherry, watching the logs blaze upon a heart of red hot coal.

"Sea coal," said Matthew. "The mine runs right under the sea. It used to be shipped in colliers to London. Goes by rail now."

A log shifted in the fire and wide caverns opened up. I leaned by in my chair watching the picture. It looked like a building burning. The log sank still further on the bed of coal, and the picture disappeared in a flurry of sparks. One shining star fell on my skirt.

"Here, you're alight—careful, let me do it." Matthew leaned over to brush the spark from my skirt. I turned my face towards him, my cheek brushed his, our lips came together in a kiss that seemed easy and inevitable. The quickness of my response surprised and alarmed me.

Matthew drew away. In the firelight his face looked serious. I wondered what he was going to say, but he pulled me to my feet. "Come on," he said. "The shift at the mine stops work at noon. Binyon has told them we're turning up soon after, but they won't wait. Get your coat on. I'll drive."

In the car I must have dozed, because the journey seemed to pass quickly. "You all right?" asked Matthew.

My head ached, but I put this down to lack of sleep. "Yes, fine. Why?"

"You were muttering a bit as you slept." He was driving the car through the main gates of the colliery. "Something about blood." He looked at me with concern.

The colliery yard was deserted and quiet. There was no sound, no engine at work, no stamp and rattle of machinery. But through the archway, from the inner yard, came a low deep-clamouring roar of many voices.

Matthew parked the car as Mr. Binyon came hurrying across to us. He asked us to leave; he thought it would be best if the meeting was abandoned. "It'll only be asking for trouble meeting the men now. Forgive me, ma'am, but I think you'd be better gone."

Matthew looked at me, I nodded, and he took me firmly by the arm and walked me towards the inner yard. "We'll go ahead, Binyon."

The inner yard was small; the crowd of men gathered there were still sweaty and black from their shift. An ominous silence fell as we walked in. A pathway was politely opened for us to four orange-boxes laid together to make a platform. Matthew helped me on. Another stage, I thought to myself. Could I perform?

They were quiet while Matthew introduced me. I studied the

184

faces in front of me. Some in the crowd were boys, wild and lean. Others, the majority, were older and weary, men with families, men who had gone to France, served in the trenches, survived the slaughter, and come home again. Home to what? I could read that question in their eyes.

The silence continued and now felt hostile. My throat was dry; I tried to speak and could not. Matthew stepped forward, as if to take over. I held my arm in front of him, holding him back.

"Are ye sheltering behind a woman then, Master?" yelled a voice from the front.

There was a wave of derisive laughter. I heard Matthew swear.

But I found my voice. "No," I called out. "No, he is not. And *I* am your master."

"Are you now, miss?" called that voice again.

"Listen to her, damn you," said Matthew.

"You'll no damn us, Mr. Charlecote," said an elderly man quietly. He turned to his comrades. "Listen to her, lads, give her a hearing."

I talked quickly, telling them all I hoped to do, trying to explain my plans. But I seemed I wasn't carrying convictions. They didn't want to hear about pit-head baths, and a sports-field with showers.

"What about our jobs, miss?" a voice yelled. "Can you promise we can fill our bellies?"

I was making them angry. Matthew pulled me back and started to speak. I had said the wrong things in the wrong voice, but now I could hear Matthew talking quietly, and persuasively, making no false promises, but carrying to them his hopes for the mine. They heard him out in peace.

The meeting broke up quietly. Matthew apologised for bringing me there. "I shouldn't have exposed you to it. Sorry."

"No. I'm sorry I let you down. How did it go, do you think?"

Matthew shrugged. "What do you think, Binyon?"

Binyon shook his head.

"Oh, you're always a pessimist," said Matthew shortly.

On the way back to Causley, an elderly man in a cloth cap waved the car down.

"John Thornton!" said Matthew shortly.

"Afternoon, Captain Charlecote."

"Not Captain any longer, Sergeant."

"Those were the days, eh Captain? Bloody, but better than now."

Matthew looked at me. "Alice, this is Sergeant Thornton. We knew each other well in France. What is it, Thornton? You haven't stopped us just for a chat."

"I'll talk to you on your own, Captain, if Miss Charlecote will excuse me."

Matthew got out of the car, and they walked up and down the road, Thornton talking, as I watched. Then Matthew got into the car, waved at Thornton, and started the car.

"What is it? What did he say?"

Matthew drove on in silence, then he said, "Thornton believes that there will be an attempt to fire the big house. Some of their men are wild enough to do it. They know it's empty." Before I could manage a word, he said, "And don't advise going to the police, because I won't do it. I'll deal with this on my own."

Before going to my cottage, we drove to the big house so that Matthew could inspect it. Everything seemed in order.

We made a circuit through the stable yard, onto which the kitchens and pantries opened. "This would be the most likely area for arson," he assessed. "A blaze could be well under way without notice. All well locked up, of course, but easy enough to break in. I'll be around here tonight and keep watch."

"I'll come too."

"*No*, Alice." He was firm, tucking me back into the car. "You will go back and get some rest. You look all in."

A soft mewing, plaintive and prolonged, attracted his attention. A kitten was rubbing itself against his legs. He bent down and picked it up, a tiny black and white creature with wall eyes.

"It must be one of the stable cat's offspring, one of old Minnie's kittens. She had generations of them. This little beast must have been overlooked when the house was closed. Been scratching a living ever since." He stroked its head. "Older than it looks. Half starved and stunted, poor wretch." He tucked it into a deep pocket of his overcoat. "You come with me, puss."

At the cottage, he plucked the kitten from his pocket and dropped it in my lap. "Here, you take her. I think it's a her; they usually are. Keep it for tonight and I'll pick her up tomor-

186

row. She'll give those mice of yours a run." He started the car.

"Matthew—about the miners."

"See you tomorrow. I'll tell you what goes on—and for heavens sake, have a meal and some rest."

I hadn't eaten for some time, I realised, but it didn't seem to matter. I gave some warm milk to the cat, and lay down on the sofa in front of the fire.

My head ached very badly; the pain got worse, and I felt very hot. I closed my eyes. I remember thinking that I would have a rest and then a bath. When night came I would join Matthew at the big house to keep watch. He didn't want me there, of course, but I would go. It was my responsibility too, wasn't it? They were my miners, after all.

The room was dark when I awoke. I woke with a start as if by a noise. The fire had died down, and the little cat had crawled onto the sofa with me. So much for the mice, I thought, stroking its head. I struggled to sit up; a wave of heat mixed with dizziness forced me back for a minute. I felt as though I had a double set of arms and legs, none of them quite coordinating.

I looked at my watch; it was later than I expected. Outside night had fallen. The sky was dark and cloudy, but there was a moon. I wondered what noise had roused me. Then it came again: a soft, rattle of the door handle. It was the back door. The first noise must have come from the front door. I stood up, listening. Silence. Then I heard a motorcycle start up and move away down the drive, which was a few yards away from my cottage. Behind the first cycle went another. Then another.

I knew then that the attack on the big house was under way. I considered telephoning the police, but I understood Matthew's motives for excluding them. If the police came in, then arrest, trial and prison for the men would inevitably follow. They were young, wild and reckless, but Matthew owed them a life.

I opened the door, and stepped out into the night. A path through the woods led to the big house; it was a shorter route than down the drive. The moon came out from behind a cloud to light my way.

It took me longer than I expected to get to the house. I lost my way twice in spite of the moonlight. Once I stumbled and fell. Too late I was realising that I was ill. A fever was making my head thump and my mind race.

I reached the stable yard to see a scene silhouetted by the

187

lights streaming from the range of kitchen windows. Matthew was standing, back to the kitchen door, facing three young men. He had a gun.

I stood watching, swaying a little. Matthew was talking to them. He was gradually talking them into order; he had them under control. Then I saw a figure creeping round the corner of the house; I thought he had a gun. I sped forward, my head felt as if it could fly, but there were weights on my legs. I collided with the figure, and fell back, winded.

I had a confused impression as I fell of voices raised, of Matthew shouting, "Pick her up, for God's sake, Thornton. Here, stand aside, you fools, and let me get to her."

He picked me up. "Help me to the car." I was struggling to assure him that I was all right, but I was still gasping. Dimly, I realised that it was John Thornton I had collided with, and that he had been helping Matthew, not attacking him.

Now all the men seemed to be clustering around, helping me and Matthew to his car. The anger seemed to have drained away from them.

"Thanks," I muttered. "I'm really all right. Honestly."

Matthew did not speak while he drove me to the cottage. He helped me inside; I had left the door unlocked. The little cat now slept by the fire.

He touched my forehead gently. "You've got a raging fever. You should never have come out. Now go to bed. I'll bring you a hot drink."

I tried to undress, but my fingers trembled too much. I leaned against the bed trying to steady myself. When Matthew came in he exclaimed, and came forward to help me. Gently he eased me out of my clothes and slid my nightgown over my head. "I'm all right," I kept saying.

"You are not. Here, we've got to get this temperature down. I ought to get you to the doctor."

He returned with aspirin, but I couldn't get it swallowed. "I'll sponge you down, that'll reduce the temperature."

I muttered a refusal, but Matthew brushed me aside with the peremptory order not to be prudish. I let him roll back my gown and sponge me with tepid water. Then he wrapped me up and plopped the little cat beside me. "Here, have Minnie Mouse, she'll comfort you. And the other business is all right. No one's going to burn the house."

"They're good lads, really," I muttered sleepily.

I came slowly to consciousness with the pale dawn. I lay testing my body: I was awake and in one piece. Matthew was asleep beside me, his head cradled on one arm and the little cat sleeping within the curve of the other. I looked at him and knew that I wanted him as my lover. I wanted him very much. It was a feeling I had never known not even with Frederic. It was as if everything I had experienced before was leading up to it. But I was still weak from the fever and a little afraid.

It had been a night of incredible intimacy and closeness with Matthew, but it was at an end. I couldn't let it lead to anything, though I desperately wanted it to.

I slipped out of bed to wash and then made some coffee. When I returned to the bedroom, Matthew was still asleep. Tenderly I stroked his hair. It had been his gentleness to the little cat that had been my cue to understanding him.

I thought he hadn't felt my touch, but with eyes still closed he murmured "Shall I purr?"

I took my hand away. "Matthew, here's some coffee. You'd better get away before the village gossips know you're here. They already have me down as a scarlet woman. I'm better, quite recovered."

He stretched, dislodging the cat. "It's Sunday, and they lie-in on Sunday, but I expect you are right." He got up, yawned, and drank his coffee.

"Dearest Alice, I'll see you later. I'll telephone."

When he'd gone, I stood thinking. At the back of my mind my secret worry about our relationship had stirred. I'd have to get away from Causley. I was not sure, I had never been sure, exactly what weight I ought to put on Randolph's words about his nephew who might also be his son. And yet I found I could not put it out of my mind. I was surprised at how strong the primal prohibition was.

I was still standing there when the telephone rang in the office. For a moment I considered ignoring it, on the grounds that the call was probably for one of the Charlecotes anyway. Then I remembered that the office had its own telephone number and that I had given it to my grandmother since I often worked here myself. I picked it up.

"Hello."

A crackle in the line. "'Allo, 'allo? Ici Paris." A distant voice asking for Miss Alice May Charlecote—the names came through clearly.

189

"Parlant," I said.

"Alice, my girl, it is you?" Paul Poiret's voice vibrated across the line. He was speaking English. "It is so important I speak with you. I have your telephone number from your grandmother."

Sadly he told me that he must ask for the repayment of the money he had invested in my management of the Albion. His own circumstances demanded it, alas, but he knew I was now a woman of substance, eh?

Of course I would honour his request, but it came at a bad moment—though it is always a bad moment for the repayment of debts.

"I'll return to London at once, and arrange it," I assured him.

Then I wrote a short note to Matthew explaining that urgent business about the Albion recalled me to London. I put it through the door at the Dower House.

I returned to my cottage, packed my things, tucked the kitten in with me, left out some cheese for the mice, and set off in my tiny car for London.

9 Chapter Ten

I had plenty of time to think about my relationship with Matthew on my journey to London. He was hurt by my rapid departure, as he made clear in a telephone call to me in my office some time after my arrival—a call ruthlessly put through by April who was clearly on his side.

"Did you have to run quite so fast?"

Apologetically I explained, "I had an urgent phone call that

I couldn't ignore. Business. I had to get back to London." I had already arranged for the despatch of the money to Paul Poiret.

"You could have rung me before you left. I'd have driven you to London."

"I had my car." I couldn't tell him I was frightened of all the emotions he aroused, that I was running for cover.

"Damn you, Alice, you've got more imagination than that. And so have I. Think of a better excuse!" And he slammed down the receiver.

He was right to be angry, but I was torn. On one side was Matthew and Causley, on the other the Albion. I didn't see how I could really have both. Causley represented security and a social standing such as I had never thought to have. It stood for an ordered and responsible way of life I only partly understood, but deeply admired. The sheer physical beauty of the place drew me. Matthew was part of this: he had an authority and self-confidence which drew me to him. But the Albion was my own sun shining on my own life. I was a maker, an artist, and only through the Albion could this side of me find expression.

An ordinary woman might have managed, but I wasn't an ordinary woman. I was Alice May, who had inside her the canker of guilt at what she had done in Paris, a double guilt, now doubly secret. Guilt had operated in my relations with Frederic, and it was beginning to turn itself against Matthew. And Matthew was understandably puzzled and hurt. I went back to work after our telephone conversation, but April soon interrupted me: "Your cousin Maida is here. Says she must see you."

"Oh, show her in." I looked up. "What is it, Maida? Sit down, do." I drew up a chair. Maida had got her figure back after the baby and she was wearing a pretty new dress, but there was a pinched look about her mouth and deep shadows, cleverly masked with rouge and powder, under the eyes. She looked frightened. "April, go and get some coffee for us." And then leave us alone, my eyes said.

Nervously, Maida said, "I won't beat about the bush: can you lend me some money?"

"Of course." I reached out for my cheque book. "How much? I'd have been giving the baby a christening present, anyway. How is he?"

191

"He's with your Gran. Fine, he is," said Maida mechanically. Her eyes met mine. "I need three thousand pounds."

"What?"

"More, really." Her tongue moved over her lips as if they were dry. "But that would do."

"I haven't got that much money in the world."

"But you've got this theatre. Everyone says the new show is making thousands. And you've got that place in the north."

She explained she wanted to use the money to redeem some jewellery she had pawned. I suspected Bobby had got money out of her: if she had pawned the jewellery, then he had helped her spend the money. It was a measure of her desperation that she had come to me, because she didn't like me and never had.

"Are you frightened of Frank Dawes?" I asked. "Or Bobby?"

But she wouldn't answer. And I didn't give her the money. I hadn't got it to give, whatever she thought.

Suddenly I was irritated by her. "It'll have to stay pawned, Maida, as far as I am concerned. Yes, I've got the Albion, but the Albion has a big mouth."

"It's got a *hungry* mouth," she said with a shiver. "That dead man. Don't you think about him? I do."

I sent her away with barely a kind word. I'll never cease to blame myself for that.

April came back in and collected the cups to wash. "You didn't drink your coffee. Either of you."

"Emotion," I said.

"I can always eat or drink. Nothing ever puts me off. She was crying as she left," April said as she left the room.

I would have let Maida have the money if I could, but I couldn't spare it from the Albion. And now that I had seen how much money Causley could absorb I was nervous about money in general. I could imagine how income could drain away. "I haven't got that much, not in the way people think," I said to myself, as I made up my face for the evening. "Why should I redeem Maida's pledges?" My face stared back, sceptically. "You know it's more than that," it said to me. "Maida didn't tell all the truth."

I was seeing Francis that evening. He was trying to persuade me to advertise his cinema in the foyer of the Albion, for which service he would promote the Albion on the reel of advertisements he ran before his main films. I was dragging my feet because I felt it was just another spider's strand by which Fran was reaching out to bind me and the Albion closer to him.

"You don't take the cinema seriously," Fran said. "That's your trouble. Or one of them. The other is that you don't take me seriously."

"I assure you, Fran, I take you very seriously indeed. About the cinema, well, I don't know."

He leaned forward. "You don't keep up to date with the news, you poor little rich girl." I had told him about my worries over money. "I can tell you that within the next twelve months the cinema is going to take a giant step forward. It's going to find a voice. The films are going to talk." He sat back in his chair. "Think about that."

"Talk? You mean like a gramophone record?"

"It's going to be better than that," he said confidently. "We're going to have singing films, laughing films! And that is the reason," he went on, "that I am laying my hands on as much capital as I can."

I looked at him in surprise.

"Yes," he said. "You thought I must be in debt to Wally Cook, didn't you? Wrong. *He* owes *me*. I know how to handle my money, and I don't gamble with it when I've got it." He gave me a crooked smile across the coffee cups. "I mean to get my money out of Wally."

"What about Maida? I had her round here trying to get money from me to get some jewellery back. Are you behind that?"

"Ah, Maida. So you wouldn't lend to her? Well, why should you? It would leave the Albion dangerously exposed, and you'd never do that, would you? Not you." He shook his head. "Poor Maida. Silly girl. I know a bit about it because I'm involved. Wally owes me money, which I've asked him for. I'm afraid Wally Cook may be putting on the pressure to that gangster friend of his for some money owed him for services rendered, so that he, in his turn, may want back some valuable jewellery he gave to Maida when they were together. He really loved that girl at the time. She could have done anything with him, but she hadn't got the sense she was born with. She had to fall for a man who was bound to exploit her. The jewels were not a gift but a loan. That's what her former protector says, and now he wants them back. But I think Maida's let them out of her

193

hands. Silly girl, because that man is not nice where his possessions are concerned, and he's prepared to use force to get what he wants."

"You are a devil, Francis," I said. "I think you know exactly what you are doing." With energy, I added, "Any debts I had to you, I'd pay, I swear I would. And think twice about borrowing. You won't get your hands on the Albion."

"How do you know it is the Albion I want?" he said, with that crooked smile.

I couldn't get Maida out of my mind that night as I walked home. I wouldn't let Fran see me back to the Albion; I was as near to quarrelling with him that evening as I ever was. I wondered what Maida had done with the jewels entrusted to her by her ex-lover. I hoped she hadn't given them to Bobby Charlecote, though she was silly enough and infatuated enough to have done so. And he was self-indulgent enough to have taken them.

The telephone was ringing when I let myself into my empty flat. I walked across and answered it, sitting on the bed as I did so. A mirror hung on the wall facing me and I could see my reflection: a tall, long-legged girl with shingled hair, wearing a beige wool dress and white jade earrings. Everyone else that season was wearing green jade. I decided that mine should be white.

"Hello," I said.

"Alice? It's Maida." I scarcely recognised her voice, it was so hoarse and hurried. "Can you come round to me?"

"Now?"

"Yes. It's not far away. Derby Street," I knew Derby Street, for it was where Frederic and Maria now lodged. "There's something I must tell you. Number five, first floor."

"What about?" I asked bluntly.

"Money," she said, and laughed. Or if it was not a laugh, it was a cough of pain.

I threw my coat back over my shoulders and walked round the corner to Derby Street. I was unable to stop myself looking up at the windows behind which Maria and Frederic lived, but no light showed. They were probably in bed. I did not torment myself with thoughts of their deep, secret life. Frederic and his great physical beauty were things I could not think about.

Number Five Derby Street was a lodging house and the door

was unlocked. I went into the hall which was lit by one dim gaslight. A man hurried down the stairs.

"Bobby," I said in surprise.

He stopped about a foot away and stood looking at me. "Who are you?"

"It's Alice." I realised that in the dim light he couldn't see my face.

He laughed. "Alice? Fancy you turning up. What do you want?"

"I've come to see Maida. She asked me to." There was a wildness on his face that frightened me.

"That bitch." He had come right up to me, and suddenly reached out and grabbed me. "Don't bother. I want you with *me.*"

"Bobby!" I tried to push him away; I could smell the drink on his breath.

From the basement stairs the landlady's voice shrilled. "Who's that? What do you want?"

I called. "I'm Maida's cousin, Alice. I've come to visit her. Which is her room?"

"First on the left up the stairs." The landlady padded along the hall on slippered feet. "Who's that with you?"

Bobby dropped my arm and ran out, leaving the front door open.

"He's gone now," I said mechanically.

I went up the stairs, and knocked on Maida's door. There was no answer.

"She's there, dear," called the landlady up the stairs. "Try the door."

"Maida?" I pushed open the door and walked in. "It's Alice."

The light was on, showing a bed-sitting room in considerable confusion. A chair was overturned, a table knocked over, and a mirror broken. A black ebony walking stick lay among the shards. Maida was stretched across the bed with her hand still clutching the sheet. There was blood all over her face, and her eyes were closed. She was quite dead.

Like a reel from a movie in one of Francis's cinemas, the next scenes shot by. I seemed to see them in a shade of sepia, soundless but sharply focussed. The landlady's terrified face, myself telephoning for help, and then the arrivals. The room was suddenly full of new faces. First, the doctor and the police arriving simultaneously, and myself explaining. Then my grandmother arriving, white-faced but composed, to take me away. She took me back to Ladybrook Grove and put me to bed. "Poor girl, poor girl," she said. "Let's hope they get him quickly. They want him for the dead man in the Albion, too. Oh, yes. He was there as well. Oh, a violent man."

I didn't have to be told who killed Maida. I knew. Bobby Charlecote was picked up by the police on the Dover to Calais ferry, trying to escape to France. The police treated him as a gentleman, and took him back, unhandcuffed, in a first class railway carriage to Victoria. First, he confessed to killing Maida in a fit of fury because she had been trying to get back the jewellery she had given him, and also to murdering Thomas Wooler and hiding his body. The police knew that Bobby took cocaine, and that Thomas Wooler had been getting drugs for him in France and bringing them back when he got leave.

At Victoria Bobby excused himself and went into the cloakroom, where he shot himself through the mouth.

The postmortem on Maida said she had died because of internal bleeding flooding her lungs from an injury to her throat. Poor Maida: a chain of events that had started with Francis, had forced her into a violent collision with Bobby Charlecote. Between them they were all responsible for her death. I too had refused to help her, giving priority to the Albion.

Because of Maida's death, Francis laid off his demands to Wally. Francis was no vampire; he wouldn't actually drink blood. I knew that the ultimate object of all his manoeuvres had been to weaken my hold on the Albion Theatre. So by her death Maida had paid a price for me.

This was the bleak outcome of an affair that exploded into a cause célèbre, adding to the notoriety that I and the Albion acquired. It was a notoriety that was never to die away completely. Added to all else that was to happen it made me a person the newspapers never forgot.

There were three inquests, beginning with Maida's. The publicity hounds crowded the court and lined the streets to watch the principal witnesses arrive. There was no hostility towards me, just intense curiosity. One woman pushed her head through my taxi window, as the crowds halted us, and stared right in my face. "She henna's her hair, Lou," I heard her say to a companion as she withdrew.

At this inquest I was, of course, required to give evidence about Maida's telephone call that had led to my finding her body. A frightening picture emerged of Maida's last day, as I and her landlady testified. She had spent all of it locked in her room, only emerging to telephone me. To her landlady she had confessed that she was afraid of two men: Bobby Charlecote and Frank Dawes, from both of whom she feared physical violence.

Then Frank Dawes appeared. Maida's former protector was a stocky, dark-haired man wearing a black suit with a thin white stripe. He admitted to the relationship with Maida, and to having handed over to her the jewellery, which he claimed was "on loan" only because they represented his "savings." I saw the judge's eyebrows go up at that.

In a husky voice Dawes agreed that he had made threats of violence against Maida in order to get the jewels back, because he was in a tight spot and needed cash. He didn't amplify this point, but I knew he meant he was under pressure from Walter (and behind Walter, Francis). Clearing his throat unhappily, Frank Dawes swore that he would have never, never have translated these threats into action against Maida because he'd "really loved the kid." The coroner let him stand down.

A Harley Street doctor appeared next to say that he had been treating Bobby Charlecote for addiction to cocaine and "nervous" disease over a long period. His evidence was concluded quickly because it was apparent he would have more to say at the inquest on Bobby himself. But he said enough to let us know that Bobby was violent and unpredictable.

The jewels—sapphires, diamonds and pearls—surprisingly turned out to be worth some ten thousand pounds and had been pawned in two separate lots by Bobby for the miserable sum of five hundred each time. The police speculated that he had handed over the money to his drug supplier, who was probably also blackmailing him.

I did not go to the inquest on Bobby, nor to the reopened inquest on Thomas Wooler at which the coroner's jury decided, on evidence provided by the police, that he had been killed by Bobby Charlecote. There was a history to Thomas Wooler which showed up at the inquest. A clever, rebellious boy, he had worked as a groom on Bobby Charlecote's father's stables, been thrashed for ill treating a horse, and had then run away to join the army. There, too, he was soon mixing with criminals.

197

He met Bobby again in the war and became his drug-supplier and eventually his blackmailer. Bobby both hated him and depended on him. There was even a hint of a sexual bond between them.

With each inquest public interest increased. I did not go to the last two, but that didn't mean I wasn't forced to know all about them. It was a hateful time.

Josie sent a letter from Australia full of sorrow and horror at Maida's death, followed by the news that she had become engaged to an Australian: "a bit of a rough diamond, but he's made his money the hard way."

I grieved for Maida, and, to my surprise, missed her. It is amazing how some people build themselves into your life. Liking seems to have nothing to do with it. Matthew Charlecote came to her funeral, looking sombre and miserable in his dark suit. Our eyes met over Maida's coffin as it was carried past. Maida and Bobby had levelled the score between the Mays and Charlecotes. Josie and I had suffered once, but the Charlecotes were eating bitter aloes now, and I could see the taste of them in Matthew's face. But I didn't talk to him, although I could see he was trying to force an opportunity. I evaded him; I knew we had to talk eventually, but I wanted it to be later.

After the funeral we went back to Ladybrook Grove. A funeral tea party there was a recognised occasion, and my grandmother had done her duty. In the front room was a round table set with ham sandwiches and salmon rolls, with decanters of sherry and port on a silver tray. If the men wished for whisky they had to go to the next room to get it, as convention demanded. Half an hour after our arrival, tea and fruit cake were served. Half an hour after that, one could go. The whole ceremony was hideously poised between pleasure and misery.

"What about the baby?" I asked Gran, who had taken off her hat and was preparing to clear the tea things away. "Sit down, have a cup of tea, and tell me."

"I will take the weight off my feet for a bit," she said, sitting down. "I'm looking after him, of course."

"Of course." Truly, we were a matriarchy. "I'll help about money, but I don't want to see him."

"You needn't bother about the money side of things: Matthew Charlecote has made arrangements," said my grandmother shortly. I knew she resented the way I felt about the child. But that child was *me*, couldn't she see that? And not only was it me, but also the child that had not been born in Paris.

One good thing came out of Maida's murder: it brought Maria and me close together again. Maria came round to the Albion as soon as she heard the news; she (and to a lesser extent Frederic) were a comfort during this time.

"It was bad that you did not help her to get the money," she said soberly. "But how could you know what would happen? And you have not done many bad things in your life so far, Alice." I shook my head. "You are *too* generous with giving as a rule: you give and do not take. It has been your trouble."

"With Frederic, you mean?" I shook my head. "It was always you, Maria. I see that now. I don't hold it against you. After all, I still have the Albion."

"Yes, you still have that," she agreed gravely, as if it were something she did not envy me. "And Causley." But she had Frederic.

Then she told me that she and Frederic were going to New York, where Paul Poiret could help her obtain a position with a New York designer. He was there himself. "He would like to see you. Why not? You are a free woman. New York, no?"

I shook my head. "No," I said.

Ours had never been one of those friendships where we confided in each other all the time. I was not that sort of woman and neither was Maria. The way we had both been brought up encouraged a solitary spirit, but nevertheless we had a deep understanding of each other. Maria knew the worst behaviour I was capable of and would never despise me. For my part, I comprehended why she had kept her silence over her relationship with Frederic: she had put his interests before her own. We were two creatures who had suffered and that had created a powerful bond.

As I had suspected, *Maid in Chancery* now began to run down. The play had had splendid reviews, and for a long time we had had packed houses, but gradually numbers thinned out. Some said it was the weather; others said prices were getting so high that people were thinking twice about going out for an evening.

At the same time both Meggie and Marie Tempest were offered tremendous openings, Meggie in New York again. They could not both possibly be expected to turn them down. So I would be left with an empty theatre and not much chance of bringing a show in. I had expenses, because the theatre staff and April remained to be paid, but I would have no income. I could have let the theatre to another management, but I desired, passionately, to keep total control of the Albion.

So we closed: Meggie, in triumph, to put together her personal wardrobe for New York and take some singing lessons, and Giles and I to create the next production: *Rendezvous with Destiny*. While Meggie fitted dresses at Molyneux, Giles and I once again embarked on a round of auditions. I had given him and the author freedom with auditions, since this had worked so well with *Maid*.

Theatre discipline teaches you to put personal miseries aside. They are with you still, of course, but you can't think about them all day.

"You're keeping pretty cheerful, considering," observed April.

I recognised the force of "considering," but I ignored it. April was well on the way to becoming an Albion institution. Never mind if what she knew was wrong (only it rarely was); she knew it.

"It's my new hair-style," I said. The style had smooth waves, a little soft fringe, and curled forward on my cheeks.

"Did you know you'd got a club of supporters?" asked April. "Some of the gallery-girls have got together and called themselves the Alice May Club. They dress like you and wear their hair like yours. You'll upset them with that new cut—but they won't take long to copy it. Haven't you noticed?"

"I have seen something," I admitted. "Do they sing a song?"

"No. They chant 'Alice, Alice,' and hand in boxes of chocolates."

"Do they?" I was laughing, which was perhaps what April intended. "And what happens to the chocolates?"

"You always say, 'Oh, give them to stage-door Stan for his children.'"

"And do you?"

"No, Miss May. He's an old bachelor and always has been. I keep them myself."

No wonder she was getting fat. I was getting thinner. As work responsibilities piled up, I ate less and less.

Rendezvous was a difficult play to cast. Set in a school, it called for a large number of young women. There were plenty of young actresses around, since every deb with intellectual hopes went either to the Slade or RADA. But to find the ones who could act and wouldn't take a day off to go to the Eton and Harrow match was difficult. However, Giles and the author, Miles Mortimer, professed themselves happy with their cast choices.

I did not realise then that Giles had succumbed completely to Miles Mortimer's hypnotic charm. I believe he was one of the first authors to fix you with his eye and dangle a gold charm when discussing terms. I've met others since. Nor did I realize that Miles was one of the worst judges of acting ability in the business. As far as young women were concerned, he was a sucker for the well-turned ankle and the well-tuned voice. As a result we lined up some of the best voices and the worst actresses of the time. One of them, a pretty little blonde, fluttered at me that she was a "sort of" cousin of dear Matthew Charlecote's, and thus a sort of cousin to me. She seemed to think it was funny; I ought to have smelled trouble then.

The female star was Sybylla Seldom, who thought merely being a woman in a man's world—which the theatre was then and still can be—was a marketable commodity. She used to madden me, but as Giles said, she had star quality and could throw it across the footlights like confetti.

Unfortunately, Giles reengaged Tim Braby, then at his Marxist-Leninist worst, for the male lead—the role of a young music teacher. Between Tim and Sybylla—who sported a Russian sable coat and a lot of cheek—sparks were bound to fly. I don't know if he actually called her a "capitalist whore" but rumour said he did, just as she is said to have replied, "And don't you wish you could afford me." The result was that, while Tim behaved with his usual impeccable stage manners, Sybylla was as bitchy towards Tim as she could be. She upstaged him frequently, altering her cues, and sometimes ad-libbing altogether, so that he floundered and was reduced to tears.

This understandably upset the author. I dropped in to a rehearsal to hear him and Sybylla. "But darling, that line makes me sound like a lesbian, and I won't say it."

As for our chorus of well-bred school girls, they hardly knew a cue when they heard one. We organized this chaos by appointing a cheerleader for them to follow—a raucous girl called Bryony, who later became a duchess.

Despite these troubles, rehearsals were proceeding quickly.

Then the Lord Chamberlain struck: he had come to the conclusion that certain passages of dialogue suggested moral turpitude of the worst sort. "Told you so," said Sybylla in triumph. The author dug his heels in and wouldn't cut.

So off we sailed—Sybylla, Tim, Giles, Miles Mortimer, and I—to the Lord Chamberlain's office to show him how wrong he was. Meggie sat in the car, smoking and gossiping with a beautiful policeman on duty outside St. James. She had the best time of all of us, I should think.

Tim and Sybylla went through the lines that were under scrutiny. As I watched Sybylla act I realised how unwise I had been to let Giles and Miles have casting control. I should have exercised my own judgement. Miles had mesmerised Giles into accepting Sybylla and now she was deliberately slanting her acting to confirm the Lord Chamberlain's worst fears.

His office was a very masculine affair of dark leather and polished wood against which Sybylla projected suggestions of unnatural sex with gusto. Thank God we hadn't brought the little girls with us, I thought. Without hesitation the Lord Chamberlain ordered the cutting of the whole scene.

We left in silence. Tim was almost in tears; so was Miles. In fact, they were very nearly crying together. "It's my best scene, all my best lines, the reason I took the part. How can you cut it, Miles?" Miles said he couldn't—it took the heart out of his play.

Giles and I looked at each other grimly; we knew the position better. No cuts, no play; no play, no money. It was as simple as that.

"Of *course,* it's Tim's best scene," observed Meggie under her breath. "That's why the bitch is doing it. She can't bear anyone else to have a good bit, especially a man. Say what she does about the lesbian bit, she certainly does hate men."

Such an atmosphere upsets everyone, even those who enjoy chaos. Backstage I had a pair of star-crossed lovers whose quarrels and moods could foul any production if they were given the chance, and Sybylla's tantrums gave them that chance. Their feuds with others in the company, and with the suppliers of wigs, costumes and props were worthy of the Capulets and the Montagues and very nearly as lethal.

Thus maimed by self-inflicted wounds, *Rendezvous* limped to its first night. I stood at the back watching, not daring to relax in a seat. The polite trickle of applause, the steady dribble of people leaving early, the quietness of the critics—all these told me the truth. The reviews next day merely confirmed it. *Rendezvous* wouldn't last the week out if the box-office figures did not lift.

I picked up the rumour in the Domino that the Alby was an *unlucky* theatre. Meggie told me everyone was saying it. "Of course, I tell them it's rubbish. But you know how it is . . ." She shrugged her thin, elegant shoulders wrapped in brown faille from Molyneux and topped with mink. And not a penny of it paid for, either, I thought. "Working at the Alby hasn't done *me* any harm, has it?" she continued. "I'm off to New York to play Sarah Standish in *Postscript*. Beat that if you can."

"Yes. It's a good part, Meggie," I said seriously. "I congratulate you."

"I owe it all to you, love," she said generously. "Tell you what: you ought to go to New York. See what they're doing over there. They say the stock market's rising so fast that money grows like the flowers."

"I'll think about it."

"I hope you'll have showers put in the old place when you can afford it," she said as she rose to go. "I had to have a sponge-down every night in my dressing room. Ah, well, I shall get showers and hot water in New York. Not like that dark brown stuff that comes out of the Alby taps. I had to use oodles of Guerlain to make it bearable. Oh, my America, my new-found land," and she spread out her arms wide in a loving and beautifully theatrical gesture. "Cheer up love—why not be indestructible like me?"

Meanwhile, I was worried about my own finances. Money was very tight. With his excellent intelligence system, Fran got to know and called with an offer of help. "It's your due, anyway."

"What do you mean?"

For an answer he drew a little leather pouch out of his pocket and threw it on the table in front of me. Out of it rolled a ring set with a big, dark sapphire, a diamond brooch and a sapphire and diamond bracelet.

"Maida's. I know the chap Bobby hocked them to, and he sold 'em back to me. He was glad to. He owed me a favour." He pushed them towards me. "They are for you."

"I couldn't touch them. There's blood on them."

"Yes. My blood. Your blood. Come on, Alice, we've all bled for these jewels. You don't have to wear them. Sell them. Use the money."

"For the Albion?"

"If you like."

I was turning them over in my hands. They felt cold and heavy. "And what's *your* price, Fran?"

Meditatively he said, "You've changed. You were such a quiet, shy young girl when you first came to London."

I shrugged. "Oh? And now?"

"And now sometimes you've got such a sharp tongue on you that you could cut bacon with it."

"You mean I've got hard," I said.

"No, not hard. Sophisticated." Still thoughtfully, he said, "And I don't know if I don't like you better that way."

I pushed the jewels back. "I couldn't take these things. You never thought I would. It's just one of your little gambits, Fran."

"Go on, take them. Sell them if you won't wear them."

"The money from them could never be anything but dirty money. Don't you ever feel guilty about Maida's death?"

"No. I don't feel guilty about other people's greed and foolishness, only my own, and I have enough of that to keep me going."

Next day Meggie was taken ill. She must have been getting sick for some time but kept silent because she didn't want to run any risk of losing her chance in New York. Any actress would have done the same.

That afternoon she sent for me to come and see her. I hurried round to find her stretched out in bed with the curtains drawn against the light. Her face was flushed and, while not exactly swollen, had lost its fine contours. When I touched her arm her body seemed oddly rigid.

"Have you had a doctor?" I asked.

"No. Not yet." She moved her head restlessly on the pillow, as if it was uncomfortable. "I thought I'd be better."

I turned to the door. "I'm going to get one."

"I must get to New York."

"Yes, Meg, I know, but you are ill, really ill ... Meggie, you haven't been ... I mean, it isn't that you've ..." I stopped.

"No, you fool." Meggie even managed to sound amused. "If

I'd had an abortion I'd tell you. I'm not stupid. I don't want to die."

On the staircase outside I found her landlady looking anxious, and I sent her for the doctor. When he came—a thin, youngish man—I saw a look of alarm cross his face before professional calm descended.

Within a few minutes she was being carried down the stairs on a stretcher to hospital. Her eyes caught mine in a frantic appeal. "I'll come to see you, Meggie," I said quickly.

That night Meggie became unconscious and died. I never saw her face again. A hospital doctor told me that she had died from amoebic meningitis. When I stared at him in uncomprehending silence, he said, "Very rare, but contracted through infected water. Probably through the nose."

Infected water, I thought, my mind going at once to the Albion and Meggie's "washing all over with a sponge." Sure enough, within the day the theatre was being inspected by health officials. Without much difficulty they traced the source of the infection to the ancient water channel, through which the modern pipes ran. A pipe had been cracked, probably when the bomb fell on the theatre, so that seepage had been possible. Darling Meggie, my bright star, had been killed by the Albion. I grieved for her bitterly. And it was all my fault. I had brought her into the Albion, a theatre she might never have played except for her friendship with me. Guilt for Meggie's death was a heavy burden to bear.

"I don't know why you haven't had other cases," I was told. "You've been lucky."

Luck was a relative term. Yes, I was luckier than Meggie, so tragically dead, but otherwise I was not in luck. The theatre was closed until it received a clean bill of health. And to pay for the reconstruction of the plumbing was going to cost me all I had. I would probably have to borrow from Fran as well.

I had to see Matthew Charlecote to talk. We had, of course, been meeting all this time, but I had always taken care to see that there were other people around so that intimate talk was impossible. Now we met for lunch at the Savoy. Somehow, in London, it seemed impossible for Matthew to think of meeting me except for a meal. He said afterwards he didn't know how you could court a girl without taking her out to something. It was complicated for me by my strong attraction to him. Somehow meeting across a table made it worse.

205

"I'm sorry we're up the creek about money," I said. "I know it's my fault. Or mostly. But I promise I won't ask for a penny of Charlecote money for myself. Not a penny. And you can have a free hand with Causley. I'll leave it all to you. I'll tell the lawyers so."

"Forget all that rubbish," he said. "Alice." And he gave a look at the waiter who at once ceased pouring wine and disappeared. "Darling Alice, I can't let you go like this. I thought we were beginning—Alice, what went wrong?" He took my hand.

Nothing had ever been right. I could hear what he was saying, and there was only one answer. I drew my hand away from his.

"You ran away, Alice. Why?"

"I did run away; I've run away from a lot of things."

"But from me most of all," he said bitterly.

"I ran away from you, yes. But don't take it personally. The trouble is in me, not you. There is something inside me that won't let go. I want it to—I promise I do—but it won't. I have a sort of devil inside me sometimes that reaches out for what it wants."

Diffidently, he said, "Alice, I know a bit about your life in Paris, more than a bit. You were very young. Can't you forgive yourself?"

But, of course, there was more than he knew. I made a little obeisance to the memory of Randolph.

"Life plays some rotten tricks, Matthew," I said. "I hope you never find out how rotten."

"Marry me, Alice."

"I can't marry you, Matthew. *Never*. Honestly. Sadly and definitely, no."

I hadn't been thinking about Fran at all, but after I'd left Matthew, his image rose in my mind and would not go away. And with it came a definite physical ache. I tried to get rid of it by work, but it was no good. This was the first time such a thing had happened to me. Perhaps it did often with other women. It was something I could have asked Meggie. God, I missed her. I can see now that it was my reaction to stress and that I should have got drunk or driven myself madly about the countryside. Instead, I went round to see Francis. I had never called on him unannounced before, and never at the set of rooms he had created for himself above his office. I found him smoking and listening to some music.

"Popular music," I said, as he helped me off with my coat, "does have its appeal."

"I was thinking of you, as a matter of fact."

I sat down, and took the cigarette he offered me. "I've just come from lunching with Matthew. A disaster all round. Everything's a disaster at the moment."

Fran had the sense to keep quiet.

"Fran, you remember you said to give you a chance?" I crushed out my cigarette and looked up at him. "Fran, I'm giving you that chance now."

Relief from pain, exorcism, a simple obliteration of self— what did I want from him? I don't know. But whatever it was, it was too much.

In the dim light of that room Fran used as a bedroom, so sparsely furnished that it didn't seem like a room of his, I buried my face in the pillow.

"That wasn't any good, was it," whispered Fran, "not really good."

"Yes, it was." I took his hand.

"No. No, I know it wasn't. How does it compare—?"

"I haven't had all that much experience, Fran," I said softly.

"No, come to that, you haven't, have you? Your experience has been confined to the dumb and the incompetent. Poor kid, you deserve better than that."

I took his hand and kissed it. I think he was crying. What a monster I was. Worse than Sybylla.

I wondered if Fran would forgive me; I had an idea that men did not forgive you for failures of that sort, and if he did not, what toll would he exact?

Part Three

⚓ Chapter Eleven

If life goes in cycles, I was now right down at the bottom of one. I managed to pay all my debts, but the Albion was dark and I had no immediate prospect of bringing on a show. Worse, it was labelled an unlucky theatre. For the first time in my life I did not look forward to the future.

My bank account was empty. I had a cheque due from the Causley estates shortly. I could have asked for it sooner, but I knew they had troubles themselves, so pride forbade the request. I could also have asked Fran to help, but there were reasons against that too. And in fact we hadn't met lately, for which I didn't blame him. Or I could have gone home to Gran and lived on her for a bit. But the Depression had started to bite and I knew she was battling herself to keep the Ladybrook Grove home afloat. Josie was far away on tour in Australia and about to remarry. As usual, she was no help.

So I decided to go it alone. I used my last shilling on a loaf and decided to stick it out until the Charlecote cheque came. I'd manage without food if I had to. After all, I had my apartment. Perhaps a couple of jubilant letters from Maria and Frederic describing New York and saying they were going on to Hollywood made me even harder on myself.

The first day was easy: it was extremely hot, and it seemed easy and sensible not to eat anything (except for a roll at breakfast). I strolled the streets until the heat drove me inside, and then I crept out again when the sun went down. As the evening came on, the clatter and the hustle quietened down. You could take walks in the streets and look in at other people's lives through open windows and doors. If you passed a pub or restaurant, the doors were pinned back and you could see the people inside, framed like a picture.

The next day I was conscious of hunger: real hunger pains

211

made it hard for me to think of anything else. But I found that if I drank a great deal of water this kept the pain away for a while. I walked and walked that day, so that when night came I should be able to sleep.

I didn't sleep, though. People seemed to be having an argument in the street below. I could hear their voices, on and on, into the night. Finally, they stopped, the night was quiet, and I dozed.

I was brought out of a troubled dream of Meggie by a tremendous flash of lightning, followed by a long rumble of thunder. The storm raged until dawn, to be followed by a heavy but not cooling shower of rain. I opened my window wide, so that the rain splashed through upon me as I lay stretched out on my bed.

The next day my head ached violently, and I felt unsteady. When I picked up a cup to drink some water, I dropped it, and it fell to the ground and shattered. I left the shards there, and drank from the tap. My headache grew worse towards evening, so I went out again to see if a walk would improve it. I felt shaky, but well able to walk. I found myself, I don't know how, wandering down Shaftesbury Avenue in the dark, just as the lights were coming on. Before my dazzled eyes the signs flashing on the theatres formed patterns of electric-light bulbs: blue, ruby, emerald and yellow. I suppose they were words, advertising the name of the play and the stars. But to me they were like a kaleidoscope, constantly making new shapes, brilliant and provocative, like wounds in the sky. The tall buildings behind looked like sombre tombs.

I closed my eyes. My nostrils were assailed by a multitude of smells. Onions frying, sausages, the smell of pickles, and then the excessively sweet smell of the air fresheners used in the cinema on my left, just now opening its doors for the evening house to come out. Suddenly, a gust of hot air shot up from the Tube rumbling underneath through a grille at my feet. I felt sick.

"You all right, miss?" asked a voice. A hand touched my elbow.

I opened my eyes to see a policeman, helmet on the back of his head, truncheon under his arm. "Yes. I was just resting."

"Don't rest in mid-street then, miss. It's dangerous," he said. His tone was kindly.

I took his advice and walked on. Snatches of conversation drifted across to me—"Did you see Jack Buchanan at the Coliseum?" "Oh, that Elsie Janis, what a girl!", and then a voice saying crossly, "I said chocolate cake, not chocolate ice-cream." Chocolate, chocolate, chocolate. Chocolate with onions. The sickness that had been sitting at the pit of my stomach suddenly rose up sourly into my throat and overcame me. I grabbed at a lamppost and vomited as the world spun round me. But since my stomach was empty, I vomited nothing. No one took any notice. The crowds approached me, then divided and walked past on either side. Perhaps they didn't see me. I felt distanced from the noisy world that was rattling on all around me.

London was still a rich city with goods flowing in from all over the Empire. In New York the stock market had collapsed and the Great Depression had begun, but here in the heart of London, such troubles were not yet apparent. I felt ashamed of my poverty in the middle of the abundance.

I went home to bed and spent the next day in sleep. I was roused the next morning by the sound of feet on the stairs below. I didn't open my eyes; I was too tired to bother. The footsteps approached briskly. I knew the tread, but I couldn't remember whose it was. Then a hand touched my shoulder.

"Alice, lass, what's all this?"

I opened my eyes and saw a concerned, kind face. "Dickie! Oh, Dickie!"

"I've been looking for you, love. You haven't been easy to come by. What's been up? Where have you been?"

"I've been walking, I think," I said vaguely.

"For how long?" His voice sounded very far away. "Heave ho, my dear." He had his arms round me and was helping me sit up. "Let's get under way."

I heard myself giggle. "Not so nautical, Dickie. You were never in the navy."

"Yes, I was, dear. In *Anchors Away*," he said, straightfaced. "The old Portsmouth Hippodrome, in 'twenty-two. That's right. Now, sit there and I'll give you a cup of tea.".

I heard him in the kitchen. "I don't know what's been going on here," he shouted, "but I'm just popping out to get some vittles. Let yourself run a bit low, haven't you?" There was a severe note in his voice.

In no time he was back with bread, cheese and ham from the Italian grocer's round the corner. Then he bustled into the kitchen to put on the kettle.

I smelled the ham, rose to my feet and began cramming the food into my mouth, swallowing it without chewing. I heard Dickie swear from the door. He was looking at me in horror. For a moment I stared back, then my stomach gave a heave, and I started to vomit.

I was appalled at myself. "Sorry, Dickie," I managed to say. "Sorry to be so disgusting."

He was sweet to me, calming me and cleaning me up, then sitting me in a chair and making me sip some soup, laced with sherry.

"I won't ask you what's been going on, because I can work it out for myself," he said in a sober voice. "Now you listen to me: don't ever do anything as silly as this again. Whatever excuse you gave yourself for starving—"

"I didn't want to ask for help. It was only a temporary thing," I began.

"Whatever excuse," he said severely, "it was rubbish. You were sick in your mind, that's what it was. Well, that's it. You've been down to the bottom. Perhaps we all have to go there once. I know I did."

"You, Dickie?"

"Yes." He gave me a level look. "When my Elsie died. I took to the bottle. Your Gran got me out of that hole. But once up I didn't go down again. Nor must you. You could have killed yourself."

In a way I *had* been killing myself.

"Don't tell Gran," I whispered. I didn't mind Josie knowing, but not Gran.

Dickie did not answer. His gaze shifted away, and he cleared his throat. "That's it, love," he said. "That's why I came looking for you: your Gran died this morning. Sudden. Heart, it was." Tears were rolling down his cheeks, and he made no attempt to hide them.

Presently he stood up. "This is no good, girl. Get you to bed. And come over and see me in the morning. Things to talk over. I'll get Francis to bring you."

He helped me to my bedroom, and I heard him depart. As I got ready for bed, I heard the quiet murmur of voices. I realised that Francis had been outside all the time. I supposed Dickie had contacted him. With the tact he could sometimes show, Fran had waited outside to see if his help was needed.

The next day he called for me and drove me across the river. He had on a dark suit with a black tie, his face serious. "I was fond of your grandmother. She was good to me when I was a nipper. Saved me from a hiding from the guv'nor many a time. He was a ready man with his hands, was my dad."

I knew he was talking to save me embarrassment. He drove me to the house and left me with some tactful excuse of work.

Dickie Davenport met me at the door of the house in Ladybrook Grove and led me into what had been Gran's front parlour. Without her it already seemed empty of life. Dickie was wearing an apron and carrying a feather duster. He took me in, and sat me down on the big sofa.

"The funeral will be Saturday," he said, his narrow, gentle face looking solemn. "We chose that day so everyone could come. There will be a big turn-out. She was much loved. We'll give her a good show," he said proudly. "Flowers, hearse with plumes, the lot, just what she would have wanted. I know how she liked things done."

"I know you do, Dickie; I'm grateful. Oh, it's rotten that Josie couldn't be here."

There was surprising news. "She's on her way. She was coming home anyway." Then he looked at me. "Your grandmother left Ladybrook Grove to me. I am going to run it just the way she did." He was very serious. "She knew she could trust me. I'm going to retire, so this is my life now. We talked it over." He got up and went over to a bureau, from which he extracted a document and a bank book. "That's her will, and that's her bank book. She had quite a bit, more than I knew. She's left that to you. For the Albion."

"Oh." I looked down at my hands; I was trying to control my tears. "Why not Josie?"

"Well, she's provided for, isn't she, with her new husband? Besides, I reckon, one way or another, she's had her share." He got up. "I'll make a pot of tea. Nothing like a decent cup of Indian when you're down."

"Do I look down, then, Dickie?"

"Absolute bottoms, duck," he said.

"I do feel wretched." I was trying to sort out my emotions. "Oh, I shall miss Gran."

"As we all will. As we all will," Dickie said solemnly.

"But with me, it's that everything is churning up inside me,

215

and a lot of things are coming to the surface, and I don't know if I want to think about them or not. Things I've hardly talked about."

"Want to talk now?"

"Thanks, Dickie, and yes."

I told him the whole story, beginning with my meeting with Randolph in Paris. He listened quietly while I unloaded it all on him. I felt as if a burden of guilt had been lifted. He didn't say much, nor did I expect him to, but at least someone now shared my knowledge.

My cup of tea tasted ten times better afterwards.

"Another cup?" Dickie asked, hand poised above the brown pot. "And as for what you've told me—that's life, love, I shouldn't dig too hard. Leave it be." He started to pour another cup of tea.

"Wait a minute, Dickie—what about the child? Maida's kid. Where is he?"

Dickie looked surprised. "She's left him to you and me: it's up to us, Alice. She knew she could count on us." He sounded proud. "He's very nice. You'll like him. And clever . . . sharp as a needle, that little chap." He tapped my shoulder. "Look, there he is in the garden."

I caught a glimpse of a small figure walking along a path, then I shook my head. "No, no, I don't want to see him."

Dickie put a hand on my shoulders. "Why not, Alice? Why not?"

"I don't know," I said with conviction. "But that's how I feel. And I feel rotten about everything."

"Seems to me you ought to find out why. You'll be off then, I suppose?" I was groping for my bag. "Saturday, then? Get back to work at the old Alby. You'll have a bit of the ready from your Gran and I'll stand in as well if need be."

"Thanks, Dickie," I muttered. "I'll pay you back." He knew I didn't mean money only.

"Open it up again, that's how you can pay us back," he said. "And stop that Francis Hollman turning it into a cinema."

The funeral was as large an occasion as Dickie had predicted. Ten carriages of mourners followed the hearse in addition to the many who made their own way to the ceremony. The church was crowded with faces I knew. Some were faces

216

from the history of the theatre, like Lady Dudley, who had been Gertie Miller. Beside her stood the faded beauty Lily Elsie. Mrs. Patrick Campbell was there and Gerald du Maurier. The Music Hall was represented by Tick Baxter and Gus Whelan, the Froby Sisters, and Boby and Max Winter, the comedy pair. And there were neighbours and friends, as well as family.

Josie, with her new husband, just got there in time. He was a tall man, sun-tanned and quiet. He looked dependable. I thought Josie might be home and dry at last. We did not talk until we were back at Ladybrook Grove.

"Dickie's put on a good show," Josie said, wiping her tears away and looking around her at the spread of food and drinks. "He would, of course. He knows what's right to do." She couldn't resist adding: "Fancy Stella Campbell coming on here. It's the port, I suppose, she always likes her glass."

"You don't mind the house going to Dickie?"

"Not a bit of it. It's what I expected. Besides, she told me: money to you for the Alby, and the house to Dickie to run as she did. She trusted him. 'You've had your bit,' she said to me, and I *had*," admitted Josie honestly. "Besides, I'm on my way to Hollywood. I've had an offer at last. They want the English voice, my agent said. It's the talkies, you see."

She looked towards her husband. He was standing on the edge of the crowd, a little out of things, but perfectly relaxed and happy. "I'm a lucky girl," she said. "Fred's one in a million." Hurriedly she said, "Of course, I loved your father."

"Of course you did, Josie, but he's dead." Suddenly bold, I asked her if she knew the tale about him fathering a son on one of his sisters-in-law. Had she ever heard him say so?

To my surprise she laughed. "Well, he did say so once in the booze, the dear boy. One of his fancies, I thought. But it could have been little Edward's mother. An aristocratic tart, she was, if I do say so. I didn't hold it against him."

I don't suppose she did, either. There was little sexual jealousy in Josie.

Across the room I could see Mrs. Patrick Campbell neatly feeding ham sandwiches to her white Pekingese, Moonbeam. She caught my eye and bowed like a queen. The old duck, I thought, suddenly tender.

"What's up, kid?" asked my mother. "You look peaky."

"I've been pretty run down," I had to admit. "It hasn't turned out as easy to be the little queen of the Albion as I hoped."

"That's the theatre for you," said Josie philosophically. "Down one day, up the next. It's not a dull life, I'll say that for it. Provided you don't weaken."

When everyone had gone, I went to the graveyard to put a bunch of roses on the grave, my own silent tribute. Then I took a tram to the embankment.

I walked along, looking at the Thames, wondering where I could find the courage to start the Albion again.

"Alice."

I turned round quickly. "Matthew! You? Here?"

"I thought you might be here. You've been here a lot lately, haven't you?"

"Yes, I suppose I have." It was true, the river had drawn me to it lately.

"I haven't been following you," he said quickly. "Don't think that. But I have been worried about you. I was at your grandmother's funeral today, but you didn't see me."

"You should have come on to the house," I said. I was breathing quickly.

"No. I couldn't meet you in a crowd. Alice . . ."

"Yes?" I felt suddenly shy.

"I feel as though you've been far away. Almost in another time, another country."

In spite of what he said, he must have been watching me. I found it touching. In Frederic (how far away he seemed now) it would have been irritating, but in Matthew I loved it.

"Come back, Alice," he said.

"I want to." In spite of myself, my voice wavered.

"Come and walk along the river with me."

He put his arm round me and we walked in the moonlight in happy silence.

"I'm going to start up the Albion again," I said suddenly. "I've been out of circulation too long. And now I've got money from Gran as well as what's coming from the Charlecote estate."

He walked me back to the theatre. Outside we kissed. Then he walked briskly away.

"I'm happy," I called after him. "Happy, Matthew." I don't think he heard; I don't think I meant him to.

With the money my grandmother had left me, I paid my debts and had some working capital. The news that Alice May was back in business soon got around. My telephone started ringing almost at once. Francis Hollman was one of the first to ring.

"So you're back on the scene? Three cheers. Well, I have news for you. We are now the best talking picture-house in the West End. We are wired for sound!"

"No cinema here, though, Fran," I said. "I hear you were enquiring from William Grigg. But I won't let you have the Albion just yet."

"Did you hear that?" he asked mildly. "Just enquiring. Negotiating is too strong a word. Just sounding him out about the freehold. But it's still yours."

"And I mean to use it."

"Times are hard, baby. You'll find out," he said, and rang off. There was no embarrassment shown on either side, and nothing was said about anything in the past.

But he was right. The economic slump that had started on Wall Street had now arrived in England and was working its havoc in the theatre. Noel, whom I met briefly in the Double Domino, told me that in his casting for his new show he had been saddened by the names famous in the theatre—former stars and principals—auditioning for crowd parts. With conviction he announced he was therefore having enormous crowds. He always gave old friends a part if he possibly could. As for me, he said, it was my bounden duty to reopen the Albion and provide work for the profession.

With the assistance of money raised by Matthew from a consortium of theatre-loving City friends, I put on a modest revue in tribute to my grandmother. I had begun to see what a lot I owed to her, and how much I had loved her. I used as many of her old friends as I could in the cast.

Realism had set in. I was no longer the new little princess of theatre-land; I had my feet much more firmly on the ground than before my crisis. And as I grew more confident, Matthew and I grew closer and closer to each other. I began to feel easy and giving and loving. One afternoon, some months after my

219

grandmother's death, he telephoned me and asked me to dine with him. I accepted, and in return told him I had tickets for the opening night of the new Coward show at Drury Lane. We would go together.

Seeking a dress to wear, I made my way to Louisa, who greeted me with cries of joy and kisses. "But I've nothing to wear. What have you got to show me, Louisa?"

She clapped her hands. "Follow me."

I went after her to the workrooms at the back where Ellen May was sitting at a large wooden table threading silk through a needle. She looked up, smiled and nodded as we entered. "What is it, Louisa? Hello, Alice. I work here now."

Louisa led me to a rack of some half a dozen dresses: a plain white silk evening dress with a glittering silver fringe, a black dress with a panel of emerald sequins diagonally across the front, a day dress of Kasha wool with a little fur-lined jacket. They all looked beautiful.

"They're models we buy when a lady's done with them," said Louisa confidentially. "It's often done, when things are tight. Why waste these, when you can turn an honest penny? We copy them cheap." She nodded to Ellen. "Ellen's going to cut us a toile, and then I'll get them run up in a workshop I've got sewing for me." She turned to me exultantly. "Gene and I are doing really well. Expanding. Times are bad, but women *will* buy clothes. And our's have style. I see to that." Proudly she added, "I'm an equal partner now with Gene, and I want to put some money into the Albion. It's always been my ambition. Will you let me?"

"I surely will. I'd like to have you and Gene behind me." I was examining the rack of clothes. "These are beautiful, Louisa."

"You can have one. Have the white Molyneux. What suits Gertrude Lawrence, ought to do for you."

Matthew and I met for a quiet dinner, talking in the dreamy way of people who are really saying something quite different underneath. Our hands touched over the wineglasses as he lit my cigarette, and we both knew what the contact meant. I smiled. "Lovely dress," he said.

The first night of *Cavalcade* was an important event. Everyone who was anyone in English society and the English theatre was there. Matthew and I arrived a little late and started to move through the crowd to our seats. The crowds parted and

220

there was Gertrude Lawrence. We were face to face. A look of surprise crossed her face as she took in what I was wearing. I wondered what she was going to say. Her temper was quick and her tongue sharp. But she was also a famous giggler, and this time she simply burst out laughing. I began to laugh too. Matthew looked puzzled; he had no idea why we were both so amused. Later she told me I wore the dress better than she did.

From the moment that the curtain went up on the view of the troopship leaving for the Boer War to the sound of "Goodbye, Dolly Grey," I knew that this was an historic evening in the theatre. At the close of the scene where the honeymoon couple move aside to reveal the lifebelt with the name *Titanic* on it, I found myself gripping Matthew's hand. By the time the curtain came down after the final speech, I was openly weeping:

> Let us couple the Future of England with the Past of England. The glories and victories and triumphs that are over, and the sorrows that are over too. Let's drink to our sons who made part of the pattern and to our hearts that died with them. Let's drink to the spirit of gallantry and courage that made a strange Heaven out of an unbelievable Hell, and let's drink to the hope that one day this country of ours, which we love so much, will find dignity and greatness and peace again.

Noel appeared in front of the curtains and said in a sincerely modest and tentative voice that it was a "pretty exciting thing to be English."

There was a party backstage afterwards, but Matthew and I walked away together to look at the Thames, dotted with craft—here a line of barges, a river steamer; there a tug moving through the dark night. Behind us the City was rosy with light as if there were myriad fires, starting at its heart by Trafalgar Square and spreading outwards. But the Thames was dark quiet. On its banks Matthew formally asked me to marry him.

9 Chapter Twelve

It was too much to expect that my wedding would be like other people's. We were married very quietly in St. Paul's, Covent Garden—the actors' church—in a ceremony attended by a very small family party. Louisa provided my dress of ecru lace, with which I wore a big green hat. No one had wanted a wedding with any publicity since the Mays and the Charlecotes still eyed each other with cautious neutrality. In any case, we had a special reason for quiet. A few days before we were due to be married, the boy Edward had died, and the baronetcy was Matthew's.

We emerged from the church to the sight of a horse-drawn London omnibus loaded with friends from the theatre and music-hall, all cheering and toasting us with champagne. Giles was blowing a horn. Behind him I could see the famous faces of Edna Best and Herbert Marshall, both of whom had become my friends. Surely that august figure alongside them was not Dame May Whitty? I felt as if Queen Mary had come to my wedding.

Movietone News had come to cover the event and they raced along beside us. When the horses took fright and we began a helter-skelter gallop down the street, the cameras filmed us for posterity. It's all there in the archives—me with my hat blowing off in the wind, and Matthew handing me up with a broad grin on his face.

For our wedding trip we went to the South of France. Matthew was still very conventional about such things. In his class you took your bride to the most expensive hotel you could manage, preferably on the Riviera, and gave her a good time.

We had the sunniest balcony overlooking the sea. We breakfasted there and had cocktails there in the evening after swimming and sunbathing. After cocktails came dinner, and dancing. Sometimes we had a flutter at the Casino. One night we won five hundred francs and Matthew bought me a bracelet. It was the only sort of honeymoon he could imagine.

I was Lady Charlecote (although I would not use the name professionally) and proud of it. There was a strong, true depth in my feeling for Matthew. I never doubted I was lucky to be his wife, but I wondered if I was good enough for him.

We swam every day; I had a red and black swimming costume from the shop Schiaparelli had opened in the town. Perhaps it was the constant swimming that made me dream. I swam out of a sea of sleep to find Matthew stroking my hair and trying to calm me. "Poor love, why are you talking and crying in your sleep?"

"Was I?" I was only half-awake. "I always dream when I sleep on my back. I dreamed I was swimming in a sea of fire. But that couldn't be, could it?"

"You're still deep in that dream," he said fondly. "No, of course not. No seas of fire. Not anywhere."

"But I didn't sink; I came through."

"I'm sure you did." Even in the dark I could sense his smile.

On a honeymoon there is only one way such a wakening can end. I remember thinking that he was marvellous, tender and joyful, that only a really good person could bring those qualities to love.

But I went on dreaming about seas of fire.

By the time we returned to London, I had all my plans for the Albion arranged in my mind. It was as if they had been unconsciously forming themselves during this long time of inactivity. But my plans did not develop in the way that might have been expected.

I had seen a gap in the theatre that I was determined to fill. I would take a risk now. I had learned to be braver.

We had moved into the flat at the top of the Albion. It was the sensible place for us to live, since Matthew had given up his bachelor rooms and was often in the north of England looking after the estate at Causley. In fact, for a newly married couple we were apart a good deal. Eventually, I supposed, we would have to find a family house, but that time seemed some way off. I knew that Matthew was worried about the finances of the estate at Causley, even doubtful if the Charlecotes could carry on living there at all. Farming was very depressed at this time in England—rents and profits were very low—and Causley had to be subsidised from other investments.

Francis was one of my very first visitors. He sat himself down on a chair in my office, and adjusted the crease in his trousers. He was, if possible, more dapper than ever and exuded an unmistakable air of quiet prosperity.

"You're Lady Charlecote now," observed Fran. "Not that I bear you any ill will for passing me over. He's ten times the man I am, your Matthew. Well, twice anyway. I give you twice. Except financially, of course." And he shot out a wrist and looked at his heavy gold cuff-links. "I shall be a millionaire before I'm thirty-five. But what does a girl like you care about that. You're in love."

"Yes, it is rather nice to have that side of things settled," I said, absently. "Now I can get on with what I really want to do."

Half-admiringly, Fran said: "My word, you really are a toughie."

"I'd marry you tomorrow, Mr. Hollman," said April. She handed him a cup of coffee.

"I know you would, dear, and I'd have you if I wasn't set on breaking my heart over this creature here. Three lumps, dear. So what are you going to do with yourself, Lady Charlecote, now you and the Albion have slipped from my fingers?"

"I'm going to put into it the money my grandmother left, for a start," I began eagerly.

"I could get you five percent, easy," he said, "maybe more. Why not let me handle it."

I ignored this, which was, indeed, only a routine call for attention from Fran.

"And I'm going to start a Theatre Club here—use the area of the two shops to create the Club room, and sell preferential seats to Club members. Of course, I'll still have two shops, but just little ones. I must go on selling."

"Of course," agreed Fran, with gentle mockery.

"But no longer luxury goods; I'll probaby sell books and editions of plays. Anything connected with the theatre. I might have a little theatre curio shop—you know, Sarah Bernhardt's slippers, Ellen Terry's fan."

"My word," said Fran, repeating himself for once, "you have

224

got things worked out. Don't run so hard you meet yourself coming back, will you?"

"Oh, all this is only the fringe; the real thing is I've noticed that the English will always go to a play that makes them feel intellectual and amused at the same time. Barrie did it at first. They thought he was deep. Shaw did it once he started to make them laugh. Chekhov, too. Once they saw Chekhov was funny, and you didn't have to *believe,* then they came. I'll keep that sort of play going on repertoire ... and the newer writers, O'Neill (not funny, but all that sex, that'll do instead); Samuel Beckett, O'Casey, Odets ..."

"I've never *heard* of some of those names," protested Fran. He waved a hand. "Oy, oy, the money. It'll eat it."

"I'll get it back."

"And who's going to produce, direct and act? You're not going to run a regular company?"

"Yes, I think I am. There's a lot of unemployment in the theatre. I'll get good actors cheap," I said.

"Sometimes you make my blood run cold," said Fran, getting up from his chair. "Those poor actors."

I shrugged. "They'll eat, won't they?"

April said when he'd gone that, although she had offered to marry Francis and probably meant it, she thought that for any deal involving property with him, she would want counsel's opinion and three witnesses before she trusted him.

"I expect you're right," I said absently.

"It's ever so good of Sir Matthew to give you the freedom he does," said April. She knew all about my affairs, of course. No one ever succeeded in keeping anything from April. "Not all men would. He lets you have your own way."

I gave her a bleak look, and she put her head down over her typewriter, murmuring that she was sorry if she'd spoken out of turn. She had, but perhaps it was as well she said what she did, because it alerted me. But it was Dickie Davenport who unwittingly provoked the first explosion between me and Matthew.

My plans for the Albion began to take shape quickly. There was so much unemployment in the theatre that everyone was eager to help. Giles Oliver came forward at once to say it was the sort of project he had always wanted. I knew I could work with him. I got a lot of publicity. The Albion, with its past history and its future hopes, was worth a paragraph or two in most newspapers. Giles and I started to draw up a list of possible ideas. We would create a modern West-End repertory.

"You can always make money out of the British if you amuse them while kidding them they are being intellectual," I said to Giles. "The Albion can't compete in the froth-and-bubble commercial theatres, we just aren't big enough, and we're on the edge of the smart area. Too near Covent Garden! But we can form our own audience and keep it."

"You've got so much self-confidence these days," said Giles. "It must be marriage."

"Maybe. I still miss Meggie, don't you?"

He nodded. "She would never have come in on this, though—it wasn't her idea of theatre life at all. But she would have hovered over us like a beautiful butterfly, occasionally adding colour. Darling Meg." He pushed over a list of names. "These are suggestions for people we approach. I've already sounded them out. And you will notice it includes dressers too. It's very, very important to get good dressers because that's what keeps performers happy. H. M. Tennent's have had a stranglehold on all the best ones, but unemployment is hitting them too, and I know of several first class dressers who are free. We must get them on a long term basis. It makes us fully professional."

"I quite agree. There's one other thing too, Giles. I want a diverse programme. I agree we must start with a first class good, serious play—say the new O'Neill, if we can get it. But later on, for a summer season, say, I want to go back into the history of the Albion and do some productions of Victorian melodramas. Not hammed up, Giles, but played straight. Scholars are beginning to take them seriously now. Social documents and all that. We should play to *that* audience, in that way."

He looked at me with respect. "Where did you get these ideas?"

"I thought of them myself." But that wasn't quite true. At a party given by Matthew's friend Lady Ottoline, I had listened to a pair of literary historians talking—one has to pluck ideas from somewhere—and I thought this one was a winner. Nineteenth-century popular theatre would be a rich field for reaping.

226

"I wonder if we could do a summer run of old-fashioned music hall," said Giles with enthusiasm. "I loved it when I was a kid; I'd love it still. I know a chap at the B.B.C. who's a real enthusiast. We might get them to broadcast it."

"Marvellous publicity," I said.

"Ring up dear old Dickie Davenport—he knows about the old times."

"I haven't seen much of Dickie lately. He's been busy with one sort of thing, and I've been busy with another."

"Like being married," smiled Giles.

"Yes." I know Giles wanted a gossip, but I didn't want to talk about my marriage with anyone. I ought to have seen this as a danger sign.

"Give Dickie a tinkle, dear."

"I will." I was reluctant, and I knew why, but again this was not a subject up for discussion.

On the telephone Dickie sounded bright and cheerful, but that was his professional face. He never let you see what was underneath.

"Hello, Alice. Nice to hear your voice. I was thinking about you. Rather not talk on the telephone. Can I come over?"

"Yes," I said cautiously. "Come to the Albion tomorrow. Midday?"

"I'll be there." He had assumed I was making a friendly family call. Leave it thus. We could talk business later.

"Come on your own," I said.

"Of course." He sounded slightly surprised. "How's Matthew?"

"Splendid, bless him. But in Northumberland. He telephones every night. I'll see you tomorrow then." And I didn't think about it till then.

I spent the rest of the day working with April in the office, only going out to the Double Domino to get some supper. The place was getting seedy; its day was over. I would have to find some other place to eat. I saw several people I knew, and all of them asked me about Maria and Frederic. I could tell them little except that Maria was growing rich in Hollywood and Frederic was writing a book. I felt suddenly irritated and could not finish my meal. I pushed the plate away and lit a cigarette, not enjoying that much either.

I went back to work, reading a pile of play scripts that had started to arrive immediately after the Albion was known to be

227

back in business. I was still reading when I felt a hand on my shoulder.

"Hello."

I swung round. "Matthew. You're back? I wasn't expecting you."

"Yes, you were. Or so I thought," he observed mildly. "We arranged to meet at the Savoy. I waited an hour."

"Oh darling, how awful of me. I forgot." I leaped to my feet, anxious to make amends. "Let's go now."

"No, don't let's bother. I'll eat something upstairs." He didn't sound cross, just tired.

"Come on then, and I'll make you an omelette." I was full of self-reproach. How could I have forgotten? I, who remembered every appointment in my desk diary at the Albion. "I ought to have written it down—about meeting you, I mean."

"Well, I'm glad you didn't. I don't think I want to be written down among your other appointments. 'Meet husband at nine at the Savoy.' No, it's more distinguished not to be written down." He still didn't sound angry, only amused. At least, I thought it was amusement.

In the kitchen I busied myself with eggs, cheese and salad.

"Did you have a rotten time at Causley?"

"Fairly rotten." He broke off a piece of lettuce and ate it. "The money side of things is depressing. Agriculture shows no sign of picking up. Investment income is down. The Charlecote Trust is pretty nearly broke."

"Oh, Matthew." I felt guilty that I was so detached.

"Never mind. We'll pull through; we always do," and he grinned. He must have made a splendid soldier, I suddenly thought, always ready to pack up, move on and fight the next battle. "Don't worry, we won't take the Albion away from you."

I looked up sharply. "No, I know you wouldn't do that." *Couldn't,* I thought.

"The other trustees are kicking up a bit of a fuss. We could raise money on it, you see. But don't worry: I'll win them over."

I went back to my omelette-making in silence.

"Do you want me to mortgage the Albion?" I asked suddenly. "I suppose we could." But it might be dangerous. Francis Hollman would offer a loan in a minute. Matthew knew this.

"Do you want to do that?" He was studying my face.

"No." The answer popped out before I could stop myself. I knew quite clearly that I would not endanger the Albion in any way. "And to Francis least of all."

"The answer's no, then," he said briefly, turning away.

I had delivered a blow, and one that had gone deep. But then, I'd had one too: the Albion was mine, in a way the Causley estates were not. I'd gone through quite a lot to get it. I wanted it. More, it needed me. Without me the Albion might founder, go under as a theatre. Let Fran get his hands on it, it would be a cinema in no time at all. I had to hang on.

I put the omelette on the plate with great care; it seemed important not to break its gentle roundness. I poured some coffee for him and took a cup for myself. As I went past I stroked Matthew's hair, soft and thick. He took my hand and kissed it.

We were happy in our lovemaking that night. It was very private and remote in my eyrie on the top of the Albion. I felt like a princess in her tower, ravished but triumphant. Nevertheless, I woke in the middle of the night from another dream of a burning sea. I dragged myself from bed and went to the window to look down on a dark, quiet London. The city was not burning.

I went back to the bed and sat down on the edge of it, to look down on Matthew sleeping deeply, his dark head buried in a pillow. I touched it fondly; he did not stir. I got into bed and slid down beside him, my bare thigh touching his flank. Matthew had never mentioned Frederic, nor asked any questions. But while we were on our marriage trip, he had sent in Sybil Colefax's minions and had the bedroom redecorated. My bed, my own painted furniture, had gone, and all was new and glossy. Later he told me that all my stuff was in storage and I could have it when I wanted it, but he offered no other explanation. None was really needed. This was his room now.

I turned to him, "Matthew," I said, suddenly urgent. "Matthew, come to me."

We were late rising the next morning. Matthew made some coffee and brought it to me in bed.

"Did you have your fire dream last night?" he asked as he offered me the cup.

"Yes. How did you know?" I sipped the coffee. "This coffee tastes funny."

229

"It's the usual sort from Fortnums. We ought to find a cheaper grocer. You talked about fire when you dropped asleep."

"I thought I'd exorcised it."

"I thought we had too," he said ruefully.

I pushed the coffee away, almost untouched. "I don't think I'll finish it. Somehow it doesn't taste right." I was beginning to dress. "How rotten my face looks this morning." I reached out for rouge and powder. Fortunately, life in the theatre had made me an expert with cosmetics. "There's a new beauty shop opened in Bond Street. I shall get them to do me a completely *new* face. You don't mind, do you?"

"Provided you keep the old one behind it. I've got rather fond of it."

I turned round and reached out to him. "Oh Matthew, you *are* nice."

After a while I said, "You know, I'm going to be terribly late."

"Does it matter?"

"No, no. I have nothing important to do at the Albion this morning."

I thought I heard him say "damn the Albion" under his breath.

We were both about, dressed and more or less in our right minds, when the apartment door bell rang loudly twice.

"Open the door, will you?" I said to Matthew. I was checking the seams on my stockings: they had to be straight. "Who can it be? Not April, she knows never to bother me here."

But Dickie's voice was as loud as his check suit, and I heard it as soon as the door opened. He was talking as he walked into the living room.

"Waited as long as I could downstairs, and then I came on up. Twelve o'clock you said, and twelve I was there." He was looking around. "You've got it nice up here."

Matthew had followed Dickie into the room, and closed the door behind them. Dickie had brought someone with him.

"I thought I told you to come alone," I said through stiff lips.

"I did," said Dickie in surprise.

"You've brought him."

Dickie looked down at the small figure whose hand he was holding. "But he's a *child,*" he protested. "A child doesn't count."

That one does, I thought. It was all I could do not to turn away. But I found myself drawn to the boy. He had big, bright, intelligent eyes and was subjecting me to a searching scrutiny. He had a look of my grandmother about him, but—thank goodness—nothing of his father or of Maida. He looked at me with the face of an intimate stranger.

"Send the boy away, Dickie," I said.

"Pop off, lad," ordered Dickie. "Truck off down to April, she's got some biscuits for you."

Silently the boy took himself off, walking backwards till he got to the door, keeping his eyes on me.

"It's him I want to talk about," said Dickie, "so maybe it's better he's not here. Kids do pick things up and I don't want him to feel not wanted."

"Nice little chap," said Matthew.

"Sharp little nipper. We've got a brainy one there. And that's what I came about: a brain like that needs educatin'. Now your lot have been very good, Mat, my boy. You've helped us with money."

"We owed him that."

"True enough. But he's growing up, and now Mrs. May's gone, it's not right he should live the way he does. I gave you time to get your wedding over, but now I think you should come forward and do your bit, Alice. He needs a woman, that little lad."

"I'm not going to look after him," I said at once.

In a few short words Dickie let me know that he wanted me to take some responsibility for the boy as a human being, and a member of the family. I never heard Dickie swear before, but he did then.

Before I could stop him, Matthew said, "I'll take full responsibility. We'll manage the money side somehow. And his way of life. You needn't bother Alice with it."

I looked at him, wondering what his reason was for acting so quickly: whether he was protecting me, or whether he simply couldn't bear the argument to go on any longer.

Dickie departed happily, having shaken hands with Matthew on what he blithely called a "gentleman's agreement." He *was* a gentleman, Dickie, and so was my husband. I very greatly feared I *wasn't* a lady.

Two issues in our married life had come out into the open: my dislike of Maida's son, and the strength of my feeling for the Albion. Matthew seemed to take both quietly. I had forgotten Lady Ottoline's words about the "violent Charlecotes," or if I remembered them, I thought they only applied to the dead Bobby. But Matthew had been standing with his hands on the back of an antique ladder-back chair, and when he moved away I saw that a slender wooden bar was broken. Snapped in two pieces like a fractured bone. As I looked, a wave of sickness welled up inside me. Matthew looked at me in alarm. "Darling?" he asked.

I rushed past him. When I came back, he was very anxious. "Are you all right, darling?"

"Oh yes. I think I'm going to have a baby. Damn, Damn and Damn. I *can't* have a baby now." And then I caught sight of the look in Matthew's eye. "Don't look at me like that."

Six months later I stood at the back of the Albion looking over a hushed and darkened auditorium as the curtain went up on the new O'Neill, the first play to be presented under my new term of management. Giles paced nervously up and down, rushing out every so often to be sick. "I'm the pregnant one," I muttered, "not you."

I think I would have chosen to be a fragile and delicate mother-to-be, but I remained stoutly healthy. "Strong as horses, all you May women," commended Dickie Davenport. He had been very agreeable to helping put together a vaudeville show for later in the year—"variety" they called it now, and I was negotiating the broadcasting of it by the B.B.C.

Money was very hard to come by, but slowly and patiently I put my jigsaw together, scraping the sixpences and shillings in as I could. My Theatre Club was a great success and a source of money and strength. People paid to join it, paid to buy drinks and food at the bar, and then paid again for theatre tickets. I got a lot of volunteer help (April had organised a sort of demi-Club of her own here), but I had to be careful how I used it because there was so much unemployment in every sphere of the theatre.

Thanks to the Club, Giles was able to launch his first production of an O'Neill play at the Albion and could fuss about details like the set and the costumes, done by Motley, and the orchestrating of the spots and the sight lines. We hoped to persuade the author himself to visit London for the opening.

But while I was slowly climbing up the ladder with the Albion on my back, there was a widening division between me and Matthew, glossed over for the moment by my pregnancy. I could tell that he was increasingly abstracted and concerned, although he said little. Finally he admitted that the problem of what to do with Causley was almost insuperable. He poured it all out to me late one night when I got back from a talk with Giles.

Matthew earned a good income in the City where he was a member of a firm of jobbers on the Exchange. In addition there were various family investments in New Zealand, Australia and Canada: the Charlecotes kept their money strictly in the Anglo-Saxon world. But the depression had slashed the income from these investments. At the same time agriculture had never been so poorly rewarded. Even the big grain producers of the world like America were suffering terribly. It was impossible to make Causley pay without a fresh infusion of capital to buy labour saving equipment, but that in itself would throw the estate workers out of employment.

"And they already earn pathetically little: thirty bob a week," said Matthew. "And a tied cottage. So if they lose their job, they lose their homes as well. Anyway, there's no capital to put in." He did not refer again to Fran's offer of mortgage, but no doubt it was in his mind.

Finally, and reluctantly, he told me that he had decided that the only thing to do was to leave his job in the City, and put all his energies into the Causley estate and the mine. I was very doubtful, but I did not argue. I was staying with the Albion in London; I made that clear. I had dabbled with Causley once, but once was enough. The theatre was my life.

We left it at that; Matthew would devote his life to the welfare of the Northumberland estates and I would stay with the Albion. We would divide our lives between the two. I suspect that Matthew thought I would change my mind once the child was born. I could almost hear his grandmother in the background saying, "My dear, she's pregnant, don't upset her." But the division was emotional as well as physical.

When I told Giles what we were going to do, he raised his eyebrows. "My dear, I hold no brief for the married state, you know I don't. But I hope you realise what a wedge you are driving between you?"

"It's the modern way of living a marriage," I said defiantly.

"Well, I love Matthew, don't think I don't, but he doesn't

233

strike me as at all the sort of man to sit down under that arrangement."

Giles was apprehensive, Fran watchful, and my old friend and adviser Noel was openly amused. "What a splendid source of theatrical material you are in yourself, dear Alice," he said. "I find I make use of you time and time again. The jokes are my own, of course."

I remembered our conversation as I watched the production of Eugene O'Neill burst into life on the stage of the Albion. The audience was a far cry from the smart, bejewelled and befurred people who flocked to the Coward and Novello openings; I was tapping an entirely new world of people with some money to spend—but not too much—intellectually ambitious, and demanding. I even aimed the time the curtain went up at these people from suburban homes. Not for me the chic hour of eight-thirty, with time for dinner at the Ritz first. No, my curtain went up at seven-thirty smartly, and I got them out in time for the last train home. We'd go up at six, if we had to.

I felt the warmth of their response.

"Giles, if you can't see what sort of a success we're on to here, you don't know anything."

Even Giles admitted triumph as we listened to the audience while they filed home. He grasped my hand and pumped it up and down. "You were right. We're home and dry. I feel tremendous. I say, you look pretty peaky."

"It's that bloody baby," I gasped.

"Oh dear, oh dear." Giles started to rush backwards and forwards. "Where's Matthew?"

"In the North. Where did you think?"

"It won't be for ages yet, will it?" said Giles hopefully.

"Quite, quite soon," I said. "It's been on its way since early this morning, but did you think I was missing this opening?"

"Oh, I've got a pain," said Giles. "I think I've invented couvade."

"You should feel it from my side," I gasped.

Louisa came to see me in the hospital, bearing with her a beautiful layette made in her own workrooms. She looked eagerly at the baby in her basket at the bottom of my bed. "What a lovely little girl. Oh, you are lucky, Alice." She was wearing a blue velvet coat trimmed with squirrel and looked pretty, plump and prosperous. "It is so sad that I don't have a child. I

234

pray every day, but nothing happens. We are doing so well in business, too," and she sighed. "Three more shops, but barren. Oh, how I pray."

"It happened to me without praying," I said. Twice, I thought.

Louisa was examining a huge bunch of roses. "Lovely, who are these from?"

"Fran." I wondered if she'd read the note: "To my two beautiful girls."

"What are you going to call her?"

"Matthew wants her called Aldwyn, for some family reason," I said indifferently. "I don't care."

"Don't you love her?" asked Louisa.

"I shall like her all right when she's grown up, I expect, but I don't fancy babies. I shall just have to put up with that stage."

Louisa gave me an odd look. "You ought to get in some practise."

Her words and her look gave me a sudden shock, and when she had gone, I thought: that's just how Josie must have been with me, and I know how it feels to be on the end of it. I wasn't going to have it that way. I *would* be a loving mother.

I crawled to the end of the bed and looked my child in the face. Her hands waved and I put a finger forward; she grabbed it. "O.K., daughter," I said. "This is a bargain. I will be your loving mother."

After the christening Matthew suggested that I leave the Albion to look after itself and bring Aldwyn to Causley to have "a proper life in the country." I said she could have a proper life with me in London, and he disagreed strongly. It was quite a quarrel, but it was I who reacted most violently. Our division had come out into the open.

He returned alone to Causley and we did not speak for a week after that. But all the best marriages have quarrels, and I was not seriously concerned.

Josie sent a telegram conveying fondest love and congratulations, together with the prophesy that Aldwyn would be a lucky baby. She must have been right, because the Albion and all its allied concerns prospered. I was tapping a new and hitherto unsuspected market. We began to attract patrons from far out in the provinces. School teachers, bank clerks, engineers and housewives from Woolwich to Wigan joined the Theatre Club and came regularly to swell the audiences for our plays.

235

We attracted good actors, too, because they were assured of an intelligent, sympathetic reception. God knows we did not pay much, but the actors felt that they were taken seriously. And they were doing their careers good, of course. We launched several notable stars: James Mercury, for one, and Matilda Stott for another. We did not have to look for plays, they came to us, attracted by the excited buzz going around the theatre world about us.

The price of our seats was kept low, and we were greatly helped by the growth of cheap transport. The new Green Line Coaches brought in many of our patrons, and the cheap suburban "Theatre Specials" of the Southern railway added others. We were careful to time our curtains so that everyone got away in comfort. We weren't a fashionable theatre, but we were beginning to be important.

The truth was that Francis Hollman, Eugene and Louisa and I were specimens of the rising new class that was prospering through the Depression. I was selling liberation, Francis was selling dreams, and Gene and Louisa were selling cheap, pretty clothes. Matthew, who was selling cheap food, was doing less well than any of us. But I was able to help him. It was pretty funny, I thought, but the Albion was now subsidising Causley.

Josie arrived on a visit from Hollywood, where she was now permanently settled. "I shan't come back to England for good. I'm well established there and get regular parts. Only character, of course, but it's well paid." Fred had lost what she called "a packet" in the Depression, but Josie was delighted to support him. He'd had a little illness, which left him not quite as strong as he might have been. Josie did not mind this either. "I look well, don't I?" She was painting her lips a delicious red. "This is the outdoor girl look, all sun-tanned and casual. I find it suits me to look casual. Gypsy, they call it. Maria's using it too. We go to the same beautician." She had reported that Maria prospered and that Frederic was still writing his book.

"Suits me, doesn't it?" She put down her lipstick.

"You look marvellous," I said, truthfully.

"I haven't even had my face lifted," she said. "Ever so many do, but not me. I've always had a good skin. Well, she's a beauty, your girl, but got a little paddy on her, hasn't she?"

"She is strong willed," I said. There had been a scene between them, with Aldwyn screaming at her grandmother. It was the gypsy make-up, really, but we couldn't say so.

"You ought to look after her yourself more and not leave her to that nurse too much. I always did."

"No, you didn't. Not to notice."

"I kept you with me as much as I could. You don't hold that against me, do you? I mean not all that old business?"

"You did the best you could, I suppose," I said.

"I did, Alice. I really did," she said earnestly. "I was on my own, you know."

We had always been a matriarchy, not strong on fathers. In a way, I was reproducing the situation with my own daughter.

"It's a nasty old world too, at the moment, isn't it?" asked Josie thoughtfully.

Germany had a new ruler in Herr Hitler and in England we had the Fascists and Sir Oswald Mosley. There had been a scuffle in Albion Walk one day between the Communists and the Fascists when we staged *Green Pastures,* but in general I found politics easy to ignore. Down in Ladybrook Grove things were not quite so healthy, and Dickie said he was thinking of selling.

That year a civil war broke out in Spain that roused thousands of households in Britain.

I was staggered when Matthew said he was going out to Spain to see for himself. "It's not our affair," I said. Other people's lives got broken into, other people's windows broken, but not mine. "It's nothing to do with us."

"I think it's everything to do with us."

"You can't leave us."

"You won't miss me. You haven't missed me for a long time."

"Matthew!" I was really hurt. "Oh come on, Matthew, grow up. The world isn't the Englishman's responsibility anymore. Pax Britannica is dead. Let them get on with their own affairs. The Albion and Causley, that's the real world. Anyway, for us."

"Oh, you're a child sometimes. And a selfish one at that."

I felt as though he was tearing away the success and happiness of all the last few years. There *had* been happiness, days, weeks and months of it, made up of hard working periods for both of us. Occasionally I visited Causley. I came to appreciate the house that represented the other side of my character, the

237

love of permanence and tranquillity. Unluckily I was a May as well, and they have a destructive side to them.

Does a marriage crack all at one time? Matthew did go to Spain. There was no violence that time between us. But when I was alone I gripped the chair which Matthew had once broken and let the wood snap between my hands. I was surprised at my own strength.

When Matthew eventually returned he was more sombre than before and not particularly communicative. Not that I asked questions, but I was very generous about the way I funnelled money from the Albion into Causley. I felt I had to give him what I could in this way because I seemed to fail him in other ways.

Behind me lay restless nights, when Matthew had been away and when I tramped the apartment, lonely and unhappy, bumping into the furniture and pushing it away from me. I broke another chair that way. The nightmare of swimming in a burning sea began again, too.

Within a few days of his return, Matthew had come into my office.

"I've come here on what I suppose you could say was business," he said. "I want you to give this up and come to Causley to live. I'm going into politics, fighting the parliamentary seat there for the Conservative party. There is going to be a by-election. I've been adopted as candidate. I shall need your help."

It was an ultimatum to which I gave no answer then.

Shortly after this, I was dining with Noel and assorted friends at the Savoy. The Savoy was always for high times and pretend high times: this one was pretend. We were both nursing miseries. He had, so I had heard, family troubles.

Noel, calling me his little Queen of the Theatre, told me he was sorry to hear that I had succumbed to the popular malaise of the time and was allowing my private life to interfere with my empire. He had heard from his Court and mine, that I felt divided.

"I would never abdicate," I said.

I think I heard him mutter that we never did, people like us, but that the price went up every bloody time.

Matthew fought his election and won, without much help from me, although his grandmother and Flora did sterling

238

work. I was very proud of him, but I found it hard to say so and his disappointment in me was evident. He showed it in a characteristic way: he refused any future help for the Causley estate. It had always gone against his grain to accept it anyway. Now he shut that door in my face with a bang. He would no longer take as a dole what Albion Enterprises Ltd. could spare.

It was true that in England, anyway, the Great Depression was slowly lifting. Fran and Eugene and Louisa were growing rich. In America, where things were still much tougher, Maria at least was prospering in Hollywood, and when Frederic's book did at last appear it had a surprising success.

Matthew did well, in a quiet way, in the House of Commons. He knew how to win the respect of that masculine forum. He had a particularly unobtrusive but decided way of behaving that went down well in that community. I went to listen to his maiden speech in the dignified, frozen company of his grandmother and Flora. The House of Commons wasn't as good theatre as I had expected: as performers they threw too much away. Nevertheless, I got something out of it—I met an impecunious young M.P. with theatrical ambitions who wrote me a play.

The play did well (although Matthew said the M.P. concerned was only second-rate), but was ultra conservative in tone, so we followed up with *Waiting for Lefty*, and then we did Galsworthy's *Strife* to keep the balance. People began to credit me with launching a "politico" theatre.

"The receipts are good," I said to April. She was in charge of my office arrangements and had secretaries under her now. As I had prospered, so had April. We had gone up in the world together.

"Still rising, and it's summer, too, when we usually take a drop. . . . Mr. Hollman's waiting to see you." She looked at me brightly.

Fran and I had inevitably drifted apart, but the underlying bond was strong and secret. I went eagerly to greet him.

He had come to tell me that he was off on an extended tour to establish a chain of cinemas of his own in Australia and New Zealand.

"But don't worry," he said. "I'll be back before the war starts."

"There's not going to be a war," I said at once.

239

"I saw your husband giving a nursery tea-party in Gunter's last week. Your daughter and that boy of Maida's out to tea together. Nice-looking boy."

I was surprised and showed it. I didn't like the picture they conjured up.

There was a glitter of malice in his eyes. "Good-bye darling, see you when I get back."

This nursery tea-party was the occasion of one of the biggest and noisiest quarrels between Matthew and me, in which I said that I never wanted Aldwyn to meet the boy, and in which Matthew called me stupidly prejudiced and hostile. The truth was that Matthew and I were two people facing each other on opposite sides of a valley, through which a raging torrent was about to burst.

The blow-up came on a warm autumn evening in October. Matthew and I had arranged to go together to the first night of *Dear Octopus* by Dodie Smith. Dame Marie Tempest headed the cast. At the last moment Matthew had telephoned me to say that he would not be coming.

"The crisis, I suppose?"

"Yes," he said briefly. "I'll be in the House. I'll join you halfway through if I can."

No explanations were needed. Rumours of war had been circulating all day. In the theatre the audience was strained, concentrating on the stage with difficulty. Suddenly, between acts one and two, the news flashed around the theatre. Mr. Chamberlain was flying to Munich.

Immediately the mood lightened, the cast caught the clearing of spirit and played to it. At once it was obvious that the play was another huge success for the author. I began to wonder whether I could get Dodie Smith to write a play for the Albion.

Matthew slid into the seat beside me. I reached out and pressed his hand. He smiled. "Isn't the news good?" I said.

He did not answer.

When we got back to the apartment on top of the Albion, I was jubilant. "Let's open a bottle of champagne," I said, throwing my fur wrap on the sofa.

"No."

"No? Oh come on, we must celebrate a little." I turned on the radio. The B.B.C. Dance Orchestra was broadcasting some music.

"Let's dance. Do you like my dress? I treated myself to it from Hartnell." I swirled around to let him see the blue and gold pleated chiffon skirt.

Matthew leaned over and snapped off the radio. I stopped short.

"Matthew! Turn it on again, please."

"No. I want to talk."

"I want not to talk. We only quarrel when we talk. Let's drink some wine, dance and make love; we never quarrel then."

"You must listen to what I am about to say: I'm giving up my seat, leaving the House of Commons."

"What? But you're doing so well."

He ignored this. "I think the Government is quite mad to seek any terms with Herr Hitler. I absolutely disagree."

Angrily I said, "It's like the bloody Spanish Civil War all over again: you take your own line, never mind anyone else."

Again he ignored me. "I'm going back into the army. My old regiment will have me, I expect. There's going to be a war; I want to be ready."

"There's not going to be a war. We're all going to be sensible and get on with our normal lives . . . and as for the army, you're too old."

"I'm not. And I'm going to do it. I just wanted you to know."

"No, Matthew—please," I implored. "Let's have another child—I want that very much. We might have a son. We ought to have a son." To replace the one I killed, to push aside the image of Alexander.

"This is no time for another child, for any child to be born. Shut up, Alice. You're just playing games."

"Well, thank you very much."

Matthew gripped my arm so hard it hurt.

"Shut up, Alice. I told you before. Don't shout."

"Let go of me." I dragged my arm away and his fingernails tore the skin so that it bled. I stared at it, then I slapped his face.

A lamp on the table fell to the ground, dragging a little china ornament with it. I picked it up and threw it at him.

Matthew took one look at me, turned and went out of the room, slamming the door behind him.

I ran to the door, calling out "Come back. You can't go away like that."

He did not come back. I raged round the room, kicking the

furniture, sweeping the clutter of little ornaments off the mantelpiece with an angry gesture. An oval Florentine mirror tumbled down and cracked.

It took some time for my fury to spend itself; then I slumped in a chair and faced the unpalatable truth: I had behaved abominably to someone I loved and respected.

Well, Matthew wouldn't be back. I picked up the mirror and looked at my face. I knew whose daughter I was now all right. What was it Lady Ottoline had said about the Charlecotes being violent men? I had their blood and their violence with it, and it had suddenly erupted in my face. If Randolph Charlecote had still been alive I could have reassured him about my paternity: I was his daughter.

The next day all sorts of rumours began to circulate about Matthew having tried to murder me. This, they said, was why he had gone off to join the army—nothing to do with Chamberlain and Munich at all. I told everyone I could this was rubbish, and tried to set the score right, but all I got was sympathy.

Thus Matthew and I parted, as far as I knew, forever.

♫ Chapter Thirteen

I let myself in by the side door of the Albion and walked slowly up the narrow stairway that led to my own apartment. I opened my front door, noted that April had left a pile of letters for my attention—including a note in her own writing—but that otherwise all was in good order, and went through to the kitchen to make some coffee.

I took the letters with me and flipped through them quickly

to see what they were. No letters from Matthew. They tended to come in batches; the theory of cluster, we called it, and it applied to bombs also. But there *was* an envelope from Aldwyn addressed in careful, cursive style.

When war was declared, Matthew and I made a formal peace between us for the sake of the child. We decided she needed all the stability we could give her. Our marriage was broken, but we kept up a front. All over Europe couples were doing the same thing.

Matthew had gone to India. Although strictly speaking his destination was a secret, a Charlecote was serving in the Indian Civil Service and we had channels of communication open to us. He had been gone for almost a year. I guessed he worried about us. When I had the energy to spare, which was not often, I worried about him. But at the moment it seemed safer to be a soldier in India than a civilian in London.

As I waited for my coffee to drip through, I noticed that there was a faint, gritty layer of dust over everything, which bespoke a bomb not too far away. I hadn't noticed any new gaps in the Strand or Albion Walk as I drove past, but it was getting toward dusk and I was too exhausted to notice much. Travelling was very difficult at the moment, and I had just spent twelve hours in a darkened, crowded train with no seat from Exeter to Reading. A young soldier had finally offered me his kitbag for a rest. We had spent the rest of the journey smoking and talking. He was philosophical about the war.

"It's got to be, I reckon. We've got to beat Hitler. I feel as though he's been there, a bloody nuisance, all the time I was growing up, and we've got to get rid of him. I just want to get on with it and get it over."

"I never thought about it until I had to," I had admitted.

"Oh, I did. We did up in Brummy—that's where I come from. We make guns there, you see, and so we always know before anyone else what's coming. Plenty didn't believe it. Can't touch us, they'd say. But I grew up believing in it." He was about twenty. "And I knew I'd have to fight. Didn't want to, but would have to." Not like my father's generation, I thought, who had gone into it like knights riding into battle. This young man was matter-of-fact and without illusions. "It'll take some doing though. We'll have to have the Americans in, I reckon. Wonder if we'll get an invasion?"

We were just then coming into Paddington Station, and

243

through the train windows criss-crossed with brown strips of paper against flying glass, I could see people emerging out of a shelter, followed by an air raid warden taking off his helmet and slinging it over his shoulder while he wiped his forehead.

"There must have been an alert," I said. "I didn't hear the warning, did you?"

He shook his head. "Wouldn't in the train." He stubbed out his cigarette very carefully before saying, "Wouldn't like to come dancing tonight? I'm a better dancer than I look, and I can tell you're nimble on your feet. There's always a good dance at the Troc."

I wanted to make my refusal easy for him to take. "Sorry, I'm meeting my husband on his leave—but I tell you what . . ." I looked in my purse, found a card and scribbled a note on it. "You go to the Albion Club, right next to the Albion Theatre in Albion Walk. They have a Servicemen's dance every night, and you'll find a dancing partner there far better than I could be." And more your own age, too, I thought.

He had looked pleased, and pocketed the card. We parted friends.

I poured the coffee, made myself a sandwich. April had shopped for my rations while I was away, added some home-grown tomatoes and some of her own apple jelly, and left it on the kitchen table for me.

The coffee restored me to something more like cheerfulness. I had been on an exhausting Entertainments National Service Association tour of the West of England, ending up in Plymouth. I had taken a little group of actors and performers from the Albion on a circuit of some dozen one night stands at camps and garrison towns, with servicemen and women, soldiers, airmen, and, in Plymouth, the navy as tough but receptive audiences. That old stager Dickie Davenport had been the main prop of my little band.

"Ducks," he said to all those of faint heart, which had included me, "no audience can be worse than Liverpool on a bad night, and no lodgings worse than a Blackpool boardinghouse in a wet winter, and as for travelling, well, this is comfort to some Sunday calls I've had."

Thus bullied and cheered by Dickie I had taken my troupe of dancers, singers and actors on with some success. We had billed ourselves as "The Albion Walkers" and based the performance on old-style variety, with a short melodrama in the

244

middle. *Lady Audley's Secret* went well, as did *Maria Marten and the Murder in the Red Barn.*

Darling old Dickie, I thought. He was a great cheerer-up. We had become much closer lately, and he quite often stayed in the apartment in the Albion when he wasn't working. He had neither retired from the stage nor sold the house in Ladybrook Grove, but the house had been bombed in the very first raid on the London docks and was, at present, uninhabitable, except by a few determined cave dwellers who clung on in the basement. Ellen May was there with her cat. "Moggie will not leave what has been his home for fifteen years, so I cannot. Hitler cannot bomb *us* out." Her employers, Eugene and Louisa, had not been bombed, but had prudently removed their workrooms to Oxford, while keeping the Soho head office going. The coffee I was drinking came from a shop near Louisa's office.

In the bombing of Ladybrook Grove, Wally Cook, air raid warden, had performed bravely, rescuing Ellen and her cat and as many personal possessions from the house as could be salvaged. It just showed you could never judge people.

I now had strength to open my letters, wondering as I did so how my young soldier friend was getting on in the Albion Club. I read Aldwyn's first. She was living at Causley with Flora and her great-grandmother, who was now very old but still indomitable. "Darling Mamma," she wrote, "I am learning to keep bees, this is my war work. I am growing food for Britain; that is, the bees do the work, really, but I help Flora look after them. Flora got stung yesterday, but I did not because I wore a mask. I tell the bees all the news. Did you know you must tell the bees everything? Then they carry the messages when they fly out, so Great-Grandmamma says."

I raised my head from the letter, blinking away tears. The sight of the eager syllables pouring across the page reminded me vividly of the writer herself. I missed Aldwyn passionately, but of course it was impossible for her to be in London now with its air raids and the threat of imminent invasion.

Then I opened April's note, and the impact was like a kick. April wrote, "This cable came over the telephone from India and I took it down. The message is: PLEASE BRING ALDWYN AND JOIN ME IN INDIA. PASSAGE BOOKED ON 'ORIENT STAR,' P. & O. LINE. CHECK SAILING DATE LONDON OFFICE. WILL MEET AT BOMBAY. IMPERATIVE GET OUT BEFORE INVASION. URGE YOU TO ACCEPT. MATTHEW."

245

I didn't bother with the rest of my letters. I put Matthew's message on my desk and started to pace the room. The telegram changed everything, stirring up emotions that had been buried.

"I don't want Aldwyn to live through a war with parents at loggerheads," Matthew had said at the beginning of the war. "We'll keep up a show for her. Such protection that being married to me can give you in what I suspect is going to be a terrifying time, you shall have. When it is over, if any of us are still alive, we can divorce." I had thought that was the end of my marriage to him.

He had a bleaker picture of the future than I had. I remained blindly and obstinately optimistic, even when the war had begun, through the period of the "phony" war, and through the terrible spring when the Low Countries were invaded and the British Expeditionary Force fell back upon Dunkirk. Inside me there was still a little voice that said it was going to be all right. My optimism had enabled me to refuse Josie's invitation to join her in Hollywood. I could have sent Aldwyn off on her own—many children were being evacuated to the United States and Canada—but to me that seemed like running away. I wouldn't go myself, nor would I send Aldwyn. Instead she went north to Causley. Since then, with invasion looking likely, I'd asked myself about how much risk I could let her run.

I had stayed in London with the Albion Theatre. Matthew had once written me that the Albion was my only love anyway. Not true, I thought. But I was beginning to realise how much I loved Matthew, probably more than he loved me. I seemed to be best at loving in absence. In my lowest moments, I thought I was even better at killing love in those who loved me: I had done so with Frederic, probably with Fran, and now again with Matthew. All of them had started off by loving me, I was sure of it, but I hadn't held them. What was wrong with me?

I couldn't answer that question, so I had thrown myself into work designed to get the Albion successfully through the war. I had admitted my failure on one front, but I was absolutely determined to win a victory on another. Briskly I organised the Albion for war, and brought in the sort of shows that suited my wartime audience, shows that were astringent in tone but in no way defeatist. I set up a Club for servicemen in the old Albion Theatre Club, which was languishing.

I picked up April's note and transcript and read it again. Then I saw that it was dated five days ago. For four days Matthew's urgent request had waited for me here while I had been travelling. Perhaps he had already given me up or changed his mind.

The pain this thought gave was a revelation. Is that what I really wanted after all? Just to rejoin Matthew? Not to need the Albion theatre? How time brings its revenges.

I washed the cup and saucer I had used for my coffee and gave the plate a run under the tap. Then I went to unpack and get ready for bed. These mundane, everyday tasks soothed me a little, and reminded me that tomorrow I could act.

I was half asleep when the telephone rang; I reached for it across the bed, my heart banging. We all knew, in those days, that the call in the middle of the night could only be bad news. All across Europe the summons in the small hours was feared.

"Hello?" I said fiercely. Nervousness always made me sound gruff and intense. Women are cursed with their voices, I think; we always go high and shrill in tense moments, or gruff and hostile.

Far away, as if his voice was projected through space, I heard Matthew. "Is that you, Alice?" He sounded fully as cross as I. "Where the devil have you been and why didn't you answer my cable?"

"Government tour," I gasped, a giant hand squeezing my chest so that I was breathless.

"What? I can't hear. Speak up. Have you any idea of the pull I had to exert to get this call put through?"

"I was away," I said, getting my voice under control. "Where are you speaking from? Are you in India?"

"Of course I am. Don't waste time asking damned silly questions."

You might have thought we were quarrelling, but I knew we were making up, and my heart sang.

"Just get on that bloody boat."

I cleared my throat, "Yes, darling."

There was a silence. "Oh, Alice," I heard him say, "do just get out here."

His voice sounded faint and distant, disappearing with every syllable. Desperately I shouted, "Don't go away. I want to go on talking."

The line went quiet except for a faint hum. I went on talking frantically into the hum until the operator broke in to say that the connection was broken and could not be restored. The call was over.

"Oh Matthew, did you hear anything of that? Any word of what I said?" I said aloud, tears running down my face.

An airplane droned across the sky. There was the crackle of anti-aircraft fire, and after that the wail of a distant siren, then a nearer one, and finally our own horror down in the Strand joined in.

In general, I was not at all brave about the raids, and I hated the cry of the bombs as they fell even more than the solid thump with which they landed. People said you never heard the one that hit you. But tonight I was in a trance. I was utterly confident that I would survive to be with Matthew. I closed my eyes to sleep.

In the morning I telephoned old Lady Charlecote, told her of my plans, and asked her to get Aldwyn prepared. Could she herself, or Flora, bring the child to London in time for the sailing? If not, I would make arrangements. She was bleak but cooperative.

Then I went down to break the news to April.

"I knew you'd go," she said philosophically. "No surprise to me. And good luck to you. Hitler might come any minute, we all know that. What will you do about the Albion?"

"I don't know yet."

"Dickie and I can keep it ticking over. For a bit, anyway. And if we're invaded, there won't be anything to keep up, will there?"

"I hate clearing out."

She was decisive. "No, you're right to go. You've got the kid to think of. Besides . . . you've missed him, haven't you?"

April and I did not go in for confidential talks, but we knew each other inside out.

"Thanks, April," I said. "It's decent of you."

She reached out a hand for the telephone. "I'll check all the details of your sailing date. You'll have plenty to do coping with all this lot," and she nodded towards the theatre. "And clothes—you'll need hot weather clothes for India."

Clothes had gone on ration earlier that summer, but I knew Louisa would see me through. Tears came into her eyes when I told her I was going, but she helped me select a wardrobe with her usual enthusiasm.

"They are all samples, not soiled, but they have been shown, so I can let you have them quite legally on fewer coupons. What a mercy you have such a perfect figure. Here, take this blue cotton to the window. That's prewar quality, we shan't get that easily again. And this dress of French silk . . . take it."

Together we chose clothes as if they were for a trousseau— not for a woman fleeing from a war zone, about to leave behind her friends in what might become occupied territory. But all over England people were behaving in the same almost matter-of-fact way.

In the evening I telephoned Causley to see how Aldwyn was taking it all.

Flora spoke to me first. "Oh, I'm so glad you're going, Alice. Just hang on, I'll get Aldwyn for you. She's terribly excited. Aldwyn, it's your mother."

An alert, enthusiastic voice chirruped across the line. "Oh, isn't it good, Mummy. Oh, I'm so pleased. To see Daddy again. And India, too. Oh, I am looking forward to it. Annie-in-the-village says there'll be submarines, but I don't mind that."

"Oh, the ship will be looked after. We'll have an escort from the navy."

"You *do* sound happy, Mummy." She seemed surprised, which made me wonder how I had sounded in the past.

"Oh I am, love, I am." And I was. Wildly, unreasonably, unpredictably happy.

April had confirmed that we had bookings on the *Orient Star.* The precise date of sailing was not announced; we had to be ready on board at a required time, and that was all we knew. "You'll just slip out in the blackout when the tide is right," said April. "You won't be alone, anyway. Quite a few parties of mothers and children going off. Yours will be one of the last ships out, I guess."

Flora agreed to bring Aldwyn to the port of embarkation and meet me there, so that the child need not come to bomb-torn London. In a slightly embarrassed way, she asked me if I could do a task for her in return: would I take Alexander to see his opthalmologist in London? He would travel up from his school by train, and I could take him to the appointment. Of course, he was a big fellow by now and could have done it

249

beautifully on his own, would have preferred to, but in wartime the school insisted.

Naturally I agreed, although I had not seen Maida's son since that day when Dickie had brought him in to the Albion. His eyes had looked sharp enough then. Of course, there might be nothing wrong with him, so Flora said, but one must make sure. He was so very musical, she added inconsequentially. But then, both his parents were.

The last week before we were due to sail was busy, but I duly met the boy's train at Waterloo. He was as tall as I was now, broad-shouldered and very good looking. If he remembered me, he did not show it, remarking cheerfully that the school "quack" thought he should have his eyes checked, but that he personally thought it a good device for a day off and that "M'dame" had provided jolly good sandwiches as a picnic lunch. Until I heard him talk I had not realised how firmly he had been integrated into the Charlecote family. He spoke of them all with easy intimacy and mentioned Aldwyn with the friendly patronage of an elder brother.

"I can stay to tea and then get the eight o'clock train to Windsor," he announced.

"It'll be dark then."

He ignored this, with the scorn of someone who, if the war demanded it, would fight himself.

"Flora says you're very musical."

He laughed. "Flora only says that because she's all but tone deaf herself. Now, I tell you who *is* musical, and that's Aldwyn: got a regular ear, that little kid. I'm glad you're getting her out. All civilians who can leave ought to go."

"And you?" I asked.

"I expect to be doing some fighting. I can handle a gun."

Of course, I thought, he's a Charlecote.

The hospital where he had his appointment was the one where Frederic had been nursed, and it called up memories despite its wartime face, its heavily protected windows and the sandbags at the door.

Alexander was soon out of his appointment with the report that there was not much wrong after all. We returned to my apartment for tea, and I was just getting ready to take him to the train when the siren went. We had been lucky lately; the Luftwaffe had been treating us lightly. Anyway, I was still invulnerable. The spell of Matthew's telephone call had not yet worn off.

"We'll wait for a minute and see," I said to Alexander.

Suddenly in the silence I could hear the sound of many planes, low in the sky and very steady. It was a horrible sound, rich in menace.

"We're in for a pasting," said the boy. He sounded excited.

"I don't suppose it will be much," I said, without believing it. "We'll wait for a lull and then get you to the station."

No lull came. I realised we were in for a bad night. There was no point in trying to get Alexander to Waterloo Station. Bombs were already falling; I could hear the dull thud, quite unlike the heavy rumble of anti-aircraft guns.

"Like to see the show?" I asked, as casually as I could. "It'll be starting soon. Don't know how much of an audience we'll get, but the performers will be there." I said it proudly. "Let's go down then?"

I led Alexander to the stage box. The first act, a warm-up, consisted of two popular singers, supported by some high kicking dancers. It was cheerful, colourful and noisy—a great help during a raid. As we sat down, I assessed the audience, mostly servicemen and their girls. I was always surprised at the number we got in, air raids or not. The roaring songs were succeeded by a comic scene about evacuees and got some good laughs. After the comedy, romance in a blue limelight got its turn with a crooner and trio of girl dancers in feather skirts. Rather poor, I thought, but the audience liked it and joined in.

In a quiet moment I heard the unmistakable whine of a bomb and the crack as it hit the ground. The building shook. The audience went very quiet. The first of a stick of bombs, I thought, and very close. Two more to come. I caught the eye of the comedian. He stepped forward, motioned to the conductor of the orchestra, held out his arms to the audience and led them into a thundering chorus, which obscured the next two bombs. The building shook again, but we were not hit. Afterwards the comedian called for volunteers to come onstage and sing with him. I was proud of the Albion then. It was part of my life which I was loath to leave behind even for Matthew.

In one of the raid's quieter moments I went onstage to announce that the show would be ending now, but that the theatre would remain open, so that anyone who wanted to stay on

251

for shelter would be welcome. They gave me a tremendous hand.

I looked at the boy; he was asleep. I touched his shoulder. "Let's go back upstairs. We might be able to go to bed."

As we walked in my sitting-room, I could hear the steady drone of bombers above. A new wave of attack was about to begin. I looked up at the ceiling. On the top floor of the Albion we were unprotected. Directly above us was a small flat area of roof where I had once thought of making a Venetian garden. Access was through a small door by the kitchen.

"We'll play cards," I said, "while we wait."

I pulled up a small table and took out a pack of cards.

The first bombs sounded several miles away. We played a hand or two of whist. I don't remember who won—I expect he did—then I heard a plane so close that it seemed to be flying level with the top of the Albion. One bomb came down with that sinister scream I knew so well; the Albion shook. Then there was another bomb, even closer.

"We'd better get downstairs," I said. "It's silly being up here."

"Right." He didn't make any fuss, but calmly collected the cards and picked up his overcoat.

I turned out the light, picked up my flashlight, and held the door open. We were standing in the dark at the end of the stairwell when a strong flash of blue-white light seared across my eyes. I stared right into it, wondering if I would be blinded but was unable to close my eyes. I hardly heard the noise that must have followed.

I remember the Albion shaking and trembling around me, and my own hand reaching out to grab the boy's arm. He did not make a sound. Then there was a smell of explosive and a dusty exhalation, as if the very building itself had exuded its waste.

It was quiet for a while. Then came the sound of tinkling glass and the drone of another bomber overhead.

"Is the building moving?" I whispered, my voice shaking.

His was quite calm. "No. It wasn't a direct hit. Close, though."

I was terrified now; my sense of safety had evaporated. "We must get down the stairs."

"No, wait. Look." He pointed towards the skylight through

252

which came a red glow. "I think they must have dropped some fire bombs. We'll have to put them out."

"I can't. I can't!" I was shaking.

"Yes, come on. Have you got a stirrup-pump?"

"There's one in the kitchen, with a bucket."

He dragged me to my feet. I hadn't realised I was crouching on the floor, and the action brought me to myself. He got the bucket. I went ahead and pulled open the skylight and scrambled through.

A fire bomb had fallen on the roof, failed to penetrate it, but had ignited a wooden cupola with a weather-vane that crowned the roof of the theatre. Another fire had started on the far side of the roof, but was much smaller.

All around me, from this vantage point, I could see flames and away to the east there was a richer glow of a big fire. In the streets below I heard the arrival of ambulances and fire engines. I thought the bomb that had shaken us had dropped in the corner where the pub stood. I wondered how many people had been in there and how many had been friends of mine. Our stage doorman often took a drink there, as did Minnie and Bea, two of the dressers.

Alexander had the water ready for me. I inserted the pump and pushed it up and down while he directed the thin stream of water at our fire. I was hindering more than I was helping, but I couldn't stop shaking. A tongue of fire spurted out, licking at me hungrily; I brushed sparks from my skirt. I felt my hands sting and burn. Alexander's face was covered with black soot. A bomb came whistling past, landing not far away. It seemed a long while, but was probably only minutes before the flames collapsed into a red glow and then to blackness. Then we turned our attention to the second fire. All the time the sound of the fire engines and the noise of ambulances floated up from the street below, while anti-aircraft fire and bombs and searchlights rent open the evening sky.

I had steadied now. Working as a team, we put out the second fire with some speed. For a minute I leaned against the railing. The Albion seemed to be an island of darkness floating in a sea of noise and fire. I remembered my dream of swimming in such a sea.

"We must get down," I said, praying that the staircase was not blocked. We really had no way of knowing if any damage

253

had been done to the theatre itself. In my dream I had survived, and I wished to do so now. "It's madness to stay up here."

Alexander was standing close by me. Neither of us moved but at the same moment we both heard the gentle, sinister slither of someone or something else up there with us on the roof.

"Look," said Alexander. His voice was very quiet.

I turned to where he pointed. Draped across the cupola was a large parachute, caught in the weathervane. Suspended from it, swaying gently on the wind, was a long, dark, metal object.

"It's a land mine," I said.

The mine was between us and the skylight which was our route of escape from the roof. I started to tremble uncontrollably.

"Come on," said Alexander. "I think we ought to go down now." He sounded anxious.

"They explode on contact," I said. "Land mines explode on contact."

"This one hasn't," he said.

"I can't pass it. The vibrations might set it off."

"We've got to risk it." I could see him eyeing me apprehensively.

"I can't, I tell you; I can't move." And it was true: I could not control my legs. I could order them to move with my mind, but they did not respond.

Alexander put his arm round my shoulder. "Come on," he coaxed. "Move. We'll go past very slowly. We must."

I shook my head. "No, I can't. Can't."

I sank to my knees. The boy stood for a minute, then he dropped down beside me. "Good idea," he said, "we'll do it crawling."

Hysteria took over and I began to laugh. Softly at first, and then loudly. "On our knees, on our knees to the bomb. What a way to go."

With great deliberation Alexander hit my face. Because I was turning it towards him at the time, the blow hit me with more force than perhaps he intended. I cried out in pain; blood began to run from my nose. Crying and bleeding, with Alexander pushing me, I crawled towards the skylight. I think Alexander carried me the last part, but I can't be sure.

I remember stumbling down the staircase and out into the street, into the arms of an air raid warden, who said, "My God, what got you? I thought the Albion was all right."

Suddenly, a great white flash came from above, and the roof split apart. We had been that close to death.

After getting my hands dressed at a first-aid station, we spent the night at the Savoy, which nobly took us in—grubby and without even a toothbrush between us—and made us comfortable. I recall Alexander eating a large supper before going to bed. I regained enough self-command to telephone his housemaster, who sounded remote and calm. "He's a sensible lad. Send him back in the morning."

I lay in bed, unsleeping. I had never felt so passionately possessive about the Albion, not even in my early days. I saw it now, and all the theatres that clustered in the neighbourhood, as part of that great English carnival that went back through Irving and Garrick, to the travelling players of Shakespeare's time, and beyond to the mummers of mediaeval England. It had to survive. And I felt wretched that I was going to leave it all behind, although I wanted ardently to be with Matthew. I was torn in two directions. Whatever I did now, one part of me was going to be destroyed.

Nor did I feel any better about my relationship with Alexander. I recognised that he had inherited all the good qualities of his parents and none of their bad ones. I acknowledged that he was a handsome, clever, resourceful, brave boy. But I couldn't like him. And now he had seen me at my worst, a worst I had hardly known I possessed; he had seen me as a beaten coward. Alexander had saved me. No, it was too much. I didn't like him, and I don't think he liked me. I had a black eye to prove it.

The next day he returned to school and I prepared to join Matthew. But shortly before we were due to sail, a liner full of escaping mothers and children was torpedoed and most of the passengers were drowned. The government cancelled all such sailings. The gods had taken up the dice and made their throw. I was to stay with my theatre to the end.

For a good many weeks I was miserable, but as the autumn and then winter of the Blitz rolled on, I found my life had taken up a new pattern. In my small way I was mirroring what was happening to the whole nation. A year and more passed. The Albion was repaired, bombed again and repaired again.

Nearly all the time I kept a show of sorts playing—sometimes serious and sometimes frivolous.

It was a way of life that satisfied me without making me particularly happy. I was contributing to the war effort, and I was working for the Albion. My days were full, but I wasn't really living.

I did as much tour work as I could pack in, taking troupes to the most lonely and isolated coastal defence stations as well as to the big training areas. I organised my Servicemen's Club in the Albion on a proper professional footing (no small task in itself), even while I kept the curtain up at the Albion. When the Americans arrived I worked even harder.

During the first winter of the bombing I worked one night a week in a hospital as well. The hospital was the one to which I had taken Alexander and with which I had an old acquaintance. The tasks I performed there were humdrum and modest—to free more skilled hands for better work—but I saw enough of blood and dying to feel far away from the girl who had watched over Frederic's unconscious body and flinched from the sights of the hospital. It had taken a war to make me grow up, but I conceded that it had been so.

On top of all this I, with the rest of the adult population, did a regular fire watching stint at the Alby. We took turns: I was usually on with Marie, the dresser, and an elderly scene-shifter called Richards, and we got on fine. Marie made the best cup of tea in the business. When nights were quiet we slept in camp beds in my office, but when there was a raid we went up to the Albion roof to keep a look-out.

The Albion stood higher than most of the buildings in its neighbourhood and was thus a splendid vantage point for other fire-watching groups. Fran, taking his turn with the rest, was in one of these groups. We encountered each other regularly and began meeting for supper or drinks as we had done in the past. It was natural, I suppose, that we should take up our old friendly ways where we had left off. Fran slowly moved closer and closer to me.

My first letter from Matthew after the blow was full of the same sense of disappointment that I felt myself. I answered, but his reply seemed to put a distance between us again. I don't know what went wrong. Maybe my own letter did not convey my grief. Or perhaps Matthew met someone else just then and fell in love. The idea did occur to me as an explanation and I think I understood how a man far away in another country might need the protection of a present love. Gradually his letters dwindled until I hardly heard at all.

Fortunately for me, perhaps, the strains and fears of war dampened any sexual desires on my part. Only slowly, as time passed and the war position stabilised, did my body come alive again. There were no perfumes to buy, and hardly any cosmetics, but I recognised my reawakening when I bought a new dress from Louisa. It was prewar cotton, pretty and utterly feminine, miles away in style from the utility clothing we were all now wearing and from the uniforms that Louisa and Gene were, with much profit, manufacturing.

She helped me slip the dress over my head. "Lovely," she said. "Going anywhere special?"

"No," I sighed. "Nowhere at all. The Alby tonight, fire-watching tomorrow."

Once the heavy raids had stopped, my services were no longer needed at the hospital. And, of course, with the British Isles one great armed camp of British, Imperial and American troops training for battles few of them had as yet seen, there were no military casualties. In the air force, the losses were tragically high, but not many came back to need nursing.

"I shall wear the dress, though. I'll keep it on."

"Oh do, darling. You look lovely."

So I went back to the Albion wearing the dress and delighting in it, thinking I might telephone Fran. I was so very fond of him, and I was a fruit ripe to fall. But I was not to fall at Fran's feet. "Always the bridesmaid and never the bride," he commented with wry self-mockery later on.

When I got back to the outer office April met me. "You've got a visitor." She nodded towards my inner office. "He's in there." She looked amused.

"He?" I started to move through to my own room.

"Oh yes, it's definitely a he." No doubt about her amusement.

I flung open the door.

"Hi," said a voice, low, friendly, indubitably masculine.

He was taller than I, but not really very tall for a man. Fair haired and sun-tanned. Hardly anyone was sun-tanned in England then; we were all pale grey with the war. He was wearing an American army officer's uniform. He had a letter of introduction from Josie, who said he was "a darling" and the son of a very great friend of hers and would I look after him. Never had I seen anyone who needed less looking after.

"Josie knows my father, Ed de Carrière. She said to look you up."

"Oh yes . . . I remember." I smiled. "He has a house next to Josie's with a swimming pool."

"I'm an actor, too. Or I am when Uncle Sam allows."

I shan't give his professional name because it came to be very famous and because for private and personal reasons I always called him Sam, just as he always called me Lennie. Private jokes, private memories. He was also younger than I.

"This is a fine theatre you've got here."

"Yes." I smiled briefly. "I love it."

"Difficult to run in wartime, I'd guess."

"We're prospering. Packed audiences. People are buying books and going to the theatre. There isn't much else for them to spend their money on. Of course, tastes have changed. They want to be amused, but I take that into account."

"Yes, Josie said you were a good businesswoman."

I laughed. Compared with Josie I was. At least I hung onto things.

His eyes were amused. Later on, he told me that what Josie had really said was that she was worried about me and wanted him to find out how I was. He never told me what he reported back, but I imagine now he was selective on what he told her. Josie got an edited version.

I knew now why I was wearing my pretty new dress. We went out to dinner and then went dancing because that is what soldiers on leave are supposed to do. Then we went back to the Albion apartment to play music and talk about the sadnesses of war.

"I have an old friend in Paris who is dying." Noel had come home from Paris and told me that Paul Poiret had Parkinson's disease, but was not giving in.

He reached over and turned the gramophone off. "I have twenty-eight days before I am incarcerated in a training camp. I thought I was trained, but apparently we all have to learn how to cross the Channel. And when we have learned, they aren't going to let us out till we cross. I'm not even supposed to know I have twenty-eight days left."

"Is this day one of the twenty-eight?" I asked, breathless suddenly.

"No," he drawled, "this is an extra."

"Twenty-eight days then. Almost a month. Break that down into hours and minutes and it's quite a long while."

We did not try to hide the instantaneous physical attraction. That was not the way in wartime, and probably never would have been our way. April was the first to know of our relationship, and Fran, of course, the second.

He was a friend as well as a lover. There were so many things I wanted to show him about myself and about England before the hours ran out. I took him to see some of the places that I loved. We went by train and bus (petrol was rationed) to Woodstock to walk in the great parkland of Blenheim laid out by Capability Brown. I didn't say anything corny like "this is what we are fighting for." We were fighting just as much for the stones of Whitechapel and the tenements of the Gorbals. But I wanted to show him a beautiful place. Paul Poiret had first drawn my attention to Woodstock and Blenheim; he had made a dress for one of the Duchesses. "Such style," he had said of the Park. "So English."

I took Sam to Greenwich and made him walk up the hill and look down through the trees to where Wren's great buildings for the old Palace line the river. The river was crowded with invasion barges, and seen close-up looked workaday and industrial. But from the heights its curve shone like a jewel.

"If you have good eyesight," I said, pointing, "you can just see Wren's other masterpiece, St. Paul's, from here."

"I have good eyesight," he said. But he was looking at me.

We went back to the Albion on a tram, banging through the dirty but fascinating main roads of a great city at war. We sat on top, at the front in the curving prow and I stared out happily. It was a strange argosy for the two of us.

Sam said, "You know, all these places you're showing me that you love so much have something in common: they are natural beauty improved by man."

"I suppose that's it: art."

"You know, you're a pretty civilised lady."

"Is that what I am?"

"With here and there a touch of savagery," he added thoughtfully.

"Just as well we're alone on the top of this tram," I observed after a minute. I tidied my hair.

"Lucky for us."

259

Only smokers came up on the top deck out of rush hours, and cigarettes were in short supply. The Americans had introduced Camels to the English scene; you could nearly always buy them on the black market, but the English smoker despised them and searched desperately for their own harsher brands.

"We'd better smoke," I said presently, to get my breath. I'd always smoked Abdullas myself, and you could usually buy them during the war since they were expensive. If Sam had stayed round long enough I might have got to like Camels; it was certain he was not going to like Abdullas.

But he didn't stay. At the end of the month allowed, he went away into one of those great troop concentrations from which there was no exit except the ramp down an invasion barge.

"Good-bye," I said, on that last day.

Sam said nothing. He just looked at me.

"Really good-bye. We promised," I repeated.

"That's not what I want."

"It will be."

"I rather think I'm faithful unto—"

I clapped my hand across his mouth. "Don't say it." I suppose I thought he *would* die. Or that I might.

The day after Sam left, April handed me a bundle of letters from Matthew. For months there had been nothing from him, and now there were nearly a dozen, all at once. I read them quickly; they were short but friendly in tone. "Nothing much in them," I said to April. "Rather incommunicative, really." As if he had moved a long distance from me.

"As yours are to him, I suppose."

"Funny, the things wars do to you," I mused. "I suppose we're all changed."

"You haven't changed one iota since I first knew you," declared April. "Still determined to have what you want, and then pay. And pick up everyone else's bill, too, if you can."

I was puzzled. "Is that such a bad thing?"

"It makes it awfully difficult for you to take what's offered you," said April with a sigh.

I rang Fran after I finished my usual fire-watching stint and he took me back to the Albion.

"Get into bed and I'll bring you breakfast," he said. He had lately developed a domestic side.

Fran had become an air raid warden as well as a fire-watcher

260

and was still wearing his uniform. It looked clumsy on him after his usual elegant, well cut clothes, but somehow it only emphasised how familiar and dear he was.

"Bless you," I said.

I crawled into bed gratefully and was sitting there propped up on the pillows, glad to be at rest, when I heard the key turn in the front door of my apartment. Only one person had a key to that door.

"Alice?" I heard Matthew's shout. He came straight into the bedroom, dumped his travelling bag on the floor and hugged me. He looked fit and well, although much thinner and with an unexpected touch of grey at his temples. "You still in bed? Did you get my cable?"

As he spoke, Fran came through the bedroom door carrying the breakfast. "Here you are, love," he said cheerfully, "let me be mother."

Then he saw Matthew. Fran said not one word: he went very white, settled the tray carefully on my legs, sketched a sort of salutation and went out. Afterwards he said to me, "I felt so guilty. Oh, not about anything between you and me, of which there was nothing, as you well know. But because he had been fighting and I had not." There was a note of irony in his voice. I thought an earlier memory was stirring: once again he had been humiliated by me.

Matthew said, "My God, what was all that about?"

It was the classic situation: the soldier from the war returns and finds his wife . . . and so on. Except that it was Fran, and not like that at all.

I remember Matthew sitting on the edge of the bed with his head in his hands, saying, "But, I thought we were together again." I remember my desperate voice; I remember the quarrel that exploded and echoed round that apartment for hours. It produced another crop of rumours that Matthew had tried to kill me. "This time he really meant it," went the tale. April heard it and let me know. But by that time Matthew was far away with his regiment, part of the invasion force of Europe. This time no letters came from him at all.

In April 1944 Paul Poiret died in Paris, just before I had a chance to visit him. Late in that year I took a revue to France. It felt strange stepping on French soil again. But there was no mistaking that the war was still on. Soldiers, armoured cars and guns were everywhere. Fighting was not far away. We were the smallest and most advanced troupe at work. Quite by chance we were not only entertaining close to the battle line, we actually found ourselves mixed up in it.

We were a party of five: Dickie Davenport; two girls, a singer and a dancer; and a pianist. I was in charge. Two large trunks carried our costumes and equipment. Such personal possessions as we had with us we carried ourselves as hand luggage. Through everything the two girls and I hung on to our make-up bags; we felt if we had our false eyelashes and lipsticks we could put on a show. Our pianist was a man named Tom Gelding, who said his real ambition was to write plays and that he had one ready. I promised to read it for him.

All of us had crossed the channel in an L.S.T. in a convoy accompanied by mine sweepers. We were wearing the army uniform of trousers, shirt and loose jacket, and had been issued with "Geneva Cards" entitling us to be rated as lieutenants in the British army in case we were captured. I had never heard of a tour group being captured.

Once we had landed, our little group split from the others and drove off to a clearing depot. The rest were going south; we were going up the line. The first show we put on was at a place called St. Clare de Mer. The Germans had only been cleared out a week ago, and everywhere there were shell holes, mine craters and blasted houses. But there was also a theatre, the Casino, and there were troops, none of whom had been entertained since well before D Day.

The girls' song and dance act went down explosively well, as did Dickie's jokes and soft shoe shuffle. But the pianist complained bitterly about the quality of the piano which, judging by its appearance, had certainly seen a varied life. I acted as manager, and as dresser and chaperone to the girls. They were surrounded by a cluster of soldiers wherever they moved. So was I, for that matter.

After St. Clare we went on to St. Jean le Beau. They went in for saints in this area, and there were plenty of churches to match. The Germans were pretty close to St. Jean. We could hear the guns. The French villagers could hear them, too, and were not very friendly. They thought the Germans were sure to come back to drive us out.

"Had so much propaganda they don't know where they are," said Dickie charitably.

"They're still numb, I think," I said. "And can't believe they're free."

St. Jean le Beau had a sickening stench to it. I fancy that not so far away were unburied bodies. How strange it was to put on a show with the dead within hearing distance. The sanitary conveniences there were minimal—just three little boxes standing in a row, without water. These were used by everyone, troops and civilians. We all had the Normandy trots. I longed for a hot bath and a soft bed.

It turned out that the French peasants were not so far wrong after all, for the Germans attacked and broke through. In the middle of the night there was a knock on the door. I opened it. Outside was a tired but determined young officer.

"Lieutenant Baker. You're to come with me."

We were bundled into a truck, and, with a Jeep as escort, were driven off along a dark country lane. We seemed to be part of a procession. There was certainly traffic ahead, and I sensed movement behind. All lights were dowsed, so it was hard to be sure, and the lieutenant would not talk much. "I'm just detailed to see you safe," he said shortly. "Rather be going the other way." He meant he hated to leave the fighting behind.

We had a frightening drive through the freezing, foggy night, wondering if the noises we could hear behind and in front were the Germans. The French roads were deep and lined with thick hedges like a Devon lane. Presently we had to pull to the side to let a stream of vehicles pass unhindered. When I saw the armoured column I knew this was the counterattack going in; I understood the young lieutenant's frustration at not being part of it. The strength of the armour driving forward made me feel more confident of the outcome of the battle ahead.

The next day we continued our tour, but in a different direction. The German counterattack was beaten back and the Allied armour pushed on. By the time we got to our base I was thoroughly unwell and not up to going to my dear Poiret's grave in the family mausoleum in Montmartre cemetery. I had permanent dysentery; the army doctor whom I consulted looked alarmed, pumped me full of some new wonder drug and sent me off home.

"See your own doctor when you get back," he advised, "and

get that area tidied up or you won't have any sex life to speak of."

In London I groaned to April, "I feel I'm about to die."

"Not you," she answered. "Here are the latest bills from the Alby for you to pay. And a batch of letters to answer. And a new play has arrived. Get on with it."

After I'd paid the bills, I read Tom Gelding's play and felt my spirits rise. "A few changes, a few cuts, and we're in business," I announced.

Sick I might be, but I was not defeated.

♬ Chapter Fourteen

The war was over; it was a time for new beginnings. I achieved one of the first theatrical successes of the peace. Judging the taste of the times finely, Tom Gelding's play ran and ran. *The Magician* established Tom as a new, serious dramatist and me as the mistress of the new theatre. *Magician,* which Giles produced, was a serious play, but it was also very witty, and—no small advantage—it was a detective story. You could read it—as thousands did—simply as a mystery, but you could also read it as a morality play, and thousands did that, too.

"You go on working like this, you're going to get hard," Fran warned, "and you won't like that."

"Yes, I will. Why not?"

"Oh no, Alice, not you. It's what you've always feared. What you didn't want to happen to you. It's your secret worry."

"Not so secret if *you* know, Fran."

"I know you inside out," said Fran. "Inside out, my love, and don't you forget it." There was a note in his voice that stopped me for a moment. A hint, perhaps, of what he could do, if he wanted. And I guessed there were moods in which Fran did desire to hurt me, old friend as I was. I had always eluded him, and he would not forget.

I didn't need any money from him at the moment. I was riding high and that never pleased Fran. So I let him put a little money into my affairs to keep him sweet and because I loved him in my own way. But I thought he was watching and waiting.

The London theatre just after the war was dominated by two big groups: the Stoll Theatre Company, and Howard and Wyndhams. Between them they controlled about half a dozen London theatres. The figure of Prince Littler, who was also chairman of Moss Empires, was a commanding one. The firm of H. M. Tennant were the leading theatre managers. It was no longer the theatre of Cochran, Jack Buchanan, and Ivor Novello. The world had moved on. But I held my place. Slowly I was becoming a personage.

I had a theatre and I had a policy, together with a little money. These things together enabled me to create a style that was respected. Not everyone liked it, but they knew it was genuine. In my heart I acknowledged my debt to my old master Paul Poiret, who had taught me what style was.

The young doctor's warning about my sex life proved not quite accurate. Placed as I was, the patron of a popular theatre, able to influence the careers of young actors, I did not lack for suitors. The person to whom I naturally drifted for love and attention was Giles Oliver. It seemed a matter of course that we should become lovers. It happened with almost absentminded affection during a try-out for a new play in Manchester. The play was a disaster, and we both needed comfort. For a time he lived in my apartment above the Albion, and I got used to seeing his dressing-gown hanging on the back of the bathroom door and his toothbrush next to mine. This was the nearest I came to a permanent relationship at the time. It was ended by Giles.

He took me to the Ivy one night to tell me he had been offered the Artistic Directorship in a new theatre in Toronto.

"Darling, I'm pleased. I'll miss you, but I'm pleased."

He drank some Chianti. "There's something else to tell you."

I stared.

265

"I'm going with Matilda Vernon. We shall be married before we go."

Matilda Vernon was the youngest and brightest recruit to the classic theatre. At the moment, she was playing Ophelia at Stratford. I almost said, "I didn't know you'd been seeing her," but I just stopped myself in time and drank some more wine.

Giles was my own generation; we'd been colleagues for a long time. His departure hurt. I think it was meant to. Later I discovered that the money behind the Canadian venture had come from Fran. I wondered if his love for me was turning sour. He had never had a permanent relationship with anyone else. Perhaps that was my fault. I think I took a little step downhill at that moment. It was a vulnerable point in my life as a woman.

The pattern of my life for sometime to come was established during this period. I was attractive, well-dressed, and a power in the theatre; I could pick and choose my lovers. None of them stayed long in my life; I never even wished one to do so. I thought life owed me what I could take.

Matthew had not returned to Parliament after the war. Instead he took a partnership in a friend's business. He said Causley needed the money. When did it ever not? We met politely to discuss Aldwyn's education. During the war Aldwyn had necessarily grown away from me. Now I had to get to know her again. She was a dear girl. As she grew up—the figure of the child that might have been—Frederic's child—disappeared into the shadows and ceased to haunt me. Aldwyn's complete reality drove away his ghost.

Matthew asked that Aldwyn be sent to Heathfield because this had been his grandmother's school and she had wished it. I said I preferred St. Mary's, Wantage, because I had observed that the best mannered debutantes and the young married women who formed the largest and happiest group of friends seemed to come from that school. We compromised on a small coeducational school near Oxford, which was Aldwyn's own choice. After this she went on to Miss Drayton's finishing academy in St. Giles, Oxford.

Three years seemed to pass with great speed because I was so occupied with building up the position of the Albion. I suppose I was at the peak of my powers. If I wasn't happy, I was successful, and I accepted the substitute. You can't have everything all at once—at least not for long—and although the postwar generation tried very hard to do so, just as we had done in our generation, I was old enough, and canny enough, to know better.

But between me and Aldwyn there was total love and trust. Which made what happened even more of a shock. Every so often, Matthew and I met briefly to discuss her future. Viewed from a distance as we met over lunch at the Caprice, then the best eating place in London, we must have looked a lovely couple, beautifully dressed, sophisticated and poised. But in fact, we were awkward with each other.

"Before we go on to Aldwyn there's something I want to say," said Matthew. I looked at him over my martini. "I want a divorce," he said. "All right with you?"

"Of course," I said coolly. "I don't know why we haven't done it before."

"Which of us provides the evidence?" he said.

"I will, if you like," I said, trying to appear cool.

The waiter arrived with the cold consommé. I was watching my diet.

"I won't ask if you plan to get married again."

"You have already asked . . . the answer is yes."

"Oh!" I crumbled the thin toast. "Anyone I know?"

"An American," he said briefly. "Very young, very attractive."

"Very unwise," I said, eating a bit of toast. "Sounds it, anyway. For you, I mean. She'll wear you out."

"Thanks."

I consulted my diary. "Now, let me think. I'm very busy this month, but I can give you evidence next month, if you're not in too much of a hurry." I smiled sweetly. "That suit you?"

"Beautifully," he said viciously. "Now let's talk about Aldwyn."

We agreed that Aldwyn should go to Florence to study fine art and learn Italian.

When I reported to Fran—whom I still saw, but at increasingly irregular intervals—that Matthew wanted a divorce, he raised his eyebrows. We had met by chance at a Charity Ball, each of us with different parties, but we danced together.

"That's not what I heard," he said, thoughtfully. "I heard he'd bought a bachelor apartment in Manhattan." What he said made me realise how closely Fran kept an eye on my life and Matthew's.

267

"Well, he's changed his mind then."

"And you're going to provide the evidence?"

"I am."

"I hope you're wise," said Fran.

Though I'd been chaste for three years, I hadn't expected any trouble about providing the necessary evidence. I asked Reg Powys; we were fond of each other. Reg was a young actor with whom I had an easy, on-off relationship for years. But when I asked him, I could see the thoughts go through his mind: I was so much older; he'd look a fool. I thought he was about to refuse. Then he raised his head and said huskily, "Be proud to, darling." He went on, "We all love you. I owe you a debt. The theatre owes you a debt. The vitality we've gotten from you, love. Gladly—anything for you."

"I think your metaphors are getting confused," I said, my voice unsteady. "But perhaps I won't call in my debts just yet. Forget what I just asked. I'm going away to think things over."

Over the next few days I let my mind ponder on the past. I remembered how Matthew had been in those early days. The day at Causley when there had been the attempt to burn the house and when he had handed me the kitten. The first night of *Cavalcade.* The night we got engaged. Our wedding. If it had gone wrong, I thought, the fault had been mine. Then my pride rallied, and I thought, hell, it takes two to break a marriage. So I sent a telegram to Matthew saying: "If you want a divorce, provide the evidence yourself." That'll settle it, I thought. Let him get on with it.

But after a few weeks I had a letter from my solicitor (still William Griggs, though this was from a younger partner in the firm), telling me that Sir Matthew "had decided not to proceed with the matter." I was angry, but I did not move in the suit myself.

The news had come with the post brought up one morning with my breakfast tray. I always took breakfast in bed these days in my gaily painted and gilded bed. April usually brought me the mail, and sometimes the breakfast tray as well, which was prepared by a daily housekeeper. Then we would sit and discuss business while I sipped my coffee.

"How's Aldwyn?" I asked, looking over my letters. There was one from Louisa, which I hurriedly put aside. "Still asleep? She was out very late last night. Dancing, I suppose?"

268

"I suppose," said April in a noncommital way.

Aldwyn came into my bedroom at that moment. I looked at her with pleasure. I thought her the prettier because she was not in the least like me, except in her height. Her bright russet-coloured hair and hazel eyes must be a throwback to an earlier generation. Her bones were elegant and would see her through to old age. I thought the person she truly reminded me of was Gertie Lawrence. Since Gertie was the person in the whole world I had myself most wanted to resemble myself, perhaps there was something in prenatal influence after all.

"Darling, I think I'm going to come out to Florence with you and settle you in. Give myself a holiday. After all, it's ages since I had one."

Aldwyn sat on my dressing-table stool and looked at herself in my mirror, then she sprayed herself with my scent. "Sorry, dearest," she said, "but I'm not going to Florence."

"Not?" I was bewildered. "What are you going to do then?"

"I'm going to work."

"What at? What can you do?"

Aldwyn stood up; she looked radiant. "I'm going on the stage."

April kept very quiet, so she had known already. Of course she had, I thought with irritation. Aldwyn was always talking to her.

"I shan't pull any strings," I said. "No influence." I suppose I was angry and showed it.

Aldwyn got up. "I don't need any. I'll manage. Contacts." She went out closing the door quietly.

"What did she mean by that?" I demanded of April.

"Why don't you ask Francis Hollman?" She consulted my diary. "You are dining with Mrs. Milling. He's going to drive you there."

Louisa and Gene now lived in a lovely new house overlooking Hyde Park. When I looked back, how ridiculous it seemed that we should all be so prosperous. Eugene had joined a City Livery Company, was about to become an alderman, and so might become Lord Mayor of London.

Fran arrived in his green Rolls that he drove himself. I got in beside him silently.

"Lovely frock, Alice," he said. "Balmain, isn't it?" He always noticed things like that. Fran had a house in the West Indies, a

269

flat in Rome, and a conscience that he kept quietly to himself. He lived by different rules from the rest of us. "You must have been in Paris."

"Only by proxy," I said. "Louisa brought it back." Then I spoke about Aldwyn.

"I don't know what you are expecting," he said, giving a delicate turn to the wheel. "With four generations of theatre behind her, you didn't think she'd be an accountant or a vet, did you?"

"I shan't help her," I said. "She must make it on her own."

"She won't need your help, love." He sounded amused. "She's coming in on my side. Films. *I'm* helping her."

I knew that Fran had been putting money into the production side of films, but this was his first intimation that he had major influence.

"Francis, you devil," I said. I meant it, too. At times, I had the feeling he wanted to take away all the things I really loved, and then give them all back, but only as his gift. It was high price for me to pay just because he had failed in bed with me once.

He followed me into Louisa's house, where her careful taste had arranged English antique furniture and glazed chintz. Nothing could have been further from my own colourful style of interior decoration, which still bore the imprint of my days with the Martines. "I love the girl," laughed Fran, putting his arm round my waist, "like I do her mother."

"No strings?"

"Have there ever been?" he demanded, before turning to greet Louisa. "But you ought to keep an eye on her."

I held him back. "What do you mean?"

He shrugged. "You've picked sides in your family. 'You, you and you,' you said, Alice, 'and *not* you.' How do you know she's picked the same side?"

"I still don't understand."

"Go to the Double Domino some night and find out. You don't go there much now, do you?"

"No, too many memories."

"Well, she does." He went on to Louisa. "Lu, you're putting on weight, and this girl here never gains an ounce. Thinner, if anything. It's all that pasta and garlic you eat."

I sat through the whole dinner party wondering what it was that April and Fran appeared to know about Aldwyn that I did

270

not. And why? All my friends loved me, but my family did not, it appeared. That told me something about myself that I preferred not to examine. So I took a second helping of Louisa's risotto and drank some more wine.

The next evening, taking Fran's advice, I went to the Double Domino. I sat down and ordered a drink. They seemed surprised to see me and made a fuss. I was important in the theatre now; someone to be courted. How the place had changed. Everyone was so young. But then we had been young when we had started the Domino.

Aldwyn was sitting at a table against the wall with a tall young man who at first had his back to me. Then he turned so I could see his profile. How like his mother he was, and yet how like all the Charlecotes. Alexander.

I could see enough of Aldwyn's expression to read how she felt about him. She loved him, but there was a restraint and dignity in her demeanour that I found both painful and touching. She was holding back, but she wanted him. Alexander's attitude was harder to read. But he was there, and I thought he wasn't the sort of young man to go anywhere he didn't want to go, or do anything which didn't fit in with his plans for himself.

I hesitated for a moment, then I walked across to them. If you are going to lose your daughter, I told myself, then you will do so with dignity.

"Hello, you two," I said. They were holding hands. Alexander stood up. "Oh, do sit down; I just thought I'd look in here. Haven't been here for ages."

"I know," Aldwyn said.

"I used to come a lot once. We all did." I sighed.

"Nostalgia never works," Alexander said.

How clever of him to say so—and how unkind. I think he was telling me he knew how I felt about him and didn't care. He didn't have to care: he was a young man born to be successful, just as his parents had been born to fail. Life had evened things up.

"You're at the Bar now, aren't you?" I asked. "In very good chambers? Will you go into Parliament? You got a first at Oxford, after all."

"Oh, a Law first." He shrugged dismissively, as if anyone could do that and it meant nothing at all. "And anything else is a long way ahead. But yes, I have ambitions."

I finished my drink, said good-bye to them, and went home.

271

That's the end of a relationship for me, I thought. Where am I with Aldwyn now?

I was still up when Aldwyn came home that night, although it was late. I didn't ask what she had been doing.

She entered my sitting room, lit a cigarette and sat down and looked at me.

"I didn't know you smoked." I didn't raise my eyes from the book I was pretending to read.

"I've learned. Do look at me . . . Thank you. I know how you feel about Alexander. I've always known."

"Of course. Everyone has."

"But I find it hard to understand."

"His father killed his mother," I said bleakly.

"You can't hold that against *him.*"

I put my book down and started to move about the room. I am always restless when I am unhappy.

"He is the child of two of the weakest, most violent and criminal people I knew," I said "I hold *that* against him. I fear him."

"We have almost the same ancestry," said Aldwyn. "You ought to fear it in me."

"I do."

Instead of being angry, Aldwyn just laughed. "You don't understand me and Alexander at all."

Maybe not, but I certainly understood now how Josie must have felt about me.

Aldwyn finished her cigarette. "Look, dearest, I'm moving out of here. I've found a tiny place in Gerald Road."

"Near the police station? A good idea. Can you manage the rent?"

She nodded. "I've signed a contract for Maxim Films. For seven years. Not much money, but it'll keep me going. Fran helped."

I was beginning to dread the sound of his name.

In a deliberate voice Aldwyn said, "I think that you ought to get back together with Dad. You've never ceased to love him. I've never understood what broke you up."

"It was the Albion," I said. "I *think.*"

"No." She dismissed that with a wave of her hand. "No, I've talked it over with Alexander and we don't see it that way. We think you've always felt guilty towards the Charlecotes—that lawsuit, the will, all that stuff—and that was what did it."

I didn't know whether to laugh or cry. "Oh my dear," I said sadly. "As if I hadn't known that for years and years. But it does no good to know. Perhaps I should go out and stand on the steps of St. Paul's and make a general confession."

"Yes. Why don't you?" She was merciless.

"You'd like that, would you? I'll tell you who would: Francis Hollman." She blinked at that. "But do you think it would bring your father back to me?"

I looked round the room of my beloved apartment. It had seen too much, this place. "I think I'll find a cottage in the country. Not be here so much by myself."

Aldwyn nodded, said she understood. She didn't. No one could but me.

Thus we set out the demarkation lines of our new relationship, defined our territory. Two sovereign powers had reached a tacit agreement to disagree with each other. But naturally I was wretchedly unhappy about it.

Thus I had to watch Aldwyn build her life apart from me. I saw her in various films, in which she had small but worthwhile parts. One heard of her as a serious, dedicated young actress. I did not know what her relationship with Alexander was; no one mentioned him. But in her sort of world silence was often as golden as praise—and as significant.

The Albion prospered greatly. I was almost rich; but I was also lonely. Everyone assumed that because I was so successful, I must be having a very social life. In fact, I often spent my evenings alone, with supper on a tray and a book to read in bed.

Flora stayed with me when she was in London. I had got really fond of her, although she did have frightful clothes. Even Louisa's impeccable taste and gentle good sense couldn't make much impact on her, although for my sake, she tried.

Early in Coronation year I learned that the Coronation Honours would make me a Dame of the British Empire. I decided I would accept the honour, but not the title. I was already Lady Charlecote, though I still called myself Alice May.

It was about this time that Fran decided to settle abroad. He said that it was because he thought he had paid enough in tax, but it was probably because he had had a mild heart attack, which we were not allowed to mention. There was so much about Fran one was not allowed to mention. When Eugene and Louisa told me of the dinner they were going to give in my honour at the Mansion House, I hoped he would be there.

273

All these good things were happening to me, but my mood was dark. The sun did not seem to shine in my world as warmly as it should have. I ought to welcome this mood, I told myself. I have been here before at the bottom of the well and dug myself out. The digging was the good part. I enjoyed it, really. But I couldn't seem to summon up the energy this time. After a bit, I thought that perhaps it was something physical, so I made an appointment with my doctor.

He sent me into the London Clinic for a few days to do some tests. April came to see me each day, bringing me my mail, and Aldwyn telephoned. In the post, of all extraordinary things, was a letter from Matthew, asking for us to be reunited. "There never was anyone else," he wrote. "I tried, God knows I tried, to separate myself from you, but it can't be done."

His letter was the first I answered when I got back to the apartment. I walked out to post it in a box in the Strand by the Law Courts. "It is too late, my darling," I wrote. "Too late." But I asked him to join my party for Coronation Day. If I lived so long.

There are some things one must manage on one's own. When you come down to it, you are always alone with your own little bundle of responsibilities and guilts to bear. I had built my whole life on a lie I had acted out in Paris and kept to myself ever since. Suddenly I realized I didn't care a damn anymore: whether I had lied or not, it had been *my* life and, for the most part, a good one.

And so I felt, even more strongly, as I lay in my bed at the top of the Albion the night after the reception in the Mansion House, thinking back fondly on my past and ahead to the operation that might take me from all I loved.

I opened my eyes to the ceiling of the operating theatre and heard a voice say, "She's coming round." The ceiling faded away and I sank back into the dark, but during that one moment I had time to notice an emptiness, a cold void below my heart. I felt no pain, but sensed air and movement where there should have been none. "An operation is an invasion of privacy," I shouted. I think I heard a laugh from God, stationed above me, and he said, "Just time for a cup of coffee before stitching her up." I was thinking about the funniness of God drinking coffee—so now I knew what ambrosia was—when the darkness turned to warm water and rose over my head. "The

274

frozen section was clean, nonmalignant. Good-oh," God said. I was swimming in the warm water, and it was very hard to breathe. I opened my eyes.

Matthew was standing there, looking down on me.

"You're not God," I said. "God's an Australian."

He didn't hear me. "You must never do this to me again, do you hear?" His voice was angry. "Never, Alice."

"Ah you are God," I said, closing my eyes. "God with Matthew's face on."

"You really should not have faced this on your own." His voice was gentler now. "But then you've always faced things on your own. That's been the trouble. Well, you've got to stop." He banged his fist on the bed table so that the nurse came hurrying up, saying "Sir Matthew" in a shocked voice. I knew I was on earth then. In the recovery room.

"How do you think it feels for your husband and daughter to come back and find you here, in this state, and not to have known?"

"We're not married now," I protested weakly. "Not really."

"We are. Always have been and always will be. Divorce would have made no difference. Separation has made no difference. Never mind the things we both said. Didn't you realise what a terrible thing you were doing to us, not telling us that you were about to undergo a major operation. Going off like this, on your own. How could you?"

"I thought I could see it out by myself." I had always given myself a physical pain when it was an emotional one that I was really suffering. This time the doctors had cooperated. "Work through it on your own," I repeated.

"That's it, that's exactly it: you always have to do it on your own."

Distantly I seemed to hear Maria saying to me: "You always give; you cannot take." She little knew, I thought dreamily, how I could take, how I had taken.

"Yes, I do see it would make you angry," I said aloud. "At least I can see it now."

I could feel myself drifting away, Matthew's face retreating from me.

"She's going off again," I heard the nurse's voice.

"On the contrary." Matthew's voice had a note of satisfaction in it. "She's coming home."

They had me up and walking around the next day. I could

275

walk well enough, but I certainly felt empty. Wryly, I wondered if that far-off doctor in the services troupe had not been right about his warnings. But my Australian surgeon was jolly and forthright. "No, no, girlie, don't you believe it. Tightened those muscles up this op has; made you good as new."

A week later I returned to Albion Walk to complete my convalescence in my own bed. Matthew and Aldwyn were there waiting for me.

The apartment was full of flowers, and the sun was shining. All the furniture looked gleaming, and over everything was a smell of my Rosine scent.

"Sprayed it myself," said Aldwyn, "although I prefer Miss Dior, frankly. But somehow, this scent is you."

April arrived with yet more flowers. "A lot more downstairs," she said. "I'm only bringing them up by degrees."

There were flowers and messages from the whole entertainment world, spanning the alphabet from Agate to Zoltan Korda, people I wouldn't have expected to think of me."

"I'm so surprised," I said, my arms full of flowers and letters.

"You're surprised? It's nothing to the surprise you gave us," and April sat herself down beside me and handed over a square packet, wrapped in Asprey's violet paper. Inside was a suede box, and inside the box a small clock made in blonde tortoiseshell, its face encircled with small diamonds. It was an enchanting object, and I exclaimed it with delight. On the back was engraved "With love from Fran."

"He's given me time. What a lovely present."

"And he's coming in to see you before he flies," continued April. "He's still in London." She sounded as though, for some reason, there was no cause for celebration.

"Oh good, I can thank him properly then." I looked at Matthew, he showed no sign of jealousy, but seemed thoughtful. He still didn't like Fran. April didn't smile either, as she usually did when she spoke of Fran. Something was up.

When the door had closed behind April, Matthew said, "Maria put me right about one or two things. Fran, among others. She seems to know a lot about him. It was she who told me about the operation."

"Maria always did interfere." I wished I hadn't let her know about it.

"She's your oldest friend," he said mildly. "She knows you better than you know yourself."

276

"Or thinks she does."

"Now, now. She loves you."

"Yes, I believe she does. And I love her. That's remarkable when you realise how long we've been apart. But I think we do better that way. When we're together we compete too much."

Still mildly, Matthew said: "You're going to have a chance to start competing again."

"What?"

"She's here in London. And Frederic. They came over with me, but until you were recovered Maria thought they should keep away."

On cue, as if she'd been waiting in the wings for the right lines to be spoken, Maria pushed open the door and marched in.

It *was* a march; my old friend had lost nothing in energy and aggression. She was as handsome as ever. In fact, more so, because she was now very thin, with a slender elegance that old Maria had never possessed. There was a tiny frosting of silver on her dark hair, but it just added to the glitter. Maria had come through yet one more war, and yet another peace, and survived with triumph.

I liked her for that resilience, saluted her mentally for it. "Maria." I gave her a hug with all the strength I had. The years we hadn't seen each other suddenly seemed wasted.

"You haven't changed," she said, with surprise. "You look the same, sound the same. Now *me*—I have changed."

Not essentially, I thought. But I didn't say so.

"Where's Frederic?"

"He's outside. He's too shy to come in."

I went out into the hall. For years I had wondered what I would do when I met Frederic again, if I ever did. I need not have troubled. So much of human behaviour is unrehearsed and irrational. Now I simply walked forward, put my arms round him and kissed him.

He kissed me back. With Frederic and me our bodies had always known best.

"Dearest Alice. How wonderful you look. Maria said you would." His voice was husky, but he was talking fluently. "Alice rises above everything, she said."

Matthew came to the door, holding a bottle of champagne. "Come along, you two. We have to celebrate."

"Your arrival and my recovery," I said gaily, pulling Fred-

277

eric into the room. Maria had removed her smart hat and was prinking her hair in front of the mirror. It's nearly a lost art prinking, but Maria still had it to perfection.

"Friends must stay together in times of trouble," she said, nodding sagely, just as the old Maria might have done years ago in Vienna. "So here we are to give our support."

"Well, I'm better now." I spoke happily, taking the glass that Matthew held out to me.

"I didn't mean your health," began Maria.

I saw Matthew and Aldwyn exchange warning glances. Matthew gave Maria a glass of champagne, and she stopped talking abruptly.

Maria drained her glass. "So you haven't told her?" she asked.

I had a flash of premonition of what it was going to be. So after all these years my luck hadn't held. I could see in their loyal, tolerant eyes that they were determined to forgive me even if what Wally Cook said was true. Suddenly it made me angry.

"Damn it," I said. "You needn't forgive me before I've been found guilty."

Matthew remained calm, "Pipe down," he said. "We're going to get this cleared up and out of your life. You may have been a fool, Alice, but by God, I won't have you called dishonest."

We lunched on grilled salmon and cold chicken à la Elizabeth at the oval glass table with baroque golden legs I had designed. After the chicken we had a lemon parfait that I recognised to be of Aldwyn's making. We drank champagne.

Over our lunch we talked about our times and old friends. Annette Lucifer, now in New York and a neighbour of Maria and Frederic, was discussed. I told Maria about Eugene and Louisa. Then Francis Hollman's name came up and I noticed a look pass between them. I forced them out into the open with the story that Matthew and Aldwyn had so obviously wished to keep quiet till I was stronger, but which Maria had blundered into.

"Come on," I said. "Tell me what the trouble is. It's Fran, isn't it?"

They let Matthew do the talking.

"You know, or perhaps you don't, that retired or not, Francis has been buying up the property all round you," he began.

278

I shrugged. "I had heard. But he's done that before and then sold again. Every so often he goes on a shopping spree."

"This time it's serious," said Matthew. "He's got a hold on everything round the Albion."

"Some of that property he must have had for donkey's years," I said sceptically, "and never done anything with it. Is that all?"

"He has everything around you. You are on an island," persisted Matthew. "He can't force you to sell, of course."

"Indeed not," I said.

"But he can make you glad to."

"Ah!" I said.

Aldwyn got up nervously. "Let's have coffee in the drawing room. Alexander said he'd come in."

I sat where I was. "No, we'll have it here. Let's finish what we've begun."

I could see Maria was about to burst out with something.

"He says he has evidence that the letter your father wrote to his lawyer about you inheriting the Albion was forged. That *you* wrote it, and confessed as much to Dickie Davenport years ago."

So at last, my final, pathetic secret was out.

"Dickie swore he'd never tell," I said.

"He didn't," said Matthew. "But he wrote it in his diary. Wally Cook found the diary when he was in Ladybrook Grove at the time of the Blitz, and he kept it. Before he died he gave it to Fran."

"There was always a strong link between those two." For a moment I wondered what was the origin of it. Some other secret there, that I would never know. "And Wally was so marvellously brave in the Blitz, we all said so."

Matthew shrugged. "People don't change. They simply show other sides of their character."

I had never seen Dickie's diary, but I could imagine it. No doubt he had written down the words he had spoken to me. "Clever little thing you always were," he'd said, half admiringly, half shocked. "So good with your hands—but forgery!" I could almost see the page.

"I expect Wally sold the diary," I said calmly. "So what is my old friend Fran going to do with it?"

"Nothing through the law," said Matthew. "You own everything now in any case."

"And if I didn't, *you* would," I answered. "I suppose that letter, if it still exists, could be examined. I imagine it does exist. Lawyers never destroy anything."

In a low voice Maria said, "Behind that letter must lie a tale."

"Don't harass her," whispered Frederic.

"Fran will use that letter, spread the news of it, if you do not sell to him. Blackmail."

It wasn't so much that Fran wanted the Albion anymore, I thought, he just wanted to get even with Alice May before he died. He loved me, but he resented me, too. I'd known it for years.

There was a ring at the door and the sound of a voice.

"It's Alexander," said Aldwyn, with relief. "We can talk to him about the legal side."

"Haven't you already?"

"No," she said indignantly.

"Let him in." I got up and walked through to the drawing room, golden in the early afternoon sun.

Oh Dickie, I thought. Because you were such an honest little man and had to tell the truth somewhere, what have you let me in for?

The others came into the room behind me. Alexander was already standing there. Aldwyn ran forward and he kissed her. Alexander reminded me of Randolph Charlecote—his looks went directly back to that generation—but there was a strength of bone that I thought came from the Mays. "I'm taking Aldwyn to the opera tonight," he said. "Gala performance."

"She's an unmusical girl," I said. "But I expect you'll train her. We've been having quite a performance here ourselves. Sit down and we'll tell you."

Alexander absorbed the information relayed by Matthew and me with professional ease. He didn't seem particularly surprised. But then I realised Aldwyn *had* told him, whatever she said.

"Of course, we must get hold of Francis Hollman at once," he said.

"Agreed." I stretched out a hand for the telephone. "I'll ring the Savoy."

Before I could dial, the telephone rang. I picked it up, and to my surprise, I heard Josie's voice.

"Josie, where are you?"

"California, love. Where I live, you know!"

I covered the receiver. "It's Josie," I mouthed to Matthew. "I expect she wants to ask how I am."

Matthew shook his head. "I didn't tell her. Did you, Aldwyn?"

Once again I had underestimated my mother.

"Alice? Are you there? Lovely to hear your voice, darling. How are you? Don't bother to tell me, darling, because I'm in a hurry. Guess what?"

"You've won an Oscar."

"Be reasonable, ducky. If I had it would be in the old trouper's class. No, I'm hitting Broadway at last. In *Quadrille*, with the Lunts. How many years is it since I said I'd play in New York? That would be telling."

A circle had come full round in my life and Josie's. She was "going to New York," and my place in her world was still peripheral. Things were as they always had been.

But this time it would be different. As Josie finished, amid protestations of love on both sides, I said to Matthew, "And now it's time to take on Fran. I'm going to ring him." I reached for the telephone.

"No," protested Matthew. "You're not up to it."

"I'm going ahead *now*—Fran? I'm back, and thank you for that lovely present. I am going to use the time you gave me . . . Fran, can you come round? Yes, the Albion, and *now*. We have business to discuss." I heard him draw a breath—perhaps the dying gasp of a friendship.

He was there surprisingly quickly. I heard the noise of the lift coming up to the top of the Albion, and then the ring at the door. "I'll go," I said.

The hall in my apartment at the Albion ran across the width of the building, so it was both long and broad; all the main rooms opened off it. If I looked towards the kitchen I could see the flat roof where Alexander and I had put out the fire-bomb during the Blitz. Today it was a peaceful garden with tubs of flowers. The hall I had decorated myself in the style I had learned at the Martines, with a frieze of figures walking through a London Park. Some of the figures were easily recognisable—Noel, Gladys Cooper, dear Meggie, and Giles, killed in an air crash a few years ago. Eugene and Louisa were there too, selling flowers from a stall, and Franny. So much of my past, so much of myself, was in that painting.

"Come in, Fran," I said, opening the door. "You've been quick."

"Walked round." He was panting a bit. "Quicker than getting a taxi in this traffic."

He came in and shook hands and greeted everyone, cheerful and composed as ever, my old friend, my dear Judas.

Then he took a small, leather-bound book out of his pocket and put it on the table. "Dickie's diary. I suppose that's what this meeting is all about?"

I looked at it. Memories of Dickie and Ladybrook Grove came vividly into my mind. "Yes. What have you done to me, Fran?"

"Not me." He was unrepentant. "You. You yourself."

I looked at him, without a word.

"All right: so I'm using what I know to get something I want. You seem to have heard all about it."

"I have been told that you now own all the land around the Albion, but I've heard this tale before."

"This time it's true. To complete the area, I need the land the Albion stands on. You can forget all the talk about turning the Albion into a cinema, that's out. Those days are gone. But I do plan to develop the whole piece of land: offices, a hotel, shops. That's what I want it for. I'm rich now; I shall be ten times richer afterwards."

"You really are ruthless, Fran. It's not really the land and the Albion. You just want to settle an account in your favour."

He moved the diary towards me. "If you can't beat me, join me. I'll give you the diary, and you sell me the Albion. Then you get your solicitor to destroy that letter. Because it's still there. I've seen it. Don't ask how, but I have."

"Unscrupulous, too?" I said. "Franny, I never knew you. This is blackmail."

"I didn't know you were going to be ill." He shook his head. "I feel bad about that."

"Will you really make a public issue of it?" I said. I could hear Matthew murmur something in the background. Alexander was trying to stop me talking. "Be quiet, you two. Will you, Fran?"

"I won't have to," he said quietly. "It can all be between you and me. Of course I don't want to spread the story about; I'm sorry as much has got out as it has. But I wasn't thinking of

282

publicity. I know you, girl, and I knew who you'd want to keep the story from."

I looked around the room. "Yes, my friends and relations. The people who love and hate me most."

"Mother," Aldwyn protested.

"Well, you've all been quick to assemble and pass judgement on me. With love, of course," I said ironically. "But judgement, nonetheless."

"Please, Alice," said Matthew.

"No, even you Matthew. Possibly you most of all. All of you, the people closest to me, have decided I am guilty. Well, now you can hear what really took place."

I had all their attention now.

"I did forge that letter: it *is* in my hand. I confess. I tell you that freely."

I heard Fran give a sigh; he knew he'd lost his game.

"But I did it at Randolph Charlecote's request. He asked me to do it. He wanted that letter written."

Fran sighed again. "Why didn't he do it himself?"

"Because he was too bloody drunk," I said vehemently. "He did start the letter, but he couldn't finish it. He told me to write it for him. He knew he was going to die, but he wanted me to have the Albion." I was almost shouting. "It's one of the reasons I have tried to hang on to it, because he wanted me to have it. Keeping my faith was the last thing I could do for him, for all who died in that war."

I shuddered into silence, unable to go on. Far away and long ago, that scene of the young Alice and the desperate, frightened, drunken Randolph Charlecote still moved in my memory. There was one thing I would *never* tell them: it had been fear, not drink, that had immobilised Randolph Charlecote. I had had to help him walk to the cab that took him away. I hadn't cried then—I was too young for the right sort of pity— but I was crying now.

There was relief in the tears. The terrible doubt I had nursed inside me all those years that Randolph had been too drunk to know what he was saying—or even the nagging worry that I had invented what I wanted to hear—suddenly cleared away. I *had* done what he had desired.

Matthew covered his face with his hands. Aldwyn came and stood by me silently, giving me a handkerchief.

283

Fran flipped the diary across the table to me, and stood up. "Your game," he said. "Forgive me?"

I stood up too. "Oh Fran. You're the one I mind least of all. After all, you were protecting yourself." That arrow went home, I thought. "I understand."

"I knew you would," he returned imperturbably. "I said to myself: Alice is the one who will understand." He reached for his coat. "Good-bye, all of you. Look after this girl. She's worth the lot of you."

He walked towards the door. We both knew it would be a long time before we met again. The thought "if ever" was carefully repressed.

"Thank you so much for the clock."

"You know why I chose it?"

"Indeed I do: we've both learned the value of time. Of life."

"Clever girl." He picked up the clock from where it stood on my desk. "Look, I'll show you something. Here, at twelve o'clock, I've had them put a tiny diamond. Think of me when you look at it."

"Oh Fran." There were tears in my eyes. "Dear, dreadful Fran . . . so it *was* partly me that you wanted all this time, and not just the Albion?"

"You, darling, you, every time. But I always knew it wouldn't do."

Then a flash of the old Fran showed again. "All the same, I'll get the Albion yet."

"Never," I said. "Twenty-five years from now, the Albion will still be a live theatre and playing to packed houses. You'll see."

"Think I will?" Fran grinned. " 'Bye love, be seeing you."

When I came back into the room, exhausted but triumphant, it was to hear Matthew tersely asking the rest of them to go.

I kissed Maria and Frederic fondly. "See you tomorrow. I am tired now, and Matthew and I have to talk. Good-bye Aldwyn. Write to your Aunt Flora for me, will you? Ask her what colour Randolph Charlecote's eyes were, will you?"

"Yes, but why?" Aldwyn was bewildered.

"It's a question of genetics." My eyes were brown, and I couldn't have gotten them from Josie. Hers were blue.

"They were brown," said Matthew. "Brown." He pulled at

my arm. "That is, I really have no idea, but he was certainly your father."

"Sit down. And say nothing for the next half hour."

He sat down on my Ruhlmann sofa and put his arm round me. When he tried to begin a protestation of apology and love, I put my finger on his lips. "Forget it," I said. "As I shall."

Matthew looked around him. "Funny to be back here. Nothing seems changed, although I suppose you must have replaced things as they wore out. You're a great one for creating atmosphere, Alice."

"Poiret taught me."

"I want to take you back to Causley," he said firmly.

"Yes, a holiday would be nice."

"No, not a holiday; forever." He hurried on before I could interrupt. "Farming is prosperous these days, in case you hadn't noticed. Also, I've made a fair amount myself. I set out deliberately to do it, after the war, and now it's done."

"Well, lovely for you," I said. "I've succeeded too." I hoped we weren't going to fight again. "That's what all this has been about, hadn't you noticed?"

"There are some old buildings at Causley that I want to turn into a theatre. It could be done. Small, but commercially viable. I want you to leave here and come north to create it for me."

I was staring at him, speechless.

"We'll plant roses all round it. A theatre in a rose garden. The Rose Theatre. What about it, Alice? A cultural centre for the north. You could do it."

"And leave the Albion?"

"Yes, leave it to the next generation, to Aldwyn. Why do you think she's been sweating her guts out learning to act, to produce, to arrange finance?"

"In films," I said quickly.

"Just so as not to cut across you. But it's the Albion she really wants. Let her have it, Alice. Let her have her turn."

In a calm voice, not showing the excitement that must have been there, he outlined the plans for using the old barns of the Home Farm as the nucleus for the theatre he planned, which he thought could also be used for music. "Oddly enough, they tell me the acoustics are excellent. We shall have to be careful not to lose that quality. The building goes back to the fifteenth century, perhaps earlier."

285

I did not answer him directly, but I knew an answer was shaping itself inside me, and that I was going to accept his offer of a theatre in a rose garden. Nor did I say anything about Alexander and Aldwyn, but I could see that I would accept their relationship too. What they had, and how it would grow, was their own affair. At last I had learned a lesson that I had taught Josie long ago.

Benjamin Britten wrote an opera for the Queen's Coronation called *Gloriana,* Diana Wynyard appeared as the divine Helen in *The Private Life of Helen,* and Noel Coward starred in Shaw's *The Apple Cart* at the Haymarket. *The Seven Year Itch* and *A Woman of No Importance* jostled for attention with *Airs on a Shoe String.* But at the Albion I had chosen to put on *Trelawny of the Wells.* Tony Repton played Sir William Gower, Peter Harper was Arthur, and a rising and delightful young actress, Aldwyn May, was Rose Trelawny.

I chose the play because it seemed to me to offer a tribute to the theatre itself. I left Robert Carewe's play, *The Garden of the Goddesses,* for Aldwyn to bring in, a sure success to start her off.

We collected marvellous notices, and after an initial surprise at our choice of play, audiences were good. Repton directed, and I did the décor. By the end of the summer ours was one of the acknowledged successes of the Coronation Season.

By now the word was around that I was leaving. It was sad packing up my possessions from my apartment above the Albion, but as Aldwyn's possessions began to take their place in the rooms, it seemed so natural and inevitable that my spirits rose. Unbelievably, I was happy to go.

The night before I was due to leave for Causley I was in the Albion as usual. From certain hints and secretive smiles I knew that I was going to be given a farewell party. Everyone thought they were keeping the secret, but I knew when Aldwyn insisted on a visit to Elizabeth Arden for hair, face and nails and when Louisa came in with a dress from Dior. I knew for sure when Matthew fastened a necklace of diamonds and pearls around my neck. My own private gifts to myself were the loveliest underclothes of satin and lace.

But I was totally unprepared for the word that went round just before the curtain was due to go up: "Look in the Royal Box." That secret had been well kept by the front-of-house manager, although he had certainly known, and so had April

286

and Aldwyn. I could tell from their grins. Of course, I was delighted. I only discovered the full enormity of what they had planned for me when the curtain went down at the end and then rose again, and Repton and Aldwyn took one of my hands each and dragged me forward between them to the stage.

There was a wave of clapping, then silence, and then I was staring into the warm darkness of the auditorium, facing rows of expectant, hopeful faces. I remembered Paul Poiret; I remembered Maria and Frederic; I remembered Dickie and Meggie and Noel, and I remembered Sam. I thought of the Werkstaette, and Ladybrook Grove, and Causley and my beloved Matthew. But most of all I thought of the Albion itself: its past, its present and its future. I remembered Noel saying how it was pretty exciting to be British. I stretched out my hands to my audience.

"Dear friends," I said. "Dear friends."